CW01523005

WHISKEY & SIN

EMILY RATH

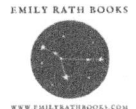

EMILY RATH BOOKS

WWW.EMILYRATHBOOKS.COM

To the stretch of I-95 between Jacksonville, FL and Columbia, SC. You mystical, magical, wonderful piece of highway. This book is yours...as much as a stretch of road can claim a book as its own.

A NOTE ON THIS OMEGAVERSE

This is an Omegaverse novel. If you're new to the Omegaverse, let me explain a few things. All humans have an alternate biology that includes heightened animalistic traits adapted to a romance premise. Think strong mating instincts (urges to bite, rut, claim), pheromones, heats, fancy peens with knots, and bonding marks.

In the Omegaverse, all humans are divided into three biological categories:

- **Alphas:** They are powerful, possessive, and prone to leadership roles. Alphas prefer their own company, often forming packs of other alphas (and sometimes betas).
- **Omegas:** This is the rarest designation. Omegas are the emotional/sexual glue that holds alpha packs together. Omegas need alphas to care for and be cared by. Every three months, omegas experience a mating heat, which is a 3-day cycle of heightened fertility. If an omega is bitten by an alpha, this will 'bond' that omega to the alpha.

An unbonded omega is highly sought after. In this universe, male omegas *can* get pregnant (Google 'MPreg').

- **Betas:** This is most of the population. They are average people. They can be subjected to the pull of alphas and omegas. For example, an alpha's 'bark' can command them, and an omega's perfume/heat will heighten arousal. Betas can also be bonded to alphas.

There are as many types of Omegaverse as there are flavors of LaCroix. If you want more background, Google it. Aside from the biological distinctions, this book is *NOT* a paranormal romance. There are no shifters and no magic.

TAGS & CONTENT WARNINGS

Tags: tattooed loner alpha, sensitive beta, male/male romance, small town, sad boy fall vibes, Chris Stapleton's *Traveller* album as a novel, forced proximity, mutual pining, who hurt you, knotting, omega heat, *MINE*, I can't express how I feel so let's stare into each other's eyes instead, touch him and die, we've both got a lot of trauma so let's unpack it together

Content Warnings:

There are multiple dark themes discussed in this book, including: sex trafficking and forced drug use. There are *no* detailed scenes of sexual assault, but there are flashbacks and mentions of past acts. A character suffers from PTSD and experiences several active symptoms including heightened startle response, fear of physical touch, flashbacks, nightmares, depression, and memory loss/confusion.

Other warnings include: descriptive sex scenes with knotting, brief mention of MPreg, use of firearms, cinematic violence (a deadly car crash, gunshot wounds, blood, death), parent death (off page), vomiting (no description).

At its heart, this book is about healing and survival. There is hope in this book. There is joy and peace and—ultimately—happiness. You will get a happily ever after.

AUTHOR'S NOTE

This is a fictional world. There is no sexism, no racism, and absolutely no homophobia. None of my characters are burdened with the weight of these stigmas. All characters can be read as queer/pansexual. Love is love.

1

This was rock bottom. Silas stood in the middle of a disgusting gas station bathroom and the sinking feeling hit him: I never want to leave. Sure, it smelled like a urinal cake in here, and there was nowhere to sit except the toilet with a broken seat. But it was better than walking back out that door.

Yep, rock fucking bottom.

A heavy fist pounded twice on the door, rattling the bolt in the latch. Then a deep, male voice barked, "You got *one* minute, Si. Hurry the fuck up!"

Silas flinched, gripping tighter to the sides of the sink. Letting out a shaky breath, he glanced up, meeting the gaze of his reflection in the cracked mirror. Above him, the fluorescent lights buzzed. A fly crawled in a lazy spiral pattern across the glass. He watched it flick its iridescent wings.

Halfway.

That's what Dallas said before he got out of the SUV to start pumping gas. They were halfway to Bridgeport. Halfway to Silas's miserable fate. And now Silas was locked in a dirty bathroom, halfway to a panic attack. He sucked in another breath through his nose, blowing it out his mouth, watching his reflection do the same.

Just breathe. You're not there yet. There's still time.

Time to do what? Escape? Not likely. Floyd and Dallas were worse than a pair of bloodhounds. He couldn't even walk from the SUV to the bathroom without one of them holding him tight by the arm. Silas didn't exactly blame them. He was a known flight risk, after all. He suppressed a shiver, choking back memories too painful to relive.

Don't look back. Never look back.

There would be no running, but Silas didn't want to go to Bridgeport either. The only thing waiting for him there was getting force-bonded to a pack of drug-running alphas, trapped for the rest of his life with a pack he didn't choose. Everyone thought the life of omegas was so glamorous. Welcome to the real world.

Silas focused on his reflection in the mirror. He always wore a hoodie if he could help it. He didn't like it when people stared at his scars. His beanie was pulled low over his forehead. His brown skin was sallow, his dark eyes empty.

This is what numb looks like, he thought to himself, gripping tighter to the sink.

But Silas didn't want to be numb anymore. He'd spent the last seven years suffering the effects of a hormone suppressing treatment. The lying sons of bitches at the Omega Center told him it was a flu shot. Everything that made him an omega was erased in an instant. Cut off. Numbed. Full sensory castration. He couldn't sense pheromones, couldn't go into heat, couldn't bond or breed. It was a fate worse than death.

Well, being sold out of the Center and forced to turn tricks was a close second...

BANG. BANG.

"Come on, OB. We're burnin' daylight!"

OB. Omega/Beta.

Only Dallas called him that. He gasped, hurriedly tapping the knob on the hand dryer to set it off. The sound roared in his ears, and he called over it. "Be right out!"

Floyd may be mean, but Dallas was sadistic. If Silas didn't leave this bathroom in the next ten seconds, Dallas would be coming in after him. And then he'd have a raging alpha on his hands.

He flicked back the latch on the door. Dallas immediately banged it open, filling the small space with his presence. After seven long years, Silas's suppressant shot was finally wearing off. He just had no control over the how or when. He was like a busted radio, only catching static unless you jostled him just right. In this moment, the alpha's scent was sharp in his nose, like a floor cleaner, metallic and lemony.

Dallas shoved him up against the wall, one hand at his throat as he squeezed. The pale, freckled skin of his arm was exposed up to the elbow, showing off his detailed gang ink —all symbols of his status and affiliation with Pack Rainier. "Don't ever make me wait for you again. We got a schedule to keep."

"Sorry," Silas rasped, his pulse racing as Dallas leaned in closer, giving him a long sniff. Silas's gut twisted as he fought to contain a whimper.

"You're starting to smell good, OB." Dallas's nose brushed against his jaw as he helped himself to another whiff of Silas's faint omega scent. "About time too. Ava was worried you'd be a dud forever." He loosened his hold on Silas's neck, but Silas didn't dare move. "You excited to meet your new pack?"

3

Silas nodded.

"I bet they treat you real nice," Dallas crooned. "Fill all your sweet holes at once, have you begging for more. That'll be fun, right?"

"Yes," Silas said on a soft breath. "So much fun."

In truth, the thought sickened him.

Dallas leaned in again. "You keep smelling this good for me, and maybe we'll practice when we get to the motel. It's been a while since you and I had some fun, hasn't it?"

Fear spread through Silas's veins like ice, freezing him to stillness. He pressed himself against the wall, Dallas's hand still at his throat. He was suddenly drowning in a sea of memories. Dallas was cruel. Dallas was selfish. He took and took. He liked to harm. Pain with his pleasure, always pain first—

Stop. Silas sank into that numb place inside himself and nodded again. "Yeah, we can do that."

"A little goodbye party," Dallas added with a smirk.

Numbness. Stillness. "Yeah...that'd be nice."

"Good, now get in the car. I'm done waiting for your ass." Dallas dropped his hand to Silas's arm and tugged him out of the bathroom, dragging him towards the idling black SUV.

Floyd stood waiting by the open back door. He was a beefy alpha, built like a linebacker. He had his arms full of junk food—bags of chips, jerky sticks, powdered donuts. "Si, I got you a couple chicken and corn taquitos and a banana. Ava says you need more fruit. And there's a Beast Blast in the cupholder."

Silas grimaced. Gas station taquitos and an energy drink? Yeah, omegas really out here living the life. "Thanks, Floyd," he replied, climbing into the backseat.

4

"I'm not eating any of that shit," Dallas snapped as he shut Silas's door.

"Well, what are you gonna do?" Floyd replied, climbing into the front seat with his horde of junk food. "Not a lot of options in there."

"We'll get burgers or something."

"With him?" Floyd jabbed a thumb at Silas.

"We'll do drive-thru." Dallas rolled the SUV out onto the two-lane country highway. "You'll behave, won't you, OB?" he added, glancing back at Silas in the rearview mirror.

Silas had come to hate the sight of those icy blue eyes. Worse than that was the creepy smile that spread from ear to ear as Dallas watched him. Swallowing down his nerves, he nodded. "I'll be good."

Not like he had much choice. They child-locked the back doors so Silas couldn't get out on his own. And they only took country roads and strictly drove the speed limit. Fewer checkpoints out here. Fewer cops. Fewer people to notice if Silas got creative and started calling for help. But no one was going to help him. Silas Wright was on his own. It was the most resounding lesson of his life.

From the front seat, Dallas slurped on his drink. "Keep your yap shut, OB, and we'll get you a milkshake to wash down those shitty fucking taquitos."

Floyd chuckled, tearing into his bag of chips. "If he didn't have the shits before, he will soon," he said through crunchy mouthfuls.

"Good point. Better skip the milkshake if we're gonna party later." Dallas cranked up the radio, blaring his metal music.

Silas looked down at his lap to where he was holding the pair of warm taquitos in a piece of wax paper. Sounds hummed all around him—the radio, the rumble of the tires hitting the road, the grunt of the engine. He tuned it all out, his every breath and being focused on that one word. *Halfway*.

Halfway to his final destination.

Halfway to the slow dying of a new life, force-bonded to a pack of criminal alphas.

Halfway...

He set the taquitos aside untouched. Taking another slow, even breath, his resolve hardened. There are moments in life, when you're at rock bottom, and your only choice is to stop digging down and start digging to the side instead. Staring at the back of Dallas' head, a new thought settled in Silas's mind.

There's no way in hell I'm going to Bridgeport.

Silas

At Dallas' insistence, they stopped at the next exit for burgers and fries. While Dallas was reaching in his pocket for his wallet, Silas's eye settled on his hip. That's where he saw it: a *gun*.

Dallas' gun was just sitting there. All Silas had to do was reach between the seats and he could pull it from its holster. He'd seen enough action movies to know shooting the driver of a moving car could be disastrous. His mind flooded with images of cars on fire, rolling down the road, wrapping around trees. The idea of such a horrible death chilled his anger.

It took almost an hour for him to build up his courage to try for it. In fact, he had all but given up on himself. But then Dallas had to look at him in the mirror with those icy blue eyes and say, "So...who do you want first?"

Silas didn't need to ask for clarification. Dallas had a belly full of food, he was amped up on energy drinks, and he was nursing his third cigarette. He'd be looking to pull over soon. Silas knew what would happen once he did.

Floyd chuckled, popping back handfuls of chocolate-covered raisins. Glancing over his shoulder at Silas, he flashed him a knowing wink. The image of being spit-roasted by these two alphas churned him up inside.

Try it, and I'll bite it off.

The radio sparked with static, a loud crackling that set Silas's teeth on edge. Dallas leaned forward, fiddling with the dial.

"Let me do it," Floyd grunted, dusting his fingers off on his shoulder before poking at the buttons. The static got louder.

Dallas slapped Floyd's hand away. "Leave off it."

This is it.

Silas didn't think, he just moved. With both alphas distracted, he lunged for Dallas' gun. It slipped easily out of the holster and Silas jerked it back between the seats.

"*Hey*—"

"What?"

"Oh—fuck—*FUCK*! He's got my gun!"

IN MOVIES, ACTION SEQUENCES ALWAYS SLOW WAY DOWN. Bullets fly from the end of a gun, and you watch them spin through the air. Cars leap barriers and flip and turn with the grace of breeching whales. But real life is very different.

Silas didn't know what happened from the moment he snatched the gun to the moment he was hanging upside-down, suspended by his seatbelt in the back of the smashed-up SUV. He blinked awake, his senses flooded with all the smells of a car crash—burning tire rubber on asphalt, the tang of twisted metal in his mouth, the chalky airbag dust coating his nose and making him sneeze.

He groaned. How long had he been out? He needed to

move. Needed to flee while he still had the chance. It might already be too late.

An echoing groan from the front seat sent his pulse racing as his hand flailed desperately for the buckle of his seatbelt. Finding it, he tried to brace against the roof with his other arm as he gave the buckle a hard press with his thumb. It clicked loose, and his body sank like a sack of potatoes. He swallowed his cries as he righted himself onto his hands and knees in the cramped space. A searing pain stabbed down his left leg sharp enough to bring tears to his eyes.

Please, don't be broken.

How was he going to run on a broken leg? He flipped over onto his butt, reaching gingerly for his left leg. He only had the headlights to see by, but it was enough. No blood. No shaft of white bone sticking out. He ran his hands down the length of his shin. It hurt like crazy, but felt intact. Enough to risk running.

And it was time to run.

The two alphas were still strapped in the front seats. Silas scooted forward, peering between the seats. Dallas was unmoving, his eyes open and unfixed. Blood streaked down the side of his pale face into his bleached blonde hair. Thick droplets dripped onto the grey roof in time with the blinking headlights. He was dead.

Good. Fuck you, alphahole.

Floyd was still alive. His head was all but touching the roof as his seatbelt fought to hold him suspended. Shattered glass peppered his face and chest like the spray of buckshot, but he was still breathing. At any moment, he might open his eyes and try to take control of the situation.

Not wasting another second, Silas wedged himself between the front seats and stretched out his arm, reaching desperately for his prize. Dallas' gun rested by the rearview mirror in a pool of broken windshield glass. Silas pinched the muzzle of the gun between two fingers and dragged it over the glass back towards himself.

Floyd groaned again, louder this time.

Silas swallowed his panic. Jerking the gun the last six inches over the glass, he palmed it and scooted back into the safety of the back seat. Heart racing, he raised the gun and pointed it at Floyd. "I'm done," he muttered. "I want out. I never wanted *in*." He blinked back his tears, trying to control the shaking of his hand as he pressed the muzzle against Floyd's sweaty head.

He had to do it. He had to pull the trigger. If he didn't, Floyd would find him. He'd send Ava to find him. Floyd *deserved* to die. He'd done so many terrible things. Silas had witnessed them with his own eyes. His hand shook as his finger curled around the trigger. "Do it," he muttered to himself. "Come on!"

He was about to shoot a man.

Killer. Murderer. Criminal.

"Silas...Dal..."

Holy fuck.

Floyd was talking. He was waking up. "Silas...you 'live?"

Silas held his breath, staying quiet.

"Dallas..."

Silas looked around, wild-eyed. The child-locked doors were still shut, the glass intact. Thank god, the crash shattered the rear window, because Silas really didn't want to climb over a dead man. He would do it, if it meant freedom, but it would be one more shitty memory to haunt his restless dreams.

"Si, help me," Floyd muttered. "Legs hurt."

No way. Silas was done. Leaning forward, he tapped the

gun against the back of Floyd's head again. "You feel that, Floyd? I've got a loaded gun to your head."

Floyd groaned. "C'mon, Si—"

"It's my turn to talk," he snapped. "I'm out. Do you hear me? I'm gonna let you live, and you're gonna go back to Ava, and you're gonna tell her I'm dead. I had the chance to kill you, and I didn't, Floyd. Because I am *not* like you. I will *never* be like you. I'm done with this life. Don't try to find me, or I will finish what I fucking started."

"Makin' a mistake, little omega," Floyd muttered. "She'll never stop."

Silas scowled at the back of his head. "Neither will I." Raising the gun, he slammed the butt of it against Floyd's temple, knocking the big man unconscious. He didn't know how much time that bought him, and he wasn't waiting around to find out.

Careful of the glass, Silas crawled under the back row of seats towards the broken rear window. All the stuff in the back of the SUV had been tossed around, including Floyd's backpack. Silas had no idea what was inside, but even if all he found was a pack of smokes, it was more than what Silas currently had in his pockets. He dragged it with him out the back window.

His left leg ached, but he rolled out of the SUV and stumbled to his feet, swaying in the tall grass next to the wreckage. He slung the backpack over his shoulder and tucked the gun in at his waistband. Then he did a little half turn, wincing as he put too much weight on his injured leg. The smell of rain hung thick in the air. In the distance, thunder rumbled.

Perfect. Caught in the rain with nowhere to go.

He had no idea where he was. Somewhere in the gently sweeping mountains between St. Albans and Bridgeport.

Silas's eyes followed the signs of chaos up the sloping hill back towards the road. The scene was illuminated by the red glow of the blinking taillights. Deep divots in the ground told him they rolled all the way down the hill before smashing into the trees. Silas was lucky to be alive.

And now, Silas had to disappear. Off the grid. He was going to become a ghost. The invisible man.

Oh, Silas Wright? Yeah, he died. An omega who never reached his full potential. Tragic.

Turning away from the wreckage of the car—the wreckage of his entire miserable fucking life—he tucked his other arm through the backpack's shoulder strap and stumbled back up the hill just as the first drops of rain started to fall.

3

Bear

Rain pelted the windshield in heavy sheets, limiting visibility to nil. Bear lifted his foot off the accelerator, letting the truck slow to twenty-five miles per hour, as he flicked his brights on.

Now I can't see a damn thing.

The glare from the rain made his visibility even worse. He flicked the brights back off, resigned to coasting his way home down the winding mountain road. He grew up on these roads and knew his way blindfolded, but deer were antsy this time of year. The last thing he wanted was to hit one and have it bang up his truck.

As the thunder rumbled, he reached for the volume knob, cranking the music louder. He hummed along, drumming his thumbs on the wheel. The truck cruised around a tight bend in the road and—

"Shit!"

Bear swerved left, heart pounding. He swerved right to overcorrect, and his back tires squealed, fishtailing on the slick mountain road. Once he was back in control, he slammed on his breaks, his eyes darting to his rearview mirror.

I almost hit someone.

What the hell was someone doing walking this road at night in a thunderstorm? He slowed his truck to a stop as he looked for the dark silhouette of the hitchhiker through the pouring rain. He turned off the music and waited.

"Where are you?" he muttered, still looking in the mirror. Throwing his truck in reverse, he pressed the gas, his engine grunting as the truck rolled back uphill a few dozen feet. As soon as his taillights lit up the hiker, Bear tapped the break, surveying the odd scene.

It was a man in a dark hoodie. Average height and build. His face was hidden in the shadows. He wore a backpack, his hands clutching tight to the straps. The man stood against the guardrail, watching Bear watch him. Bear couldn't see his eyes, but he felt his gaze. The indecision, the fear...Bear could smell it.

Suddenly, the man turned and tried to run across the road. He only got about three steps before his left leg gave out. He stumbled forward, crying out in pain as he fell to his knees. It was a sharp, panicked sound that pierced Bear straight through the chest. His throat went dry, and he felt the uncontrollable urge to help.

Damn alpha instincts. This isn't your business, Bear.

Whoever he was, and whatever he was doing on this road, the man was hurt. In an instant, Bear shifted fully into protector mode. Throwing his truck into park, he flicked on his hazards, and shoved open his door. The rain pounded down, drenching him in seconds.

The man was crawling on his knees, desperate to get away.

"You alright?" he called.

The man stilled like a startled deer.

Bear walked towards him. "Hey man, were you in an accident?"

"I'm fine! Just go!"

"Where's your car?" Bear called again. "Let me help you—"

"I don't need help!" The man scrambled back up to his feet.

With his heightened alpha senses, Bear could practically taste the man's pain. It gagged him, the tang of nervous sweat mixed with the thick, iron taste of blood. "You're gonna get killed out here. I didn't see you until I was right on top of you."

"I'll stay off the road," the man grunted, still trying to hop away. His jeans were ripped at the knees, and he was trying not to put any weight on that left leg.

"You're not fine," Bear replied, letting the cold autumn rain soak him down to the skin. "You're hurt. Bad from the looks of it. Let me help you," he repeated.

"I don't need help." He was breathing hard and heavy, licking his lips as he tried to stagger away. "I don't—don't need—I—fuck—" He swayed and then stilled. Doubling over at the waist, he vomited all over his shoes and the road.

Oh, shit.

Bear was on him in three steps, catching him as he fell. The man was dead weight in his arms, passed out. "Perfect," Bear grunted, shifting the man until he could lift him in a fireman's carry.

The man whimpered as Bear walked back over to his idling truck. The sound had Bear swallowing a growl. It was hard to tell in this rain, but Bear was pretty sure he was a beta. Other alpha scents burned his nose, sharply acidic, while omegas bloomed almost sickly sweet. This guy just smelled like a dirty, unwashed guy.

Bear threw open the passenger door and shoved him inside, backpack and all. Slamming the door shut, he ran around to the driver's side and got in. His shoulder-length hair was a wet mess. Ashy, brown strands hung in his face, plastered to his neck. He dragged his fingers through it, slicking it away from his face. Then he flicked off his hazards and threw his truck into drive.

The man groaned again, his breath fogging against the window.

"Never a dull moment," Bear muttered.

As soon as he got where the shoulder was wide enough, he turned the truck around. Spring Hill was the closest town with an after-hours ER. Bear was going to drive him straight there and drop him off.

"And that's it," he told the unconscious man. "I can't be involved after that. Got it?"

The man didn't reply.

4

Silas jerked awake. His entire body screamed in pain, and he was shaking uncontrollably. Wet, cold, aching all over. His memories were all messed up. Dark shit he usually swallowed down deep was floating right at the surface, mingling with other memories that felt thinner than wisps of smoke.

Hours spent trapped in the car with Floyd and his noxious junk food farts.

Dallas' gun on his hip.

The fight.

The crash.

The pain.

Oh god, the pain.

Silas didn't know how long he'd spent hobbling down the dark mountain road in the pouring rain. Using the guardrail as a crutch, he put as much distance between himself and the crash as possible. A few cars passed but didn't stop. Silas wasn't surprised. People don't help other people, at least not for free. And Silas had nothing of value to offer or trade if anyone *did* stop. Just another drifter. Alone. Dangerous.

Yeah, he'd probably drive on by too. He was on his own.

Wait...no...

He was in a moving car. Panic burst in his gut, stealing all his air.

"You should probably stay awake," said a deep voice to his left. "I think you might have a concussion."

He spun to face the voice. On the other end of the truck's bench seat, a huge, tatted up white guy sat behind the wheel. It was the guy from the road. He was wearing a pair of jeans, a dark t-shirt, and motorcycle boots. Like Silas, he was soaking wet. His shoulder-length brown hair was still dripping.

"Who are you?" Silas rasped. "Why the hell did you pick me up?"

"You were stumbling through the rain on a broken leg," the man replied in that deep voice. "I wasn't leavin' you out there. If you don't like it, there's the door. But I'm not slowin' down. If you want out, you'll just have to tuck and roll." There was a music to his voice, gravelly, yet smooth.

Silas's eyes were getting used to the soft glow from the dashboard. He could make out more details now. The man was tall, easily over six feet, and broad shouldered. He had a hipster lumberjack vibe, with a full beard and that long, brown hair. Silas was sure he probably pulled it up into one of those stupid man buns. Tattoos stretched from the tips of his fingers, all the way up his sun tanned arms, peeking out the top of his t-shirt on his neck. Geometric patterns, a pinup girl, a lion on his bicep, a spiderweb on his elbow. All in black. If any of them were gang or pack signs, Silas couldn't tell.

He took a deep inhale, trying to breathe past the pain in

his ribs. His senses were a mess, but he still picked up the unmistakable scent of dominance and control.

Alpha. One hundred percent. He sighed. *Fucking perfect.*

"You get a good sniff there, beta?" the man joked.

"Where are you taking me?"

"There's a 24-hour clinic in Spring Hill. They'll be able to take a look at that leg."

"What—a hospital?" Panic flooded him again. "No hospitals."

Tats gave him an incredulous look. "What part about 'broken leg' are you not hearing? I know you're committed to your death march, but you need two workin' legs for that and—"

"I said *no*! I'm not going to a hospital. Let me out." He reached for the door's handle and opened it a crack. Rain pelted inside.

"Shit—*whoa*—hold on," Tats barked. "I was joking about the whole 'tuck and roll' thing. Shut the damn door." He reached across the bench seat, trying to pull the door closed himself.

The quick movement sent Silas's pulse racing. The big alpha was suddenly so close. His scent was overwhelming, spicy and woodsy and...whimsical. Shit, Silas had never used that word to describe another man in his life. But it's like Tats secreted Christmas morning from his glands.

Silas held his breath and leaned away. "Get the fuck off me." He slapped his arm away, trying to ignore the feel of their skin touching. At the same time, he slammed the door shut.

Tats immediately dropped his arm.

Silas took a deep breath. "Please, don't touch me."

"Alright, man. No problem." Tats moved back over to his side of the truck. "I was just tryin' to shut the door—"

"Just stop the truck," Silas panted. "Let me out."

"I'm not leaving you on the side of the road in a thunderstorm," he countered. "I may be a cold, heartless bastard, but I'm not a complete monster."

Feeling his anger rise, Silas reached up under his hoodie, tugging loose his gun. He pointed it straight at Tats. "I said no hospitals. Now, pull over, and let me out."

Across from him, Tats went still as stone, one eye on the gun, while the other watched the road. "Okay...let's just walk this back a step. There's no need for the gun. You say no hospital, it's no hospital. I'll just...drive you to town. There's a motel. You can get a room for the night. Get out of the rain. A hot meal. I'll pay—"

"I don't need anything from you," Silas snapped. "I didn't ask for anything, and I won't fucking take anything either. And what the *fuck* is this fucking music?"

Some kind of weird country boy polka music had been playing during their entire conversation. The sound was setting Silas's teeth on edge. Between the music and the *squeak squeak* of the windshield wipers, the pounding rain, the pounding of his tumultuous thoughts—it was all too much. He was going to be sick again.

The corner of Tats' mouth curved into a smile as he reached over and turned the music off. "There. Now will you lower the gun?"

"Are you gonna take me to a hospital?" Silas replied, his finger still curled around the trigger.

Tats shook his head. "Nope...but you gotta let someone tend to that. I can practically taste the break. It's been making me gag since I put you in my truck," he added with a grimace.

There was no way Silas was going to a hospital. For an unbonded omega with a criminal record, there was no place less safe. Hospitals wanted detailed patient information. Hospitals took blood and ran tests. They had mandatory reporting procedures, to the police *and* to the nearest Omega Center. Silas knew what all unbounded omegas know: he went to a hospital, he didn't come out again.

Not to mention, Ava had cops on the take all over the place. And she had a whiz tech guy who would definitely notice if Silas's name alerted in any hospital database. It was only a matter of time before she snatched him back out of whatever padded room or cell they held him in.

"Listen, I can't go to a hospital, okay?" Hating himself, he cast the last tattered threads of his pride aside and begged. "Please...sir. Don't take me there. Please."

Tats let out a low breath, his hands tight on the wheel. "Can you tell me why?"

Silas swallowed. He'd been rehearsing his story as he stumbled down the road just in case someone stopped. He couldn't tell the truth. This alpha probably wouldn't believe him anyway. But he had to be ready with an excuse that didn't expose him as an unbonded omega on the run. Something about this alpha was making him choke back his lies. There was something in his voice, the comfort of his scent, like wrapping up in a blanket on a cold winter's day. Silas let himself unravel a few thin threads of his truth. "If I go to a hospital, my pack will find me."

Tats was quiet for a minute. "And...you don't want them to find you?"

"No. I'm *never* going back. You take me to a hospital, the hospital reports me, and the pack finds me. That can't happen. I'll pull this trigger on myself first." He tapped the muzzle against his temple.

Tats glanced over at him. "Are you bonded? Are they gonna come looking either way?"

"No pack owns me," Silas replied, lowering the gun.

"What's your name?"

"Silas." The word slipped between his lips without conscious thought. *Shit. Fuck.* Why did he give this alpha his real name? What the hell was wrong with him?

Tats just nodded, eyes on the road. "You got a last name, Silas?"

Again, Silas felt the urge to spill his guts. He shook his head, physically biting his bottom lip to keep the word from coming out of his mouth. "My first name is enough," he managed to get out.

"Why are you here?"

That voice. So deep. So soothing. So...compelling.

"Just passing through. I was on my way to Bridgeport. Now I don't know where I'm going—"

Shut up. Shut UP.

Silas swallowed the rest of his words, his chest heaving as if he'd just run a mile. Recognition suddenly dawned. With a scowl, he pointed the gun back at the alpha. "What the hell is this? Are you pulling some kind of sneaky alpha bark on me right now? You forcing me to answer you?"

Tats had the audacity to shrug, even with the gun on him. "Sorry. Old habits."

Silas clenched his jaw tight. There was nothing he hated more than an alpha taking advantage. Not that he expected any less. Alphas just couldn't help themselves. "Don't make me shoot you," he snapped. "Fair is fair. What's your name then? I know I don't have alpha powers to force it out of you."

"I got nothin' to hide," Tats replied quietly. "I'm Bear."

Silas blinked. "Bear...as in the animal?"

"Yup."

Silas snorted. It sent a sharp pain across his sternum, and he grimaced. "You're joking, right?"

Bear reached into the cupholder and tossed something at him. He caught it one-handed, still holding the gun with the other. It was a wallet. Smooth brown leather, well-worn from his pocket. Silas flipped it open and read aloud the name on the driver's license. "Henry Calhoun Beresford III...fuck, that's a mouthful. So, I'm guessing Beresford became 'Bear?'"

"Pretty much," Bear replied, taking the wallet, and slipping it back into the cupholder.

They were both quiet for a moment. Silas could see the glowing lights of a town shining just beyond the trees. He was running out of time.

As if the alpha could read his thoughts, Bear glanced his way. "I may have another option."

"Another option for what?"

"For that leg. I'm invested now. I didn't risk my own neck to just dump you someplace. Call it alpha overprotectiveness."

"I said no fucking hospitals—"

"And I won't take you to a hospital," Bear said, cutting him off. "My friend is the vet in town. Lord knows he owes me a thousand favors." He reached for his cellphone in the cupholder. "Let me just call—"

"No," Silas barked, raising the gun again. "No phone calls. I let you touch that, you'll call the cops or-or text your pack, and they'll come jump me in the motel parking lot."

"I'm not gonna call the cops, and I don't have a pack," Bear growled. "But I *am* getting really sick of having that damn gun in my face. You've clearly been through some bad shit, and I feel for you, but my patience is wearing thin. I'm wet down to my damn socks, I'm tired, my dog has probably

23

shit on the rug, and at this rate I won't be home until sunrise. So lower that goddamn gun, or I *will* drop you at the clinic." Alpha bark laced every syllable of his little speech, and Silas fought the urge to whimper.

"They can treat my gunshot wound while they treat your broken leg," the alpha added. "Just know they'll have to leave us alone at some point, and then I'll rip the heart rate monitor off your finger and garrote you with the cord. You hearing me, little beta? Now, lower the damn gun."

Shit...this Bear has bite.

Silas shakily lowered the gun, choosing to believe it was his decision. They both knew otherwise. He considered what the alpha was offering as pain throbbed up his leg. "He's a vet? Like, dogs and cats?"

"Dogs, cats, horses, cows. Any animal, really," Bear replied, his tone softer now.

Silas couldn't think. He was still feeling dizzy. He placed a hand to his aching head, closing his eyes. "And he won't ask questions?"

Bear laughed. "Oh, he'll ask a thousand questions...that doesn't mean we have to answer any," he added. "I trust Jared. If I ask him to keep quiet, he will."

They took a turn and the edge of town stretched before them. The soft yellow lights of the motel sign flickered in the rain. VACANCY. FREE WIFI. NO PETS. Across from the motel, lights lit up a gas station, a pawn shop, and a dry cleaner. More shops stretched down the main drag.

Bear glanced his way again. "So...what's it gonna be? Are we going to Jared, or am I leaving you at the motel?"

Silas let out a breath. It was a roll of the dice either way. At least he still had the gun. "Fine. Take me to the vet."

"This will go smoother if you let me call him first," Bear

replied, throwing on his turn signal even though they were the only vehicle on the road.

"No calls," Silas replied.

"Alright." Slowly, a smile tipped his lips. Then he was laughing again. "You know, maybe this *is* better. I'm never gonna live it down though. I hope you know this will eat up every favor I've earned over a fifteen-year friendship."

Silas frowned. "You want me to apologize?"

"Nope," Bear replied with a shake of his head. "But I *do* want you to put that gun away. And know this: If you pull it on Jared, I'll finish whatever was started on you tonight. We clear?"

Silas nodded, slipping the gun inside his hoodie pocket.

"Good. We're here."

5

Bear

I f someone at the bar earlier had asked Bear how he planned to spend the rest of his Friday night, the last thing he expected to say was that he'd be standing at the back door of Jared Larson's veterinary clinic helping a runaway beta with a broken leg.

Raising a large fist, Bear rapped several times on the back door.

"I'm good," Silas muttered, dropping his arm from around Bear's shoulders.

Silas. The name felt real enough when he said it. Bear had a gift for tasting the truth on people. It was a skill he honed for six years in the military as an intelligence officer. He probably could have gotten the answers he wanted from this beta without using his subliminal alpha bark, but there was a gun in his face at the time.

Speaking of guns—

"I said I'm good," Silas said again, breaking through the fog of Bear's thoughts.

"Hmm?" Bear shifted his arm on his waist. Damn, this

beta smelled good. Bear actually had to fight the urge to lean in.

The beta inched away from him. "You can let go of me."

"Stop squirming or you'll fall down the steps," Bear warned, keeping his arm firmly around his waist.

Jared threw a window open upstairs and stuck his head out. "Bear? What the hell are you doin' here? Who's that with you? I can't see his face—"

"Open up," Bear called up to him. "We need your help."

There was a pause as Jared stared down at the pair of them. Then he cursed under his breath. "Hold on. I'm comin' down."

The window snapped shut. In no time, the lock chain rattled inside the door. It swung open, revealing Jared standing in nothing but a pair of sleep pants. Like Bear, he was a big guy. They played football together in high school. Bear was maybe broader in the shoulders, but this beta was tall—unnaturally so, given his biology.

"What the hell, man? You hurt?" Jared said, his blue eyes blown wide. Bear could taste his anxiety on his tongue, tart and bitter like an unripe blackberry.

"He is," Bear replied with a grunt. "This is Silas," he added, shuffling sideways inside the door, pulling the beta along with him.

"*Ow*—shit," Silas groaned, tripping over the threshold.

Bear got him inside and Jared shut the door.

"If he's injured, take him to the clinic. They're open 24 hours—"

"No hospitals," Silas grunted. At the same time, Bear said, "I need you to look at his leg. We think it's broken."

Jared was still standing there, wide-eyed. "Where'd you find this guy? Who is he?"

"Side of the road," Bear muttered.

"Shit." Jared dragged a hand through his short blonde hair. Turning, he led the way down the narrow hallway and through a door into his clinic. "This isn't cool, man. I work on animals."

"I wouldn't ask if this wasn't important," Bear replied, helping Silas down onto a chair. "You can x-ray and do a cast and shit, right?"

Jared huffed. "Oh, did you suddenly go to med school? Broken legs usually require surgery, asshole. I'd need a team of people here, anesthesia, I'd have to open him up. And I'm not licensed to practice on people. I could lose my license. Hell, he could press charges against me for assault."

"I won't press charges," the beta muttered, gingerly adjusting his leg.

"Oh, well that's alright then," Jared scoffed. "Thanks, drifter man. I'm glad I have your permission to torch my fuckin' career."

"Jared...will you just look?" Bear murmured. "Visual exam only. Let us know what we're dealing with."

Jared glared at them both, jaw clenched tight. Bear knew him well enough not to push. He had to make up his own mind. Bear knew what *he* would do...but Jared wasn't Bear.

"Fuck, alright—" Jared dropped to one knee in front of the other beta. "Are you a rapist?"

Silas gasped, eyes wide. "What? No!"

"You rob any banks around here?"

Silas glanced sharply from Bear back to Jared. "No."

Jared narrowed his eyes. "You into kiddie porn or some twisted shit like that?"

"God—*no*," Silas panted.

"Then what's your story, asshole? Cause I'm not risking my career on some meth-dealing, bank-robbing, piece of shit beta drifter. How'd you break this leg?"

Bear watched Silas carefully. Now that they were inside, he could finally get a good look at the guy. The beta was around 5'10", maybe 180 pounds. He was young and handsome—medium brown skin with round, dark eyes, thick black brows, and a dusting of facial hair. His navy-blue hoodie had some faded university logo on it. He still wore the hood up over his head. A grey beanie covered his hair.

Taking a breath, the beta's shoulders sagged. "I...escaped my alphas."

Bear went impossibly still. It tasted like the truth, even if only a thin version of it. He couldn't fight his alpha urges, which were screaming like a fire alarm to protect this guy. The urge was so strong in the road it was almost like Bear had lost control of his own feet. It had been a long while since he'd ever felt that lost to his instincts. He didn't like it. Didn't like feeling out of control. Didn't like this beta for making him feel it.

"You...escaped?" Jared asked for the both of them.

Silas nodded.

"I'm sorry, but you're gonna have to give me more than that." Jared sat down and wheeled his chair forward. "Were you being held hostage or something? Are you a missing person? Did they do *this* to you?" He gestured to Silas's leg. "Did *you* know about this?" he added, his gaze shooting up to where Bear stood by the door with his arms folded over his chest.

"I know what you know," Bear muttered.

"Well, I don't know a damn thing!" Jared turned back to the beta. "Look, if you're in danger, you should go to the hospital. Hell, go to the police. Let them help you—"

"The alphas I ran from own the cops, alright?" Silas snapped. "They've got guys on the take from Bridgeport to St. Albans. If I could trust the police, I'd be there already.

And hospitals aren't any better. My name would alert in the system, and the pack would find me."

Truth.

Bear leaned in, eager for more.

Apparently, so was Jared. "Why do they want you so badly?" he asked with narrowed eyes. "I mean...you're just a beta, right? Am I missing something?"

Silas just shrugged. "Betas have uses too," he muttered. "And if you buy something, you think you own it. No one walks away once money is exchanged. It's bad for business."

Truth...veiled, but true enough.

Shit, this was getting heavy fast. Bear stepped forward, trying his best to keep the bark from his voice. "Were you being trafficked when you got away?"

Silas blinked, immediately looking back down at his hands. "Something like that."

Truth.

Jared let out a breath. "Holy shit. This is..." He glanced sharply up at Bear. "We need to call the police. Call Terry. This is serious!"

Bear saw the beta's hand shift to the front of his hoodie where he was hiding his gun. At the same time, his fear spiked, stinging the back of Bear's throat. Bear groaned, dragging a hand through his hair, trying to breathe through his urges. "No."

"What do you mean 'no'?" Jared cried, launching to his feet. "Some pack of alphaholes was trying to *sell* this guy, Bear! He's in serious trouble—"

"And he's tellin' us the police'll make it worse," Bear replied.

Jared blinked, open-mouthed. "And you're just gonna believe him?"

"Yes."

Bear felt the wave of relief flood through Silas. It wasn't enough to wash out all the festering pain and trauma, but it made Bear feel better too. Damn, what was with this beta? Bear had never felt so sensitive towards one before. Even with Jared standing here, all Bear was scenting off him was frustration and a bit of worry. He turned to Silas. "Do you have anywhere you can go after this? Someplace safe? A friend, maybe?"

Silas swallowed and nodded, still looking down at his hands. "Yeah...yeah, I got options. I have friends back in St. Albans."

Lie.

It tasted bitter and weak, like over-brewed tea leaves. Bear felt his whole body tensing as the taste flooded his mouth. A broken beta, wounded and alone. Afraid to go to the hospital. Afraid of the cops. Deathly afraid of alphas. Bear had been tasting his fear since the moment they met on the road. He glared at Jared. "You gonna work on that leg, or what?"

Jared glanced back over at Silas. "Well? Can I take a look?"

Silas's shoulders fell with relief. "Yeah. Thanks, Doc."

"Right...well, give me a minute. I gotta wash up and get some gloves...and a shirt," he added. "Bear, help Silas out of his shoes and pants. I'll be back and—"

"I'm not taking my pants off, and the alpha's not touching me," Silas snapped.

Jared glanced from Bear back to Silas. "I can't treat your leg with your pants on..."

"You only need from the knee down," Silas countered. "You got scissors?"

Jared pulled open a drawer. He rifled inside, handing

over a pair of scissors. "Don't kill each other with these while I'm gone."

Before Jared was out the door, Silas had the scissors in hand, cutting his jeans off at the knee.

ONCE HE WENT INTO DOCTOR MODE, JARED WAS CALM AND efficient, helping Silas remove his shoe and sock. The cut-off piece of jean sagged down to his ankle, and Silas winced as Jared slipped it off. The leg was bruised and swollen, but the skin was intact. If anything was broken, it was all happening inside the leg. Jared helped Silas hobble down the hall to the other examining room. Silas hopped up on the table as Jared got his portable x-ray ready.

Now that Silas's adrenaline was zapped, fatigue was taking over. His scent shifted from panicked and alert to broken and deeply tired. Bear fought the urge to growl as Jared's helping hands made Silas whimper in pain.

"Sorry, I know it hurts," Jared murmured, getting Silas's leg into position.

The poor beta was shaking like a leaf. He was still damp, and now he was stretched out on a cold operating table. Bear glanced around the room.

Jared raised a brow. "What are you looking for?"

"Blanket," Bear muttered.

"Cabinet," Jared replied, rolling the x-ray into place. "Left side, on the bottom."

Bear grabbed two hospital style white blankets off the shelf. He tucked one under his arm and unfolded the other, handing it over to Silas. "Here. You're gonna make *my* teeth rattle."

Silas took the blanket, letting it fall over his top half. "Thanks," he sighed with relief.

Bear layered the other blanket on top and stepped back, arms folded as he watched Jared work.

"Hmm...it's definitely broken," Jared said some minutes later, looking at the images on his computer screen. "But it's not that bad. You're really lucky. This looks like a hairline fracture."

"Yeah...lucky," Silas muttered. His shivering was less now, which only enhanced his fatigue. He was on the edge of consciousness.

Bear came around to stand behind Jared.

"These can be hard to pick up on x-ray, but the angle is just right in this image. See it there?" Jared murmured, tracing over the faint line with his finger. "If you'd tried to do anymore running on it, you might have split it open."

Bear narrowed his eyes at the black and white scan. "Does it need surgery?"

"I don't think so, actually," Jared replied. "I would get it casted. Stay off it for a month, maybe six weeks."

"Great," Silas grunted, shifting under the blankets with a wince. "Look, Doc...if it's not too much trouble, can I maybe get a pain killer? Or a horse tranquilizer?"

Bear smirked.

"Are you an addict, drifter man?" Jared replied with a raised brow. "Do you pop your grammy's back pills when she's not looking?"

The beta heaved a sigh. "No, I'm only asking 'cause of the whole broken leg thing."

Jared glanced over at Bear, seeking his permission.

Bear gave him a curt nod.

"I've got something here for pain relief. Not the hard stuff, but it'll work to take the edge off."

"Perfect," Silas muttered.

Bear snagged Jared's arm as he passed. "Will you cast it for us?"

"Bear, I..."

He lowered his voice. "Don't make me say 'please.'"

Jared rubbed his head with a tired hand, then let out a slow exhale. "If I say no, are you gonna bring up our junior year spring break?"

Bear smirked again. "That depends...are you gonna say no?"

Jared muttered a curse under his breath. "Why am I such a good fuckin' friend? You know you don't deserve it."

"I know," Bear replied. He let his eye drift back over to the beta huddled under hospital blankets on the operating table. "I know."

6

Bear

An hour later, Silas was passed out on the table, too weak and exhausted to stay awake. Jared was finishing up the cast. "So, this needs to stay dry," he explained. "Wrap it in plastic for showers. No sand and no dirt. Nothing that might get in there and irritate the skin—"

"I know," Bear muttered. "I've broken my own share of bones. Remember?"

Jared set aside the rest of the casting materials. "Right... well, I don't have any crutches here. Most of my patients wouldn't know how to use them," he added with a smirk.

"I have a pair in the shed from my ACL tear a couple years ago."

"I can slip you some sleeping pills, but I'm not getting involved in hard pain meds. I'm sorry, bud, but I draw the line at dealing to drifters."

"It's fine," Bear replied. "This has been more than enough. Thanks, J."

"Rest, lots of fluids, and keep him off the leg for at least the next four weeks. Six if you can manage it. No weight or he can break that fracture right open."

"I'll tell him."

Jared wheeled his chair back, turning to narrow his eyes at him.

Bear's body tensed under Jared's visual assault. "What?"

Jared pursed his lips, saying nothing.

"What?" he barked. "Spit it out."

"You'll tell him? Meaning you're gonna turn him loose? You'll gift him your old crutches and watch him hobble off to find his friends in St. Albans?"

Bear matched his frown. "Yeah, of course. Why do you care?"

"I care because I just risked my fuckin' license to treat a person...and I care about *you*," he added, shaking his head as he cleaned up the mess. "I know you, Bear. You can't let shit like this go. I see your wheels spinnin' already."

Bear couldn't help feeling defensive. "Alpha's have an innate need to protect—"

"Fuck your alpha nonsense. This is just...you," Jared countered, slapping down his tray of equipment. "You do this, Bear. You've got a savior complex deeper than anything your alpha genes cursed you with. Plenty of alphaholes would have driven right by this guy and not even blinked."

Bear's scowl deepened. "You saying I shouldn't have stopped? He's being trafficked, and that's not my problem? I guess I should just drive on by, huh?"

"I don't want you to get hurt," Jared replied.

"I know what I'm doing."

"Do you?" Jared challenged, crossing his arms.

They were both quiet for a moment, staring each other down. In moments like this, Bear could almost forget Jared was a beta. Shaking his head, he dragged both hands through his hair. "You didn't see him on that road, J. You don't know. He looked..." Words escaped him.

"Hurt?" Jared offered.

Bear shook his head again, swallowing the bile that had suddenly risen in his throat at the memory of how Silas's fear had tasted in the road...the haunting look of him crawling to his feet, desperate to get away. He looked at the beautiful man on the table. "Hunted," he murmured. "He looked hunted."

Jared glanced warily over at the man on his table. "And you really wanna get involved with a guy being hunted? What happens when the hunter comes knockin' on your door?"

"I can't just walk away." Saying the words out loud, Bear's decision was made. In truth, he knew he made it the moment he opened the door of his truck and stepped out into the rain. Wherever this road led, he was on it now.

"Well, I've done all I can do," Jared replied. "And I don't wanna sound like an ass, but can you get him out of here now? And if you breathe a word of this to anyone, I'll be the one that comes knockin'," he added, leveling his finger in Bear's face. "If I lose my license thanks to you two, I may as well get creative, and I've always wanted to try a kidney transplant. You hearin' me?"

"I hear you," Bear muttered, moving over to Silas's side.

"And we're even for like...ever," Jared added. "However many favors you think you had on me, you just cashed 'em all. We're square."

Bear hefted the unconscious Silas into his arms in a bridal carry, blankets and all. "Yeah, we're square, J."

"Good. Here, let me—" Jared rushed around the room, gathering up Silas's discarded sock, shoe, and strip of cut jeans. He shoved it all in a plastic bag, adding a rattling bottle of pills. "Anxiety meds," he explained. "And this one has a couple more sleeping pills in it," he added, tossing in a second bottle.

"Thanks." Bear shifted his hand so Jared could slip the handles of the bag over his wrist.

"I'll help you get him out to the truck."

Outside, it had finally stopped raining. A bad bulb in the parking lot made the light flicker and buzz. Silas stayed passed out in Bear's arms as they crossed under it. Jared opened the passenger door for them, and Bear shoved Silas inside. He groaned, his body flopping down face-first on the bench seat. Bear tossed the bag in at his feet.

"Just...take care of yourself," Jared said softly. "You don't owe this guy a damn thing. You're not a pack leader anymore. He's not yours to protect. You made your choices, Bear. Don't let this drifter drag you back where you don't wanna go."

Bear shut the door, pressing his hand against the cold metal. He didn't turn around.

"There, I said what I wanted to say," Jared muttered. "Alright, well...see you when I see you."

Bear didn't reply. He just stepped around the front of his truck and got inside the cab. Turning the key in the ignition, the truck roared to life. When he glanced back, Jared was already back at the door, slipping inside.

Bear looked down at the beta passed out on his bench seat. "What the hell am I gonna do with you now?"

Shifting his truck into drive, he turned up his radio, and headed home.

7

Bear

Thirty minutes later, Bear pulled up the gravel drive to his cabin. The handsome A-frame sat nestled in the woods right at the lake's edge. The lakefront windows all glowed a welcoming, golden yellow. It reflected down onto the edge of the dark water.

The sight of his cabin always eased his mind. It was his own design, and he built a lot of it himself—the kitchen, the stone fireplace, the floors, most of the furniture. He had his uncle's company do the actual construction, but the rest was all Bear, even down to the deck that stretched across the front.

He turned off the truck and took a deep breath, glancing to the right. The beta hadn't moved the entire drive home. Bear dragged himself out his side of the cab and went around to Silas's side. Doing his best to be gentle, he pulled the beta out.

Silas groaned, shifting away from his touch. "Don't fucking touch me," he mumbled.

"Okay, tough guy. I won't," Bear replied, shifting to get him in a better hold.

"Hurts—"

"I know," he soothed. "Let's just get you inside." He shuffled sideways up the steps of the deck.

Inside the house, Zeus was barking like crazy, knowing Bear was home. He was a sweet dog, but dumber than a box of rocks.

"I'm comin'," Bear called up the steps.

The front door was set against a wall of glass, exposing the open-plan kitchen and living room. Zeus stood there, tail wagging. Bear had to shuffle Silas to get a finger free to jab in the key code. The lock beeped and the deadbolt retracted. Bear shoved open the door, and Zeus darted out, his nails clicking on the deck as he zoomed down the steps.

Bear moved through the living room, weaving between the pair of leather couches. Off to the left, behind the massive stone chimney, were the bedrooms. His room was directly behind the chimney, sharing it on the other side of the wall. It had amazing views of the lake too. But like hell was he sharing. He turned right in the hallway, bringing Silas to the back bedroom.

"Don't touch—" Silas whimpered.

"I know. I'll put you down on the bed, and I won't touch you again, okay?" The door was open, and he didn't bother turning on the light. He just flopped Silas down on the queen bed, right on top of the quilt. Silas had the hospital blankets around him already. If he needed more than that, all he had to do was roll over.

Taking a chance, Bear slid his hand under the blanket and reached for the front of Silas's hoodie. He slipped the gun out, palming it as he took a step back. He glanced down with a frown, clicking the magazine out. He tipped it towards the light, seeing it was full of rounds. He racked the gun and nothing came out.

"Figures," he muttered.

He put the magazine in his pocket and tucked the gun into the back of his pants. With one last look at Silas, he stepped out and shut the door. He walked with purpose back across the living room, out the front door, and down to his truck.

He had to know more about this beta.

Snatching up the plastic bag and the backpack, Bear locked his truck and went back inside, depositing the bags on the granite kitchen island. He pulled the gun from his pants and clicked it down on the island too, setting the magazine next to it. The faint smell of alpha wafted out of the bag as he unzipped the front pocket, dumping all the contents at once onto the island. A pack of gum rattled out first, followed by a set of keys, a pack of smokes and a lighter, and the real prize: a wallet.

Bear flipped it open, and his frown deepened. The driver's license inside was for a Floyd Rainier: alpha, 40 years old, 280 pounds. If this was Silas's attempt at making a fake ID, he had more than a few screws loose. For starters, this alpha was easily three times larger than Silas. His skin was also about two shades darker. Bear shuffled through the other items in the wallet: a couple credit cards in Floyd's name, a hotel keycard, and a club card for a deli that was one stamp away from a free meatball sub.

Oh, and seventy-two bucks.

"Score," Bear muttered, replacing all the stuff in the wallet.

He set it aside and opened the main compartment of the backpack. The stench of alpha reeked—a pungent mix of sweat, menthol cigarettes, and pastrami. It churned Bear's stomach.

He'd never fared well around other alphas. Since first

presenting back when he was seventeen, he'd yet to meet another alpha with a scent signature he could stomach. He tried for so long to make pack life work, but he just... couldn't. The mix of scents, the closeness, the need for constant direction and support from his pack mates. Even alphas crave an alpha. For three years, Bear twisted himself inside out, trying to be what everyone else needed. All the while, he was miserable.

In the end, he walked away. That was three years ago. He'd finally resigned himself to being alone. His family may not understand, his pack definitely didn't understand, but Bear was done trying to be the alpha he wasn't.

He tipped the backpack over, dumping the rest of the contents. Sifting through it, his suspicions were quickly confirmed. A change of clothes three sizes too big for the beta, including a pair of underwear that smelled so thickly of alpha jizz Bear almost gagged. An old Dopp kit full of sundries. The heaviest thing was a pair of boots in a men's size thirteen. Bear reached into the plastic bag and pulled out Silas's shoe. Checking the tongue, his frown deepened.

Size: Men's 10.

"This isn't your backpack, little beta."

So, Silas was stumbling in the dark on a broken leg, desperately clutching to a backpack that wasn't his. A backpack full of another man's clothes. The only thing worth anything in the whole bag was the cash.

It fit Silas's story at least, what little Bear knew of it. Silas escaped alphas and was on the run. This Floyd definitely smelled like an alpha worth running from. But why did Silas have his bag if he couldn't use a damn thing inside it except the cash?

It bothered him. For the hundredth time that night, Bear felt that indescribable itch to know more. He had to physically fight the urge to go wake the beta up and demand answers.

"You're too curious for your own good," he muttered to himself.

The smell of this alpha was choking him. Shoving back from the island, he went straight to the cabinet under his sink and got a trash bag. Snapping it open, he shoved all the contents of the backpack inside. He tied it closed and carried it downstairs into the garage, holding his breath all the while. He set the trash bag on the top shelf next to an old cooler and stepped back, sucking air into his lungs.

"I can still smell him," he muttered at Zeus, who stood at his side. He went straight back upstairs to the kitchen sink and flipped on the hot water tap, scrubbing at his hands and arms. His gaze drifted back over to the end of the island. The gun bothered him. Watching Silas with it had bothered him even more. Having it waved in his face wasn't the problem. It was *how* the beta waved it. Bear would bet any money the beta had never fired a gun in his life.

Snatching up the gun in one hand and the magazine in the other, Bear marched to his room, through his bathroom, into the walk-in closet. In the back of the closet sat a large gun safe. He tapped in the six-digit code, waiting for the double beep before he clicked it open. His personal stock of rifles sat neatly arranged within. Handguns each had their own boxes on the top shelf. Some were heirlooms, others were things he'd bought for target practice or hunting.

He set Silas's gun on the top shelf, leaving the magazine beside it. Giving it one last look, he slowly shut the safe door and waited until he heard the lock click into place. All the while, his mind buzzed. It wasn't like Bear to be reckless. He needed to calm down and focus. He wasn't going to let his alpha instincts control him.

The beta couldn't stay here, that was for damn sure. Bear had no room in his life for running a safe house for weary betas. He'd give him a day or two to sleep off the worst of his injuries, but then he had to go. Bear would do all he could to help, but the beta couldn't stay.

8

Silas

S ilas cried out, clawing at the air with both hands, trying desperately to stop them from binding his arms. "No, *no!*" He gasped awake, heart racing, a sheen of sweat covering his body. He wasn't bound, just tangled in his blankets. He wiggled his shoulders, loosening the blanket enough to free himself.

Just a dream. Breathe.

He took a few shaky breaths. He was so hot. Sweltering. Why did he still have on his hoodie and beanie...and only one shoe?

Two shoes? No—one shoe and one—what the hell?

He blinked his eyes open, glancing around the room... the dark room he'd never seen before. He bolted upright, choking back a cry of pain. His whole body was one big bruise, and his left leg was throbbing. It felt like someone had taken a bat to it.

Slicked in sweat, he tugged off his hoodie, letting the cool air kiss his skin. He dragged his beanie off too, rubbing his hand over his buzz cut. He let his mind fill with recent memories. A face sharpened immediately into focus.

Bear.

Stupid name, but an okay guy...for an alpha. Silas clearly pictured the lines of the tattoos going up his arm. His hipster beard. Those piercing hazel eyes. That deep voice, brimming with alpha confidence.

And his scent. God, but he smelled so fucking good. Silas wasn't used to having such sharp senses when it came to alphas. He'd lived most of the last seven years feeling like he had cotton balls shoved up his nose. As the cotton finally loosened, he was getting whiffs of alphas for the first time. Turns out it was a real mind fuck.

He dragged a hand over his face again. This had to be Bear's house. Even with the curtains closed, Silas could make out the features of the room: a big bed, wooden chair in the corner, side tables with lamps, a dresser with a mirror.

He tossed the white hospital blankets off his lap. He was still wearing his jeans. They felt stiff and dirty. His left pant leg was cut off at the knee, and his leg from the top of the shin down to the foot was now wrapped in a thick white cast.

Reaching over with a groan, he turned on the lamp. A bottle of water sat on the table with a note taped to it: DRINK ME. Next to the water was a plate of pills and another note that said TAKE ME. Next to the plate was a red apple with a note: EAT ME.

"Smart ass," he huffed, downing the pills and chasing them with the water.

That's when he noticed the crutches. They were wedged between the bedside table and the bed. A note was taped to those too: BATHROOM IS DOWN THE HALL.

"This guy thought of everything except a change of—" But the words died on his lips, because there, folded on the chair next to the bedside table, was a little stack of clothes and a final note: SMALLEST I COULD FIND.

Silas frowned again. He didn't know why it bothered him, but it did. He wasn't used to people doing things for him. At least, never anything he *wanted* them to do. Since meeting Bear, it was like the alpha couldn't stop doing things for him. Getting him out of the road, taking him to the vet, bringing him home, leaving him water and pills. If he expected anything from Silas in return, his alpha ass would be disappointed. Silas was done with that life for good.

Shrugging himself back into his hoodie, he slipped his legs off the bed and reached for the crutches. Bracing for pain, he curled forward and tried to stand. He wobbled a bit, trying to get the crutches under his arms. If he didn't get to a bathroom, he was gonna piss his pants.

He shuffled down the hall and turned at the open door into the waiting bathroom. In his exhausted state, he wanted nothing more than to sit like an old grandpa, but it was too painful to get back up. Instead, he swayed awkwardly on the too-tall crutches and did his business.

He was halfway back down the hall when he heard a door slam from somewhere near the front of the house. A dog barked. Curiosity got the better of him. Peeking his head around the corner, his mouth dropped open in shock. This place was...*amazing*. The walls arched up to a curved point, like the whole house was a big triangle inside.

And then there was that view. The far side of the house was a wall of glass leading all the way up into that pointed ceiling. Stretching out from end to end behind the glass was a perfect view of a mountain lake. It looked like a painting with the autumn leaves splashing bright colors all around—

apple red, golden yellow, burnt orange. And the water was a deep, sapphire blue.

The view made Silas's heart feel tight. He wanted to see how far the lake stretched beyond the windows. But he didn't feel ready to see Bear. He was sure the alpha had more questions. And if Silas was completely honest, he wasn't ready to be hit in the face with that scent again.

If he wasn't careful, Bear was going to figure him out, and then where would Silas be? It was one thing for Bear to help a beta who couldn't keep his story straight. But if Bear knew the truth...if he knew he was actually harboring an unbonded omega with fucked up, suppressed hormones? An omega who only yesterday had killed a man? Would he turn Silas in to the police? An Omega Center?

Silas chilled at the thought. With so few omegas in the world—and fewer born every year—they were monitored closely. Omega Centers were meant to be safe spaces for newly presented omegas to find protection and support. They offered free housing, health services, and screenings for alpha pairings...at least on paper.

But Silas knew the truth: not all Centers were created equal. Sure, some of the private Centers were better than a hotel spa—private rooms, monitored heats. But those were expensive and exclusive. Most Centers were run by the government. They may show a clean face to the world— sappy documentaries about finding your pack, promises of free education and job placement—but the truth was less rosy.

Silas's Center only cared about selling its omegas to the highest bidders. The scent books were all bullshit. The only options were politicians and other well-connected people. And the job training he was promised? Yeah, that didn't happen. Instead, his Center jumped at the first opportunity to volunteer him for a medical experiment. Lies and manipulation. Pain. Suffering.

I'll end it first, he thought darkly. *I'm never going back to another Center.*

Maybe Bear would be all too happy to return Silas to his captors. Ava was always generous. No doubt she'd pay Bear handsomely for his trouble—

"Hey there," Bear called from the kitchen. His deep voice tasted like warm honey on Silas's tongue. Did voices have tastes?

A quiet moment stretched between them as Silas's mind spun.

"You gonna come out here so we can talk?"

Silas sucked in a sharp breath.

Fuck.

9

Silas

Taking a deep breath, Silas tugged up the hood of his hoodie and swung around the corner. His eyes settled immediately on the alpha standing behind the kitchen island. The shirtless alpha.

Bear's arms were massive, his shoulders toned, and he had an eight-pack you could wash clothes on. The wet t-shirt gave most of it away last night, but it was totally different seeing him in the daylight. Both arms were fully sleeved in tattoos down to his fingertips, and they connected across his hairless chest. A few patterns stretched down his ribs and up his neck, but his stomach and hips were untouched by ink.

The alpha's deep summer tan ended at his hips, showing off a strip of creamy white skin that led down to—

Oh shit...is he naked?

Silas swallowed, eyes going wide. But then Bear turned around and reached for something on the counter. That's when Silas saw his low-slung shorts.

Thank fuck.

Bear had his brown hair tied up in a man bun. A few unruly tendrils framed his face. He turned back around, holding some kind of green smoothie. He slipped on a pair of glasses with black, square frames. The corner of his mouth tipped into a smile. "You gonna come over here? Or you wanna just stand there swaying?"

Taking another breath, Silas swung forward on his crutches. "How long was I out?"

"About thirty-two hours," Bear replied, taking a sip of his weird green smoothie.

Silas paused with a sharp hiss of pain. "What?"

Bear just shrugged, stroking a hand over his beard. "We got back around four am Saturday morning. Now it's around one pm Sunday afternoon." He glanced at the oven. "Yeah, 1:15pm."

"Fuck," Silas muttered. "Sorry."

"Don't be. You clearly needed it. Jared said you shouldn't do much else but rest."

Jared. That was the name of the vet. Big white guy. Sporty. Snarky.

Suddenly, a dog barked, nearly making Silas jump. It was a big dog. Looked like a lab, but it was a caramel brown color with weird wavy fur. It had cool amber eyes. It came trotting over to him, sniffing his pants, his cast.

"Whoa, easy there," Silas muttered.

"That's Zeus," said Bear from across the room. "He's an idiot."

Silas couldn't let go of his crutches to shoo the dog away, so he just let him nose his crotch. The dog soon lost interest and trotted away, flopping down on a massive pillow.

Silas turned his attention back to Bear. "I'm sorry to be such a bother," he said again.

"You're not a bother," Bear replied. "Why don't you sit down. Want anything? I can make you one of these," he added, gesturing to his smoothie.

Silas grimaced.

He laughed. The sound was deep and low. "I'll take that as a no."

Silas just shuffled forward. "You're a health nut, aren't you."

Bear took another sip of his smoothie. "You only got one life and one body to live with it. I take care of mine, so it'll take care of me."

"Yeah, yeah. All that 'my body is a temple' bullshit. I know the type. Alphas love being strong in mind, strong in body. Easier to dominate the rest of us." As soon as the words were out of his mouth, Silas wanted to bite them back. Fuck, why did he have to say that? He glanced up sharply. "I'm sorry. I didn't—"

Bear raised his free hand. "Don't. You're right. A lot of alphas keep fit to appease our urges for power and control. It's shitty, but it's true. We make great athletes, bodyguards, soldiers. I've done a bit of all of it myself. But you're wrong if you think all alphas seek to dominate others," he added. "A true alpha wants to protect others. We're strong so you don't have to be."

Silas didn't know what to say to that. It was so opposite of everything he'd ever experienced with alphas. And he knew a *lot* of alphas.

Bear seemed fine to let it drop. He checked something on his phone and glanced back up. "Want some coffee? I have some left from this morning."

Silas nodded.

"Sit down, and I'll bring it to you," he replied, busying himself at the counter.

Silas glanced around at the options of furniture. Two cozy leather couches framed the massive stone fireplace. A pair of chairs by the windows completed the square. The kitchen had a row of stools at the counter, but he'd have to climb to get on one.

And everything in here smelled like Bear.

Glancing outside, he noticed the deck had several chairs too. The urge for fresh air suddenly felt overwhelming.

"You gonna sit?" Bear said again, coming around the island with his smoothie in one hand, a mug of coffee in the other.

"Umm...could we maybe sit outside?"

Bear paused. "Sure." He walked over to the door, setting down his smoothie to unlock it and swing it open. The dog darted out, running the length of the deck and leaping onto the patio sectional in the corner.

Silas swung himself across the living room and out the door, taking a deep breath of fresh air. It cleared his senses, calming his frayed nerves. The September air was cool. It felt good with his hoodie on.

Bear shut the door and stepped around him, heading for the closest pair of deck chairs. He sat down on the far one, placing the cup of coffee in reach of the closer chair.

"What lake is this?" Silas asked, moving towards the empty chair.

"Lake Beresford," Bear replied, sipping his smoothie, eyes back on his phone as he tapped away with his thumb.

Silas paused. "Wait...so are you named after a lake...or is a lake named after you?"

Bear smiled, tucking the phone in his pocket. "Not after me, exactly. After my family. The Beresford's have lived here for over a century."

"Uh-huh. And is your daddy the mayor then? Did you go

to Beresford High? Were you prom king in your own little kingdom?"

"No...but this *is* Beresford County," Bear replied. "And my uncle is the sheriff. Does that count?"

"Fuck me," Silas muttered, sinking awkwardly down onto the deck chair. He winced, losing control of one of the crutches.

Bear caught it before it toppled, taking both from him and propping them along the deck rail. He sat back down, content to look out at the lake and drink his smoothie.

Silas let his eye drift over to him. This alpha was living next to a lake named after his family, in a county named after his family, and his uncle was the sheriff.

Yeah, I'm fucked.

He reached for the coffee and gave it a sniff. "You lived here long?"

"All my life," Bear replied. "At one end of the lake or the other. I only built this place about three years ago. Where are you from?"

"St. Albans," Silas replied, taking a sip of the coffee. He immediately regretted it. He coughed. "*Gah*—shit—is this just black coffee?" He peered inside the mug to see a pitch-black liquid, thick as molasses.

"You didn't tell me you wanted anything added," Bear replied with a smirk. "That's an expensive roast. It tastes great black."

Silas was still trying to suck the bitter taste off his tongue. "Liquid spinach and black coffee...no wonder you're alone out here," he muttered, setting aside the mug of coffee he definitely wasn't going to drink.

"I don't mind being alone," Bear replied. "The question is...are *you* alone?"

Silas turned slowly to look at the alpha. "What?"

Bear held his gaze with those piercing hazel eyes. "Who is Floyd Rainier?"

10

Silas sucked in a breath, his heart racing out of his chest.

"I asked you a question," said Bear, that deep voice pressing at the corners of Silas's mind. "Is Floyd Rainier your alpha? Is he who you're running from? Did he hurt you?"

The sound of Floyd's name on another alpha's lips set something off in Silas's mind. He dropped his head into his hands, elbows balanced on his knees, and rocked, trying to press down the memories flooding him in waves. The crash. The drive. Floyd's buckshot-splattered face. More memories. Dark memories. Memories that belonged in the numb place.

How the hell did this alpha know Floyd's name? Silas scrambled, trying to make it make sense. Did he say it last night? He wouldn't...

Then it hit him.

The backpack.

He jolted upright in the deck chair, eyes narrowing on the alpha next to him. Bear took the backpack. He went through it. What else did Bear take while Silas was passed out?

Oh shit...

Silas's mouth went dry as he dropped his hands to the front of his hoodie, patting the pocket. Empty.

Where's the gun?

He patted his jeans pockets. Did it slip out onto the bed—

"I took it," came the alpha's voice.

Silas stilled, eyes darting back over to him. "Give it back."

Bear took a sip of his gross smoothie. "No."

Silas's anger rattled in his chest, echoed by his fear. "Give me back my fucking gun."

"We both know it's not your gun, little beta. And I take gun safety seriously. As long as you're in my house, it stays in my safe."

"I'm not gonna shoot you with it," Silas snapped, crossing his arms in frustration.

"Oh, I know," Bear replied, finishing the last of his smoothie. "You couldn't even if you tried."

"What—"

"You've never shot that gun before, have you?" Bear pressed, now holding his gaze.

"I didn't need to. I got away just fine. But I *would* have pulled the trigger...on myself if no one else," he added under his breath, dropping his gaze down to his mismatched feet.

"I believe you." The alpha stretched out his long legs, folding his tatted hands over his bare stomach. "For future reference though, the pistol you were waving around has a manual thumb safety. You need to disengage it before it will fire. Also helps if you chamber a round."

Silas sank back, anxiety and embarrassment clenching tight in his gut. Bear knew. The whole time Silas had the gun out last night, trying to boss the alpha around, Bear knew he didn't even have the safety off. All he had to do was slap it out of his hand and shove Silas from the moving truck.

Oh god...and what if he'd really needed to shoot it last night? What if Dallas had—

"It's no big deal," Bear said, his voice low and soothing. "You didn't know, because it's not your gun, and that's okay. Next time, you'll know."

Silas sucked in a gasping breath, dropping his head back to his hands.

"Just breathe," Bear said after a minute. "You did your best, and your best was enough to get you out. You can be proud of that."

Out.

Silas was out. Was that really possible? Could you ever really be out of a life like that? Or would the taint of everything he'd done, everything he survived, follow him forever? The body may be out, but the mind never escapes. The soul? That's locked in too. Forever in. He was broken pieces now. No tape. No glue. Shattered.

Emotion overwhelmed him. He didn't even realize at first that his cheeks were wet. "Oh, god. I'm such a fucking— disaster," he panted, sucking in air. "I'm—still in. I'm—" He covered his face with both hands. "I'm so messed up. I'm so—"

A gentle hand on his shoulder made him go still as stone. The alpha was touching him. He glanced at the tattooed hand on his shoulder, noting the rune markings on the fingers, the mountain sunset pattern on the back of the hand. Stars. A name along the outside of the wrist: Georgia.

Silas's whole body trembled as his senses were invaded with a wave of rich alpha scent. Bear was pumping out pheromones meant to help calm him down. God, it felt so good. Like slipping into a hot bath. That spicy, forest smell filled his senses. Silas wanted to climb out of his chair and wrap himself around the alpha, bury his face in the crook of his neck, right where he knew the scent would be strongest. Silas could hardly believe it. This quiet alpha was tending to him like...

Like Silas was an omega.

Oh...shit.

Was he perfuming? Could the alpha smell it? He couldn't stay here. He wasn't safe. No alpha would let an unbonded omega slip through their fingers. He didn't care how nice Bear was being now. Once the truth came out, he'd be like every other alphahole. If Silas didn't plan his exit now, he was going to find himself trapped all over again.

"Get your hand off me," he muttered, his voice a low growl.

An omega growling at an alpha. What a joke.

Bear dropped his hand away.

They both looked out at the sapphire lake.

"Is Floyd going to come looking for you?"

"He might be," Silas admitted. "I don't know, and that's the truth. I could have killed him. The gun was in my hand. I...I *should* have killed him," he whispered. "But I didn't and I'm...a fucking idiot." He buried his face in his hands again, letting out a low groan. "I couldn't do it. I was right there, and I couldn't pull the trigger."

"Is there anything else you can tell me? Anything I need to know? I'm not compelling you, Silas," the alpha added, his voice soft. "You've taken enough shit from alphas. You tell me only what you want me to know."

You mean, like the fact that I'm a hormone-suppressed omega who's been trafficked for the last seven years between the worst scum of criminal alpha packs...

Oh, and my suppressant is wearing off...

And a pack in Bridgeport bought me and expected me to arrive, like, yesterday...

Oh, and last night I killed a guy...

Yeah, nothing to see here, alpha. Look away.

Silas closed his eyes, pushing all those truths deep down inside. "No," he replied. "There's nothing."

Bear gave a slow nod. "Silas...I'm sorry, but you can't stay here."

Silas tried to pretend the words didn't hurt. Bear was right, this was too dangerous for them both, but Silas needed a minute to breathe and come up with a plan. Daring to look over at the alpha, he let Bear see his vulnerability. "Give me another day or two? I'll stay out of your way. I'll just sleep and...I won't make trouble. If Floyd comes, you can hand me over to him."

Bear held his gaze, those hazel eyes depthless in their intensity. "I'm not doing that."

Silas sighed, shaking his head. "Then give me back my gun, and I'll end it."

A muscle twitched in the alpha's jaw. "Are those your only two options? You stay here, or you beg me for a gun?"

He scrambled to come up with an answer. A lie. Instead, he simply said, "Bear, I just...I need another day."

Letting out a slow breath, Bear nodded. "You can have three." Pushing himself out of his chair, he stomped away across the deck and entered the house, leaving Silas alone in his misery.

11

Three more days. Bear was going to let this beta crash at his cabin for three more days, knowing a criminal alpha pack was out hunting for him? What the hell was he thinking?

You're thinking that beautiful beta needs your protection.

He stormed inside, leaving the beta out on the deck. Zeus followed him in, flopping down on his donut. Bear slapped his smoothie cup and Silas's cold mug of coffee into the sink, gripping the granite countertop with both hands. He let out a low groan.

What the hell was that out there? What was this beta doing to him? It's like Silas spoke, but all Bear could focus on was the fullness of his lips, the sweeping arch of his cheekbones, the smooth slope of his shoulders.

Fuck, get it together.

Bear didn't even realize he was touching him until Silas told him to stop. He knew Silas was twitchy around alphas, and for good reason. But Bear still felt this uncontrollable urge to comfort him. He was drawn to him—his voice, his natural beauty, his simmering strength. The man was like a hurricane in a box—all quiet stillness on the outside, chaos within.

And damn, but Bear liked the way he smelled too. Betas all carried scent signatures, same as alphas and omegas. It was usually just softer. That made it harder to read emotions off beta scents unless the alpha was bonded to them. Bear liked this beta's scent. It was a strange sensation, but the scent just...fit. Warm, like his voice. Sweet and smooth like the look in his dark eyes, his soft lips...but with a kick too, perfect for that sharp mouth.

Bear needed to be careful. The last thing he intended to do was let himself get lured in by a beta, especially *this* beta. But when Bear's hand was on him, Silas had reacted, his scent growing stronger too. Bear could still taste it on his tongue.

In contrast, an omega in heat cast off a scent so cloying, so sickly sweet, it filled a room. Alphas were drawn to it like moths to a flame. For a while, he held out hope he could help Pack Beresford find an omega to replace his mother. That was one more reason he felt called to walk away. The pack was never going to settle so long as their alpha turned his nose up at every prospective omega. The pack was better off without him.

Silas would be better off too.

He's not your problem.

Bear repeated those words, a mantra in his mind, as he held tight to the countertop. When Silas broke down, Bear felt a surge of anger course through him. He'd wanted to put his fist through the wall. Alphas had hurt this beta. Repeatedly. Even now, some shitty pack was probably using its power to torture and control other betas like Silas.

He may not be able to change anything about Silas's past, but he could do his best to try and help set the beta on a path towards a better future. Silas could stay a few more days. Bear would get him some supplies. He could start over. A new life in a new town. He'd find a better pack if that's what he wanted. Or he could mainstream. Most betas lived outside the bounds of alpha packs.

In the meantime, Bear wasn't taking any chances. He pushed off the counter, striding down the stairs into the basement. As soon as he opened the door to the garage, his eyes settled on the white plastic bag tucked up on the shelf next to the cooler. He tugged it off the shelf and opened it up, fishing through the dumped contents until he found the wallet.

He hated doing this, but he had no other choice. Slipping his phone out of his pocket, he opened his contacts, flicking down the list until he found TERRY BERESFORD. He thumbed it, holding the phone up to his ear. The line rang a few times.

"Sheriff Beresford," came a deep voice on the other end.

"Hey Terry, it's me. It's...Bear."

Silence on the other end. Then Terry sighed. "Well...shit. This is a surprise. How's the north end of the lake treatin' you?"

"It's fine," he muttered.

Of all Bear's family, his Uncle Terry had been the least supportive of his decision to leave the pack and move twenty minutes up the lake. With Terry so busy at the sheriff's station, it fell to his son Boyd to take over as pack leader. They both knew Boyd wasn't the right choice, but their pack was old school. A Beresford always won in questions of succession. It was bullshit, but alphas got set in their ways like that. Bear wanted them to have a vote when he left, but Boyd squashed that pretty quick.

"So, what do you need, Bear? You wouldn't be callin' me if you didn't need something."

Bear cut right to the chase. "I need you to run a name for me. I need anything you have on the guy. And I need you to be on the lookout for him. You see him, you let me know."

"Shit, kid," Terry grunted. "No 'Hey, Uncle Terry'? or 'How's the bad back?' You just dive in, wanting me to break the rules for you?"

This had always been Terry's style. Guilt, passive aggression...sometimes aggressive aggression. And when he *did* help, he expected fawning gratitude. Bear was only willing to play his games up to a point. "I wouldn't ask if it wasn't important. Will you run the name or not?"

The line went quiet again. Bear waited. This was a negotiation.

"Three Sunday dinners," Terry said at last.

Bear swallowed his frustration, squeezing tight to the phone against his ear. "One."

"You want it to be four? I'll own your ass for the whole month. Three Sunday dinners, starting tonight," Terry barked.

"I can't do tonight," Bear said quickly, his mind already distracted thinking of the beta up on his deck.

"Well, then I can't help you. Willow is bringing the new baby. You'll meet your nephew and eat dinner with the pack, or you can call some other sheriff to do your dirty work. What's it gonna be, kid? Decide, 'cause I got important law enforcement shit to do."

Bear clenched his jaw tight, letting his eye fall to the wallet in his hand. The beta was in trouble. He needed protecting. That mattered more than Bear's beef with his uncle. "I'll do it," he muttered. "I'll be there tonight. Six o'clock."

"Good," Terry grunted. "Give me the name you want run."

Bear flipped open the wallet. "Name is Floyd Rainier. ID number is 775-217-340. You got all that?"

"Yeah, I got it," came Terry's muffled voice.

"Can you have something for me tonight? It's important, Terry."

Terry huffed. "You tell me it's important one more time, and I might just grow a curiosity. I'll get to it when I get to it. You wanna run names for fun, come pick up an application. We're hiring."

Bear rolled his eyes, knowing his uncle couldn't see it. "I'm good. And...thanks, Terry."

The line was quiet for another minute. "See you tonight. Don't be late." With that, Terry hung up.

Bear tucked his phone back in his pocket and tossed the wallet back in the trash bag.

Looks like I'm going to a family reunion.

12

Bear

Bear had only been at the pack house for twenty
minutes, and already he was desperate to leave.
Growing up, the house was home to his omega mother and
her three bonded alpha mates. Their combined scents
soothed him, a rich tapestry of family, love, and acceptance.
Even with three mates, Georgia only managed to have two
kids. She had lots of health issues, a couple miscarriages.
She had Bear and then, seven years later, his baby sister
Claire.

Mom died while he was away at basic training. Breast
cancer. It was awful. It left Claire alone with their dads.
Losing an omega is cataclysmic for bonded alphas. Mom
dying broke the pack's spirit. Bear's father Henry turned to
the bottle. He found the bottom one too many times and
landed himself in hospice for liver failure. When he passed,
Reed walked out and didn't look back. That just left Liam.

That's when Terry moved into the house, determined to
rebuild the pack. He brought his beta mate and kids. Then
Leo joined, a loner alpha looking for somewhere to land.
Jake and Liz were twins from the other side of the lake.

Terry was always taking calls over at their place. Drugs, domestic violence—it was a total shitshow. He dragged them out at fifteen. They both presented a year later. Now they were the barnacles on his ass for life.

By the time Bear left the military, the pack house was bursting at the seams with six alphas, two bonded beta partners, and a handful of kids yet to present. With Claire gone, only Liam's scent provided any comfort to him. Now he looked around, feeling like a ghost haunting his own home.

"How you been, Bear? It's been a while."

He glanced down into the bright, smiling face of his cousin Willow, Boyd's beta mate. She was a sweet thing. She reminded Bear of peaches and cream—her peachy orange hair tumbled down her back in spiraling curls, while her skin was white as cream, dusted with freckles. And she was fertile like an omega. They'd been bonded six years and she'd already pumped out five kids—though none of them would present as omegas. The omega gene was restricted to omegas.

The newest baby, a boy they named Boyd Jr. was tucked in her arm. Boyd had already proudly told him they'd be calling him 'BJ' for short. Bear could only shake his head. It was just like his cousin to give his kid a name that made you think of sucking a dick.

"I'm fine," Bear replied, taking the basket of bread from Willow's free hand.

"Nothing new up your end of the lake?"

He pushed all thoughts of the beta from his head. "Nope. I'm gonna plant a winter garden. Backed up on orders. The usual."

He followed her through into the dining room. The table was all but hidden under the Sunday dinner spread. It was the one night a week the whole pack was expected to be home and hungry. Two massive trays of lasagna sat steaming at either end, while the middle was a mess of salad, garlic bread, chicken wings, and sliced watermelon.

Bear set down the basket he was carrying, trying to keep his body relaxed as the alphas all started pressing in, finding their usual seats. A presence behind him made him tense. He smelled him first—overripe bananas and engine grease.

Boyd was tall and stocky, like Bear, but that's where the similarities stopped. Bear looked more like Terry's son than Boyd. He was the mirror of his mom, Janine—midnight black curly hair, warm green eyes, and olive-toned skin tanned almost brown from all his time in the sun. He elbowed Bear in the ribs. "You don't mind if I sit at the head, do you Cuz?"

Bear shook his head.

"Bear'll sit by me," came a soft voice.

He turned to see his dad Liam leaning against the doorway. Tall and lanky, with dark skin and salt and pepper hair trimmed short on the sides, he still kept that damn mustache. Georgia always hated it. Bear's heart squeezed tight. Damn, but it was hard to see Liam like this.

Bear crossed over to him, wrapping him in a hug. He took a short breath, just enough to catch a whiff of that pumpkin spice smell. How was it possible that even *that* was fading? Bear had to let him go or he'd embarrass them both and start crying right here in front of the pack.

"How you been, Little B?" Liam murmured.

"I'm good," he replied, not meeting his eyes.

"You smell different."

Bear stilled. Liam's own scent might be fading, but apparently his senses were as sharp as ever. "Different how?"

Liam shrugged. "I don't know. Different. Sweeter. You got somebody new in your life?"

"This old hermit?" Boyd barked, breaking their private moment by clapping his hands on both their shoulders. "Hell will freeze over before Bear lets anyone into his cozy little den. Bear the loner bear," he added with a chuckle.

Liam gave Bear a sad look, his dark eyes seeing through him with such ease.

"C'mon, the chow's getting cold." Boyd dragged them both to the table.

Dinner passed by in a blur. Seven alphas and three betas rubbing shoulders, all talking over each other, while a mess of kids ran around the table asking for seconds and stealing thirds.

Terry showed up over a half hour late, still in his sheriff's uniform. Janine, his beta mate, launched from the table to go greet him. With his arms wrapped around her, his eyes trailed the table, landing on Bear. They looked alike—same height and build, same hazel eyes. Only difference was the hair and about twenty years. Terry was clean-shaven, going bald at the top. He gave Bear a little nod.

"We got company tonight, Pop," Boyd called, waving his fork at Bear.

"I know," Terry replied. "Good to have you home, nephew."

"So good," chimed Willow, patting the squirming baby in her arms.

Liz, Janine, and Liam all echoed their agreement.

Janine gave Terry her place at the full table, dishing him up a plate of food, while Willow got him a beer, and Boyd too. Bear watched with a frown as the betas darted around, catering to their mates' every unspoken need. Down the table, Liz sat next to her new bonded beta Ryan. He was doing the same thing, rubbing her back as he refilled her drink.

The new dynamic of the pack had never sat well with Bear. He didn't fault the alphas for finding beta partners, but it was odd to see the betas always fawning over them. When Georgia was alive, she was the center of the universe. She didn't have to lift a finger if she didn't want to. Her alphas would have pulled down the moon if she asked for it. Henry was the cook. Liam kept them all organized. Reed was the fun.

Bear liked seeing an alpha willing to tend to their mate. He missed it. Without an omega, alphas grow cold, demanding. This pack needed an omega to shake them up and recenter them. He tucked the thought away, keeping his eyes on his plate and answering questions in monosyllables.

An hour later, dinner finally ended, and Bear escaped to the back deck for fresh air. He stood against the rail, looking out at the dark lake. Beer in hand, he waited. If he pushed Terry, his uncle would only push back. Bear had to wait. He was the one asking for the damn favor. But he was itching to get home. He was sure the beta was probably sound asleep, but Bear couldn't suppress the urge to check on him.

Finally, Terry stepped up behind him. "We need to talk."

Bear followed him back inside the house. Terry had taken over Henry's old office. It was decorated in his memorabilia now—law enforcement certificates, pictures, trophies, military medals. Terry sat down behind the desk and pulled a folder out of the drawer.

"You asked me to run a name," he began. "You do any digging yourself?"

Bear shook his head. "Not yet."

Terry sucked his teeth. "Well, you should. This alpha is a real piece of work."

"How so?"

Terry glanced down, flipping open the file in front of him. "Drug possession, distribution, soliciting sex, unlicensed carrying of a firearm. It's all minor charges...what they actually caught him on. But this guy is just one cog in a very dangerous machine," he added, tapping his finger against the file. "Pack Rainier is rotten to the core. This file hardly scrapes the surface." He leveled his eyes at Bear. "Now, you tell me what the hell you've gotten yourself into."

Bear set down his beer. All of this lined up with Silas's story. Floyd was a mid-level foot soldier in a criminal alpha pack. It made sense. The top alphas wouldn't bother with something as trivial as driving a beta from St. Albans to Bridgeport. If they were caught, they'd be looking at serious charges. Trafficking was no joke. Floyd had to be expendable. Which meant he was the least of Silas's problems. Bear stiffened in his chair. Who else might come looking for this beta? He leaned forward. "Can you give me everything you have on the pack? Names, positions—"

"The fuck you say?" Terry growled. "Son, I asked you a damn question." He slapped the file closed. "How are you twisted up in Pack Rainier? Why is Floyd Rainier lookin' for you?"

"He's not," Bear said quickly. "I got nothing goin' with any alpha pack. I'm asking for a friend."

Shit. Too late to take it back now.

He hated lying to his uncle, but he had to give him something. And he wasn't ready to let anyone else know about Silas.

Terry's frown deepened. "What friend of yours is runnin' sideways from an alpha pack that deals in drugs and prostitutes?"

Bear emptied his mind. Terry might not be as accomplished a human lie detector as Bear, but he was still a sheriff, and he'd dealt with this shit for thirty years. He held his uncle's gaze. "He's just an old military buddy. Got in with the wrong people when he got out. Trying to make a clean break now. Apparently, Floyd is looking to reel him back in."

Terry narrowed his eyes. "And apparently you think I was born yesterday."

Bear just waited.

After a minute, Terry grunted, shoving the file across the desk at him. "You still owe me two more family dinners."

Bear nodded, taking the file. "And you'll find out more for me? Other pack details?"

Terry crossed his arms. "What are you gonna do with more details?"

"Knowledge is power. Can't outsmart an opponent you don't know."

"Your friend is playing a dangerous game, Bear. My advice?"

Bear raised a brow. With Terry, everything eventually became a poker metaphor. "Fold?"

"Damn straight," he said with a slow nod. "The house has all the cards. Your friend doesn't stand a chance against this pack, Bear. Change towns, change names. Fold."

Bear stood, slipping the folder off the desk. "I'll tell him." He turned to leave.

"Hey..."

He glanced over his shoulder.

Terry stood now too. "Take care of yourself all alone up there. And don't go poking into business not yours."

Bear smirked. "You're the second person to tell me that in two days."

"Good. Maybe I'll be the first you listen to."

"Yeah...maybe."

13

B y the time Bear returned home, it was almost ten o'clock at night. He was desperate to shower. His skin crawled with the smell of alphas. He parked in front of the garage, juggling two bags of leftovers and the bottle of wine Janine forced on him. And Liam gave him a case of his homemade spiked apple cider. He tucked that under his other arm, the bottles rattling as he shut the truck door with his hip.

He'd say that much about pack life—he missed the food. Good food and strong libations were the heartbeat of Pack Beresford. Living on his own, Bear usually didn't make anything that took time or effort. It was only him to impress, so why bother?

He marched up the deck steps, juggling his plunder as he worked his thumb on the keypad and opened the door. Zeus tore past him, rushing down the stairs to bark at the bullfrogs. He got the leftovers squared away. Then he cracked open one of the ciders, breathing in the familiar smell of spiced apple. It reminded him of fall bonfires with the family, Liam's arm around his shoulders, pointing out constellations.

An odd sound made him pause, bottle halfway to his lips.

Was that Zeus? He glanced outside, looking for the dog. When he didn't see him, he flicked on the exterior flood-light. There the doofus was, ankles deep in the lake. Bear sighed, taking another swig of his cider.

Suddenly, a wail came from the back bedroom, stabbing Bear in the chest with its urgency. He was rocked back, smacking his bottle down on the counter.

"Please—*please*—don't—"

Bear was moving, his only thought getting to the beta. He charged into the dark bedroom, flicking on the bedside lamp. Silas was on the bed, using only the thin hospital blankets as his covers. He was still wearing that disgusting hoodie and ruined jeans.

Silas twisted in the blankets, his handsome face a mask of deepest anguish. "Stop—"

"Hey, hey. Wake up." He shook the beta's shoulder. "You gotta wake up."

Silas's dark eyes shot open as he gasped for air. As his gaze settled on Bear, he squawked, flailing backwards as if expected Bear to hit him. His hand dove under the pillow and he came out swinging with a knife.

"*Shit*—" Bear stumbled back.

"Stay the fuck away from me," Silas cried, swinging the sharp blade again.

"Put the knife down!" Bear barked.

Silas immediately opened his hand and the knife clat-tered down onto the floor. The poor beta let out a cry, closing his hand into a fist, powerless to resist Bear's full alpha bark.

Bear narrowed his eyes on the blade. He recognized the handle and the stain design. It was one of his knives. The beta stole it right out of the knife block in the kitchen. "Why are you sleeping with this under your pillow? You're gonna cut your damn fingers off." He picked it up, setting it on the bedside table just out of the beta's reach. As a show of good faith, he stepped away from it too.

Silas was still panting, one hand clutching at his chest. "Oh god, I'm so sorry. I wasn't gonna hurt you," he gasped, fear lacing his words. "I wouldn't—I didn't—sometimes when I wake it's all still...fuzzy..."

Bear raised a hand, recovering his own breath. "You don't need to explain."

Silas's face turned to a grimace as he puffed out a sharp exhale. "God, you stink—"

"What?"

"I'm sorry." Silas closed his eyes and shook his head. "You smell like alphas. It's...so strong. It's messing with me a little." He rubbed his face with a groan. "Can you uhh...can you step back, or take off that sweater or something? I—I can't calm down—"

Bear knew how much he hated the smell of alphas. He had to remember this beta felt the same. Without hesitation he tugged his knit wool sweater off and tossed it through the open doorway into the hall. For good measure, he stripped off his black t-shirt too, tossing it out after the sweater. Now he stood half naked in the beta's room. "Better?"

Silas nodded, hands still visibly shaking. "Yeah, sorry. The smells. I'm not used to—it's a lot for me."

Bear could smell his worry, like sour milk. "It's okay. I didn't mean to startle you. You were having a nightmare."

Silas looked down, tugging his hood forward around his ears. "Yeah...that happens. Sorry—"

"*Stop* saying you're sorry!"

His anger startled them both. Silas winced, shifting away, his arms going around his middle as if he was ready to get hit. Bear groaned, dragging a hand through his messy hair as he stepped back. He didn't even know why he barked at him. He just needed the whimpering to stop. Needed the beta to be relaxed again.

Barking at him is not the way, alphahole.

He let out a slow exhale. "Look, let's just...move past this, huh? Now that you're awake, you want some food? I got lasagna, garlic bread..."

"Nah, I'm good," Silas muttered. "I'll just go back to sleep."

Bear frowned, crossing his arms over his naked chest. "Look at me."

Silas's eyes darted over to him, still wary.

"You've been with me almost 48 hours, and you haven't eaten anything. I don't know how long you went without a meal before that. You're hungry." It wasn't a question, Bear could taste it on him—that feeling of emptiness, that slow and steady ache. "Why won't you eat my food? You got allergies? You afraid I'll poison you...what? You're clearly afraid of random knife fights," he added with a wave at the blade.

Silas shrugged. "I just...don't wanna bother you. I don't want to take anything from you. And I can't pay you back."

Bear sighed, dropping his hands to his sides. "You're not taking anything from me. And you're not bothering me... well...that's not true. *This* is bothering me."

Silas winced again, holding tighter to himself. "What is?"

"*This*," Bear repeated with a wave of his hand. "This —*you*—sitting there lookin' like I'm gonna hit you, keeping a knife under your pillow to stab me if I get too close. And now you're too afraid to eat my food. That bothers me. I want you to take a breath. Let's get you out of these dirty clothes. You can shower while I heat up some lasagna. What do you say?"

Silas was quiet for a minute. "Yeah, okay. I'll eat."

"And the shower?" Bear pressed. It didn't seem right to keep the beta sitting in his own filth. "I can wash your clothes," he added. "The t-shirt and shorts here should fit you."

Silas just looked down at his faded hoodie.

"I'll shower too," he went on. "I always leave the pack house smelling like I swam in a public pool of alpha pheromones. We'll both wash away all the terrible shit of the last 48 hours. Separately, I mean," he added, feeling heat burning his cheeks as the beta stiffened. "We'll shower...you know...separate showers. I'll shower, and then I can help you wrap up your cast. Then you can shower."

"I can do it myself," Silas said quickly. "And do you...is there a hoodie I could wear?"

An alarm bell dinged at the back of Bear's mind. "Why do you need a hoodie?"

Silas shrugged. "I just like them. I get cold."

Lie.

Bear didn't even need to use his alpha senses to know. He leveled his gaze at the beta. "What don't you want me to see?"

Silas stilled, not raising his eyes. "Nothing. It's not a big deal. I can just shower later."

Bear crossed his arms again. "You mean you'll sneak into the bathroom and back to your room, hiding whatever it is you don't want me to see. So just come out with it. You got a second dick growing out of your shoulder? Tattoos you regret? I got a few of those too."

"It's none of your business," the beta muttered, putting a little bite in his words.

"My imagination is runnin' wild over here."

Silas sneered, his dark eyes narrowing at him. "My pain and suffering is a curiosity for you? Cocksure alpha, so comfortable in his own skin. Look at you," he scoffed. "God's gift to men. You really wanna see what I'm hiding?"

The beta's anger made Bear's stomach churn. He instantly felt guilty. "No, it's fine—"

"Oh no, the alpha wants to know," Silas growled, scooting to the edge of the bed. "Alphas always get what they want, right? Even if it's only their morbid curiosity satisfied." He swung his legs off the bed, facing Bear.

"You don't have to do this," he said quietly. "You're right, it's not my business."

But the beta wasn't listening. Silas sat on the end of the bed and jerked the hoodie off over his head, dropping it to the floor. Underneath he wore a ratty t-shirt. He stripped that off too, tossing it aside. The beta sat with his upper body fully exposed. His medium brown skin had a handsome, bronze undertone. His body was fit, his muscles lean. He was beautiful...and angry. Bear's gaze dropped from his scowling face down his neck, his chest, his stomach. His eyes landed on the wrists Silas held upturned for him to see.

"Satisfied?" The beta's voice was impossibly tight.

Some part of Bear was faintly aware that his hands were shaking. His breath came in short pants as he fought to control the surge of alpha instincts that rushed through him with the force of a raging flood. Anger. Disgust. Not at Silas, at the situation. At what this beta had clearly endured.

But it didn't make any sense...

He lifted his eyes to meet the beta's dark gaze, his chest rising and falling with each measured breath. Fighting to control the bark in his voice, he spoke. "Who did this to you?"

14

Silas

If his heart raced any faster, Silas was pretty sure it would burst. The alpha was staring him down, horror etched into the lines of his handsome face. Bear's jaw was tight, his hazel eyes narrowed, his mouth turned down in disgust. Silas could practically taste the rage rolling off him.

Weirdly, he felt the smallest twinge of relief. He liked that this alpha seemed to care. And Silas knew full well what had him so upset. After seven years living as a broken omega, his body was a tapestry of overlapping, oval-shaped scars with raised edges. The old ones were faded to a sepia brown, darker than his natural skin tone. Bite marks. Dozens of them.

Alphas in his past had been determined to try and force a bond, biting him over and over, ravaging the scent glands on both sides of his neck. Bites trailed down either side to his collarbone, his chest. Heavy bite marks scored the insides of his wrists too. If he had his pants off, Bear could see the way alphas had shredded his femoral arteries, desperate to unlock his latent omeganess.

"Why the hell would alphas do this to a beta?" Bear

whispered, his deep voice hoarse with anguish and confusion.

Silas just shrugged, flipping his wrists over. It was easy to say this and know it wasn't a lie. "A lot of alphas like to have the omega experience."

Bear flinched.

Silas wanted him uncomfortable. He wanted him to know the truth. "Did you know you can buy omega essence? It's like deer piss for hunters. But this is for alphas who can't get an omega to touch them with a ten-foot pole. Alphas slather it on you and rut away, dreaming of having an omega under them instead. Knotting and biting is all part of the role play. They don't care about being gentle because deep down they know you're not an omega. You're a beta. You're nothing."

The alpha clenched his jaw tighter. His eyes lingered on those bites at his neck. Silas knew they were bad, a raised mess of damaged skin. "Alphas did this to you," Bear whispered.

"Yes."

Bear tensed, as if he were suddenly in acute physical pain. "Did...Floyd did this to you?"

Silas just shrugged, reaching for the crutches. "I can't remember. Not all the alphas who fucked me bit me. It was seven years of the same shit. You start to lose track."

Bear crossed his tattooed arms over his naked chest, still clearly confused. "But...a bite still bonds you...right? Even as a beta, each bite bonds you to the alpha that gave it. Why would an alpha risk making a bond with..."

"With a whore?" Silas finished for him. "Yeah, they make drugs for that," he said with another shrug. "Blockers and shit that keep a bite from taking. No alpha is gonna sink their teeth into some beta during a scene and risk a bond. It's all very clinical in that sense."

Bear grimaced in horror. "Clinical? It's diabolical. It's torture! It's—*god*—it's so fucking wrong." He took a step closer.

Silas held his breath to avoid his intoxicating scent. There was something about his rage that spiced it sharper in Silas's nose. He had to get out of here. "I'm gonna go take that shower now," he muttered. "I'll have the lasagna when I'm done." Not waiting another second, he brushed past the alpha, swinging on his crutches towards the door.

"Wait."

Bear's soft voice stilled him. He stood there, his back to the alpha, feeling Bear's eyes on him. He took a few deep breaths, waiting for the alpha to speak.

Bear took a hesitant step forward. Silas could taste his concern. Bear's Christmas morning scent had a softer expression, as if muted by a thick fall of snow. The alpha was afraid to get too close, afraid to say or do the wrong thing and scare Silas off. It was strange to taste it and know it to be true. Silas had never felt genuine, heartfelt concern from an alpha before.

Bear was standing right behind him, and Silas's every nerve was on edge. He held his breath, praying to whatever god wanted to hear him to keep his omega scent suppressed a little longer. Silas had to protect himself. Kindness was a weakness. Kindness was a trick. Kindness is what they used to lure you in, keep you compliant, make you grateful.

Kindness gets you killed.

Bear's breath warmed the back of his neck and Silas's body lit like a fuse. The heat spread from that point of connection across all his exposed skin, raising goosebumps down his arms.

"I'm sorry," Bear murmured. "Silas, I..."

"Don't be," he said on an exhale. "You didn't do it."

"And you didn't deserve it."

Silas clenched his jaw tight, unable to keep the alpha's spicy, woodsy scent from invading his senses. He wanted to get lost in that scent. Surrender to it, never to escape. He had to shut this down.

If he knew half the shit you've done, he would kick you out tonight.

You sold drugs.

You sold yourself.

You helped the pack sell others.

You killed a man.

Liar. Criminal. Whore. Murderer.

Silas swallowed down all those truths, burying them deep. "You don't know shit about me, alpha," he muttered. "I'm not your problem. Two days, and I'll be gone. Save your tears for someone who deserves them."

Not waiting another second, he swung forward on his crutches, fleeing the room and the brooding alpha.

15

Silas

After the most awkward shower of his life—standing on one leg like a flamingo, with his casted leg wrapped in a trash bag—Silas toweled off, feeling fresher than he had in weeks. He gave his towel a check and opened the door, swinging out into the hallway. He passed his threshold to find Bear still in the room. A shirtless Bear.

"What are you still doing in here?"

"Changing the sheets," Bear replied.

"You don't have to do that," he said, balancing on one foot with the crutches against the wall as he pulled the plain, white t-shirt on over his head.

"If you're gonna be clean, the sheets are gonna be clean," Bear replied, tucking the oatmeal-colored top sheet in around the end of the mattress.

Silas ignored him, too distracted by his new dilemma. Unless he wanted his cock swinging around, he needed to get these shorts on. There was no way around it. He was going to have to drop his towel and sit his ass down on the chair. It was either that or ask the alpha for help...which would require more touching. Shaking his head, he quickly dropped the towel and plopped down, letting his bare ass settle on the cool wood of the chair. With a groan, he dragged on the athletic shorts.

"Fit okay?" came the alpha's low voice from the corner.

"Yeah, fine."

"Where are your other clothes? I'll wash 'em."

"Bathroom."

They could both win the award for Most Talkative tonight. Silas knew why *he* wasn't talking—he was too afraid to say the wrong thing. What was Bear's excuse? Silas had the sneaking feeling that Bear was actually a talkative person, but you had to earn his words. No trust meant no communication. If that was the case, Silas was going to be moored on Silent Island for the rest of his time here.

Bear walked past him, his arms full of the soiled sheets. Silas saw his t-shirt and hoodie balanced on top of the stack. "Come out when you're ready," he said as he left.

He gave himself a few more minutes alone in the room to pretend like he wasn't starving before he snatched up his crutches and swung out into the living room.

Bear was in the kitchen, pulling a dish out of the oven. The damn alpha was still shirtless, his tatted muscles tense as he balanced the dish, setting it on top of the stove. The room quickly filled with the smell of lasagna—basil and sausage and sweet, sun-ripened tomatoes.

Silas was salivating. "God, that smells amazing," he admitted.

"Tastes even better," Bear replied. "You want a beer? Hard cider?"

Silas paused. Alphas never offered him alcohol outside of sex. He had to fight down the tingling feelings in the back of his throat. He had a few bad associations with beer. And just the smell of tequila was enough to make his hands shake. "Nah," he muttered. "Water's good."

Bear set a bowl on the counter, rattling a fork down next to it. Then he bustled around, opening and shutting cabinets, filling a glass in the sink with water. "Ice?" he called, not looking over his shoulder.

"Sure," Silas replied.

Without hesitation, Bear turned for the fridge and rattled a few ice cubes into the glass. This was weird. Alphas didn't cater to Silas. *Ever.* Even when they were kind in the bedroom, it was only for their own ends, just another part of whatever fantasy they were trying to create. And the tenderness never lasted.

It was all feeling a bit too much. *Silas* was feeling too much. It had been so long since he experienced the full range of his omeganess. It felt like another lifetime, someone else's life. In truth, he spent less than a year as a full omega, and in all that time he was cloistered at a Center. He had no idea what to expect. How did he control his urges? Was that even possible?

"You just gonna stand there?" the alpha called. "It's getting cold."

Silas blinked, letting his gaze drift over to the alpha.

Bear was standing at the end of the bar, a large bowl balanced in his hand on an oven mitt, a fork in his other hand. "You ever notice how some food tastes better as leftovers?" he asked through a bite.

Silas crossed the living room over to him. He paused next to the bar. A heaping bowl of lasagna sat on the counter, already dusted with parmesan cheese. A shaker of red pepper flakes sat next to it, in case Silas liked a bit of spice. The iced water was perched behind it in a clean glass. Next to the water was a small plate with three pieces of cheesy garlic bread. Bear had tucked a napkin under the side of the plate.

"You have to stop." The words came out with no conscious thought.

Bear stilled, his fork paused halfway to his mouth. "What?"

"Stop," Silas repeated. "Stop being so damn nice to me. I can't—I—is this about sex?" He leveled his eyes at the alpha.

Bear nearly choked on his lasagna. "What the hell are you talkin' about?"

"I'm talking about you doing all this shit for me," he snapped. "The food, the clothes, changing my sheets. You picked me up out of the road, but you don't know me. You clearly don't wanna get to know me. You haven't asked me any questions. I could be an axe murderer or-or a serial killer, and you just—"

"Are you?" The alpha was all quiet calm, as he sat his bowl down on the bar.

"What? *No,* I'm not a serial killer. But *you* don't know that. You hardly talk to me, and I don't know what you want!" He was shouting now, his heart pounding. "Why are you helping me if you don't care about me? What do you get out of this?"

Bear narrowed his eyes. "Get?"

"Come on, man," Silas scoffed. "No one helps anyone for free. Especially not alphas. So, what do you want from me?"

Bear's scowl could start a fire. "I don't want a damn thing from you."

"Really? And I'm just supposed to believe you help fucked-up drifter betas free of charge? I'll eat your food, and use your shit, and you expect *nothing* from me in return?"

Bear huffed, crossing his arms tight over his chest. "If you want a list of chores, I'll be happy to oblige. There's always a thousand and one things to do. For the next two days, I'll have you hobbling your crippled ass up and down this mountain. You'll be sweatin' from sunrise to sunset—"

"Sweating on your cock too, right?" Silas snapped. "What's the deal there gonna be? A blowjob a day keeps the cops away? If I don't give you what you want, you'll call your uncle the sheriff to come drag me off?"

"Jeeezus." Bear dragged a hand over his face, stroking his beard. "Have these thoughts been rattling around in your head this whole damn time? You think I helped you because I can't wait to gag on your beta dick?"

"Alphas don't do anything for free," Silas challenged. "Ever. *Never.*"

Bear shook his head. "Un-fucking-believable. Do I look like I need help getting my dick wet?"

Silas's scowl deepened, saying nothing.

"And even if I *was* gagging for dick, what makes you think I'd want yours?" Bear growled. "You're a mess, Silas. You're a shattered, shell of a beta who's terrified of alphas. I look at you and you flinch. I reach for you and you shy away. And I'm sorry, but that's not exactly a turn-on for me. I don't get off on fear and pain. At this point, I'll shove my dick in my smoothie blender before I go wagging it at you."

"I'll shove it in there myself if you try anything," Silas shouted back. "You may have taken my gun away, but I will fight you 'til I'm dead, I fucking swear to god!"

Both men stood, mere feet apart, chests heaving, eyes wild as they stared each other down. Silas's every instinct was to curl up and whimper, but he held his ground. The alpha just looked at him, those hazel eyes burrowing into his soul. He needed Bear to look away first. He needed to win this.

A muscle twitched in the alpha's jaw. "You done? You get it outta your system?"

Silas sucked in another breath, chest still heaving. Slowly, he nodded.

"Good," the alpha muttered. His tatted hands were balled into tight fists at his sides. "I will say this once, and then never again. I will *never* force myself on you. I know an alpha's word means shit to you, but as long as you are under my roof, I will protect you with my life, even from myself. Alpha to beta, you have my word."

Bear's pledge coiled itself deep inside Silas's chest, digging in with strong roots. Like a weed it, cracked at the foundations of his hard-won resolve and detachment. Silas believed him. He believed this alpha.

There was only one problem...

I'm not a beta.

16

Silas

Bear snatched up his bowl of lasagna and stormed out onto the deck. Alone in the cabin, Silas endured the most uncomfortable dinner ever. Perched up on a bar stool, he felt the alpha's presence through the glass. The lasagna was amazing, but Silas couldn't enjoy it. His latent omega instincts were fluttering just beneath the surface. Like the bud of a plant in early spring, they were pushing against the hard frost, desperate for a glimpse of sunlight.

His omega urges spoke with one voice: *comfort the alpha.* Bear was upset. Silas *made* him upset. If Silas was a good omega, he would tend to the alpha, right?

He's not my alpha, and I can't act like an omega.

It took everything in him to let it lie, shoveling down the lasagna and eating the bread so fast he nearly choked. As he slipped off the bar stool, trying to navigate his bowl over to the sink, Bear came back in, the dog trotting at his heels.

"Let me," Bear muttered, stepping past Silas to snap up the bowl, clattering it down into the sink. He stood there, hands braced against the counter. "Stop pickin' fights with me." He said the words without turning around.

Bear's hair hung around his shoulders, slightly curled at the ends. Silas wanted to reach out and touch it, learn the texture. He could smell the crisp, fall night air on Bear's skin. He closed his eyes, keeping his hands down at his sides. "I'm sorry."

Bear spun around. "And stop apologizing for shit that's not your fault."

Silas raised a brow. "It's not my fault I picked a fight with you?"

"The reason you picked it isn't your cross to bear anymore," the alpha replied. "I think you *want* to be afraid of me. The world only makes sense if you know how to fit me into one of your boxes. The angry alpha, the fucks-you-til-you-cry alpha. Am I right?"

Silas said nothing.

"That's what I thought," Bear muttered. "Well, I'm not playin' your games. I'm not goin' in a damn box."

Silas had never felt so transparent before. So *seen.* "Alright."

"And I'm helping you because it's the right thing to do," the alpha added. "You can accept that, or not. I'm still gonna do it. I'd like to think, if the tables were turned, someone would've stopped for me out on that road." He raised a brow at him. "That enough of a reason for you?"

Silas let out a shaky breath. "I'm—" At a stern look from Bear, he swallowed down the 'sorry' part. "This is hard for me," he said instead. "I...it's been a while. I've been in the life so long. You don't just come out, you know? The body is here, but the mind..."

"Would you believe me if I said I get it?" Bear slipped his tatted hands into the pockets of his jeans and leaned against the counter. "I was in the military for six years. I'm not sayin' it's the same," he added quickly. "But it's another world. You don't get it unless you were in too. I don't know what you've been through, but I *do* know that all that shit can't touch you here. You're safe in my house."

Silas wanted so desperately for that to be true. He wanted to feel safe with this alpha. He wanted to let his guard down. He wanted to *breathe*. Suddenly the two-day timeline felt less like a ticking clock and more like a countdown to devastation. Staying any longer meant letting Bear find out the truth and risk having this alpha turn on him, as all alphas do when it comes to omegas.

But leaving meant...leaving.

"Time and sleep," came the alpha's soothing voice. He knocked his knuckles on the counter as he moved a bit closer. "When I first got out, I slept like the dead for two weeks. It helped me readjust."

Silas nodded, shifting off the stool. It felt like a dismissal, but not one infused with malice. Bear was excusing him to go rest. Bear was tending to him. *Again.*

Like Silas was an omega.

Fuck, I am in so much trouble.

17

Bear

Bear only got halfway down the long, gravel drive before he was pumping the breaks. He sat in his truck, engine running, hands clenched tight to the wheel. His heart was racing. He felt anxious and needy. It all hit him like a slap to the face when the beta came into the living room. Bear thought he had a handle on this...

"Clearly not," he muttered, trying to loosen his white-knuckled hold on the wheel.

Last night had been intense. The beta sat there, body exposed, daring Bear to look. It was an outright challenge. A test. He wanted to see how Bear would respond. Silas exposed more than his scars last night. He exposed his truth. The truth of what he'd been forced to do, of what he'd endured. Each scar represented an alpha taking something from Silas. Bear had to fight every instinct not to wrap the beautiful beta up in his arms and smother those bites with his own scent. He wanted to erase the memory of all other alphas from the beta's skin.

Shit. What the hell is wrong with me?

He took a shaky breath. To think of the beta suffering, pretending to like it as those piece of shit alphaholes—

"Fuck!" Bear slapped the steering wheel, feeling the sharp sting of it against his palm. "God—*FUCK!*" He slapped with both hands, again and again, letting the pain soak through his palms. Chest heaving, he dropped his hands to his sides and stared out the windshield.

He jerked the truck into drive and sped off, gravel churning under the tires. If he didn't leave now, he might just leap off this crazy cliff, race back to the cabin, and drop to his knees at the beta's feet. Shaking his head, he cranked up the radio and turned left on the main drag, grateful for every mile of distance he put between himself and the stranger threatening to twist his life inside-out.

BEAR DROVE STRAIGHT OVER TO LOWEN & SONS, THE BETA-owned antiques warehouse he'd been collaborating with for the past four years. The owner, Ray Lowen, was one of the original Lowen brothers that constituted the 'Sons' in the shop's name. Back before his double knee-replacement, Ray was active on the local baseball team. One night at beers after a practice, he hit Bear with the genius idea to take commissions for new projects that looked like old. Someone wants an antique dining set feel, but can't afford the hundred grand price tag? Enter Bear.

In four years, he and Ray made a killing offering vintage vibes at a fraction of the cost. Sure, Ray was spitting on the graves of his antique purist ancestors, but it was hard to care when he could afford to half-retire. And Bear was good. You showed him a couple pictures, and he cold pretty much recreate anything. With a little investment in digital marketing, Bear helped Lowen & Sons become one of the hottest spots for antiques and custom furniture.

Ray helped him unload the finished set of six dining chairs from the back of the truck, while his wife Kate ran down a list of new order requests.

"I know you said no more this year, Bear, but she's offering to pay almost double," Kate rushed. "Apparently the dressers are a gift for her daughter's new house—oh, did I tell you, the last one burned down and it's so sad—and she really wanted something to be ready by Christmas—"

"Fine," Bear grunted, carrying two chairs at once.

Kate squeaked, nearly dropping her pen. She was a sweet beta, barely five feet tall, with bobbed grey hair and kind eyes. "Oh Bear, really? You'll do it?"

"Anything to stop you hoverin' over me."

Ray chuckled. "I told you he'd do it, Katie. You didn't need to sell it so hard with the sob story."

"It's not a story," Kate said with a huff. "Moira showed me the photos. It sounds just awful. Some of that furniture had been in the family for a century—"

"I said I'll do it," Bear replied. "But if you're addin' two dressers to my list, push one thing to the new year. And *you* gotta make the call to the unlucky customer."

It took another twenty minutes before they could all agree on who was getting pushed, and an unhappy Kate stomped off to go make the call.

"She'll be alright," Ray said, turning his attention back to his restoration project.

Bear watched him work. All the shit with Silas was gnawing at him. "Hey...can I ask you a personal question?" He already regretted speaking, but now Ray was setting down the sander and looking at him.

"Sure."

Bear struggled to find the right words. "You never...did you ever seek out pack life? Did you ever want an alpha?"

Ray huffed. "If this is an offer, Bear, I may just have to sit myself down. You know I'm old enough to be your father—"

"I didn't mean me," Bear growled.

Ray chuckled. "Well, what did you mean?"

"I mean..." God, Bear didn't even know what he meant. "Have you ever been drawn to an alpha? Can't explain it. Feel like you can't fight it. Your biology is just...cryin' out, begging for relief."

Ray's eyes went wide. "*Oooh*...our boy has it bad. Who is it? Do I know 'em?"

Bear groaned. "No, it's not—"

"I never figured you for the beta type," Ray mused. "Well, to own the truth, I didn't really think you had a type. I think the last time I ever saw you with a partner was back when you were in high school runnin' with that pretty beta. What was her name...Cheyenne? Caroline? Somethin' with a 'C,' I think..."

"Her name was Christine, and that lasted all of two months. I presented right after."

"Yeah, she was a sweet girl. You know, she's married now—"

"Focus, Ray. I'm asking about you and an alpha. Have you ever felt pulled to one? Like everything they do, everything they touch, it just...you can't look away?"

Ray shrugged. "Not really. But plenty of betas bond with alphas. My brother Jeff had a bonded alpha mate. Remember Rita? She was a good gal."

"Yeah, but I'm talking about a feeling like...like I don't know," he muttered, dragging a hand over his beard with a groan.

"Well..." Ray crossed his arms. "Describe it to me. You're feelin' some kinda way about it, so let's talk it out."

Bear took a deep breath, closing his eyes. Immediately, the beta surrounded him. He could smell that soft scent. "It feels like...gravity shifts. Like they move and you feel it. You sense 'em deep. You almost know what they're gonna say before they say it..."

Ray let out a low whistle. "Sounds like some alpha/omega vibes to me."

"He's not an omega—"

Goddamn it.

"Ahh...so it's a *he* then?" Ray smiled like a fool. "And what's his name? When do me and Katie get to meet him?"

"He's no one, and never. He's just...passing through."

Ray sighed. "You know, if I could have one dream for you, Henry Beresford, it's that you'd dare to take a chance on something."

Bear stilled, glancing over. "I took a chance on you, didn't I? We work well together. I took a chance enlisting in the military. Leaving my pack. I take chances all the time."

"None of those were chances," Ray said with a shake of his head. "That was just life and the living of it. You were followin' the path you were always meant to tread. Takin' a chance looks like putting your trust in someone else. Riskin' your heart, your control."

"You do know I'm an alpha, right?" Bear said with a raised brow.

Ray laughed again. "Yeah, I know it. Don't mean you can't still take some chances in life. You just have to work a bit harder to get out of your own damn way."

.   .   .

AFTER SPENDING A COUPLE HOURS AT LOWEN & SONS, BEAR stopped by the market for some groceries. The need to tend to the beta was still simmering. He wanted to see Silas happy. Food made people happy, right? The beta had the look of someone who'd skipped one too many meals, probably not by choice. Well, Bear couldn't fix much, but he could fix that. He was going to feed his beta.

He was in the meat aisle when he sensed a familiar presence behind him. He turned to see Jared walking over, pushing an empty shopping cart.

"Long time, no see," Jared said with an uncharacteristic scowl.

Bear caught a whiff of his subtle beta scent—soft and clean like a shea butter soap. But he was clearly irritated. Anxious too and...scared? Shit, Jared Larson was as tough as they came. Why was he feeling scared?

Jared glanced around, making sure they were alone. "So...how's the dog?"

They both knew he wasn't asking about Zeus.

"Dog's fine," Bear muttered.

Jared nodded, jaw tight. "And the leg?"

"Healing. You were a big help."

"He's still with you then." It wasn't a question. Jared knew Bear too well.

"Just for another day." Even as he said the words, Bear felt a tightening in his chest. Was he really going to shove the beta out the door? He buried his discomfort.

"Uh-huh...and then where will he go?"

Bear just shrugged. He felt possessive about Silas and didn't like talking about him, even to Jared. "I assume he still wants to go to St. Albans. Said he had friends there."

Jared raised a brow, arms crossed. "And you believe him?"

No. Bear knew St. Albans was a lie. He'd been trying to come up with a better plan for the beta since Silas first brought it up. He'd be safest going someplace new. Someplace far away from the bullshit pack who hunted him.

Someplace like Spring Hill. He could start over here...live a quiet life...with you.

Bear groaned. This was crazy. He needed to get his head examined. He didn't know the first thing about this beta. Silas was even more closed off than Bear. There was no trust, no rapport...not yet.

But there could be. You could open up more. Let him in. Talk to him. Show him you care. That's all he needs.

No. Bear had to let the beta go. That was the plan. And it was always safest to stick to the plan.

Jared left his cart and came to stand next to him. "Are you making him a nice 'goodbye' dinner?"

Bear swallowed his growl. Jared was pushing. If he wasn't careful, Bear was gonna push back. He was in no mood for this now. "You got somethin' to say, just say it."

"Fine, I will." Jared leaned in close. "You wanna know who I saw this morning?"

Bear glanced sharply over at him.

"Boyd Beresford."

Bear's stomach clenched into a tight knot. Fuck, this couldn't be good.

"Yeah," Jared went on, sensing the shift in Bear's mood. "He brought in one of his pit mixes to get spayed. You know what he told me? He said he and his daddy are worried about you. Worried about the company you're keeping. Apparently, your old 'military pal' is passing through, and he's mixed up with some bad guys. Boyd wouldn't give me any details other than to say the one on the prowl likes to use pliers."

Righteous indignation burned in his gut. He'd like to see Floyd Rainier just try and come for Silas. Bear would put him six feet in the ground. He'd bury that piece of shit alpha with his favorite pair of pliers.

Irritation for Boyd simmered too. Bear hated to think of his cousin strutting around the county talking about him behind his back. "They don't know anything," he said. "Boyd likes to run his mouth."

"They know a hell of a lot more than me," Jared countered. "They know the name of the pack. They know you're worried. Should *I* be worried? Should I be sleepin' with the lights on? I mean, who the hell are these guys, Bear?"

Taking a deep breath, Bear turned to face his friend. Jared wasn't trying to be an ass, he was just scared. Bear put a hand on his shoulder. "Look, J...you're not part of this, okay? No one will come to you for anything."

Jared stiffened under Bear's hand. "You need to cut that stray loose," he demanded. "I'm sorry if that makes me Asshole of the Year, but we've got lives and livelihoods here. We've got people who depend on us, Bear. That beta has other places he can crash. Let him go."

"I said I would, and I will," Bear growled. He leaned in, trying to control the bark in his tone. "Stop pushing me."

"I will when you start thinking clearly," Jared replied. "What does he need? Some clothes...a prepaid phone? You can buy one here. I'll kick in a thousand dollars cash, my gift for being an uptight asshole. Buy the beta a bus ticket, and get him gone, Bear. Do it, or I will."

Bear's shoulders sagged. As much as he wanted to be angry and ignore Jared's warnings, he knew he had a point. Bear didn't really know Silas. What he was feeling was just some alpha biology bullshit that would fade as soon as the beta was out of his life. "He leaves tomorrow," he said, ignoring the painful ache in his chest at saying the words aloud.

Jared opened his mouth and closed it again. "I...shit, I didn't think that would actually work," he admitted. "You're usually more stubborn. I had like two more minutes of speech planned..."

"Yeah, well, save it. He'll be on a bus out of here tomorrow. So, stop worrying."

"I was less worried about me," he said quickly, one hand on Bear's arm. "I was more worried about *you*."

Bear slipped his arm out of Jared's hold. "We'll get our ducks in a row tonight."

Jared nodded, his body deflating a bit now that the fight was won. "I'll swing by with the cash in the morning, check the leg before he goes."

"Thanks."

"It's the least I can do," he said with a shrug.

Bear turned his attention back to the steaks, holding still as he waited for Jared to walk away. Long after the scent of the beta faded, Bear still stood before the buy-one-get-one sirloins, trying to control the shaking of his hands. Jared wanted the beta gone. Terry and Boyd wanted him gone. Bear wanted him gone too...right?

So why did the mere thought of watching Silas walk away fill him with so much unspeakable dread?

18

Silas

S ilas spent most of the day sleeping, curled up on the couch under a blanket that smelled like Bear. The dog joined him halfway through his first nap. The massive thing probably weighed eighty pounds. Was it weird that Silas actually found the weight comforting? That was until Zeus started snoring. Then he let out a couple dog farts that had Silas shoving him off the couch.

Around two in the afternoon, he made himself a pathetic lunch of peanut butter on bread. The only bread was some weird brown shit. The bag wasn't even labeled. Bear probably bought it at some fancy outdoor market. Silas smirked, imagining the hipster lumberjack strolling around with a basket on his arm, Zeus on a leash, complaining about the price of hemp seeds.

That was almost three hours ago, and now the alpha himself was finally home. The sound of tires crunching on gravel alerted Silas to Bear's return. He choked down his nerves, rushing to clean up the mess he'd made.

He felt Bear before he saw him. Zeus was by the back door, tail wagging. Then the alpha appeared, climbing the stairs of the deck, his hands clutching several bulging shopping bags. He had the door open before Silas could even get the water off, totally unencumbered by his massive haul. The alpha paused in the doorway, his gaze catching on Silas behind the sink. "Hey...you don't need to do that." He shut the door with his booted foot.

"I made the mess, I'm gonna clean it up."

Bear crossed over to him, setting the bags down on the counter. The alpha's mood was surly. Whatever went on in town, the message was clear. Bear was practically wearing a big sandwich sign that said: DON'T ASK.

But Silas was...Silas. He couldn't take much more brooding silence from the alpha.

"Sooo...how was your day?" he asked, making small talk like he was a bonded mate, welcoming his alpha home.

"Fine," Bear replied. "Long. Busy."

"Yeah...mine too."

Bear raised a brow at him.

"I slept all day," he admitted, turning the water off.

"Good." Bear was really working those monosyllable muscles tonight.

"Yeah, I slept for a bit. Made a sandwich. Your bread tastes weird, by the way. And your dog has rotten farts."

Fuck me, why am I still talking?

Bear just hmm'd under his breath as he unloaded some of the groceries into the fridge and pantry. He worked around Silas, never coming within a foot of him.

Feeling in the way—and decidedly unwanted—Silas snatched up his crutches. If Bear didn't want to talk, fine. But Silas couldn't stand here and absorb his bad mood. It was going to make him crazy. "I'll just get out of your way," he muttered as he hobbled off.

"Wait."

The alpha's voice stilled him at once. It wasn't a bark, but the effect was the same. Silas didn't want to leave. He glanced over his shoulder.

"I got you some stuff in town," Bear said, rummaging in a couple of the bags on the counter. "I wasn't sure about your style. I hope you don't mind."

Clothes. The alpha bought Silas new clothes. Well...actually, they were *used* clothes. He could see the tags. But still, Bear went out of his way to get all this for Silas?

"I think you can get these on around your cast," the alpha said, holding up a pair of grey joggers with a black tie at the waist.

A pair of slides flopped out of the bag. And a new pack of athletic socks. A pack of briefs. There were a couple t-shirts too—long and short-sleeved. Another pair of shorts.

"And here—" Bear pushed a bag across the counter at him. "I wasn't sure what to get, so I asked a guy at the store. He helped me pick these out."

Silas glanced warily inside the bag. His throat closed up when he realized what was in it. It was toiletries and a mix of hair products for textured hair. Of course, this long-haired lumberjack would care about appearances. Silas reached in, brushing the tips of his fingers over a small bottle of leave-in conditioner, a jar of coconut oil, and a boar's hair bristle brush. "Thanks," he murmured, swallowing down the thick knot of omega urges now sitting like a rock in his throat.

Bear shoved a third bag forward. "Last bag."

Silas looked inside to find hair clippers and a set of guards, an electric razor, a new toiletry bag, and—his heart nearly stopped—a prepaid cellphone. Silas' eyes shot up, chest rising and falling, as he looked at the alpha. He'd hardly touched a cell phone in seven years. His first pack learned the hard way: you didn't give a flight risk access to a phone. They found him, of course. They would always find him. He suppressed a shudder. "What the hell is this?"

Bear leaned over the counter, looking in the bag. "What is what?"

"The phone, alphahole," Silas snapped, fighting to shut down the swirl of anxiety and fucked-up memories suddenly crashing between his ears. He felt nauseated.

The alpha narrowed his eyes at him. Silas could taste his confusion. "You're mad at me? Hell, I know it's not fancy, but it'll work just fine."

Silas shook his head, backing away from the bag. "I can't...this is...I'm not allowed to have a phone."

Bear's brows shot up. "What—"

"Take that shit back," Silas cried, feeling the walls crashing in. "I don't want it!"

"Whoa, easy," came the alpha's soothing voice. "Just take a breath, and slow down."

Silas was swaying on his crutches. Was the room spinning, or was he? He couldn't breathe. Memory after memory crashed inside his head. Finding the phone on the table while the john slept. Sneaking it into his pocket. The pain when he was found. The hunger. The darkness.

Swirling, swirling...

"Look at me."

He blinked open his eyes, his vision suddenly filled with the calming shades of green apple and warm honey.

Bear's eyes.

The alpha was right in front of him, his tatted hands gently holding either side of Silas's face. That intoxicating alpha scent swept over him in waves, burrowing under his skin, warming him from the inside out—winter woods and spiced red wine, hot chocolate with cinnamon.

"Look only at me," the alpha murmured.

Without conscious thought, Silas wrapped his hands around Bear's wrists, holding onto him for dear life, letting himself fall into those eyes.

"Now...breathe for me."

Silas sucked in air through his open mouth.

"And out," the alpha whispered.

Silas blew out, his spent breath fanning over the alpha's mouth.

Bear's body tensed, but he just nodded. "Good. Again. Breathe in."

Silas took a couple more breaths, not shifting his gaze from the alpha's hauntingly beautiful eyes. Everything was slowing down. There was only Bear. And all Bear wanted was for him to breathe. He could do that for Bear. He *wanted* to do that for Bear.

The realization crept in slowly. Silas could almost think he was imagining it. But as his breathing slowed, and the pounding in his ears eased, he heard it. The alpha was purring. It was quiet, but deep, vibrating through their shared point of contact. It flooded Silas with a deep feeling of contentment. His alpha was pleased with him. He could die happy. It was all he ever wanted. It was—

Oh, fuck.

Silas dropped his hands away from Bear.

The alpha raised a brow in confusion.

"I'm better now." Silas pushed away.

Bear dropped his hands and the purring stopped immediately. He seemed suddenly unsure, taking a step back too.

He's upset. Tend to your alpha. He needs you.

Shut up! He's not my alpha.

Great, now he was arguing with himself.

"I'm sorry," he said. When Bear's scowl deepened, he

groaned. "Fuck—I *know*." He sighed, dragging a hand over his face. "I know, you hate me apologizing for shit, but I didn't expect to be so...triggered."

Bear softened a little. "Can you tell me why the phone triggered you?"

Silas shrugged, looking down at the alpha's boots.

Bear just waited, willing to let Silas say anything or nothing at all.

Silas glanced up, holding tighter to the handles of his crutches. "When you just pushed it on me like that I...I remembered the last time I got caught with a phone. I got lost in the noise for a minute."

"The noise?"

"The memories. I can only stay numb for so long, you know? I keep a tight lid on all that shit, but sometimes something gets out...and then it's like the omega chick with the box where all the bad shit comes out at once."

A little smile quirked the corner of Bear's mouth. "Pandora?"

"Is she the stupid omega with the box of bad shit?"

Bear nodded. "Yeah."

"Well then, call me Pandora, 'cause I got a big ol' box of bad shit up here," he replied, tapping at his temple with one finger.

Bear was quiet for a minute. "Do you have other triggers? Things you know will open the box?"

Silas let out a slow breath. "Well...basic human kindness, obviously," he said with a wry smile. It wasn't funny, and the alpha didn't return his smile.

"Other than kindness," Bear replied, mouth tight. "And cellphones...and physical touch."

"Alcohol," Silas murmured. "When you offered me a

drink last night I—" He closed his eyes and shook his head. "Don't offer me alcohol."

"Done."

Just like that, Silas knew Bear would never offer him a drink again.

"Anything else?"

"Not that I know of…but I can't always know what will trigger me. Sometimes it happens in the moment," he said with a shrug.

"That's fair. But you can always tell me. I would never hurt you, Silas."

Silas. His name on the alpha's lips. It was all he could do to suppress a whimper. He had to get out of here. "Thank you for…everything," he said, wishing he had more than words to convey just how grateful he was.

"If you'd like, you can use some of this stuff tonight," Bear said, gesturing to the bags. "I'll put the toiletries in the bathroom for you."

"Yeah…thanks."

Bear's gaze traveled over his face. "I can cut your hair if you want, clean up your edges. I know I don't look it with this wild-man hair, but I'm good with clippers."

Silas ran a self-conscious hand over his head. His hair was short, but it was still a mess—dry and brittle on top, uneven on the sides, with his edges all grown out.

He glanced up at the alpha, tasting something in his scent. Hope…expectancy. The alpha *wanted* to cut his hair. Bear wanted to tend to him.

And goddamn it, but Silas wanted to let him.

"Yeah…that would be okay."

Bear's eyes lit with pleasure. "Yeah?"

Silas nodded. "Yeah."

19

Silas

Twenty minutes later, Silas was sitting on a stool in the middle of Bear's massive bathroom, staring at his reflection in a full-length mirror that doubled as a door to the closet. This bathroom was like something out of a movie. There was a huge, slate-grey tiled shower with glass walls big enough for four people—Silas immediately pushed *that* image away. Thinking of this alpha sharing a shower with anyone was enough to make him feel physically ill.

A floor-length window was set along the wall between the shower and the toilet. Perched in front of the window was a large soaking tub.

"The glass is one-way," Bear explained with a smirk. "No creeper in the woods can watch you take a bath."

"That's good," Silas replied, holding tighter to the sheet around his shoulders. It was the best they could do for a barber's cape.

"So...what do you want?" Bear was plugging in the clippers, arranging the guards on the vanity.

Silas shrugged. "Whatever you think is good."

"You like a little length on top? We could fade it up the sides a bit. I'm no barber, but I can manage a little bit of style."

"Sounds good."

Bear slipped his phone out of his pocket and tapped it a couple times. Music started streaming out of a speaker Silas hadn't notice mounted on the wall in the corner. Classic rock echoed around the space and Bear bobbed his head, stepping towards Silas with the clippers.

"Do you trust me?" he called over the music, grinning at Silas's reflection in the mirror.

Silas held the alpha's gaze. It was so strange to see them together. Bear towered behind him, still in his henley, jeans, and boots. The sleeves of the henley were bunched up, exposing the tanned skin of his tattooed forearms. The ink slashed and swirled. He held the clippers in his right hand, a little fine-toothed comb in his left. His own ashy brown hair was up in a high bun, a few tangled tendrils framing his face.

Silas wasn't a small guy, but he felt small seated in front of the towering alpha like this. Small but...safe. Protected. He nodded again. "Yeah, do it."

Bear stepped forward, clicking the clippers on. "Right. Hold still."

It turned out Bear was something of a perfectionist, which made sense seeing as he had a career as a furniture-maker. Silas didn't know how long he sat on the stool while Bear worked, changing out clipper guards and going over and over the sides of his head, trying to smooth out the fade. He kept what little length Silas had on top, only cleaning up the edges.

"You know what'd be cool?" came Bear's voice near his ear.

Silas blinked his eyes open. The haircut was so soothing he'd started to fall asleep. Bear's scent wrapping around him like a blanket wasn't helping. "What?"

"I could do a deep part here," he said, gesturing to the line where his fade met the growth at his crown. "I've seen it on guys before. Just shave it in."

"Whatever you want," Silas replied.

Bear frowned at him in the mirror. "I want you to like it."

"I already do," he admitted.

Bear nodded, his grin tipping up on one side. "I'm doin' it." Not waiting for Silas to protest, he flicked the razor guard off into his hand and flipped the clippers on the side, shaving a line down the side of Silas's head from the temple. In no time, he was brushing his fingers over it, a real smile on his face that lit up his eyes. "You like it?" He smiled at Silas in the mirror.

Silas pulled his gaze from the alpha and focused on himself, tilting his head left then right. His hair looked... cool. Polished and styled. "I do," he admitted. "It's really good."

Bear kept smiling as he started cleaning off the clippers. "Now you just gotta get out that new razor and clean up your scruff."

Silas flipped the sheet off his shoulders, letting both his hands touch his new hair. He brushed along the grain, feeling how dry it was on top.

"You can leave this mess with me," Bear said, still putting away the clippers. "Go get cleaned up. I'm gonna start dinner. You like steak?"

Silas nodded. The feeling of being overwhelmed was pressing in again.

Kindness is dangerous. Kindness gets you killed.

"Hey..."

A warm hand on his shoulder. He followed the line of Bear's tattooed arm up to his shoulder. Then he let himself look the alpha in the eye without the crutch of the mirror.

"Breathe it out," Bear murmured.

His gaze darted away as he took a few deep breaths.

Bear handed him his crutches. "You like brussel sprouts?"

Silas scrunched up his nose. "No."

"Well, there you go then. Cling to that. I'm the alphahole who's gonna make brussel sprouts knowing you don't like them."

Silas snorted, hobbling to his feet. "Maybe I'll like the way you make them."

Bear smirked. Slowly his face fell, and he turned more serious. "If you do, I get to ask you three questions. And you gotta answer."

Silas stilled, his smile falling too. This is what he wanted, right? He wanted the alpha to care. He wanted Bear to talk to him, to show interest. But now that Bear was offering, Silas couldn't help but retreat. "One."

"Two."

He faced the alpha. "One. And nothing about shit from the box."

Bear nodded. "Fine, one."

"But you won't get to ask, because I don't like brussel sprouts."

Bear grinned. "We'll see."

20

Goddamn it, Silas liked brussel sprouts. Or he should say he liked Bear's brussel sprouts. He'd never had them prepared this way. They were roasted instead of boiled, drizzled with a bit of olive oil and cracked sea salt and pepper. Bear roasted them on a sheet with some carrots. He also grilled them each a sirloin steak and warmed bread in the oven that he slathered with herb butter.

They sat out on the deck. The late autumn night was chilly, but it was helping to keep his mind clear. Silas loved this deck. He loved the feel of the lake, the sweetly salty smell of it. He loved the fresh mountain air and the sea of stars that twinkled above. And he loved the patio lights and their soft glow over the table laden with food made by a caring alpha. A feeling of peace settled in his chest. Silas swallowed back his emotions, terrified to feel them, to give them voice even inside his own mind.

Bear sat across from him at the outdoor dining table, leaning back in his chair. "Well?" he said, a brow raised as he watched Silas try a brussel sprout.

Silas speared another with his fork. "It's good."

Bear laughed. "You really like it?"

He nodded, popping two more in his mouth. He liked the crispy crunch. The salt melted on his tongue. "Yeah, really good."

"I win," the alpha said, picking up his bottle of hard cider and taking a sip.

Silas ignored Bear's gloating and stuffed the rest of the brussel sprouts in his mouth.

"So...I guess that means I get to ask you a question now. And you have to answer."

He stilled, his mouth full of sprouts. He could do this. He could let the alpha ask him a question. Chewing until he swallowed, he choked out an "Ask."

Bear gave a slow nod, clearly taking this very seriously. He mused over his question options. Finally, he leaned forward. "If you could go anywhere, where would you want to go and why?"

Silas narrowed his eyes at the alpha. "That's...not what I expected you to ask me."

Bear's mouth twitched. "What did you expect me to ask?"

Silas shrugged. "Something from the box."

"You told me *not* to ask you about the box," Bear said indignantly, slapping his bottle back down onto the table.

"Well, I didn't think you'd actually listen."

"Too late now. I asked my question, so you gotta answer."

Silas was quiet for a minute, looking out at the dark lake. *Here*, came his honest answer. *I'd want to be here.*

He'd never spent any time in the mountains. Never traveled beyond St. Albans. There was a slowness to this place, a whispering kind of quiet that Silas never found in the city. Cicadas chirped and frogs croaked. Somewhere down the lakeshore, music was softly playing, a jazzy tune that floated on the air with the rustle of the wind through the autumn leaves.

He closed his eyes. The alpha was waiting for him to answer. "I guess...if I could only go to one place, I'd pick... the desert."

Bear leaned his tatted elbows on the table. "Why the desert? And that's not a second question," he added quickly when Silas raised his brow. "That was part of my original question. It was where *and* why. Same sentence."

Silas rolled his eyes and the alpha smirked. He couldn't quite believe it. If he'd rolled his eyes at Dallas, he'd be swallowing his own teeth right now. His smile fell, thinking about the man he'd killed. This alpha had no idea he was sitting across from a murderer.

Silas dropped his eyes to his plate, and he focused instead on his half-eaten steak...the steak that was a little bloody. His mind flashed with images of Dallas hanging upside-down in the car, blood dripping down his face, eyes open and unfixed—

"Hey..."

He glanced up.

Bear had reached across the table and taken his hand. He gave it a gentle squeeze. "Stay here with me. We were talking about the desert. Why do you want to go there?"

He swallowed, fighting to push all the shit back into the box. "I *uhh*...I just...it's warm there."

"Good. What else?"

"I guess, maybe I want to see a cactus," he added, his vision clearing and his breathing slowing. "That sounds dumb, doesn't it?" He glanced across the table at Bear.

The alpha shook his head. "Not dumb at all. The desert is beautiful. I did a human intelligence training program out in Redrock. It's some beautiful country."

Silas nodded, giving the alpha a weak smile. He glanced down. They were still holding hands. Or rather, Bear was holding the back of his hand. His calloused thumb was curled around, brushing Silas's palm in gentle strokes.

"Better?" the alpha asked, his thumb going still.

Silas nodded. "Yeah, I'm fine."

"Wanna talk about it?"

Silas shook his head. "No."

No, I'm not telling you I murdered someone on Friday night. Not while you're holding my hand, and I'm dreaming of climbing in your lap.

This had to stop. Silas didn't know this alpha, and the alpha definitely didn't know him. He was a walking book of lies. Bear deserved better. He deserved someone whole. He deserved the truth.

"I'm getting cold," he murmured, slipping his hand out of Bear's grasp.

The alpha let him pull away.

"Do you care if I go back inside? I'm tired and my leg hurts and I gotta pee."

How many more excuses you gonna pull out? Did your dog die too? Your apartment flood?

Across from him, Bear just nodded. "Yeah...anything is fine, you know that. You wanna go in, you go in. I'll clean this up."

"You shouldn't have to do all the cleaning. I'm sorry I'm so useless."

"I don't mind," Bear replied. "It's one extra plate. One extra fork. Go in. I'm gonna sit out here a while longer. Nights as pretty as this won't last much longer."

Leaving the alpha at the table with his half-eaten dinner, Silas hobbled back inside.

· · ·

Back in his room, all the stuff Bear bought for him in town was arranged on top of the bureau—a neat stack of clothes, including his freshly laundered t-shirt, hoodie, and shredded jeans; the bag of toiletries; and the bag of electronics. Silas took the razor out and put it in the toiletries bag. Slipping the straps of the bag over his wrist, he swung back down the hallway to the bathroom and shut the door with a snap.

He leaned against it, eyes closed, taking deep breaths. He glanced up, taking in his reflection in the mirror. His haircut looked good. Really good. He wanted his facial hair to match. Taking the razor out of its new package, he turned it on, feeling the buzz of it vibrate through his hand. He flicked it back off and tugged off his white t-shirt from Bear. He stood balanced on one leg in just the basketball shorts, his scarred upper body on full display. With a grimace, he raised the razor to his face, clicking it back on.

As he ran the razor over the sides of his jaw, he let himself think of Bear, standing behind him with the clippers, his fingers smoothing all over the top and sides of his head. The alpha had been very careful not to go anywhere near the bite marks on his neck. But more than once Silas saw the alpha's eyes dart to them. Each time, it made him frown. Bear didn't like that Silas had scars.

And what alpha would? What alpha could stand to be with an omega who'd been so clearly used and abused by other alphas? In the end, it was all about biology, and alphas were possessive. They wanted to be the first—the *only*—alpha to lay claim to their precious omega mate.

That's why omegas were shipped off to Centers as soon as they presented, shut away from the outside world until their perfect alpha mates came to take them to their new happily ever after. At least, that's the way the media liked to portray omega life.

There should be a huge warning label on all content made for omegas: YOUR RESULTS MAY DIFFER.

Silas had met so many omegas in the life and not one of them was there by choice. Force-bonding was a real thing. A scary, fucked up reality that all omegas needed to understand. The odds were, if Silas didn't find a way to keep himself hidden and his hormones suppressed, he'd be captured and force-bonded by one pack or another.

But he didn't want to think about that now. Tonight, he just wanted to feel pampered. He had new clothes, a new haircut, a razor. He could wash his hair, moisturize his skin. Tonight, he'd let himself indulge in his omeganess.

Bear bought all this for him. He wanted Silas to feel clean and happy. And Silas wanted to make Bear happy. He groaned, trying to push thoughts of the alpha to the back of his mind. But it was hard when the alpha's scent lingered on his skin.

He finished with the razor, inspecting the results in the mirror. He now had a clean shave on his cheeks, his jaw, his neck. The only hair left was a respectable line over his lip and a bit of dark fuzz on his chin. In a few more weeks, it would be a proper goatee.

He shuffled over to the tub, flicking the curtain back and turning the shower on. He grabbed the bottles marked 'shampoo' and 'body wash' and set them on the edge of the tub. Then he reached for a trash bag and the roll of duct tape.

In minutes, he had his humiliating foot condom on, the tape wrapped tight around the top of his shin to keep the water out. He dropped his shorts down around his ankles and sat his bare ass down on the lip of the tub. Then he swung both legs inside and stood with just his right foot, bracing with his hands on the shower walls.

The hot spray of the water hit him, clearing all his senses. He stood under the shower head, letting the water pepper his skin. Showers were a luxury in his old life, a reward for good behavior. When he performed well, he got to stand under the hot water as long as he wanted. There were times when he remembered staying inside the four sacred walls until the hot water was long gone.

Now felt no different. He knew Bear was nearby, but he wasn't *here*. Silas was blissfully alone. He took his time, slathering his hair twice with the new shampoo. He liked the feel of rubbing his hands all over his head and neck, knowing Bear's fingers had been there first.

Rinsing his hair, he picked up the bottle of body wash and a washcloth. He squirted some of the clear liquid onto the cloth. Instantly, he stilled.

Holy fuck.

The scent slapped him in the face. It smelled like Bear... or at least a layer of him. Nothing could compete with the feel of the alpha, his presence, the calm he brought Silas with a look. But still...

Silas looked down, taking a shaky breath. It was like he held a concentrated shot of Bear's essence sitting in his palm in gel form. He snatched up the bottle with his free hand, reading the label.

THE CLEAN COMPANY
SANDALWOOD & VETIVER
BODY WASH

Sandalwood and Vetiver. Silas had no idea what vetiver was, but he wanted to drown in it. He set the bottle down on the lip of the tub and held the cloth up to his nose, taking a deep breath. That spicy smell filled his every sense, burning down his throat, wrapping itself around his lungs.

"Oh god," he groaned. He glanced down, knowing what he would find. His cock was hard, growing harder.

Fuck.

His every nerve ending was on fire. Taking a deep breath, he held the cloth with both hands and folded it over, rubbing it between his palms to form suds. The motion had him fighting the urge to whimper.

Once the cloth was sudsy, he dragged it down his arm. His whole body shivered. He dragged the cloth down his other arm, but the cloth felt too abrasive. He dropped it to his feet, snatching up the bottle with both hands. He flipped it over, squirting a dollop right into his palm. The scent still hung in the air as he used his hands, rubbing them all over his neck, his chest, his stomach, letting that essence of sandalwood and vetiver coat his skin.

His cock was impossibly hard now, aching with the need to be touched. He couldn't remember another time when he felt so turned on, so needy—not since he first presented. Giving in to temptation, he wrapped his left hand around the base of his shaft and gave it a stroke to the tip. This time he really did whimper. He bit his bottom lip, swallowing the sound. Eyes shut tight, he gave himself another stroke, feeling the way his cock pulsed against his hand. It felt so damn good, his legs were shaking.

He probably looked ridiculous balanced on one leg, his cast wrapped in a trash bag, jerking off in an alpha's shower. But he didn't care. God, nothing mattered but drowning in this scent, in the feeling of having Bear all over his skin.

Stay with me, the alpha had whispered. *You're safe here.*

He let his mind fill with the memory of each touch the

alpha had given him—his shoulders, his hands. Bear's arm wrapped around him at the vet's office. Bear carrying him to the truck.

Silas leaned his shoulder against the wall of the shower, dropping his right hand down to join his left. He felt dizzy with desire as he pumped and twisted the base with his left hand, cupping his tip with the right. Silas wanted to let go. He wanted to give in to his every omega desire. Because he *was* an omega, and omegas desired to be pampered and cherished. They wanted an alpha who would tend to them, love them, make them feel safe and secure.

"Please," he whimpered.

He needed more. He needed his alpha. He wanted Bear's hands on him, his body pressed tight against him, holding him close, drowning him in his essence.

"Oh, please—" he said again, keeping the rest of his plea silent.

Please...I need you. Please, hold me. Please, alpha, fuck me so good. Make me whole. Make me yours.

He groaned, his head resting against the tile as he pumped himself with both hands. He dropped one hand to cup his balls and gave them a squeeze. Oh god, he needed these hands to be Bear's. He needed release. The wanting was almost painful now.

He bit down on his lip until it hurt, letting his imagination fully free from its cage. Bear *was* here. Bear was right behind him, his hands on his shoulders, skimming down his arms. The strong alpha with his tattooed hands was touching him everywhere. He stepped in close and Silas felt the alpha's need for him, pressing against his ass cheeks. His alpha was so big. So ready.

And god, Silas was ready too. He needed this like he needed air. He dropped one arm forward, balancing against the front wall of the shower, keeping his left hand around his shaft. But it wasn't his hand anymore. It was a tattooed hand. A mountain sunset, constellations, runes from some dead language. After, Silas would ask him what they meant. But now, he needed his alpha.

"Don't stop," he panted.

And Bear didn't. The alpha pressed in closer, his voice deep in Silas's ear, that drawl dripping sweet as honey. Silas had to taste it. He needed it on his tongue.

"You want me, Silas?"

Oh god, the sound of his name on his alpha's lips. It was heaven. Nirvana. His tip was leaking. He was right on the edge. "Alpha, make me come," he whined.

He knew that would work. Bear couldn't resist his omega's whine. He would fuck him so good. Silas was more than ready.

"Yes—*yes*—"

Bear's hand tightened on his shaft as he gave a few more strokes, his grip so firm. "Come for me, omega. Come for your alpha. Fill my hand."

And Silas could deny him nothing. With a groan, he was coming. Fuck, he couldn't stop. His whole body shuddered. The shower started to spin, and still he was coming. It felt like his entire essence was leaving his body.

Slowly, the sensation began to fade. Silas took a gasping breath, feeling the warm water pound his shoulders. He spiraled down from his high, his spirit rejoining his body. He slumped against the wall, dropping his hand away from his softly pulsing shaft.

"Oh god," he muttered, barely loud enough for even himself to hear. "God, help me."

That was the hardest he'd ever come in his life. As he

panted, letting his breathing slow, a new realization shattered his every sense.

Fuck! Oh, fuck—

He nearly toppled over in his rush to turn off the water. Silas stood there, still on one leg like a damn flamingo. He sucked in a deep breath, filling his lungs to capacity. Then he slapped a hand over his nose, pinching his nostrils shut. The smell of the Bear body wash was too distracting, and Silas had to be sure. He held his nose for a count of five and then let go, swallowing down the scent in his mouth.

"No, no, no..."

A new scent now mingled with the Bear body wash. This scent was pungent, cloying even. It was the smell of an omega's come. *His* come. It was so rich and fragrant. There was no way Bear wouldn't be able to smell it with his sensitive nose.

Fix this. You have to fix it. Now.

He scrambled out of the shower. He had to find something to mask the smell. *Anything.* He ripped open the cabinets, breathing a sigh of relief when he spotted a jug of bleach tucked in the back behind a pack of toilet paper. He snatched for the jug, slapping it down on top of the counter. He worked the cap off and dumped a helping of it all over the inside of the sink. The sharp sting of the bleach hit his nostrils first, then his eyes were watering.

More. MORE.

He hopped over to the shower and tipped the jug, shaking it back and forth until bleach coated the bottom of the tub. He took a gasping breath, throat burning, but he kept pouring. He flipped open the lid of the toilet and dumped a helping of the bleach in there too. He poured until there was less than a third of the jug left. The smell was making him dizzy. He was going to be sick. But this had to work. Bear couldn't know.

Lastly, he held his right hand out over the bowl of the toilet, coating it in bleach from the wrist down. He'd come in this hand. Bear might smell it on him. He soaked the hand in the bleach, waiting until it burned before washing it off.

He held his breath again, waiting a five count before he sucked in more air. The omega scent was completely gone, replaced by the noxious fumes. He had to get out of here.

Leaving all the toiletries out on the counter, he plopped down onto the toilet lid and tugged his shorts back on. Then, still wet, he snatched up his crutches and flung open the door. He high tailed it back to his room, shutting the door with a soft snap.

"Never again," he panted, hobbling over to the bed. He sank down on it, letting the crutches clatter against the wall.

He was an idiot. A desperate, needy omega who was going to get himself in serious trouble. No more dreaming of Bear in the shower. No more jerking off, spilling his omega seed all over the damn place. If he wanted a chance at staying here, he had to rein in his every omega instinct.

Even as he had the thought, something niggled at the back of his mind. He looked around the room, trying to figure out what was unsettling him. That's when he saw it. There was a fourth and final bag Bear had yet to formally offer Silas, but it was here all the same. This one wasn't a plastic shopping bag full of goodies. It was a duffel bag.

Suddenly, everything sharpened into focus. Bear wasn't just being nice by getting Silas new clothes and toiletries and a razor. He wasn't showering Silas with gifts to make his life *here* more comfortable.

Silas groaned, dragging a hand over his fresh haircut.

Bear had been so nice tonight. So friendly and obliging. The haircut. The steak dinner. Cleaning up everything, encouraging him to pamper himself. It was all a ploy to get him ready to leave. Because tomorrow, his three days were up. He'd bet any money Bear was going to wake him up early and drop him at a bus station.

Bear didn't want him. He certainly didn't want him to stay. And to his credit, he'd never made any statement to the contrary. Silas was just an omega-brained fool. Needy, desperate, and biologically driven to seek out comfort and safety.

But he didn't deserve someone as good and kind as Bear. He was a used up, hormone-addled whore. A scarred shell of an omega. A murderer on the run, with nothing and no one. No skills besides selling drugs on street corners and sucking dicks. He had nothing to offer an alpha like Bear. And he didn't deserve to stay here. So tomorrow, he would go. He wouldn't put up a fight. Strangely, he had more pride than that. He wasn't going to stay anywhere he wasn't wanted.

But that didn't mean tonight he wouldn't mourn.

He tugged back the edge of his blankets, slipping his legs under the covers. He kept his eye on the offensive duffle bag as he turned off the light, the shape of that bag the last thing he saw before he succumbed to darkness. Curling on his side away from the door, he wrapped his arms around his middle.

Kindness is dangerous.

Kindness gets you killed.

The sound of his own quiet weeping lulled him to sleep.

21

B ear slept like shit. He spent the whole night tossing and turning. By the time the sun was rising through his windows, he was curled up on his side, wide awake. He watched every moment of the sun's ascent over the hills. All the while, he second-guessed his plan.

After Silas went to bed, Bear had stayed up late, getting everything ready. He wanted to do right by this beta. He started by buying him a one-way bus ticket to Redrock. Then he spent the better part of three hours researching safe houses and low-income rentals. Bear planned to offer him six-months of rent, just to help him get on his feet. He made a few calls, securing Silas a bed at a beta-run shelter on the city's south side. They were willing to offer him a bed for two weeks. That would be plenty of time for Bear to finalize rent with one of the low-income complexes. It would be up to Silas to find work.

This was more than generous, right? A new life in a new city, far away from all the ghosts that haunted him. It was the best thing for him. For *both* of them. So why couldn't Bear sleep? He groaned, rolling out of bed. Maybe he'd go for a run. That always cleared his head. He checked his phone and saw a new text from Jared.

Jared: Be by around 9am tmrw with the $.

Bear frowned. So, Jared would give Silas a thousand dollars and shove him out the door. What a Good-fuckin-Samaritan, forcing a trafficking victim to leave town so *he* can be more comfortable.

Aren't you doing the same thing?

Bear slapped the phone down on his bedside table with a growl. He slipped on his sweats, not bothering with a shirt. Then he put on his running shoes. He opened the door to his room and knew immediately something was wrong. His every sense sharpened. What was different?

The hall bathroom still reeked of bleach. Bear had been too afraid last night to ask the beta what the hell he did in there. Once he checked to make sure all the plumbing was intact, he'd just pulled the door shut.

No, bleach wasn't the problem. He smelled...was that coffee?

Stepping around the corner, his large body framed the archway. The air left his lungs as his eyes immediately landed on the beta. Silas was sitting on the end of the far couch, Zeus curled up at his side. The beta had his beanie on and the hood of his faded hoodie pulled up. He stroked absentmindedly at Zeus's ears, a mug of coffee in his free hand.

Bear's gaze trailed down the beta. He was wearing the grey sweats Bear got him yesterday, the left leg bulky and stretched around his cast. His right foot sported a new athletic sock and the slip-on sandal.

"Morning," Silas murmured, keeping his eyes on the dog.

It didn't look like a very good morning. The beta looked exhausted. His smell was off. Too sweet. Bear couldn't place the emotions attached to it. The beta was too calm, and yet chaotic all at once. Like a duck gliding across the lake—all serene stillness on top, churning like crazy on the bottom.

"Couldn't sleep?" he asked, still standing in the archway.

"I've slept enough," Silas replied with a shrug.

What the hell did that mean? Slept enough for one night? For all of time? And why did Bear feel like his skin was suddenly crawling?

The beta sat so damn still. "I'll just finish this cup of coffee, then I'll be ready to go."

Bear's mouth suddenly went dry. "What?"

"I'm out today, right?" Silas still wasn't looking at him. He stroked the dog's ears and Zeus stretched out, loving the attention. "Three days was the agreement. So, I'm ready to go whenever."

Son of a bitch.

Sure enough, Bear glanced across the room and saw that damn duffle bag sitting by the door. His whole body snapped tight. So, Silas clearly couldn't sleep either and he'd just been sitting out here, waiting for Bear to kick him to the damn curb.

"You know it's not like that, right?" he said, stepping forward. "I'm not kicking you out or...you're not a burden, Silas. Really," he added, desperate to see that resigned, hopeless look off the beta's handsome face. He dropped to one knee in front of him, placing a hand on his knee.

Silas stiffened.

Right. No touching.

Bear dropped his hand away. "You know this is for the

best, right? You deserve a chance to start your life over. I've got it all set up for you."

Silas's long, dark lashes fluttered as he dared to glance up. "Set up?"

He groaned, rubbing the back of his neck with a calloused hand. "Yeah, I...shit, I would have talked to you about it last night, but I was afraid you'd try and stop me," he admitted. "Just...let me do this for you, Silas. Let me—are you holding your breath?"

He tipped his head to the side, watching the beta. Silas was sitting stiff as a board. His chest wasn't moving. He was slowly puffing out his cheeks. The beta let out a little exhale and leaned away. "Could you maybe um...sit over there," he said, pointing to the wide expanse of the free couch.

Bear blinked, suddenly realizing where he was and what he was doing. He was inches from the beta, on his damn knees between his legs, and his hand was back on Silas's knee...

What the hell?

He shot to his feet and Silas instinctively flinched. He hated knowing the beta was still afraid of him. "I got you a bus ticket to Redrock," he explained, his voice gruffer than he meant it to sound. "And I've set you up at a beta house. They've agreed to let you stay for two weeks."

Silas shot his gaze up at him, dark eyes wide with concern.

"Which is only temporary," he added quickly. "I've got requests out for openings in some low-income apartments. Once we snag you one, I'll pay six months' rent and—"

"No." Silas set down his cup of coffee, tension tightening across his shoulders. "Bear, no. I can't take any more from you."

Was that the first time the beta had said his name since

that first night in the truck? Bear ignored the way his pulse quickened. Damn biology was gonna be the death of him. "It's all taken care of," he replied.

"But I don't know anyone in Redrock," the beta murmured.

"That's the point. Silas, you can't go back to St. Albans. Or Bridgeport." He prayed the beta wasn't that dumb. "There's nothing for you there. Start over."

Silas nodded, looking back down at the dog. "And this is what you want?"

Bear stood still as stone, his hands clenched at his sides. "This is what's best. You deserve a chance at a better life."

An impossibly long moment stretched between them.

"I'll do whatever you think is best," Silas said at last.

Guilt crashed into Bear with the force of a door to the face. He could feel his anger rising. The joys of being an alpha meant that whenever something was the least bit uncomfortable, his first reaction was anger. He had to get out of here before he said or did something he'd regret.

"I was gonna go for a run before Jared gets here."

Silas glanced up. "Why is Jared coming over?"

If Bear told him about the money now, it would just upset him more. "He wants to check over your leg...and say his goodbyes. You were a one-of-a-kind patient. I think he feels invested," he added with a weak smile.

Silas just nodded, still so quiet. "I don't know how to thank you, Bear...for what you've done for me."

More guilt twisted Bear up inside. "I didn't do anything."

"That's not true, and you know it."

Bear shrugged. "I did the least that anyone else would have done."

"You're wrong." Silas raised his eyes, those dark pools

deep enough to swim inside. "Eleven cars passed me before you stopped."

Bear blinked. "You...do you remember that night?"

Silas nodded. "My memory is shit, but some things stick better than others. That number has been rolling around in my head for days. Eleven cars with eleven drivers saw me struggling on the side of the road, limping like a wounded animal, and they didn't stop. *You* did."

The beta's gaze was making Bear feel all kinds of things that were completely inappropriate. He had to get out of here.

"I'm going for that run now." He stormed off towards the door.

"I'm gonna want my gun back!"

Bear stilled, his hand on the knob. He glanced back over his shoulder. Silas was looking right at him, determination in his eyes. "We'll talk about it when I get back."

Not waiting for the beta's response, he slipped out the door and shut it with a snap.

22

Silas

Silas watched Bear storm down the steps of the deck. Apparently, the alpha hadn't slept well either. Silas could smell his nerves, his frustration and guilt. The longer he was around the alpha, the more sensitive he was getting to the subtle changes in his scent. A bond would increase his ability to read him a thousand-fold.

A bond? What the fuck are you talking about? He wants you out, idiot.

Besides, the last thing Silas wanted was to belong to someone else. Even a kind-hearted alpha that smelled like Christmas morning. Omegas lost all agency in a bond. They lost all hope of independence. Mentally, Silas understood how important it was to keep his distance from this alpha. What he was feeling was just physical. It would pass, and not a moment too soon.

Last night had been...Silas had never lost control like that. It scared him. It was like he had some kind of out-of-body experience. Sure, he often chose to leave his body during sex, but that was more of a defense mechanism. That was about numbing yourself to all sensation and surviving whatever bullshit was happening around you.

Last night was different. Last night was...pleasurable. Silas had an honest to god orgasm. An *omega* orgasm. A fucking incredible orgasm that left him weak and shaking, desperate for more. And it was all thanks to his unhealthy new obsession with a man-bun-wearing, bearded, hipster lumberjack alpha with an animal for a name.

Before he could waste too much time daydreaming about the way the alpha's ashy brown hair swept off the back of his tatted neck up into that man bun, he shoved himself off the couch. Snatching up his crutches, he moved towards the back of the house. In his five days here, he hadn't seen more than the kitchen, living room, and the bedrooms.

Behind the kitchen was a large dining room with a handsome wooden table and chairs. Silas was sure the alpha made this dining set. It screamed Bear. The table was made of two pieces of wood held together with resin made to look like flowing water. The room had a wall of windows to let in the autumn light. The other long wall opened at two ends, leading you through into a front sitting room. This room felt like a combination office/den. Bookshelves covered two of the walls. Bear's scent was just as heavy here as in other parts of the house.

There was a desk in the corner by the window. A laptop sat in the middle of the desk. A pad of paper and a pen sat next to it. An industrial-style lamp on the corner of the desk was on, letting off a soft, golden glow. It was so alpha, Silas wanted to laugh, all straight lines and organization. The only thing out of alignment was a manilla folder. When his eye fell on it, Silas suppressed a shiver. He moved instinctively towards it. Flipping it open, he choked back a gasp.

Floyd Fucking Rainier. It was a police file on Floyd. Silas flicked though the papers—Floyd's impressive rap sheet, police wires on suspected pack activity, photos of crime scenes. He paused, bile rising in his throat. A blurry picture of the Hotel Royale stared up at him. It was a favorite haunt of Pack Rainier. They rented out entire floors to turn tricks. Silas had spent countless hours and days trapped on the fifth floor of that shithole.

Why did Bear have this? Where the hell did he get it?

The sheriff.

Goddamn it, that's what Bear was doing on Sunday night. He wasn't just having dinner, he was meeting his uncle the sheriff and getting information to check Silas's story. Did Bear read all this shit and realize how dangerous the pack was? Is that why he wanted him gone?

His gaze landed on the printer behind the desk. Freshly printed papers sat in the tray. He picked them up, heart sinking. The top one was a one-way bus ticket to Redrock. The other two were print-outs for beta-run shelters in the city.

Bear's mind was clearly made up. Silas was out.

Swallowing down his flood of pain and confusion, Silas folded the papers and tucked them in his pocket.

Suddenly, Zeus launched away from his side, barking like a maniac.

Did Bear forget something? Did he want to keep arguing? Either way, he probably wouldn't like finding Silas going through his shit. Silas swung forward on his crutches, using the second doorway to cut back into the living room. As he crossed into the room, he glanced sharply over to where Zeus was barking by the glass front door. But it wasn't Bear standing on the deck.

Silas's entire body stilled. Fear strangled him as a large

man peered in through the glass. It took him a moment to recognize the vet. He was wearing a cap pulled low over his brow, dark sunglasses, and a thick jean jacket with the collar popped. The vet raised a fist and rapped on the glass.

Zeus hopped in place, mouth open, tongue lolling. Apparently, he wasn't afraid of Jared. That helped calm Silas down. The vet saw him approach and raised his hand in a wave. Smiling, he slipped off his sunglasses and tucked them into the buttonhole of his jean jacket.

Silas opened the door. "Hey."

"Hey, Silas. How you feelin'?" Jared's smile was wide, his straight white teeth gleaming like a toothpaste ad.

"I'm fine," he replied, stepping back to let the vet inside.

Jared stepped in, glancing around the cabin. "Bear here?"

"He went for a run," Silas replied. "Did you want to wait for him?"

"Can't. I just got an emergency call," Jared explained. "Apparently, a chihuahua swallowed his weight in baker's chocolate. I'm meeting the owner at the clinic to pump the lil guy's stomach. So, it was now or never."

"You didn't need to come."

"Well, I had to drop off the cash. I said I would," Jared replied.

Silas stilled. "Cash?"

"Yeah, didn't Bear tell you?" Jared's smiled fell. "Oh shit... he didn't. I'm gonna pretend that's 'cause he wanted me to look like the good guy here." He rubbed the back of his neck. "Bear and I agreed you'd need a little something to help you get back on your feet sooo...here." He reached in the pocket of his jean jacket and held out an envelope.

Silas didn't reach for it. "What is it?"

"It's just a little cash."

Silas's heart was pounding. So, Jared was in on this? He helped Bear plan it without any input from Silas. This beta was in close with Silas's alpha, coordinating how to get him gone. It made his gut twist.

He's not your alpha.

Silas flinched, closing his eyes. "I don't need any handouts."

"It's not a handout," Jared said quickly. "It's...shit, well I guess that's what it looks like, yeah. But it's totally meant in good faith," he added. "Honest to god, I just wanna help. You can't start over with nothing, man. Just...let us help you." He held out the envelope again.

Feeling like a worthless piece of trash, Silas took the envelope and stuffed it in the other pocket of his sweats with a muttered, "Thanks."

"Sure thing," Jared replied, his voice now lighter. "So... how's the leg? Still in a lot of pain? You been keeping off it?"

Silas nodded. "Yeah...it's not bad. The meds help."

"Good." Jared stuffed his hand in his pockets and pulled out a small pill bottle. "I brought you some more pain meds. These aren't happy candy, but they're better than nothing. Take two for serious pain every 6-8 hours."

These Silas took without hesitation. Anything to feel numb again. He had a feeling he was going to need it.

"Right...well, I can't really wait around," Jared said with another glance around. "You take care of yourself, okay? And did he get you a phone? Here—" He reached into the pocket of his scrub pants and pulled out a wallet, handing over his business card. "My numbers are on there. Text when you get settled, yeah?"

"Yeah." Silas took the card. He didn't even have Bear's number. The alpha gave him a phone but didn't give him his number.

If that's not a fuckin' sign of where you stand...

The vet stepped forward and held out a hand, willing Silas to take it.

Slowly, Silas shook it. Jared's hand was so smooth compared to the wood-working alpha's hand. Silas dropped it quickly.

"Right...well, I'm off." He gave Zeus a few pats on the head. As he turned to go, Silas found himself calling out.

"Hey..."

Jared turned, one brow raised. "Yeah?"

"Could you take me into town with you? Save Bear the trip?"

Jared's smile fell. "I don't know...I can't really be late."

"You can drop me anywhere," Silas urged. "Town is small enough, right? I'm sure I can find my own way to the bus stop."

"Bear won't like that," Jared muttered. "You don't even wanna say goodbye?"

Silas swallowed down the surge of emotions threatening to boil over. "This is best," he replied. "We don't need to make a show of it. I'll shoot him a text."

Lie.

Jared was considering, but Silas could tell he was leaning towards 'no' so he inched forward. "We both know this is for the best. Bear is getting too attached. His alpha nonsense is taking over. I need to get gone...before he does something we both regret."

Jared let out a slow exhale. "Fuck...fine. Get your shit. I'll drop you. But text him, alright?" He leveled a finger in Silas's face. "Don't be a total bag of dicks and leave without a word."

"I'll text him as soon as we get in the car," Silas replied with a solemn nod.

Lying piece of shit.

Jared snatched up Silas's duffle, slinging it over his shoulder.

Silas stood before the open door, taking one last deep breath. He filled his senses with the alpha's perfect scent. Then he swung out the door and closed it with a snap.

It was time to start over.

Again.

23

Bear

Bear's chest heaved and his legs burned as he pounded down the mountain trail. He wove between roots and rocks, spry as a buck, fists pumping at his sides. The crisp morning air stung his lungs, but it felt good. He felt alive, clear-headed. He was making the right decision. The *only* decision. This anxiety was just because Jared was right; he was a bleeding heart with a savior complex. The beta would be fine without him. He'd move on. Find new friends. New lovers.

Over my dead body—

"Fuck—" He nearly tripped over a root. Stumbling a step, he recovered.

Get the beta outta your head before you bust your ass!

His phone buzzed in his pocket. Pausing on the trail, he pulled it free, glancing down at the caller ID. TERRY BERESFORD.

"Perfect," he muttered, raising the phone to his ear and tapping his thumb on the green button. "Hey, Terry."

"Morning," came Terry's deep voice. "...I catch you mid-fuck? What the hell, son? Why you so outta breath?"

Bear rolled his eyes. "I'm out for a run, Ter. What do you want?"

"I'm calling to do you a favor," Terry said, a hint of a snarl in his tone. "You said you wanted to know if that shit-bird was spotted around town."

Bear stilled, his breath tight in his chest. "Who—Floyd?"

"Yeah...I'm sending you an email. Got a few images attached." Bear could vaguely hear the tapping of computer keys, as if Terry was sitting at his desk in the sheriff's station. "We took these from the cameras by Spring Hill Credit Union. The other one came from the clinic. And one at the bus depot. Apparently, he's been sniffin' around."

"Shit—hold on—" Bear dropped the phone from his ear and flicked it on speakerphone. "I'm lookin' now."

He pulled up his email app and tapped on the new one from Terry. The first image loaded slowly. It was a blurry night shot from the corner of the credit union, but the outline of Floyd Rainier was unmistakable. His face was in full view. The fucker was in Spring Hill. "When were these taken, Ter?"

"Last night."

"Fuck," Bear growled, tapping the other download. An image of Floyd sitting on a bench at the depot filled his screen. "All of these were from last night?"

"Yeah. No one was seen with him," Terry added. "Doesn't mean he's alone."

Bear nodded, though Terry couldn't see it.

Terry sighed into the phone. "I feel like I gotta ask, kid... wouldn't be doin' my job if I didn't. What's this alpha mean to you? Is your old buddy still in town? I take it Floyd is lookin' for him..."

Bear didn't respond. His brain was buzzing. Floyd was here in Spring Hill, haunting the bus depot and the clinic.

He was looking for Silas. Why was this beta so important? It didn't make any sense...unless Silas was lying about who he was.

Terry huffed into the phone. "You realize I'm the sheriff of Beresford County, right? I could haul you in for obstruction and make you tell me what the hell is goin' on..."

Bear was hardly listening. "Terry, I gotta go."

"Hey—*wait*—I'll do it! Don't fuckin' test me. I may do you the odd favor I shouldn't, but don't you go thinkin' I don't take my job seriously."

"I don't think that, Ter. And I'll fill you in," Bear added, throwing his uncle a bone to chew on. "Sunday night at dinner, you can pick my brain, okay? But now, I gotta go."

He didn't wait for his uncle's response. Lowering the phone from his ear, he tapped the red button and ended the call. Terry could rip him a new one later. Now, he needed to get back to his beta. Even the best-laid plans sometimes needed to change. Shoving his phone back in his pocket, Bear pivoted on the trail and began running home.

24

Silas

"Here we go," Jared said with a smile. He pulled his Jeep up outside the dingy bus depot. It was little more than a kiosk with a pair of benches.

The beta hadn't stopped talking the entire drive into town. He rambled on about baseball stats, his clinic, the weather, and that one time he went to Redrock for a convention and 'thought the tacos were great.'

Silas was exhausted. He barely uttered any responses, but Jared didn't seem to notice. It was all he could do to keep himself from throwing up all over Jared's cream leather interior. His senses were spinning out of control. Every cell in his body revolted at being driven further away from Bear. This was some real messed up omega bullshit. It better be over quick, or he was going to down the bottle of pills in his pocket.

It's not real. It's just biological. You don't know this alpha, and if he knew the real you, he'd call his cop uncle and turn you in. If not to his uncle, he'd turn you in to an Omega Center.

"You need help with the bag?" Jared said, still all awkward smiles.

"Nah...I got it." Silas reached into the backseat and pulled the duffle onto his lap, wrapping the strap around his shoulder. Then he swung open the Jeep door, hopping down on the gravel on his right leg.

Jared scrambled out of the car too, coming around the side to open the back door and fish out the crutches. "Remember to find someone in Redrock to take that off in about five weeks, okay?" he said, handing them over.

Silas just nodded, stuffing them under his arms. He had every intention of getting it off himself. Scissors, pliers, hammer and chisel if it came down to it. Hell, he'd chew it off. He wasn't trusting another doctor—animal or human.

A sharp breeze gusted, rustling all the leaves in the nearest trees. Silas suppressed a shiver.

Jared shut the back door. "Oh, jeez. You cold, man? You got a coat?"

"I'm fine," Silas murmured, just wishing the vet would get gone so he didn't break down in front of such a rapt audience.

"You need a coat," Jared pressed.

"I'm going to Redrock," Silas replied with a dry laugh. "That's a desert, right? I'll be fine."

"You'd be surprised how cool it can get at night. Here—" Jared shrugged out of his thick jean jacket. It had a red and black checked flannel lining. "Take this."

Silas shook his head. "I'm not taking your coat."

"Nonsense." Jared slung it around his shoulders.

The beta's scent filled his nose, contrasting sharply with his own softly sweet scent. Silas hated it—too bright and fresh, like spiked lemonade. But with his hands on the crutches, he couldn't exactly shove the jacket off.

"Wrap up warm, and your bus should be here soon, yeah? And you texted Bear?"

"I texted him," Silas replied, not meeting the beta's eye.

Jared nodded and tucked his hands in the pockets of his scrubs. "Well, I'd stay here with you..."

"Nah, man. I'm good. Really," Silas replied. "Thanks for your help. And I'll text when I get to Redrock."

"Good. Well...see you then, Silas. Have a good life." With that, the vet stepped around the front of his Jeep, slipped in the front seat, and drove away.

Silas was left with no other choice but to hobble over to the bus stop bench and wait. He wasn't sitting more than a few minutes before the stench of alpha hit his nose and a voice called out much too close for comfort.

"Hello, Silas."

25

Bear

Bear jogged up the steps of the deck and instantly knew something was wrong. The fine hairs on his neck stood on edge as he punched in the code to the front door. Zeus bounced by the door, eager to be let out. As soon as the door swung open, he darted out, barking his way down the stairs. Bear stepped inside the cabin, his hands clenched in fists at his sides. The living room and kitchen were empty. Silas's bag wasn't by the front door.

"Goddamn it," he muttered, already knowing what he'd find. "Silas!" he called. "You here?"

He stomped across the living room and down the hallway to the guest bedroom. The smell of Silas hit his nostrils, soft and sweet, like a shot of whiskey chased with vanilla ice cream. His scent brought alive the features of his face—those cheekbones Bear wanted to trace with his tongue, the full lips he wanted to bite, those depthless dark eyes...

But the smell was stale, already fading. The room was empty.

"Silas!"

But Bear knew he was gone. He shoved his hand in his pocket, jerking his phone out. Maybe the beta sent him a message, or tried to call—

Of course, he didn't. You didn't give him your number.

He groaned. He meant to do it today. The beta just left with no way to contact him? That should have been enough to stop Bear in his tracks. If the beta wanted more from Bear, he'd say something. He'd *do* something. His every action since he arrived had been to keep Bear at knife-swinging length. Bear was just the biggest fool in the world, unable to take a hint. Well, this was a pretty big damn hint. *Leave the beta alone.*

But then he saw the missed call with a voicemail from Jared. With a growl, Bear pressed the play button and held the phone to his ear. Jared's voice filtered out, all anxiety and guilt:

"Hey, man...uh...so I guess I just had a hunch that Silas didn't text you. He said he would. He's fine. I showed up early and he asked me for a ride to town. I told him no, but he kinda insisted. I dropped him at the bus depot. He's totally fine."

Bear hissed under his breath. "Fucking Jared."

Silas was at the bus depot. Alone. He was at the bus depot with no protection and Floyd Rainier was still sniffing around. Bear was already on the move. He barely registered the last of Jared's message.

"He's just gonna wait there for his bus. Okay...I felt weird not telling you, and now I've told you, and...yeah. I just...let him go, man."

Bear dropped his phone from his ear. His mind was

running faster than a runaway train. He had to play this right. He had to get to Silas. That was the first thing. The most important thing. But he also had to make sure whatever action he took didn't make things worse for the beta. They had a chance here. A real chance for Silas to disappear for good.

Bear ran to his room, tugging on a shirt. Then he threw on a utility jacket with deep pockets. Not wasting another minute, he sprinted through the cabin and out the door. He had to get to his beta.

26

Silas

"Are you Silas?" The wizened old depot attendant hobbled over towards Silas. "Silas...Beresford?" he added, squinting down at the clipboard in his hand.

Silas's heart skipped a beat. Shit, is that the name Bear put on his ticket? He swallowed down the confusing ball of emotions in his throat. "Yeah...I guess that's me."

The old alpha glanced up over his clipboard. "You're a Beresford?"

"Distant cousin," he muttered.

The alpha just checked something off on the clipboard. "You got yer ticket?"

"My bus isn't coming for like an hour."

"It's runnin' ahead of schedule, and yer the only passenger listed for Spring Hill. The driver just called. She'll be here in ten. Gimme yer ticket, and I'll get you checked in."

Silas reached into his pocket, pulling out the folded printout of his bus ticket. He handed it over to the attendant.

The alpha squinted his eyes, checking the name on the ticket against the one on his list. With a little nod, he took a scanner off his belt and scanned the barcode on the ticket. The machine made a little double beep. "Yer good to go. When the bus gets here, just hop on. You need help?" he added, glancing over at the crutches propped next to Silas on the bench.

"Nah, I'm good," he replied.

"Well, happy travels," the alpha attendant wheezed, shuffling away with his clipboard tucked under his arm.

Silas let out a low breath. Just like that, he was done. Six days ago, Silas Wright stumbled his way into Spring Hill. Now, Silas Beresford was leaving.

He slipped his hand inside the pocket of Jared's jean jacket and fished out his phone. He clicked a few buttons, opening his contact list.

Empty.

With a sigh, he pulled out Jared's business card and plugged in both numbers. Silas has no intention of texting him when he got to Redrock. If he texted Jared, then Jared would have his number...which meant Bear could get it from him. Silas didn't want to open yet another door for rejection. Every day Bear didn't bother to text Silas would be one more twisting of the knife. No, a clean break was best... but he felt a little better having at least *one* contact programmed into his phone.

He stilled, looking down at the double line of Jared's numbers glowing softly on the screen. A memory floated just beneath the surface of his mind. He closed his eyes, letting it rise to the top. It was another number, memorized back when he was seventeen, a freshly presented omega new to Center life. Without hesitation, he tapped the number into the phone and pressed the call button. He raised the phone to his ear and held his breath, waiting as the dial tone trilled once. Twice. Three times.

The line connected.

"Who the fuck is this and how the fuck did you get this number?" came an irritated voice.

Silas let out his breath. "Ollie? Is this...Ollie is that you?"

Silence.

"Holy fuck," the voice rasped, panting into the phone. "Oh, shit. Oh, holy fucking fuck! Silas?"

Silas closed his eyes and smiled, letting his vision swim with memories of Ollie Ortega. When Silas knew him, he was a tall, string bean of an omega. He presented three months before Silas, and they met at the Center. They were the only two males at the Center and so were roommates.

Ollie was a computer whiz. He was always competing in e-game tournaments and running omega chat rooms. Ollie was also the reason Silas was usually in trouble. He did shit like hack into local restaurant websites and order them takeout without paying. Mysterious bags of tacos and boxes of pizza would show up at the Center reception desk and the night guard could never catch them out because the bill always came paid.

"I can't believe you still use this number," Silas said with a relieved sigh.

"Silas...this is real, yeah? I'm not getting punked right now?"

"It's me."

"Prove it. Tell me something only he would know."

Silas thought for a second for something specific enough to convince him. "Alright...uhh...how about the fact that *you* stole Sister Cadence's tablet and filled it with A/O bondage porn. You blamed it on Ty Eastman, and he got double chores for a month."

Through the phone, Ollie howled with laughter. Silas

couldn't keep the smile from his face. He knew that laugh so well.

"Oh, man! Shit, that was funny! Where the hell are you, Si? What happened to you after..." Ollie quieted, his laughter dying, and Silas knew why. Ollie wasn't taken for the special testing. He wasn't tricked into getting a hormone suppressant shot. He was a good, marketable omega. It was the straight and narrow life for Ollie...well, straighter. Ollie was born to break the rules, but for all Silas knew Ollie graduated from the Center and was packed up, living the good life.

"What happened to you?" Ollie repeated.

Silas sighed, letting his gaze drift down the narrow, two-lane country road. "A lot," he replied noncommittally.

Ollie didn't press for more details. "Where are you now? You safe? You good?"

Silas chewed his lip, his shallow breaths sitting high in his chest. "Yeah, I uhh...I'm kinda in transition right now, I guess. Starting over."

"Starting over can be good," Ollie replied. "You got a pack?"

Silas closed his eyes and shook his head, forgetting for a second that Ollie couldn't see him. "No...you?"

"Shit man, I got four alphas breathing down my neck night and day," he said with a nervous laugh.

Silas tried not to feel the pang of jealousy that lanced somewhere under his left ribs. Not all omegas needed to suffer just because he did. "You happy?"

Ollie was quiet for a minute. "Yeah, man. Yeah, I'm not gonna lie, I am. I make sweet money doing the online gaming stuff, enough to support all my guys—not that they need it. We're a team, you know? Three of them work too. I got a doctor and an accountant in my nest. An accountant,

Si. He reads comic books and likes to do taxes and tastes like cherry pie. God, he's fuckin' adorable. Can you believe that shit? I've gone so soft," he said with a laugh. "It was a major change at first, but I'm good. I've been with my guys for five years now. They're good to me. Good *for* me. It's...pack, you know?"

Silas nodded, not caring that Ollie couldn't see it. He was happy for him. It was the dream to find a pack, have them want you, and complete the bond. All omegas were supposed to want that...right?

"How can I help you, Si?" came Ollie's voice. "You need money? A place to crash? I got a nice place here near Mercy Hospital. One of my alphas is a surgeon. I'd have to ask the pack about letting another omega crash, but it's usually whatever I say goes—"

"No," Silas said quickly. "No, I'm not in St. Albans. And I'm...I can't go back there, Ol. I'm not...St. Albans is done for me."

"Yeah, sure. That's cool. I just wanted to offer. I want to help you, man. Tell me what you need," Ollie pressed. "I can wire you cash. You want me to rent you a getaway car? You know I'm good with that shit."

Silas huffed a laugh. "Yeah...I remember." He turned somber, his mind flooding with the memories of their brief time together. "I remember everything, Ol."

"Same, man," came Ollie's soft reply.

From Ollie's end, Silas heard a slamming door, voices, the sound of Ollie dropping the phone away, hand over the receiver. In moments he was back on the line.

"Look man...this is really a lot for me...hearing your voice outta the blue like a ghost. You gotta tell me something," he pleaded. "You gotta let me help you, Si. I'm not gonna be able to calm the fuck down. My alphas already know something's wrong. Heath just came barging in expecting to see my blood on the floor."

Silas's mind was a tumble of incoherent thoughts and feelings. It was all too much. He wanted this bus to come already so he could take his sleeping pill and pass the fuck out. He needed to feel numb again.

That's it. That's what I need.

He leaned forward on the bus bench. "Hey...could you get me some scent blockers?"

"Blockers?" Ollie's confusion was understandable.

"Yeah, my shot is finally wearing off," Silas explained. "Bad fuckin' timing too. I'm kind of on my own right now. I need to be on blockers until I can figure some shit out."

"Oh my god...it's only *now* wearing off? Fuck, it's been what..."

"Seven years," Silas muttered.

Through the phone, Ollie's voice caught. "Seven years? You've been numb for seven *fucking* years? Fuck, man!" He was shouting now. "Why would you wanna stay like that? No more meds, man. Wake the fuck up. It's time to live again."

Through the phone, Silas could hear one of Ollie's alphas trying to soothe him. That twinge of jealousy sharpened to a burn. "That's easy to say when you're packed up and living comfortably," Silas growled into the phone. "Not all of us were so lucky, Ol. You spent the last five years getting fucked in a nest surrounded by your mates, eating bonbons and ordering shit you don't need off the internet. I just got fucked...and bit. And beaten."

"Silas..." Ollie murmured. Silas could hear he was crying.

"You asked me what I need, and I'm telling you," Silas said over him. "I'm an unbonded omega on the run. The pack is still lookin' for me, and I'm about to hop on a bus for Redrock. I'd like some blockers waiting for me when I get there. Can you arrange that?"

Silas could hear Ollie whispering something back and forth with his alpha. "It's done," he said into the phone. "I'll text you the location for pickup."

As Ollie said the words, the outline of the bus emerged through the trees. It came fully around the corner, engine groaning and tires squeaking as it slowed to a stop.

"Thanks, Ol," Silas said into the phone. "Look, I gotta go."

"I'll be in touch soon," Ollie replied.

Dropping the phone from his ear, Silas ended the call. With a few clicks on the screen, he saved Ollie's number in his contact list. Now Silas had two contacts. He slipped the phone back in his pocket just as the bus doors squeaked open. Grabbing up his duffle bag, he slung it across his shoulder and reached for his crutches.

The pretty bus driver gave him a wave. "You going with me today, sugar? Oh no—what happened to you?" she cried, watching him hop a step as he tucked the crutches under his arms.

"Long story," he replied, swinging forward.

"You need any help?" she called, both hands still on the wheel.

"I got it." He transferred the crutches to his right hand, holding the rail with the left as he awkwardly hopped up the steep steps.

"Ticket?" she asked, holding out her hand.

He pulled it from his pocket and handed it over.

She nodded and handed it right back. "Empty bus so far, so you got your choice of seats," she said as he passed her. "We'll be picking up a few people at the next stop."

Silas looked across the rows of empty seats. The bus smelled like stale popcorn and cleaning wipes. The seats were a faded fabric in a pattern of confetti. Silas hopped a couple rows down and slung himself into a pair of seats. He took the window seat, dropping his duffle in the empty seat next to him. With a heavy breath, he let his head fall against the cold glass of the tinted window.

The colors of the town were muted through the glass. The trees weren't as vibrant, the sky less blue. That's how life felt on his suppressant shot—muted. He was finally starting to wake up after a seven-year-long sleep. He felt things now. Bear made him feel things. But that alpha was all but a stranger. Silas had to let him go.

Feeling was awful. It was overwhelming. Silas wanted to be numb again. He'd take his pills to get him through the long bus ride, and when he arrived, he'd go back on scent blockers. He'd live like a beta. He'd mainstream. Alone and numb to the world. It wasn't much of a plan, but it was good enough. Survival plans didn't have to be flashy to work.

He stilled, his every sense prickling with dread. On the far end of the street, he saw something that made his heart stop.

Someone.

"Drive," he rasped, his voice barely loud enough for him to hear over the rumble of the bus.

The bus didn't move.

He tore his eyes away from the window, peering over the seats up at the driver. She was on her phone, her fingers flying over the screen as she texted away. He swallowed down his panic. "Uhh...are we gonna go? Can you drive?"

"Yeah, sugar," she called, eyes still on her phone. "Just gimme one sec—"

Silas looked back out the window. Floyd Rainier was

walking down the sidewalk towards the bus depot. His face was banged up and he had a limp, but he was very much alive. Distracted by the bag of donuts in his hand, he passed in front of a 24-hour diner, nearly bumping into a couple exiting the door.

Oh god...I gotta get out of here. Now!

Floyd was coming to check the bus depot. He was going to ask that old attendant if anyone got on. He'd ask for a description of the passengers. He'd see Silas's name. God, why hadn't Bear used a full alias? Too late now. Floyd was gonna know Silas was on this bus. Final destination: Redrock. If Silas knew Pack Rainier, they'd have three people waiting to pick him up at the depot.

Just as quickly as this dream lived, it died. Silas had to get off this bus.

27

Silas

"Please, can you drive now?" Silas called again.

The driver laughed, plopping her phone into her cupholder. "You in a hurry, hon? It's eight hours to Redrock. If I were you, I'd settle in." She tapped a button and with a loud *whoosh* of air the double doors folded shut.

Silas kept his eye on Floyd, watching as he moved closer down the street. Floyd thought he had time. The bus wasn't meant to leave for another thirty minutes. His window of escape was closing. Fumbling with one hand for the zipper of his duffle, Silas reached gingerly into the top of the bag, his hand closing around the handle of one of Bear's kitchen knives. It wasn't the gun, but it was better than nothing. It calmed him to have his hand on it.

"Come on, come on," he muttered, bouncing his good knee with nervous anticipation.

Down the street, Floyd lifted his gaze away from his phone screen, his eyes landing on the bus. With a gasp, Silas instinctively ducked down. It didn't matter that the windows were heavily tinted, he wasn't taking the chance of Floyd seeing him. He squirmed low in his seat, one hand still stuffed inside his bag holding the knife. He kept just the top of his head visible over the edge of the window, both eyes glued to Floyd's big frame.

How the hell am I gonna fight him off?

Floyd had easily over a hundred pounds on him. Silas's only real advantage was speed, but with a broken leg that was shot to hell. If anything, he'd use this knife on himself. Floyd wasn't taking him back alive.

He didn't get time to think too deeply about his plan of defense, because just then the bus breaks squeaked, and the engine roared to life. The driver cranked the behemoth into gear, and the bus started rolling forward.

"Thank fuck," Silas groaned, still holding tight to the knife.

He watched Floyd's eyes go wide as he stopped on the sidewalk. His mouth opened slightly, the bag of donuts sagging in his hand. He started trotting forward, waving his phone hand in the air, as if he could catch up with the bus or flag the driver down. But the bus was rolling in the opposite direction.

Silas let out a breath as they picked up speed. In moments, he lost sight of Floyd all together. With a panicked whimper, he pulled his shaking hand loose from the duffle and dropped his head against the cold glass. He needed a new plan. If Floyd worked fast, he may even be able to follow the bus. Surely, he had a new car. What if Floyd followed them to the first rest stop and dragged Silas off?

He pulled out his phone, now wishing he had Bear's number. He needed someone to know what was happening to him. Bear would have a plan. Bear would calm him down.

"What would Bear do?" he repeated to himself, both legs bouncing with nerves.

He flipped the phone over and over in his left hand, trying to remember the feeling of calm he experienced the other night out on the deck. Bear had taken his hand, held his gaze, and they breathed together. Silas couldn't plan if he couldn't breathe.

"What would Bear do?" he said again.

He let out a shaky breath.

Bear would get off the bus.

He tucked the phone back in his pocket, looking sharply out the tinted window. The mountainous countryside was flashing by, the rolling hills awash in fall colors. They were still on the edge of town, so old buildings and houses flashed by too. A gas station. A lumber yard.

"Damn driver out here tryna be roadkill this morning," the bus driver muttered.

Silas glanced up over the seats. She seemed agitated, checking all her mirrors with a huff. Meanwhile, ice settled in Silas' veins.

Something's wrong.

A car horn honked behind the bus and the driver huffed again. "Jeez, guy. I'm going the speed limit!"

Silas's hand dove back inside his duffle, desperate to hold the knife. "What's happening?" he called up at the driver.

"Oh, this asshole just doesn't like being stuck behind a bus. Keeps ridin' me," she replied.

Beep. Beep. BEEEEP!!

A triple honk, and now the driver was cursing. The bus swerved a bit and Silas wrapped his free hand around the seat in front of him, holding steady. His heart was racing, his mouth dry. Silas held his breath with dreaded anticipation.

"Shit, this guy's tryna run me off the road!" the driver

cried, a hint of panic in her voice now. "He's coming up on the left."

"Don't stop!" Silas called up to her, pushing himself up in his seat and craning his neck to try and look out the opposite windows. He had to see the vehicle hounding the bus. It was Floyd. It had to be. The alpha must have parked by the depot and come tearing after them right away. The driver of the car laid on the horn as it sped past the bus, daring to play chicken with oncoming traffic on this curvy, two-lane country road.

"Whoa!" the bus driver shrieked. She slammed on the breaks and the bus screeched.

Silas was thrown against the seats in front of him with a grunt.

"Hold on!" she cried. "He's tryna stop the bus! What the hell is this asshole's problem?"

Two more honks. Now the vehicle was in front of the bus.

"Don't stop!" Silas cried, pulling the knife free from his bag. "Do *not* stop! Keep driving!"

But the bus was still slowing.

"This is crazy! I gotta stop—"

"No!" Silas cried, heart racing out of his chest.

The driver just shook her head. "Maybe there's something wrong. Something I'm not seeing. Sometimes stuff gets up under the bus, you know?"

This was it. The end of the line. Floyd was going to come tearing up those steps any second, and Silas had to be ready to end it. He held tight to his knife. He wasn't going to give Floyd a chance to get close enough to knock it out of his hand.

The bus screeched to a halt and Silas stood. He was going to meet his end on his feet, not cowering like an animal in the seat. This alphahole was going to watch Silas drag the kitchen blade across his own throat.

The bus driver jerked the gear into park and smacked her hand down on the door button. With a sharp hiss of compressed air, the double doors whooshed open.

"What the hell?" the bus driver shouted. "You got a death wish? Why did you stop me like that?"

Silas held tight to the knife, raising it in the air. He wanted it ready to strike. With his free hand he tugged back his hood. He let the metal kiss the skin of his throat.

"Hey—you can't come on," she shrieked, leaning back, trying to slap her hand back on the door button.

Too late.

Heavy boots stomped up the stairs. As soon as the daring highwayman's face cleared the first set of seats, Silas's heart burst open like a grenade.

With a gasp, one word slipped from his lips. "Bear."

28

Silas

B ear locked eyes with Silas immediately. His sharp gaze settled on the knife at Silas's throat and his face flickered instantly into a mask of pure rage. "Get your shit, and get off the bus," he barked in the deep, honeyed voice.

Silas jolted. The alpha may as well have hooked him up to a shock collar. His entire body hummed with relief and need as he dropped the knife from his throat and reached blindly for his bag.

Bear is here. Bear is getting you off the bus.

"What the hell is your problem?" the bus driver cried. "This is all kinds of illegal—" Her sentence was cut short as she screamed bloody murder.

Silas's gaze darted back up to the front as he slung his bag over his shoulder.

Holy Fuck.

Bear pulled a gun on her. The mild-mannered, loner alpha was committing highway robbery, stealing Silas in broad daylight. Bear leaned over the driver. "What's your name?" he growled.

"De-denise," she squawked, compelled to speak by his alpha bark. She was a beta. She didn't stand a chance against him.

"Denise? I'm taking this," he barked again, flicking her ID card out of its clear display pocket on her visor. "Listen to me very carefully, Denise. This bus didn't stop. Do you understand me? You didn't stop, and no one got off. Repeat what I just said."

"Didn't stop," she mumbled, tears streaking down her cheeks. "No one got off."

"Excellent. If I find out you told anyone any other version of events, remember I have this," he growled, raising her ID card balanced between his two tattooed fingers.

"You're crazy," she rasped.

Silas couldn't agree more. What the hell was happening right now? Who *was* this alpha, and what happened to cool-as-ice Bear Beresford?

"You're doing a good thing today, Denise," Bear said, ignoring her insult. "You're saving this man's life." He threw his gaze back over to Silas. "Come on. *Now.*"

The alpha bark curled around Silas's very spine until he felt a tug. His whole body was desperate to obey his alpha. He snatched up his crutches, hopping his way down the aisle.

"I'm sorry," the driver cried, her teary face streaked with mascara. "I'm sorry."

"Don't be," he panted, tossing his crutches down to the waiting alpha as he hopped one-legged down the steps. "You really are saving my life."

Confused in the extreme, the driver just sat silently and watched as Silas got off the bus.

Bear was waiting at the bottom, gun still in hand. Stepping forward, he wrapped his gun-wielding arm around Silas's waist, crowding Silas with his overpowering alpha presence. It was all Silas could do not to whimper as Bear pulled him impossibly close, his raging alpha pheromones burrowing deep into Silas's senses. Silas filled his lungs with the alpha's scent, groaning with aching need as he let Bear be his crutch. He slung his arm around Bear's shoulders, and the alpha led him towards the idling truck.

As they passed the tailgate, Bear tossed the crutches into the back. They clanged and rattled. He didn't bother bringing Silas around to the passenger side. He just jerked open the driver-side door and pushed Silas forward. "Get in."

Silas climbed up awkwardly with his good leg, using the steering wheel to pull himself in. It was a bench seat, so he slid himself over, leaving room for Bear to climb in after him. The alpha slammed the door shut and threw the truck into gear, tires squealing as he sped off.

"Get down," Bear said, both hands on the wheel, eyes narrowed on the road.

Silas had barely had the chance to slide over. He was wrapped up in his duffle bag strap, trying to tug himself loose. "What—"

"I said get *down*," Bear growled, reaching across the bench seat one-handed to grab Silas by the collar of his jean jacket. He jerked him down.

"Shit," Silas gasped, getting himself free of his bag and dropping it at his feet. Then he let the alpha pull him head and shoulders down onto the bench seat. His head was practically in the alpha's lap.

"Stay down." Bear dropped a tattooed hand to his shoulder. "We gotta get through town without anyone seeing you."

Silas heard rather than saw a few cars zoom past in the opposite lane. Meanwhile, Bear looked like he was alone in his truck. "Without Floyd seeing me you mean," he muttered, his face all but pressed against the leather.

Next to him, Bear stiffened. "You know?"

"I saw." His breath caught. "Wait—what? How do *you* know?" He twisted his neck and shoulders, looking up into the alpha's face.

Bear's bearded jaw was clenched tight, eyes still narrowed on the road. "About an hour ago, my uncle sent me some photos of Floyd snooping around town last night. He's been checking the bus depot lookin' for you."

"He was there," Silas replied, that hollow feeling of relief making him feel light and empty. "He was right fucking there. The only thing that saved me was the bus pulling up early...and you."

"God *damn* it!" Bear slapped his driving hand against the wheel. Silas felt his rage boiling inside the closed air of the cab. "He was there? You saw him?"

"Yeah," Silas muttered. "He was coming for the bus. He would have found me. You came just in time."

"Yeah, just before you killed yourself," Bear snapped. "What the fuck was that with the knife?" He was all but shouting, his eye darting down to glare at Silas. "You're fucking crazy!"

"I thought you were Floyd. And you took my gun," Silas huffed in defense. "The knife was all I had."

Bear's hand tightened on his shoulder. "You left," he gritted out.

Silas swallowed. "Jared came early. He gave me a ride to town—"

"If you'd have waited for me, we wouldn't be in this goddamn mess," Bear growled. "I woulda seen the photos from Terry, and we coulda come up with another plan. A better plan that didn't involve me pullin' a gun on a goddamn bus driver!" His anger was making his accent thicker. It was flooding from his pores too, choking Silas like sawdust hanging heavy in the air.

"Well, this worked out okay," Silas replied, trying to soothe him. "Now Floyd will think I'm gone, right? He'll have proof of me on camera getting on that bus. He'll assume I got off somewhere before Redrock. I could be anywhere. They'll spend the rest of their days looking in all the wrong places."

Bear jerked the wheel left, making a sharp turn that nearly had Silas tumbling off the bench seat. Only Bear's hand on him kept him in place. Another sharp turn of the wheel and they were rattling down a gravel drive, the sound of the crunching was loud under the tires. They couldn't possibly be back to the cabin yet...

They didn't go more than twenty feet before Bear slammed on the breaks and threw the truck into park. "Sit up," he growled, lifting his hand off Silas's shoulder.

Silas pushed himself up off the seat back into a sitting position. He glanced around. This one-lane gravel drive stretched on into the shadow of the trees. Behind them, a country road was visible. "Where are we—"

"Just a side road," Bear muttered, both hands back on the wheel. "I needed a minute. Can't think. Can't drive." He glanced over at Silas, still wearing a deep scowl. "Take that goddamn jacket off."

"What—"

Bear growled low in his throat. "It smells like Jared, and it's messing with my head. Will you take it off before I lose my fucking shit?"

Silas huffed, stripping off the jacket. "That's implying you haven't already *lost* it."

Bear ignored him. He jerked open the sliding pane of glass on the back window. Silas handed him the jacket and Bear shoved it through the open square in the glass, letting it thump down into the bed of the truck. Then he snapped the window closed.

Silas raised a wary brow. "What's the matter with you?"

"Nothing," he snapped, both hands back on the wheel.

"Nothing? You look like you're trying not to explode. Talk to me."

Bear's alpha growl intensified, his hands clenching painfully tight to the wheel. He snapped his face over to glare at Silas. "You fucking left! No note. No text—"

"You didn't give me your number—"

"Bullshit," Bear countered. "Jared has my number. All you had to do was ask him."

"I figured if you wanted me to have it, you would have given it to me when you gave me the phone," Silas admitted with a shrug.

"You didn't give me a chance," Bear muttered. "You were cutting and running." He held Silas captive in his stern gaze. "What was your plan? Never to see or speak to me again? Our bullshit conversation this morning was it? I mean so little to you?"

Silas's breath caught in his throat as he tasted the raw need in Bear's words. "Bear—"

"Just forget it." Bear shoved open his door and all but stumbled away, pacing around to the front of the truck. He faced the open stretch of gravel road with his back to Silas.

Silas watched the alpha stand still, shoulders heaving as he gasped for air. His every omega sense was screaming at him to tend to the alpha. Bear was upset. Silas *made* Bear upset. He needed to fix this. Bear was right, Silas had been selfish and scared. He didn't want to face whatever this was between them, he didn't want a painful goodbye, so he left.

How do omegas do this? I just want to be numb again.

"Fuck!" Bear barked into the trees, scaring a few birds off their perch.

Silas took a deep breath. It was a little bit easier now that the cab of the truck wasn't flooded with the scent of Bear's anger. Maybe he didn't need to be an omega. Silas could just be a friend. Like Ollie was a friend, offering help and support.

Silas popped open his door and slipped down onto the gravel, balancing on his good foot. He hopped around the open door, using the truck as a support as he inched closer to the brooding alpha. "Hey...I'm sorry, okay? I'm sorry I left like that."

Bear stiffened.

"I don't know how to do this," Silas said, gesturing around at everything and nothing. "I don't know how to be a friend. Maybe I used to know...but a lot of shit happened between having friends and having nothing and no one... and I'm kinda drowning over here if you haven't noticed... What am I talking about," he said under his breath. "Of course, you noticed. You notice everything about me."

Well...almost everything.

"You read me like an open book, and that scares me I guess," he went on. "Because this is not a good book, Bear. I'm like a horror movie meets a true crime special over here. You don't want to read this story. You don't wanna know me."

"You don't get to make that decision for me," Bear said without turning around, his voice low. "If I want you in my life, that's my business."

Silas tried to ignore the omega inside him, purring with eagerness at the alpha's words.

Bear wants to know me.

Bear wants me.

Shut up, he muttered at the needy omega.

Bear groaned, spinning on his heel in the gravel to pace in front of the truck. "I can't believe I just did that. I chased down a goddamn bus for you. I pulled a gun on that woman for you. I committed a crime for you!" He halted, turning on his heel to face Silas.

Silas swallowed down his anxiety. "I didn't ask you to do any of that—"

"You don't think I know that?" he shouted with a wave of his tattooed hand. "You can't even *look* at an alpha without sinking into a place of fear and loathing. You tried to leave. You wanted a clean break, and here I am pulling you back in. What the fuck is wrong with me?" He dragged both hands through his messy hair, turning away.

Silas's pulse thrummed. Want, need, and fear warred inside him. He hopped a few steps closer, holding on to the hood of the truck.

"I feel like I can't breathe," Bear panted, one large hand clutching to his chest. "You don't smell like you. I had you in my arms again, and all I could smell was Jared. It's like you're here, but you're not here, and you don't wanna be here. Fuck, I don't even know what I'm saying..."

Bear was unraveling. His alpha senses were raging out of control. This was just one reason why alphas need an omega presence in their life. Omegas are meant to center and ground. Omegas are the glue. Could Silas risk it? What kind of friend would he be if he let Bear suffer and drown in these battering waves of alpha emotions?

Silas reached for the alpha. "Bear, stop," he called, trying to snatch at his sleeve as he passed by in his pacing. Silas didn't have an omega bark to command the alpha, but he had a whine. He'd never intentionally tried to use it before. Taking a deep breath, he let himself fall into his own storm of swirling emotions. He let himself sink into that aching, twisting feeling of need.

He softened his voice. "Bear...*please.*"

29

Bear

Bear froze as if he were hit with a stun gun. His entire body suddenly felt like it was vibrating with a new need. A demand that burned through him like fire.

Go to your beta.

The gravel crunched under his heel as he turned. Eyes wide, he took in Silas from head to toe. Was he hurt? What was wrong? He stepped forward, taking the hand Silas held outstretched towards him. Silas reeled him in.

"What's wrong?" Bear muttered, still casting his eyes over the beta. Standing this close, he could finally scent Silas without the distracting stench of Jared covering him. Fuck, it was making him hard. Silas was so beautiful—those wide, dark eyes, open and honest, his parted lips taking short breaths. Bear wanted to memorize his features with his hands, his mouth.

He groaned again, ignoring the twitching of his cock. He let his lungs take deep hits off that delicious beta scent—sweet, and so goddamn smooth. There was something different about it right now, sharper. It was hooking in Bear's nose like a fishing lure, tugging at his senses, demanding that he act. The beta was upset.

"Tell me what you need," he said, raising a hand to brush his tatted fingers against Silas's jaw. He simply couldn't help himself. He had to touch him. Just once.

Silas closed his eyes tight. "I need..." He didn't finish the sentence, but his intensity had Bear inching forward, desperate to climb inside his mind and see for himself what had to happen to satisfy this beta's needs.

What the hell is happening to me?

Since the moment Bear stumbled his way onto that bus and saw Silas standing with a knife to his own throat, his scars exposed, it was all Bear could do to keep the pieces of himself from bursting in a thousand different directions. His beta was ready to kill himself rather than be taken. Bear saw the determination in his eyes.

Whatever happened to this beta in his past, one thing was certain: he was strong. Silas was a survivor. He was a goddamn force of nature. This man was resilient. He didn't need an alpha to be strong *for* him. He deserved an alpha to be strong *with* him.

Bear inched closer, his body humming with the fevered feeling of having this beta in his arms. Silas's scent surrounded him and Bear fought the urge to purr. It was building in his chest. "Silas, tell me what you need."

Silas opened his dark eyes, his expression clear. He licked his full lips, Bear watching his every motion. "I need for you...to calm down," Silas said slowly.

Bear blinked. His raging emotions stuttered, like a wave hitting against a stone breaker. "I—don't—"

"You need to breathe," Silas soothed. "Alpha...look at me."

Bear's entire body pulled taut like the string of a bow.

Alpha. I'm the alpha.

"Bear...I got off the bus," Silas murmured. "I'm not in danger anymore. Look at me. Feel me in your arms. I'm here. I got off the bus."

"You got off the bus," he muttered, his senses still swimming, crashing, breaking.

"*You* got me off the bus," Silas corrected, both hands holding tight to Bear's forearms. "Bear, I wanted you to come for me, and you did. I was so scared. I saw Floyd in town. I thought it was Floyd pulling over the bus. I had my phone in my hand, cursing myself that I didn't have your number to call you. I wanted you."

"Wanted me," Bear echoed, stumbling through the fog of his mind towards this beta's soothing voice.

"Yes, I wanted to hear your voice," the beta said, inching closer. "I was going to end it, Bear. I had the knife in my hand, and my only regret was that I didn't say goodbye to you. Is that crazy? We hardly know each other."

Bear was only catching every other word. He cupped the beta's face with both hands, his tatted fingers digging into his beautiful dark skin. "Don't ever do that again. Do you hear me? Death is not an option for you."

Silas slid his hands gently up Bear's arms, wrapping them around his wrists. "I decide my own fate."

"You don't get to decide to leave me like that," Bear growled, tears stinging his eyes. He didn't know what was happening to him. Suddenly this wasn't about the intoxicating beta anymore. Silas was cracking him open, exposing him.

"Who left you?" the beta murmured, his thumbs gently stroking the outsides of his wrists.

Bear closed his eyes tight, feeling Silas touch the tattoo on his wrist. One name, a thousand memories. *Georgia.*

"Everyone." He let out a slow exhale. "My mother. My fathers. My sister. Everyone dies. Everyone leaves. There is no pack. Even you leave. I can't make anyone stay."

Silas leaned in, all but sharing breath with Bear. "All my life...not one person has ever asked me what *I* want. They only take, take, take from me. Now, for the first time in my life, I get to choose. I will not lose myself to this, Bear. I will not lose myself to you. If you want to be my friend...if you want me in your life...you have to let it be my choice. After everything I've been through, I've earned that right."

Bear let out a shaky breath. His body felt like a live wire at having this beta so close. "Then choose. In this moment, what do you want?"

"I want..." Silas dropped his hands from Bear's wrists to his chest, splaying them flat over Bear's tense muscles. "God, I want to kiss you," he whispered. "Just one taste—*please*—"

Like a pair of firecrackers, the alpha and beta ignited. White-hot need flared between them as Silas wrapped his hands around Bear's neck, pulling him closer. Bear let himself be pulled, waiting for that first touch of Silas's full lips against his own. And god, it was perfection. His lips were soft, but his determination was iron-strong. Silas consumed his every sense. Bear was drowning in this beta. They kissed with abandon, their mouths a fevered press of lips and tongues and teeth. Silas teased, flicking his tongue into Bear's mouth. Bear reciprocated, his hands dropping around the beta's waist to pull him closer.

Bear was hard as stone, and he didn't care if Silas felt it. Bear *wanted* him to feel it. He wanted the beta to know the effect he had on him. This man was everything. His taste, the feel of him in Bear's arms, the sounds of need he made deep in his throat.

Bear groaned, flicking his tongue deeper into the beta's

mouth, sucking, devouring, claiming. Silas whimpered his desire for more, his hands clinging to the front of Bear's shirt. The sound zipped straight through him. He had to have this beta. *Now.* Had to tend, knot, bite—

What the hell?

Silas whimpered again, but this time the movement he was making wasn't about pulling Bear closer...he was pushing him off. Bear stilled. It took everything in him to loosen his grip on the beta and let him pull away.

Silas jerked back, one hand going to his lips as the other reached out blindly for support from the hood of the truck. "Oh shit," he whispered. "No, no—*fuck*. What did I do?" He stumbled back a step, eyes wide with worry.

"It's okay," Bear said, his mind still in a daze. He felt drunk or high or...what the hell? Drunk off a few moments of kissing? Bear was clearly attracted to the beta, and their chemistry was electric, but no kisses were ever so good as to leave you feeling drunk after...right?

Silas was now in full-on panic mode. He was hobbling backwards, muttering under his breath. Was kissing Bear really so terrible?

"Hey, it's okay," Bear said again, taking a step towards the beta.

"Stay back!" Silas's chest was heaving, his lips still wet from Bear's fevered kisses.

Bear blinked, the haze lifting somewhat. A new sensation was piercing through his cloud of lust and hunger.

Protect.

Bear had to protect his omega. Silas was feeling deeply vulnerable and worried. Bear had to—

He stilled, his senses sharpening on that new scent that was tearing through him, burying itself right in the very heart of him. The scent was still sweet and smooth, but the spice had an urgent kick, like that first shot of moonshine hitting the back of your throat.

Protect the omega. Protect the omega.

"Silas..."

"Don't," Silas snapped, raising a shaky hand. "Just—don't come any closer. Stay the fuck over there!" By 'over there,' Silas was referring to the now nearly ten feet of space he'd put between them by hobbling backwards along the truck until he was practically at the tailgate.

Bear raised a shaky hand to his mouth, brushing his fingers over his lips. Then he let his tongue flick out to taste the ghost of Silas's kiss. God, it was perfection. Smoother than whiskey, layered with heat and sex and raw, aching need. His pulse was racing out of control. His cock was impossibly hard, desperate for the omega's touch. Bear had never had this reaction to an omega before. *Never.* He felt like his entire body was sparking and humming. But now his omega stood there in a panic, desperate to get away from him, terrified of being wanted.

"Silas," he said again. What else was there to say? Bear couldn't understand what was happening. This couldn't be happening. How the hell was this happening? He inched closer. "Silas—"

"Stop!" the omega cried, his body giving off an involuntary shiver.

"Stop what?" Bear murmured.

Silas groaned, dragging his hood back up over his head, hiding his thick patchwork of scars. "Stop saying my name like that. I can't fucking fight it."

Bear stilled. How was he saying it?

Ohhh...you're asking him to come to you. Put any more alpha in it, and it'll be a bark. Your omega can't deny an alpha order.

Bear groaned. This was insane. "Silas, what the hell is

going on? That's you, isn't it? That scent?" He took another deep breath, filling his senses with that rich omega scent. It was so completely Silas. It was the same beta scent Bear loved, the scent he craved from the moment they met on that rainswept road, just multiplied times a hundred. It was flowing off the omega in waves.

The omega.

Silas closed his eyes, shaking his head. "Please...don't come any closer."

30

"I deserve to know what's going on," Bear said, his frustration mounting. "You told me you were a beta. You *were* a beta."

"It's complicated—"

"Then uncomplicate it!"

The omega flinched, his eyes shutting tight again.

Hurt and confusion slammed through Bear—but that scent. God, that *fucking* scent. He groaned, taking a few deep breaths. "Is that what this is? This madness between us? This pull I've felt since we met in the road last week?"

"Bear, I couldn't tell you—"

"How did you do it?" he said, his eyes narrowing on the omega. "How did you hide it? Are you on blockers? You're an omega, right? Not a beta. Not at all."

"It was a medical thing," Silas muttered. "An experiment gone wrong. Look, I said it's complicated, but I have no control."

Bear's frown deepened as his mind raced. "What kind of experiment masks an omega as a beta like that?" Before Silas could reply, Bear sucked in a sharp breath. "Oh shit...

that's why they want you so badly. Pack Rainier. Floyd. That's why he's still sniffin' around. He's not here to collect a missing beta prostitute, he's here to hunt down an unbonded omega. Am I right?"

Silas crossed his arms tight over his chest, leaning against the truck with his casted leg still dangling in the air. Anger was flooding out of him, smashing against Bear and making him dizzy.

Not anger. Fury. Hate.

Silas's handsome face was a mask of righteous rage. "Fine, you want the truth? Here's my ugly truth. I've lived seven long years as a walking corpse. When I was eighteen, my Center pawned me to a medical group for an experiment that caused total omega sensory castration. When I proved useless to the Center, they sold me to a pack gang. Discount price for the omega dud," he added with a dark laugh.

It sent a chill through Bear. There was nothing funny about this. Silas was telling him the truth at last. Bear could taste it thick in the air, like spiced honey. Silas was dropping his walls, exposing his soul.

Silas the omega. The unbonded omega.

Bear couldn't move, couldn't breathe.

"I've been handed around as packs waited to see if my omeganess might ever recover," Silas went on. "After seven years, I'm finally waking up. Pack Rainier didn't waste time selling me to some shit alpha pack in Bridgeport. I was on my way there when I caused the car crash that killed one alpha and maimed Floyd. That's who I am, Bear. A drug-dealing, trick-turning, criminal who killed a man on Friday. And I'd do it again, because I escaped before they could force me into a bond, and I will *never* go back into that life. I will end it first. And *you* don't get to tell me that I won't," he added, leveling a finger at the alpha. "Until you've lived that life, you don't get to tell me it's better than death."

Silas's rage was Bear's rage now. He wanted nothing more than to hunt Floyd down and rip him limb from limb. But Silas needed him now. He wanted to take this omega in his arms and comfort him. He inched forward. "Silas, I'm sorry—"

Watching Silas physically recoil was excruciating. His entire body shook with it. Fuck, it felt like rejection.

He's not your omega. It can't be rejection if he's not yours.

"Save your pity," Silas snapped. "I'm not looking for an alpha to apologize on behalf of your entire messed up fucking designation. All I want is to go my own way and make my own choices. I want to be seen for *who* I am, not what I am. But all the world will see is an unbonded omega."

"The bite marks," Bear murmured. "Those are all from alphas trying to force a bond with you?"

"Yeah," Silas replied, his tone growing increasingly distant. Bear was losing him. He was shutting down and closing off. "Nice, huh? When they couldn't get the bond to take by tearing me open with their teeth, they forced me on hormone injections. Months of getting pumped with god knows what, all to try and kickstart my omega traits. Never worked," he added with a shrug.

These truths were tearing him apart. The alpha in him was raging, while the human in him wanted to weep. No person deserved this, no matter their designation. "That's so wrong. I can't—Silas I am *so* sorry. That's not what a pack is. That's not what a bond should be. Any alpha who would try to force a bond should have their fucking teeth pulled. No omega should suffer that fate."

Silas just laughed. It was dry, utterly without mirth. "You

know, I think I've met more force-bonded omegas than I did omegas who chose their pack? That's the real world, Bear. That's the side of being an omega they don't show you on the news. Centers are practically summer camp, and the laws are there to help us, right? It's all bullshit."

Bear's heart broke for this omega. Force-bonding was supposed to be a serious crime. Where was the effective enforcement? It made him furious.

"Look, I'm grateful to you for getting me off the bus," Silas went on, drawing Bear's attention. "You saved my life again. Second time in a week has to be some kind of record...but I need to know what happens next. I'm freaking out over here. What are you thinking?"

Bear sighed, dragging both hands through his hair. "What am I thinking? Fuck...I don't even know," he said with a shake of his head.

"Well...are you going to tell your sheriff uncle that you found an unbonded omega?"

Bear blinked. Terry was the last consideration on his mind right now. "What? *No*. Why would I do that?"

Silas just crossed his arms again. "What about an Omega Center?"

Bear let his gaze fall to the omega's cast. "I assume that's the real reason you didn't want to go to the hospital? Mandatory reporting of unbonded omegas means the hospital has to report to the police and the nearest Omega Center, right?"

Silas nodded.

"And the last time you went to a Center, they allowed for medical malpractice and sold you to an alpha gang." Bear shook his head. "Fucking hell...what a goddamn mess."

"What's your move here, Bear?" Silas pressed. "You're sitting on a gold mine. All you have to do is cash it in..."

"Cash in? What—cash *you* in? Like you're a stack of carnival tickets I can just trade for a light-up yo-yo? Do you really think so damn little of me? You think I'd be willing to sell you back to Pack Rainier or dump you on the steps of some Omega Center for the finder's fee?"

Silas held his ground. "All honor goes out the window as soon as an alpha sniffs out an unbonded omega. It's not a question of *if*...but *when* you turn on me."

Bear felt like he'd just been punched in the gut. "Silas that is...I'm sorry, but that's bullshit. You can't really think that every single alpha is so devoid of character."

"Every alpha I've met," he said with an indifferent shrug. "And I've met quite a few." As if to prove his point, he flipped back his hood to expose his neck scars and tugged up his sleeves, flashing the scars on his wrists. Each one hit Bear like a stab to the chest. *Wrong. Wrong. Wrong.*

"You show me a good alpha, and I'll show you ten more who think 'no' means 'yes.'"

Everything made sense now. Silas's fear of touch, hiding his scars, his hatred of alphas, preferring to sit outside, his wariness of strangers. This was a lonely, scared, unbonded omega with nothing and no one. Was he determined to make his way alone? Could he ever accept help from an alpha and believe it to be honest?

"What happened in the bathroom," Bear murmured. "With the bleach..."

Silas stiffened, his eyes darting down to his feet. "My omega scent wasn't under control and...I didn't want you to smell it."

Partial truth.

Bear had to know. God help him, he had to ask. "And... why did you kiss me just now?"

Silas shrugged. "I may be a broken omega, but I'm still

an omega....and you smell really good," he admitted with a weak smile. "I'm not used to scenting alphas. The suppressant zapped all that out of me. Being around you has been... a lot."

Truth.

Bear took a deep breath, glancing around at the woods. He had to make some hard and fast decisions here, decisions that may affect the rest of both their lives. This omega deserved protection. Was Bear strong enough to offer it without falling in too deep? He raised his eyes to hold the omega's gaze. "Alright, Silas. We can't camp out here all day. You need to decide what we do next."

Silas blinked. "Me?"

"Yes, you," Bear replied. "Every choice from here on out will be yours. Starting with: Do you want to get back in the truck?"

The corner of Silas's mouth twitched. "And what happens if I do?"

"That will be for you to decide," Bear replied. "Want me to drive it? You tell me where. I'll drive you home. I'll drive you to Bridgeport or Redrock. St. Albans seems like a bad idea to me, but if it's what you want, I'll take you there."

Silas swallowed, his nervous need spicing the air. "You would take me back to the cabin? Then what?"

Bear shrugged. "Dealer's choice. Sleep, eat, watch TV, paddle board on the lake—might be hard in your condition."

The omega narrowed his dark eyes, his lips slightly pursed. "You would let me stay with no strings attached?"

Bear raised a brow at him. "Do you want there to be strings?"

Silas groaned, dragging a hand over his face. "Is this a joke to you? D'you think this is funny?"

"Do I look like I'm laughing?" he replied flatly.

Silas huffed, flapping his arms. "Well—why the hell would you just take me home with you and let me stay without setting any conditions first?"

"What conditions do you want?"

Silas scowled at him. "How about the condition that I have to work for my room and board? Nothing for free. No handouts."

"I already told you that if it's chores you want, I can oblige," Bear replied, leaning against the side of the truck.

"What about timeline? You can't just let me stay forever," Silas pressed.

Bear nodded. "A timeline sounds reasonable. What kind of timeline would you like?"

Silas was quiet for a minute. "What about...five weeks? Is that—no, that's too much," he muttered, looking a little sheepish. "Two weeks is fine too..."

"Five weeks," Bear replied. "But room and board is covered. You'll work because you need the job, and I need the help. You'll work around the house and in the shop. I'll pay you twenty bucks an hour. Payout will be at the end of each week. You give me an eight-hour day, five days a week, for five weeks that's..." He did the quick mental math. "Four thousand dollars. Does that work for you?"

Silas swallowed. "You'll pay me four thousand dollars?"

"For five weeks of work, yes. You don't work, you don't get paid," Bear replied, knowing the omega needed him to draw a firm line. "No sitting around with the dog drinking my coffee all day."

Silas smirked. It fell quickly as he nodded. "Five weeks means I would stay until the cast comes off. Jared can take it off and then...I'll be ready to move on. By then, the heat here should be totally gone because Pack Rainier will think I went to Redrock."

"It's a good plan."

"And no sexual favors," Silas added.

Bear frowned. From this distance, he could still smell the omega. It was heady. Even when he was angry and on edge, Silas smelled like Bear's best wet dream. Five weeks of this was really going to mess with his head. But the truth of Silas's circumstances worked as an instant curative to any burning sexual desire Bear might feel. More importantly, Silas didn't want Bear. Perhaps, biologically, yes, he craved an alpha, but mentally and emotionally Bear knew that Silas would rather eat glass.

Their kiss was...well, not to be repeated.

He held the omega's gaze. "Silas, I swear to you that, if you come home with me now, our relationship will be purely platonic. Only you will have the power to change that dynamic. Only you will get to say if we become more. However, I have no intention of holding out hope. You don't owe any alpha the honor of your body or your bond. And when it comes to heats...well, there are all kinds of ways around needing an alpha's help with that too."

Silas scoffed. "You can't be serious. It's really all in *my* hands?"

Bear gave a curt nod.

Silas narrowed his eyes. "And if I said that right here, right now, I want you to drop to your knees and suck my dick?"

Bear did his best to ignore the way his cock seemed ready to leap into action. "Are you asking for that?"

"I'm asking for the truth! If I told you to drop to your knees right now and suck my dick, would you do it?"

Bear matched his stance, arms crossed, gaze brooding.

"Without hesitation. So perhaps make sure you mean it before you make any of those particular requests."

Silas groaned, pinching the bridge of his nose in frustration. "Why are you doing this? Why are you putting all this choice on me? What the hell do you get out of it?"

Bear considered the answer to each question before replying. "I'm doing this for the same reason I pulled you from the road in the first place: because it's the right thing to do. And I'm putting the choices on you because, as you say, you've earned the right. You need to learn to trust yourself again, Silas," he added, holding the omega's gaze. "You need to feel confident in making choices and seeing them followed through by yourself and others. And you need to learn to trust people again. What I get out of this is the chance to help someone restore their faith in their fellow man. Does that satisfy?"

Silas was quiet for a long minute. "You are a very strange alpha, Bear Beresford."

Bear just shrugged. It wasn't the first time he was told he didn't fit the alpha mold. It took him a long time to stop taking it as an insult. Too long. Now, he embraced it. "So, what's it going to be? What do you choose to do next?"

Silas looked around. Slowly, he let out a breath. "I guess...for now...I choose to go back to the cabin with you."

Bear kept his face impassive, even as his pulse quickened. "Final answer?"

Silas rolled his eyes. "Yeah, final answer."

Bear nodded, gesturing at the truck. "Fine. Let's go home."

31

Silas

Silas woke early on Thursday morning and checked his phone to find a message waiting from Ollie.

Ollie: Meds will be at address on Sat

He sighed with relief. Last night he'd texted Ollie Bear's address, begging him to find a way to send the scent blockers directly to him at the cabin. If he only had five weeks here, he needed to get them in his system.

He left his room to find Bear shirtless in the kitchen, still sweaty from his workout, his tanned muscles flexing with every move he made. The man looked lickable.

Mother fucking may I—

Silas groaned, pushing that thought deep down. He swung forward on his crutches with a gruff, "Hey."

The alpha stood at the end of the bar. He turned at Silas's approach. He had one of those gross green smoothies in his hand, and he was reading something on a legal pad. "Come take a look at this. I need you to approve it."

His curiosity piqued, Silas crossed through the living room into the kitchen. "What is it?"

Bear set the pad down on the bar and stepped back. "Work list."

Silas shuffled his crutches into one hand and tugged out the end stool, slipping onto it with a *click* and a *clack* of the crutches against the countertop. He picked up the legal pad, his eyes quickly scanning the list scrawled in Bear's narrow handwriting:

- *Feed the dog (daily)*
- *Get the mail (daily)*
- *Laundry*
- *Keep guest room and hall bathroom clean*
- *Keep all shared living spaces tidy*
- *Clean up after all meals*
- *Cut wood and stack*
- *Power-wash, sand, stain dock*
- *Prep winter garden*
- *Weed flower beds*
- *Shop work*

"That's just a few things I came up with," Bear said, pulling Silas's attention from the list. "You have final choice over what you do and in what order."

Silas felt a stirring of discomfort. This seemed like a lot of physical stuff, and he was operating at sixty percent. He'd never power-washed or sanded a thing in his life. "What is shop work?"

"I'll expect you to help me out in the shop sometimes. There's all kinds of stuff that needs doing. I didn't write it all out. But all you have to do is say no to any task you don't want to do—"

"No," Silas was quick to say. "No, I can do it." That was the deal right? To stay here he had to work. He didn't want this alpha thinking he was weak or incapable. If it was on this list, Bear wanted it done. And Silas was damn well going to do it.

BY EVENING, SILAS WAS READY TO EAT HIS WORDS. HIS ENTIRE body hurt. Every muscle. Every bone. His hands were scraped all to hell from weeding for three hours without gloves on. Bear didn't tell him there were gloves in the garage. In Bear's defense, Silas never asked.

After three more hours of pulling weeds with gloves on, crawling around in the grass to avoid the up-down-up-down motion with his bum leg, Silas was dirty, smelly, his hands were two open blisters, and he was ready to collapse. He barely had the energy to stumble his way up the deck stairs back into the cabin. That night he flopped himself down in the tub, too tired to stand for a shower. He just slung his casted leg over the side, letting the hot water soak into his aching muscles.

That was his entire Thursday, and he wasn't even finished. How did he not notice Bear had flower beds wrapping around the whole damn house? For the first night since Bear found him on the side of the road, he didn't take a sleeping pill. He didn't need it.

ON FRIDAY HE STAYED INSIDE, THINKING MAYBE THAT WOULD be easier. Yeah, try using a vacuum on crutches. Or unloading and loading a dishwasher. Dragging a hamper of laundry down into a basement and back up again. Cleaning toilets.

The only time he left the cabin all day was to do his daily mail check. That meant hauling his busted ass down nearly fifty yards of gravel drive. By the time he got down to the mailbox, he was panting and sweating, and his busted hands were aching so bad he wanted to scream.

"You don't have to do the whole list all at once," Bear cautioned him Friday night. They were sitting outside eating dinner—grilled salmon with prosciutto-wrapped asparagus and a stone fruit salad. Thank god for Bear's cooking. Silas had never tasted anything so delicious in his life.

Well...that kiss came to mind.

"It's fine," Silas replied. "I can do it."

SATURDAY WAS SUPPOSED TO BE A DAY OF REST. BEAR TOLD him he was free to do whatever he wanted. What Silas wanted to do was work. He wanted to bleed and sweat and distract his mind from all the chaos that swirled inside it. So, after he fed the dog and had breakfast, he went outside to finish up the weeding.

It helped that Bear was keeping busy too. Apparently, he was behind on his furniture orders, so he spent long hours out in his shop. It was situated a few hundred feet down the lake. A narrow stone path wove to it through the trees. It was huge, with metal siding and large, sliding doors that could be opened on all four sides to help with air flow. The shop had its own gravel drive that went up to the road.

Whenever he was out there, Bear blasted rock music and Silas heard the alpha hard at work—sanders, saws, drills, hammers. If Bear could work on a Saturday, so could Silas. He only paused in the weeding to do his mid-afternoon mail run.

He tugged out the stack of mail and stilled. The large

brown package on top was addressed to 'Reginald Crap-weasel.' Silas couldn't contain his grin. That was one of the many aliases Ollie used to order his ill-gotten goods off the internet. Somewhere in a police database, there had to be a growing fraud file on Mr. Crapweasel that stretched five miles long.

Silas tucked the rest of the mail back in the box and balanced on his crutches with his armpits as he tore into the package with both hands. Inside were three pill bottles. Silas pulled one out. Under the patient name, Reginald A. Crapweasel, there was some doctor nonsense about milligrams, but all the rest was in a language he couldn't speak.

With a huff, Silas tugged the phone out of his pocket and shot off a text to Ollie.

Silas: Meds are here. Can't read label. How many do I take?

He inspected the other two bottles while he waited for Ollie to respond. After two minutes, his phone dinged.

Ollie: Hold on a sec...

Silas waited. At the sound of another *ding*, he glanced down.

Ollie: Take 2 in the am on an empty stomach. That should last you a couple months. Lmk when you need more
Silas: Thx

Stuffing all the mail into his carry bag, he began the long trek down the gravel drive. When he got back to the cabin, he stuffed the pill bottles in his pockets and put the package straight into the big trash container next to the garage, burying it under a few of the stinky trash bags.

Then he went up to his room and searched around for the best place to hide the pill bottles. He didn't know why he didn't want Bear to know about the pills, he just didn't. It was an instinct thing. An alpha wouldn't appreciate an omega using meds to hide or suppress their designation. Silas was worried that Bear might see it as some kind of failing on his part, like he couldn't keep Silas safe...like Silas didn't trust Bear to keep him safe.

But Silas wasn't leaving this choice up to Bear. Determined not to chicken out, he cracked open one of the bottles and fished out two pills. He tossed them back, swallowing them dry. Then he tucked each bottle inside a balled-up pair of socks. Leaving the pills hidden away, he went back outside to clean up his weeding mess.

32

Twisted metal. Broken glass. The burn of acrid smoke in his lungs. Silas gasped awake, opening his eyes to a scene of horror. He was hanging suspended in the crashed SUV. The engine was on fire, the flames burning hotter. In a panic, Silas dropped down to the hood and scrambled on his side, kicking at the door to get it open. Each kick sent a jolt of pain from his foot down his leg.

"Come on—come *on!*"

He wasn't dying in this fucking car. Not like this. Not in a blazing ball of fire.

The back door creaked open and Silas scrambled out, crawling on hands and knees through the wet grass. Shoving off his knees, he swayed on his feet, turning to face the wreckage. He gasped for air, watching the flames spiral higher. The engine was gonna blow. He had to get back.

From behind, he heard the unmistakable sound of a chamber being racked in a gun.

"You're a real son of a bitch, OB," a man growled. "Turn the fuck around."

Heart in his throat, Silas turned.

Dallas stood five feet behind, gun pointed at his chest. "Any last words, you piece of shit?"

Silas raised his hands in surrender. "Dallas, *please.* Don't—"

The shot rang out, dragging Silas into the black.

"Nooo! *Ungh!* Getoffme!" Silas fought the hands that held him down.

"Silas, wake up." A deep voice called to him, urgent and firm. He wanted to go to that voice. God, he'd follow that voice anywhere. "Wake up," it called again.

I'm trying. Please, don't leave me—

Someone was shaking his shoulder. Silas couldn't breathe. He was shot, right? Dallas shot him. No, Dallas was dead. Images of Dallas's body hanging suspended in the car slammed into him. The *drip drip* of his blood. That vacant look in his eyes.

"No," he groaned. He did that. Silas killed him. Dallas was dead...but he felt the impact of the shot. It knocked him off his feet. GSW to the chest. He was dead too, right? Was this death? God, death smelled so fucking good.

"Silas, *wake up!*"

The alpha bark pierced through the chaos of his cyclonic thoughts and Silas bolted upright, his hands fisting tight to the sheets. His eyes shot open and he immediately tried to ground himself. He clutched at his heaving, sweaty chest, feeling for the chest wound.

Nothing.

"Just a dream," he muttered with relief. "A dream...just a dream."

"That's right, just take a few breaths, and calm down." Bear was here. He was standing well back and away from the bed, but he was here. Silas understood his trepidation. Last time Bear woke him from a nightmare, Silas swung a butcher's knife at him.

Now he reached instinctively for the alpha, extending out his hand in the dark. Bear took it and Silas pulled him forward, dragging Bear down next to him on the bed. The alpha sat stiffly, letting Silas hold his hand.

"You alright?" Bear murmured. "You need to talk about it?"

Silas closed his eyes tight and shook his head. His thoughts were still too chaotic. A swirling, smashing vortex of awful shit. He squeezed tighter to Bear's hand.

"Why don't you lay back down," came the alpha's soothing voice. "Lay down and just keep breathing. You're alright, Silas. I'm right here."

Silas groaned, sinking backwards. His head landed on the pillow as he fought down a whimper. Something was wrong. He tossed and turned, still holding the alpha's hand. It was the only thing grounding him. His lifeline. The nightmares swirled inside the storm of his awful memories. This was all fucking wrong.

"Silas, you need to breathe," came Bear's assertive tone. "Hey, open your eyes and look at me." The alpha leaned down, his scent swarming him. "*Look* at me, Silas."

Silas flicked his eyes open, staring up into the looming face of the alpha in the dark. "Something's wrong," he panted. "I feel—I can't breathe. I can't—Bear, I feel like I'm dyin—"

The alpha cupped his face with his hand and inched closer. "You're not dying, and you're not dreaming. Look at me and breathe. Do it. In—" Bear took an exaggerated breath in, and Silas tried his best to match him. "And out." Bear exhaled in his face.

Silas whimpered, sucking the alpha's breath straight into his lungs. He squirmed, both hands reaching for Bear's shoulders, as he tried to bury himself in that perfect scent. "Bear, *please*," he whined, not even knowing what he needed.

The alpha stiffened, trying to pull back. "Silas..." he said in that warning tone.

Bear was upset. He didn't want Silas to touch him. Silas whined again. Dropping his hands away from the alpha, he sank back onto the bed, twisting in his sheets. "I can't—"

"Silas, your omega scent is out of control," Bear warned. "You're feeling way too much. I feel like my heart is white-water rafting right now. Talk to me," he soothed. "Tell me what you're feeling. Tell me what you need."

"I feel—like I can't breathe," he gasped out. "Can't get... comfortable." He was searching for a word and that was the only one that fit. "Can't calm down. I can't—"

"What usually calms you down?" the alpha murmured, brushing his fingers over Silas's sweaty brow. "What do you like? Say it out loud."

"What?" Silas panted, gripping at his chest. He felt possessed by this feeling of panic. It wasn't him; it was his omega. Could you talk about it like a separate entity? Right now, it felt like that. Knowing he made no sense, he rasped out, "It's not me, it's the omega. I can't fight him. Bear, what's happening to me?"

Bear was quiet for a moment. Then he took Silas's hand and continued to brush his fingers over Silas's brow. "What does your omega like? What makes him happy?"

What a strange question to ask? Silas wracked his brain for something. *Anything.* "I don't know. I don't—I've never felt like this before—"

Bear let out a low breath, leaning away from him.

As the alpha's scent grew fainter, Silas felt his panic coil tighter. "No," he whined, reaching for the alpha.

"Fuck," Bear muttered. "Silas...do you like my scent?"

"*Yes*," Silas gasped.

"Okay, here...let's try this." He shifted away, and Silas wanted to die.

"No," he cried again, his hands swiping at the air.

"Just hold on," Bear soothed. "I'm not going anywhere."

Bear pulled back and Silas opened his eyes, watching as the alpha stripped out of his old rock band t-shirt, his tatted muscled flexing in the moonlight. It was then Silas noticed that the alpha was wearing nothing but a t-shirt and a pair of black boxer briefs. His hair was down and curling around his shoulders.

"Give me your pillow," Bear muttered.

Silas still couldn't think straight. "What—"

"Just give it to me—" Bear stretched himself over Silas, jerking his pillow out from under his head. Then Bear flipped the pillow onto his lap and stuffed the end of it inside his t-shirt. With a couple shakes, he tucked the pillow inside the shirt like it was a pillowcase. "Here," he said, offering it back to Silas.

Silas whimpered again. "Bear—"

"Just take it." Bear pushed the pillow at him. "Lay down."

Silas tucked it under his head. Turning on his side, he pressed his nose into the t-shirt and groaned. His senses flooded with Bear's warm alpha scent—spiced and woodsy, warm and safe. He was surrounded, engulfed. Feeling so close to him, it was like they were kissing again. Silas immediately started getting hard, blood racing to his cock.

Yes. This is what his omega wanted. He wanted to bathe in this scent, drown in it. He groaned again, rolling onto his stomach, pressing his face into the pillow. His erection grew under him, trapped between his body and the bed. He breathed deep, not caring that the source of the scent was watching him groan and writhe. He couldn't dare let himself have Bear, but he could have this. He took several long hits off the pillow, slowing his breathing as the scent acted like a muscle relaxer.

"There you go," Bear soothed. "Breathe and calm down."

Silas took a few more deep breaths, sucking in air through the fabric of Bear's old t-shirt. It's like the alpha's essence was woven into the threads. How many hours had Bear spent in this shirt over how many years?

"I think you were having a panic attack," Bear murmured. "Have you ever had one before?"

"Nothing like this," he replied, his voice muted by the pillow. He could breathe again. His mind felt clearer. He was still painfully hard. If he rolled over, Bear would see it. He could probably smell it. Alphas could always pick up on omega sex pheromones. Silas was humiliated to imagine what the room smelled like right now. But he wasn't ready to lift his face away from the pillow yet. "How did you know this would work?" he muttered into the pillow.

"Omegas need a nest to feel safe, and this room isn't a very good one. It's too sterile, too empty. You woke in a panic and had nothing comforting. Can you tell me what happened?" Bear placed a gentle hand on Silas's bare shoulder. Silas felt the roughness of his calloused fingers. The touch spread like fire across his skin, bringing every nerve ending to life.

Silas needed a distraction. Something. *Anything.* "It was a nightmare," he began, distracting himself with words. "I dreamed I was in the car again. I had to get out. It was on fire. Then Dallas was there, and he shot me. It all felt so real." He rubbed at his chest, feeling his clammy skin.

"Who is Dallas?" Bear murmured, his thumb brushing gently on the bare skin of Silas's shoulder.

"An alpha in Pack Rainier," he replied. "He and Floyd were driving me to Bridgeport. He had a gun. I saw it and I could reach it and I just...took it. I couldn't go to Bridgeport. I knew what waited for me there. I couldn't, Bear. I didn't mean to do it."

"What happened?" Bear asked softly, his voice a soothing balm.

"I just...had to stop the car," Silas replied. "We fought for the gun. I don't remember exactly but...I think while he grabbed the gun, I grabbed the wheel and...turned it. The SUV flipped off the road and down a hill. I woke up inside it, hanging upside-down by my seatbelt. Floyd was knocked out but...Dallas was dead. I killed him."

Bear's hand stilled on his shoulder. "And that's how you broke your leg? In the crash?"

Silas nodded.

The alpha let out a low exhale. "Silas, it's not your fault."

Silas sucked in a breath that came out sounding more like a sob as he gripped tighter to the pillow. "I pulled the gun. I jerked the wheel. I crashed the car, and I killed him —" His voice broke and Bear was there, sinking down onto the bed next to him.

"Hey...enough now." Bear curled his large body against Silas, holding him from behind. He wrapped his tattooed arm around him, placing his hand over Silas's chest, fingers splayed against his heart.

Silas sank into the alpha's warmth, feeling every point of contact. He pressed backwards against Bear, wrapping his hands around the alpha's arm and holding tight to him. His anchor. His lifeline.

"That alpha's death is not yours to carry," Bear intoned,

his deep, honeyed voice right in Silas's ear. "Do you hear me? Let it go. He was trafficking you, Silas. He deserves to be dead."

"I'm not sorry," Silas whispered, letting the awful truth free into the air. "I'm the reason he's dead, and I'm not fucking sorry. I'm *glad*. I'd do it again in a heartbeat. What does that make me? Am I no better than him?"

"Silas, *stop*," Bear growled, pulling him closer. "You are not like him. You're not like Floyd either—"

"I'm a killer—"

"You're a *survivor*. In the face of something truly awful, you fought and won. That alpha chose his life. He chose to hurt you. I can only imagine the things he did before he agreed to trafficking." He took a breath, his finger's flexing against Silas's chest. "I would have done the same thing," he murmured, his lips all but brushing the skin of Silas's bare shoulder. "I defy any court to hear your story and charge you with his death. Hell, my uncle is a sheriff, and he'd probably just shake your damn hand."

Silas took another deep breath, suddenly very aware of the mostly naked alpha curled against his body. Bear had molded himself to Silas's back, their bodies touching from the shoulders down, Silas's hips pressed tight against Bear. In this position, Silas could feel everything—Bear's pulse against his skin, Bear's warmth, the strength of his muscles, the hardness of his...

Oh, fucking hell.

It took all of Silas's self-control not to whimper. Silas had his ass pressed tight against Bear's crotch and he could feel Bear's hardening cock. He had to find a way out of this before he did something they'd both regret. He pulled away slightly. "I'm okay now."

Bear just nodded, relaxing his hold but making no attempt to move.

Silas let several painful moments tick by where he fought his every omega urge to roll over and stick his tongue down the alpha's throat. Now was not the time. He felt sick and clammy and he just confessed to where and how he killed a man.

"I'm okay," he said again, a bit louder. When Bear didn't move, he added, "You can let me go now."

Behind him, the alpha stiffened. Slowly, he loosened his hold. "Do you want me to leave?" he murmured in that deep voice.

No, please god. Never, the needy whore of an omega screamed inside him.

Silas shut his eyes tight. God damn this alpha and his infuriating determination to have Silas make all his own decisions! "I...I'm tired," he replied, a total cop out.

"Tell me what you want," Bear said. "Choose."

"I...you can go," he whispered, hating the words and wishing them unsaid the moment they passed his lips. But he stayed silent, and the alpha dutifully rolled away, his weight sagging the bed down as he got up.

Silas buried his face back against his Bear-scented pillow. He was such a mess, forcing the real thing away so he could cling to what remained.

"Goodnight, Silas," the alpha said.

"Night," he replied, not daring to turn around.

The alpha left, shutting the door softly behind him.

33

Bear

It was all Bear could do to stay on his feet and stumble his way out of Silas's room. He forced his legs to take him down the length of the hall back to his dark bedroom. As soon as he was inside, he shut the door and sank against it, sliding to the floor.

He was so goddamn hard.

"Fucking hell," he panted, dragging a shaking hand over his face.

Silas wanted him. The unbonded omega was writhing on the bed, desperate for him. Bear's senses were still filled with the omega's unsated desire. It was the most sensual moment of his life, feeling that raw, aching need in another person and knowing *you* are the one they want to satisfy it.

The way Silas groaned into the pillow...

The way his hips pressed against the mattress...

Bear stifled his own groan, dropping a hand to cup his aching cock, anything for a little goddamn relief. He had to get out of there. If Silas hadn't come to his senses when he did...

"No," Bear growled, shoving himself back to his feet and pacing in front of the fireplace.

Silas was nothing like the shit alphas who hurt him. And neither was Bear. He refused to be one more alpha that would hurt this omega or take something he didn't want to give. And Silas wasn't in his right mind tonight. He was scared and confused, still reeling from the events of this week.

And healing took time. It wasn't linear and it wasn't even guaranteed. Bear's mother had been a school guidance counselor. She worked with kids from troubled homes— broken families, abuse, neglect. Sometimes she talked about it. Sometimes she just carried it all. And when she carried their pain, the pack carried her.

That's what Silas needed from Bear right now. When the weight gets too heavy, you find someone you can trust to help you carry the load. Silas needed to know he could trust Bear, and that didn't happen overnight. Bear had to be patient. He had to commit to being a friend and nothing else. Because the very real reality was that, in less than five weeks, Silas could decide to walk out the door and leave forever. And Bear would have no choice but to watch him go.

That didn't help him solve his current predicament. He paused in his pacing, glancing down to see the way his briefs were tented. His precum had already soaked through the front, leaving a wet circle over his aching tip. Could he touch himself right now? Would that really be so wrong?

Yes, alphahole. The omega is in there holding himself together with tape and glue, and you're gonna jerk off?

He didn't have to think about Silas while he did it. He could think of something else. *Someone* else—

He gasped as if in physical pain, raking both hands

through his tousled hair. Even the *idea* of thinking of someone else made him nauseated. No, there was no one else. Hadn't Bear spent the last twelve years proving to himself again and again that there was no one out there for him? The loner alpha, too turned off by scent signatures to stomach a pack or even a partner.

Until now...

Now he had an omega scent surrounding him that haunted him. And it was growing stronger with each day that passed. From those first moments in the road, his soft beta scent was burrowing into Bear, sinking deep. So sweet and smooth, so...*Silas*. In the span of a week, Bear felt realigned. He felt moored to a new purpose.

He groaned again. This was a goddamn disaster. How was he going to survive four and a half more weeks of this? What happened if the omega's scent just kept getting stronger?

Bear paused in his pacing, staring out at the dark lake through the wall of glass. Why couldn't Silas be obnoxious or have hygiene problems? Bear could keep his focus if Silas was a total asshole who never brushed his teeth.

But no, Bear genuinely liked the omega. Silas was smart and hard-working. He was stubborn and clever. Not to mention beautiful beyond all reason. Visions of him swam before Bear, filling him to the brim with longing. Those dark eyes Bear wanted to drown inside. That strong jaw the omega lifted in quiet challenge.

He was so goddamn strong. Even when he doubted, even when he stumbled, Silas was strong. But he needed to learn that asking for help didn't make him weak. He was probably lying awake in his room feeling embarrassed, thinking that his nightmares made him weak too. Not in Bear's eyes. Those nightmares were proof of all the things that couldn't take him down. Silas was still standing.

No, this was *not* just about scent signatures...which meant Bear was totally screwed.

He stumbled into the bathroom, leaving the lights off as he turned on the rainfall shower head. Once the water was steaming, he dropped his briefs to the tile floor and stepped through the glass. He stood under the spray, letting the water cascade down his head and shoulders, soaking him through.

The first sensation of the hot water hitting his aching cock made him hiss. That sound soon turned to a throaty growl as he wrapped his hand around his shaft, stroking himself from root to tip.

God, it felt so good. How long had it been since he'd been with someone? Bear couldn't even think. He just needed relief. He reached blindly for the body wash, giving the handle two quick pumps. Then he wrapped his fist back around his cock, suppressing a shiver as he smoothed the cool gel up and down his hard length.

"Oh, fuck—" He gripped tight to the base of his cock, feeling as his knot began to swell. His mind raced at the unlikely possibilities. Silas on the bed. Silas in his arms. Silas whimpering and presenting for him, glancing over his shoulder to give Bear that look, *the* look. The look that said so clearly, "Take me alpha, I'm yours."

And Bear would take him. Fuck, Bear would *own* him. Rut into that perfect omega and knot him until he—

Stop.

He shook his head, trying to clear it, groaning under the spray of the hot water.

That wasn't Bear talking; it was his biology. Alphas didn't have to be dominating monsters. They could be kind and gentle, attentive. Bear would never lose control with Silas. *Never.* No ruts. No biting. He'd worship the omega, shower him with love and affection.

Yes, worship. Make him feel so good. Only cherish.

Bear pumped himself harder, giving his knot a painful twist. He groaned, biting down on his bottom lip. His hips wanted to move. They wanted to thrust. God, why was this so hard? He could think all the pretty words he wanted, but his control was razor thin.

"Bear, *please*," the omega whined in the woods, luring him in. He said it again stretched out on the bed. His omega perfume choked the air, drugging Bear with all his unspoken desires. For an alpha to leave an omega in distress like that was...Bear could hardly breathe.

Bear, please.

Alpha...look at me.

Silas called him 'alpha' and Bear wanted to die. Then he looked at him with those beautiful, dark eyes, pools of night. Bear was lost in a starless sea. Lost in Silas. Lost *to* Silas.

He was right there, right on the edge. He pumped himself harder, twisting at the base around his knot and again at the head. What might it feel like to have that omega's perfect lips around his cock? Would Silas take him deep? Would he swallow what Bear gave him? Would he ever let Bear reciprocate?

God, Bear wanted to drop to his knees right fucking now. He wanted to drown in the omega. He'd give him anything. *Anything.* The image of himself on his knees, choking on the omega's cock, finally sent him over the edge. He pictured Silas's fingers in his hair, digging in tight as he made Bear take him to the hilt.

Alpha, please—

"Silas," Bear groaned. Falling forward, he braced against

the tiled wall. With the omega's name on his lips, he came. Pain mixed with pleasure as the orgasm tore through him, taking all his air with it. He felt shredded, torn apart. Panting for breath, he sank to his knees, his hand still milking his aching cock.

When the haze of the orgasm finally lifted, he dropped his hand away with a relieved sigh. His cock twitched, hungry for more, but he couldn't bear it.

Not tonight. No more.

He was too unraveled, too out of control. And Silas didn't deserve this. He was more than his biology. Bear was no better than any other alphahole, fantasizing about an omega who didn't want him, using the omega to come. It wasn't happening again. His cock would just have to suffer.

Silas was off limits.

34

I t took Silas forever to fall back asleep. He talked himself out of going to the alpha half a dozen times, tossing and turning with his face pressed into the pillow. He woke feeling irritable and self-conscious. Oh, and he was in serious pain. Over the past three days, he really overdid it. His body needed rest today.

After he popped two of his blocker pills, he swung out into the hallway to find Bear's door still closed. Was the alpha in there? Usually, the door was open when Bear was awake. Silas swung into the living room and kitchen. Both empty. The dog trotted over to him, tongue lolling as he nosed Silas in the crotch. Silas fed him and started the coffee. While he waited, he stood at the window, looking out on the lake.

Last night felt significant. Something had shifted between him and Bear. He told the alpha his truth. He told him about Dallas and the SUV. Bear hadn't recoiled from him or called him a murderer. Instead, he wrapped Silas in his arms and comforted him, telling him he would have done the same thing. Maybe it was nothing. Maybe Bear was just being nice...but it felt significant.

The coffee pot clicked off and Silas filled up his travel mug with the dark roast. He found that when he was just moving around the house, it was easier to keep a hand free. He left a crutch propped against the kitchen island. With the coffee in his right hand and his left curled around the crutch, he let the dog out and went out onto the deck.

The chilly September air kissed his face, waking up his nerve endings and making him feel more alert. He curled up on the sectional, looking out over the lake. Zipping up his fleece against the chill, he tucked his right leg up closer to his body, stretching out the casted leg. It felt odd to have his toes exposed. He wiggled them inside the cast, wincing at the dull ache he felt in the leg. Manageable, but still there.

Before long, Zeus joined him, hopping up onto the sectional and resting his head on Silas's thigh. Silas obligingly scratched his ears, sipping his coffee with his free hand as he gazed out at the beauty of the lake. He'd never felt such a connection to a place before. He could stay like this forever.

He didn't know how long they sat there in the blissful quiet before the door snapped open and Bear came striding out. One look at the alpha made Silas's chest tighten. Bear was showered and dressed in a pair of jeans, his work boots, and an old black and white baseball shirt flecked with woodworking stains. His hair was up in his messy man bun, and he was wearing those sexy librarian glasses with the thick black frames. He wasn't smiling.

"You need to go inside," he said in greeting.

Silas sat up, sensing his worried tone. "What's wrong?"

Zeus hopped off the sectional, trotting over to greet the alpha. Bear stuck out a hand, giving him an absent pat. His eyes narrowed on Silas and a muscle ticked in his jaw. "Is that my sweatshirt?"

Silas looked down. "Uhh...yeah. Mine was in the laundry." Actually, it was dry and folded *on top* of the machine... but one touch of the fabric and Silas couldn't resist putting this on instead. How could he when he was literally wearing Bear like a hug?

"Fucking hell," the alpha muttered under his breath, dragging a hand over his beard. He caught Silas's eye again. "Ray is on his way over."

"Ray?"

"My business partner." He stomped across the deck in his heavy boots. "He's coming to drop off some stuff. I told him I'd pick it up tomorrow, but he insisted. He'll be here any minute, so you gotta get inside."

Silas reached automatically for his crutch. "Is Ray a threat? Is he an alpha?"

"Hell no, he's as beta as they come," Bear replied. "But he still can't know you're here. He's got a big mouth and his wife's is even bigger. They won't understand why we need to keep you a secret. They're good people, but they talk too damn much. Please, Si." He glanced sharply over his shoulder, hearing tires on gravel before Silas could.

The alpha's use of 'please' had Silas on his feet. His alpha needed this from him.

He's not your alpha.

He ignored the voice, swinging forward on his crutch.

"I'll go head him off at his truck for a few minutes," Bear said, already turning to trot down the stairs. "Go to your room and stay there," he called over his shoulder.

With a huff, Silas went back inside, snatching up the crutch he left by the island before he shuffled to his room. He shut the door and leaned against it, glancing around the dark space. The curtains were shut tight, making it feel cave-like, even though outside the autumn sun was shining bright. With nothing else to do, he sat down on the bed, stretching out to wait. Stripping off Bear's fleece, he leaned back against the pillows.

In minutes, he heard the front door swing open, followed by two male voices. Zeus barked a few times, his nails clicking on the hardwood floors as he trotted over to sniff and whine at Silas's door.

At least someone wants me to join the party.

Silas crossed his arms over his chest. He was being ridiculous. Bear gave him a perfectly good reason for why he needed to stay hidden. Bear's uncle was still on the lookout for Floyd, sending Bear nightly updates. Floyd hadn't been spotted again, but that didn't mean he was gone for good. And Silas wasn't taking any chances. Neither was Bear. He wasn't even sure if Bear told Jared he was still in town.

His jaw clenched tight at the thought. He didn't like the idea of the vet talking to Bear about him behind his back. Where was this resentment coming from?

It's coming from your bitch of an omega who thinks Bear is ours.

Silas smirked, knowing it was true. He didn't like the idea of sharing Bear with anyone. Not Jared. Not this new beta Ray, who worked with Bear. Certainly not Bear's uncle, the alpha sheriff.

But it was foolish to think Silas could keep Bear all to himself. Bear had a whole life here. He had family and friends. A pack. He worked in this county and went to school here. He probably knew most the families on this lake, and they knew him.

It made Silas's heart squeeze tight. There was so much

about this alpha that Silas didn't know. Did he play a sport in high school? He looked like the sporty type. Was he good in school? Did he go to college?

Silas had been with him for over a week, and he hadn't asked the alpha a single question about himself. He'd chosen to be resolutely disinterested because caring was a weakness. Caring lead to kindness, and its always kindness that gets you hurt.

But Bear was different. He made Silas want to be different too.

Silas heard Bear's deep laugh, the way his voice raised up at the end when he was asking a question. Ray was a talker. Minutes ticked by. Silas kept checking his phone. First ten minutes, then fifteen. A half hour of sitting in the dark, waiting, as the smell of something baking started to sneak its way under his closed door. Was that alphahole out there making cinnamon rolls while Silas was holed up like a mouse in the damn wall?

That was definitely the oven timer.

Opening and shutting of cabinets.

More laughter.

Silas's emotions were in turmoil. Why was he letting this bother him so much? How many times in the past seven years had he been sent to a back room to 'sit there and shut up', just waiting for an alpha to give him an order? This wasn't new to him. So why did it suddenly hurt so bad?

Turning away from the door, he rolled onto his side, wrapping his arms tight around his chest. He hugged himself, pressing the side of his face into his rock band pillow. Bear's soft scent filled his nose. Damn, it was already fading.

Reaching for the fleece instead, he bundled it by his face, taking a deep hit off it like an addict. He closed his eyes, trying to block out the sounds coming from the kitchen.

This is all you get, came the dark voice. *This small piece of him. You don't deserve more.*

SOMETIME LATER, THERE CAME A KNOCK AT HIS DOOR.

"Silas?"

Silas opened his eyes. When he didn't respond, Bear cracked the door open.

"You awake?" the alpha murmured.

He let out a soft breath. "Yeah."

Bear stepped into the room. "Sorry, I didn't think he would stay so long. Kate sent him over with a tin of coffee cake and he demanded that I bake it while we talked shop and—are you okay?"

Silas felt him step closer. "M'fine," he replied. "Just tired."

"You've been working too hard. I told you to take it easier." Bear was right behind him now standing at the edge of the bed. "Do you feel alright? Need any pain reliever?"

"I'm fine," he repeated.

Bear sighed. "You're not fine. Can you try and tell me what you're feeling? Can you put it into words?"

"Don't act like my shrink," he growled, glancing over his shoulder to glare up at the alpha.

Bear crossed his arms, his hazel eyes narrowed on him. "You're welcome to sit here and feel miserable...or you can let me help you."

"What did Ray want?"

"Just shootin' the shit. I think he needed a breather from Kate. She's an angel, but a hell of a talker. He used work as an excuse to come see me, but we didn't get to talking much about furniture." He was quiet again, but his presence loomed heavy next to the bed. "Is Ray being here what has you upset, Silas?"

The alpha saying his name made him twitch. He closed his eyes tight. His fingers still clutching to the fleece. "Did you play a sport in high school?" He heard the words same as Bear, not even realizing he'd moved his mouth.

Bear was clearly taken aback by the random turn. "Yeah. Football, baseball. Tried a couple seasons of hockey, but I was a shit skater. Two left feet on the ice...why?"

Silas ignored his question. "Did you go to college?"

"Nope. Trade school. The only classes I excelled in were wood shop and gym."

Before he could ask another question, he felt the bed dip. Bear sat down next to him, placing a tattooed hand on his shoulder. "Talk to me, Silas," he murmured. "What has you so upset?"

The feel of the alpha so close had Silas suppressing a shiver. The weight of Bear's hand on him felt too heavy and not heavy enough. Bear could body slam him and it wouldn't feel close enough. Wetting his lips, he let himself say the words. "You have a whole life here. Friends like...like Jared and Ray. They know you. They don't have to ask questions because they already know. You fit here and...I'm just a burden—"

"You're not a burden."

"I'm in the way—"

"Silas—"

"I'm gonna ruin your life—"

"Stop," the alpha growled. He tugged on Silas's shoulder, rolling him onto his back.

Silas looked up at the looming alpha, taking in his bearded face, those sharp eyes. "There's no place for me here. I belong in the shadows, and you can't live like that," he whispered. "You can't hide me away as your dirty secret—"

"Silas, look at me." Bear cupped his face. "I'm sorry, okay? This is my fault. I wasn't thinking. What I asked was unfair to you, and I'm sorry."

A shot of relief sank through Silas, warming him. What the hell was wrong with him?

"As long as you're staying here, this is your home as well as mine," Bear went on. "You should never have to give way to anyone. Not Ray, not Jared. I let you stay, and I have to respect that. It won't happen again."

"I don't understand."

"It's an omega thing. You know like, your house is your castle," he explained. "I'm not trying to psychoanalyze you or tell you how to be an omega" he added quickly. "But my mom was this way too. Your omega instincts mean you want to nest. You're protective of your space. You also want to tend anyone who comes into it. To shove you to the side like that, to keep you in the dark while a stranger was here...that was cruel. I'm sorry, Silas," he said again.

"It's not my house," he murmured, sitting up on the bed. "And you were just trying to protect me."

"You're staying here, which makes it yours," Bear corrected. "I'm out of practice, but omega rules need to apply for as long as you're here. No one comes in without your approval. I will not disrespect you like that again."

Silas let out a shaky breath, feeling the rest of the weight lift away with his words.

Bear's mouth quirked into a smile. "Better?"

Silas nodded.

"Good, 'cause I saved you some of the coffee cake. If you want, you can come help me with a few things out in the shop." He stood and turned, holding out a hand towards Silas.

Silas took it, letting Bear pull him to his feet. He hopped on his right foot, his body brushing against Bear's as he found his balance. Bear put a hand on his arm to steady him. Their shared point of connection sent heat racing over his skin.

"We'll figure all this out," Bear murmured. "You won't have to hide out forever."

"I know."

"I'll be going to the pack house tonight, and I'll talk to Terry. We'll get a better idea of what's going on."

Silas just nodded. Bear was leaving him again. He'd be alone in this house while Bear handled everything.

"We just need you to sit tight a while longer, yeah?"

Bear was so close. Silas felt himself leaning in. Bear's hand was still on his arm. Their chests brushed as Silas tipped up his chin. "I want to know you like they know you," he whispered.

Bear kept his body still. "I'm an open book, Silas. Ask me anything."

Silas held the alpha's gaze. Their chests brushed with each breath they took. Bear exhaled through parted lips, the air ghosting over Silas's mouth.

"Ask me," Bear muttered, his thumb brushing against the smooth skin of Silas's bare forearm.

"I..." Silas couldn't think of words.

"Ask."

"When you left me last night," he began before he could stop himself. "Did you take care of your hard-on?"

"Yes," Bear admitted, holding his body very still.

The truth sank deep inside Silas's chest, warming him. This alpha was all strength and quiet calm. What did it look like when he took himself in hand? What did Bear sound like when he unraveled? Swallowing his nerves, he dropped his gaze to the alpha's mouth as he murmured, "And...did you think of me?"

The alpha let out a breath through those perfect lips. "Yes."

Silas smiled, enjoying the curious feeling of power hearing that admission gave him. He held the alpha's gaze again. "I think that needs to be omega rule number two. No strangers in the house. No strangers in your head. As long as I'm here, I'm the *only* one here, yes?"

Bear nodded.

"Good." Breaking their trance, he snatched up the fleece and tugged it on. "I'll have some of that cake now. And I'm keeping this."

35

Silas

S ilas kept his distance from the alpha for the rest of the
day. The tension between them was too intense. Silas
had a slippery hold on his self-control, and he didn't want to
do anything to upset the alpha...especially if it might lead to
rejection. Silas couldn't stand the idea of wanting something
that Bear couldn't give. The idea of wanting and feeling was
scary enough on its own.

They spent a couple hours on opposite ends of the
massive workshop. Bear stood at the open end near the lake,
music blasting and tool after tool grinding and sanding and
pounding away at a stack of wood that Silas assumed would
soon become furniture.

Meanwhile, Bear set Silas up at the other end of the
workshop with a stack of sandpaper and a row of unfinished
dining room chairs. All the chairs needed sanding and the
electric sander was apparently too harsh. Silas sat on the
dusty floor, scooting from chair to chair, sanding them
bottom to top.

They took a break for lunch, and afterwards Silas stayed
in the house to rest. For the first time in over a week, Silas

sat down in the TV room, mindlessly flicking through channels with the dog.

A little after five, Silas was relaxing watching a rerun episode of *The Secret Diaries of a Teenage Omega*. It was a bullshit drama about an omega named Destiny who tries to mainstream at her local high school. Silas thought it was dumb, but the other prostitutes at the Hotel Royale were obsessed with it.

Okay, so maybe Silas was secretly rooting for Blake.

And fine, the music was good too.

Bear came down the stairs, showered and changed again out of his shop clothes. His mouth twitched as he glanced at the TV and back over at Silas and the dog. "Both rotting your brains, I see?"

Silas just shrugged, remote in hand. "Nothing else was on."

Bear smirked. "Watch what you want. I'm not here to judge."

Silas rolled his eyes, clicking the volume down. "And what do you watch then? World news and nature documentaries?"

"Sports and action movies mostly," he replied. "There's some DVDs in the cabinet."

Silas snorted, glancing up at the alpha. "You still use DVDs? Haven't you heard of streaming, mountain man?"

Bear crossed his arms and gave Silas a serious look. "I have streaming services too. I'm just saying I *have* DVDs and they're in the cabinet."

"We're fine," Silas replied, giving the dog's soft ears a few strokes. Zeus stretched out next to him, his body warm like a furnace.

"Right...well, I'm off. I'll be back later and I'll bring leftovers. You good?"

Silas nodded, turning the volume back up.

Bear just stood there for a minute and Silas could feel the alpha watching him. "You know...I always preferred Dean over Blake," he murmured.

Silas turned with a huff. "Okay, no. Dean is alpha trash, and I'll tell you why. First—why are you smiling?" He scowled, taking in the look on the alpha's face. He lowered the remote to his lap. "Oh...you were joking."

Bear laughed. "I'll see you later. You two stay out of trouble. I have my phone."

Turning on his heel, he left through the garage.

It felt weird to have the house all to himself. He finished another episode of the show before hobbling upstairs in search of a snack. He exchanged a few texts with Ollie while he ate his cheese and crackers, arguing the plot points of the last episode. Turns out Ollie was a diehard fan and watched the new episodes with his alphas every week.

After his snack, he decided to get cleaned up. Something about Bear being gone made him feel bold. He'd only been in Bear's bathroom once, and that was for his haircut. He liked the idea of showering in there tonight. It would be easier too because he wouldn't have to climb in and out of the tub.

Would Bear mind? Did Silas care?

Omega rules apply.

Resolved, he fetched his cast condom equipment from the hall bathroom and brought it through into Bear's room. The room was saturated in Bear's calming alpha scent. He had a king-sized bed along the far wall sitting low to the floor on some kind of handmade wooden platform. The frame extended up behind the bed and to the sides, where a pair of side tables were built in. Each side table had a lighting unit hanging over it. The setup was sleek and modern and screamed Bear. The bed had neutral coverings in greys and creams with pillows Silas wanted to sink into.

Nope. Look away, you needy omega whore.

Silas groaned, pulling his eyes from the bed as he swung into the bathroom. In no time he had his cast wrapped and the fancy double shower on. Hot water pounded the slate grey tile, filling the room with steam. Silas hobbled his way inside, letting the twin shower heads hit him from both directions at once.

God, how did anyone survive without twin shower heads? *This* was living. Silas had been ghost-walking before this moment. He let himself enjoy the feel of the water pummeling his back, shoulders, and face, washing all his cares and worries away. He picked up the shampoo bottle, squirting a little dollop into his hand and rubbing it into his short hair.

As he rinsed it out, Zeus leapt off his perch on the shower mat, barking like a maniac. Silas stilled, opening one soapy eye. The dog let out two more loud barks, his body coiled tight. In moments, he was bounding across the tile, skittering by the door as he darted out, still barking like mad.

Someone's here.

The dog didn't react like that otherwise. Was it Bear? Was he back early? Not likely. Bear said Sunday dinner took hours. Last week he didn't come home until after ten o'clock.

The dog was still barking. And Silas was officially panicking.

He shut both shower heads off and scrambled to reach his towel. He wrapped it around his waist and snatched up his crutches. As he hopped naked into Bear's dark bedroom he saw a green flash of light and heard a double beep. His eye darted over to the security panel on the wall by the door.

Someone was inside the house.

He glanced around wildly, looking for anything he could use as a weapon. The knives were in the kitchen. He had one hidden in his room. Could he get to it? Maybe if he moved quickly. He swung forward, determined to get to a weapon. As he was about to pass through the door he paused, craning his neck around. There, behind the open door, was a wooden baseball bat.

Better than nothing.

Silas set his right crutch aside and snatched up the bat.

"Did you find any?"

Silas stilled. That was a woman's voice. It sounded muffled, like maybe she was still outside.

"Not yet!" came another woman's voice. This one was much louder. It was definitely coming from inside the house.

Silas's omega instincts surged. More strangers in his house in the same day? He'd had enough. These women had to get out. *Now.* He clung to the bat with his right hand, swinging forward on his crutch with the other. The woman in the kitchen turned at the same time and screamed.

"Ohmigod, who the fuck are you?"

Silas wasn't expecting to see someone so young, but she was all woman—fair brown skin dusted with freckles, curvy and gorgeous, with her dark, curly hair pulled up in a high ponytail, the ends spilling around her shoulders. She'd been snooping around in the cabinets...an odd place to look for valuable shit to steal...

In a panic, she snatched for one of the knives out of the butcher's block. "Who *are* you?" she repeated.

"Who am I? Who the fuck are *you*?" Silas barked, raising his bat. The movement jostled his towel and it slinked around his knees, leaving him naked in the middle of the living room.

The intruder gasped, throwing one hand over her eyes. She split her fingers open and peered out from between them like a cartoon character. "What kind of pervert are you? Why are you wet and naked? Oh my *god*!"

It was then that her scent slapped him in the face. Bubbly and fruity and so very *alpha*. "Get out of my house!" Silas shouted, his nerves making his hands shake.

The alpha huffed. "Nice try, you naked creep! This is my brother's house and I'm calling my *uncle* the sheriff to come get you out of it. Right. *Now!*" She kept her knife-hand raised as she shoved her other hand in her pocket, reaching for her phone.

Silas's fear flipped to panic. "Don't call the sheriff!" he cried.

"Dialing!" she shrieked back, holding out the phone and dramatically pressing the green call button.

Before Silas could act, a petite woman with a sleek black bob came charging through the open doorway, both hands raised in the air. "Everyone put their weapons *down*!"

36

Silas

"Yumi, stay back," the taller girl with the knife cried, still holding out her phone.

"Oh my god, Claire, put that knife down. You look crazy." The tiny girl stepped fully into the cabin, her eyes on Silas. She had a sultry edge—thin black brows, a little pointy nose pierced with two rings, half-lidded eyes painted thick with makeup, stark against her pale skin, and pouty lips, also double pierced.

"This creep came charging in at me, and now he's naked, and I'm kinda freaking out!"

"Put the phone away," Yumi snapped. "I think you're really scaring him, C." She narrowed her focus back on Silas and flashed him a disarming smile. Her scent was beta. "Hi, we're looking for Henry. Is he here?"

"Henry?" Silas repeated, his heart still racing out of his chest.

"Yeah, Henry Beresford," the alpha called, shoving her phone back in her pocket. "Ya know, the guy whose house this is? He's my brother."

All the pieces finally snapped into place, and Silas let out a shaking breath. "Oh shit...you're Bear's sister?"

"Yeah," she replied, setting the knife down on the counter. "I'm Claire. This is my bond mate Yumi."

"And we're engaged," Yumi said in a sing-song voice, flashing a glittering ring on her finger.

Silas frowned. "Wait...so you two are Bear and Claire?"

Yumi giggled while Claire just shrugged and said, "I mean, *technically* his name is Henry. I'm just one of the last people to call him that. Yumi only does it because I do."

"Are you a friend of Henry's?" Yumi added.

"Ohmigod, are you his *boyfriend*?" Claire cried. "Don't tell me he *finally* went and bonded someone and didn't even bother to send me a text!" She crossed her arms over her breasts with a pout.

Yumi gasped. "C, shut up." Her eyes went wide as she stared at Silas, her mouth opening in shock. "Do you smell that?"

Silas stilled, his panic rising all over again as he watched Bear's alpha sister take a big dramatic sniff of the air. Like her bond mate, her eyes went wide and her mouth dropped open.

"Holy fuck. You're not..." She glanced at her mate who was grinning wide. "He is not!"

"He *is*!" Yumi squealed. She turned back to Silas. "You're an omega?!"

Claire groaned. "I move away for two minutes, and I come back and find Henry's shacking up with a drop-dead gorgeous omega?"

Yumi was giggling again. "I'm sorry...do you maybe want your towel back? I'll help you if you'll put the bat down and tell us your name."

Silas glanced down with a jolt. He was standing in the middle of Bear's living room soaking wet with nothing but a crutch and a bat. His foot was still wrapped up in his humiliating foot condom. At least the only light came from the kitchen so they weren't getting a great view. "I...yeah, thanks."

Yumi came hopping over like a bunny, darting to the floor to pick up his towel.

He tossed the bat on the couch and took the towel from her, wrapping it around his waist.

"Holy fuckballs, you smell even more amazing up close," Yumi said, bright eyed and smiling.

"*Hey*," Claire called, the slightest hint of a bark to her tone.

"I'm just saying," Yumi replied, but she still took two big steps back and flashed her alpha a smile before turning back to him. "I can smell Bear on you, but it's faint. Are you two like...just friends or something? Are you not closing that deal? Because that would be the crime of the century—"

"Yumi!" Claire cried, her tone exasperated now.

"What?" Yumi said with a shrug. "Two people as hot as your brother and this guy have *got* to procreate. It's not fair to the universe if they don't—" She went suddenly quiet.

Silas sensed her tension, his eyes darting over to her. Her gaze was locked on his neck. *Fuck...the scars.* He was in such a hurry, he didn't think to cover himself. Yumi's eyes were darting left and right, her smile falling. He quickly crossed his arms, at least hiding the scars on his wrists. And his thighs were covered in a towel.

"Ignore her," Claire called from the kitchen. She hadn't noticed yet. She was busy rattling something in a cabinet. "We've been trapped in a car for two days and it's clearly gone to her head."

"What happened to you?" Yumi murmured. "Are you... did your pack do that to you?"

He held himself tighter. "I don't have a pack."

"Then how—"

"You didn't tell us your name," Claire called, cutting off her mate.

Silas was reeling. This was all too much. The beta was standing in front of him with that worried look on her face. They wanted his name. Could he give it?

Shit, now both girls were looking at him, waiting expectantly. "I...my name?"

Claire snorted. "Yeah, you know, it's usually that thing that goes on IDs and applications to tell people who you are."

Silas swallowed. "Yeah. It's...uhh...Dean." He couldn't think of anything else in the moment.

"Well, it's nice to meet you, Dean," she replied. "How long have you been living here?"

"What?" He wasn't living here...was he? Sort of, technically. But it wasn't permanent—

"I know you're not from the lake," she said, flipping her thick curls over her shoulder. "I know *everyone* on this lake. I'd totally remember crossing paths with a hot omega. So, how long have you been here?"

"Not long," he replied, offering nothing.

She joined them in the living room, hands on those curvy hips. "Where did you and Henry meet? Is this permanent? Are you looking for a bond?"

He blinked in surprise, mouth slightly open. Damn, this alpha was on the hunt. Protective sister mode was fully engaged. She wanted answers. He hated that he was half-naked for this. *Oh shit—*

The alpha's eyes narrowed. She'd finally noticed the

scars. Up closer now, Silas could fully appreciate her features too. The similarities to Bear were uncanny—the bridge of the nose, the expression in the eyes, that dark brow that arched up just so. Bear's eyes may be hazel, but his sister's were a warm amber. They made the freckles dotting her cheeks look like little flecks of gold against her fair brown skin.

She pursed her lips, glancing from Yumi back to him. "That's a lot of bite marks there, Dean," she said, her good mood evaporated. "Did you bond an entire football team?"

"C," Yumi said in warning. "Don't be rude. He doesn't owe us his life story right when we've just met—"

"He's staying in my brother's house," Claire countered, still in alpha protector mode. "He smells like Henry, but if he's got a whole pack already—"

"I don't have a pack," Silas growled.

Claire crossed her arms, mirroring his stance. "That doesn't make any sense. All those marks, you gotta be bonded."

"Sorry to disappoint you," Silas muttered, wanting this painful moment over and his hoodie armor back in place.

Claire's mouth opened slightly in horror, connecting the dots. "Were you...attacked?"

"*Claire*," Yumi pressed again. "The poor man's not even wearing pants. The inquisition can wait until he's not in a towel."

Claire rolled her shoulders as she sighed. "Fine." She glanced back over at Silas. "I'm a little overprotective of Henry, alright? He's been through a lot, and I don't want some bonded omega bringing him any heartache."

"Jeez, C," Yumi said with an awkward laugh. "Why don't we let Dean get his clothes back on before you finish your obligatory little sister interrogation?" She turned back to

Silas, trying to keep her eyes from the scars. "We were raiding Henry's pantry looking for stuff to make s'mores down at the fire pit. Wanna join us?"

Silas hadn't quite felt the gravity shift back under his feet. He shook his head. "Umm...can I just—why are you *here*?"

Yumi groaned as Claire said, "That is a loooong story, Dean. Tug on some clothes and meet us down by the lake. We'll swap our life stories."

Did Silas really have a choice? *Not likely.* He had a feeling this alpha/beta duo would prove impossible to deny.

37

Bear

Bear stood across from his uncle, leaning his hip against the deck. Down on the dark grass, the kids were chasing each other and playing with sparklers. A single flood light on the corner of the house lit the scene, while another light glowed down on the end of the dock.

"And you expect me to believe all that?" Terry said with a raised brow.

"It's the truth," Bear replied. "My friend was in deep, but he got out clean, and they're still hounding him. He's dangerous to them, Ter. He knows the crimes they've committed. All he has to do is turn rat, and Pack Rainier is finished. They can't know how to find him. It's life and death."

Terry hummed low in his throat, arms crossed as he looked out on the lawn. "You put him on that bus out of town, yeah?"

Bear had considered this part of the story for days. Was he willing to trust Terry with the truth? "He got on the bus, yes," he replied with a nod.

Terry snorted. "And then he got off again...didn't he?" That dark brow raised as he studied Bear's face. When Bear made no reply he smiled. "Yeah...that's what I thought. It's clever, nephew. Lay a false trail. So, do you have your friend holed up somewhere? You keeping him out of sight?"

"He's safe for now," Bear replied. "We need to know if there's any more sightings of Floyd or anyone from Pack Rainier in the county. My friend is gonna lay low for a while. When we think it's safe, and the heat is off in Spring Hill, he'll take off for good."

Saying the words out loud was physically painful. Bear had to clench his teeth against making a sound. How had everything changed so completely in the span of only a week? It didn't feel real. His life didn't feel real anymore. Only one thing felt real. He couldn't voice it, too afraid to want it. Too afraid to lose it.

"Well...I won't say I like this for you, Bear. You don't need to be messed up in this. You're a good guy."

"So is he," Bear said defensively. "I'm helping him because it's the right thing to do. You know I wouldn't help if I didn't believe that, Ter."

"I do," Terry said with a nod. "You're a good man, Bear. I just wish you had an easier time of being an alpha."

Bear swallowed, saying nothing. He glanced down at the kids running in the grass.

"I wanted this life for you," Terry murmured, following his gaze. "I wanted to see you packed up with a bond mate or two, a mess of noisy kids, Sunday dinners with you at the head of the table, all of it. It's what Henry wanted too," he added softly.

"I can only be me, Ter," Bear replied.

He couldn't let himself begin to imagine the possibilities

of any of Terry's dreams for him coming true. It was too fragile. Before Silas, he had all but given up. He'd resigned himself to the life of the loner alpha. Before Silas—

He let out a slow breath.

Before Silas.

Warmth bloomed in his chest. That was his life now. There would be everything that happened before Silas came stumbling into his life, and then everything that happened after.

Terry inched closer. "Bear? You okay?"

Just then, his phone dinged and he glanced down. His heart unclenched when he saw it was a text from his sister, not Silas. He clicked the message and read it quickly.

Then he read it again.

On the third read-through, his heart dropped out of his chest.

Claire: We just saw your omega naked. Hubba hubba <3

What the hell?

Claire wasn't in Beresford County. She was still out in Wells...right?

Before Bear could recover from hearing Silas being called 'your omega,' a photo popped up in the message feed. A wary Silas was staring up at him, wedged between a smiling Claire and Yumi. All three of them seemed to be holding what looked like campfire s'mores.

Bear groaned. "Oh, shit."

Can't even leave the omega alone for an hour before chaos starts raining down.

Because that's what Claire Beresford was: a curvaceous bottle of pure chaos.

Bear pocketed his phone and cuffed Terry on the shoulder. "I gotta go."

"Bear—wait," Terry called. "We weren't done with that conversation!"

Not turning around, Bear jogged off the porch. "See you next Sunday!"

38

Bear

ear rolled the truck to a stop in front of the garage. He was out of the cab before the engine was even done turning over. Zeus was on him in a flash, hopping at his side as he strode through the dark towards the glowing fire pit. Another dog came zipping over, a copy of Zeus in a lighter fawn color.

"Hey, Hera," he muttered, giving his sister's dog a pat.

Claire had named them all as puppies. There were two more. Their aunt Janine had the one named Demeter but they all called her 'Demi.' The last one was Hades, which of course belonged to Boyd.

"Henry! Oh my *god*, there you are!"

Claire was up out of her chair, bounding across the grass towards him, her ponytail of dark curls flapping behind her. The dogs went crazy, barking and running around her as she threw herself in his arms, giving him a tight hug. Her cotton candy scent filled his lungs and he felt his own arms wrapping tight around her. Even as he did, he was looking over her shoulder at the fire pit where Yumi sat next to Silas. He leveled his eye on Silas, asking the silent question.

With the fire making his skin glow impossibly bronze, Silas nodded.

Bear relaxed, tugging his sister off him. 'What the hell, Claire? What are you doing here?"

"It's good to see you too, big bro," she said with a roll of her eyes.

Yumi was standing now, crossing the grass towards him too. "Hey, Henry," she said with a wave.

"Hey, Yumi." He gave her his customary side hug. Yumi's beta scent was sweet and spicy, like chocolate with chilies. Not offensive, but just not for Bear. Clearing his throat, he led the way over to the fire pit. "So, are you going to tell me what you're doing here? I thought Yumi's program in Wells was a three-year gig?"

Claire was a total tech geek. Her current project was some kind of online fashion app, which meant she had a lot of flexibility about where and how she lived. Yumi, on the other hand, was a doctoral archeology student. Claire may be the alpha, but she followed her beta wherever the pierced pixie led.

"Ugh," Claire said dropping into her chair. "We were just telling Dean the whole story. Dean, do you mind terribly if we start over?"

Bear's eyes held on Silas, who gave an awkward shrug. Apparently he was Dean now. Bear ignored his sister, sweeping around the back of the chairs to drop to one knee behind Silas's chair. He took a shameless hit off his omega, breathing in his intoxicating scent while he leaned in to murmur, "You good...*Dean*?"

Silas nodded, raising a hand to brush Bear's shoulder, as if he too craved the physical affirmation of Bear's closeness. That unspoken admission of need flooded Bear's senses, calming him even as it set him on fire.

"Before we dive back into our drama, I wanna hear about *you*," Claire cooed, folding her legs up under herself on the chair. "When did you two meet? How did you two meet? What's the deal?" She glanced from Silas to Bear.

"First, did you want anything, Henry?" Yumi asked. "We raided your kitchen for beer and s'mores." She gestured to the cooler by her chair.

"After two days trapped in a car with Hera, we were seriously gonna go crazy. Your marshmallows saved our sanity!" Claire added with a laugh.

"I'm good," Bear replied.

"Can you believe Dean had *never* had a s'more before? Soooo good, right Dean?"

Silas nodded. "Yeah, they were good."

"Dean, did you want a beer?" Yumi asked, holding a can out towards the omega.

Remembering Silas's hard limits, Bear's protective instincts kicked in and he found himself reaching out to snatch the can from Yumi saying "I'll take it" before Silas was forced to answer. He cracked it open and sat in the chair across from Silas, eyes on his sister. "Claire, just tell me what's going on. Did the app go under? Do you two need a place to stay, because—"

"God, Henry, you can really be the worst, you know that?" Claire groaned, crossing her arms. "Do you have so little interest in your baby sister's life that you have to ask me if my company is still solvent? Am I still that much of a screw-up to you?"

"She's doing amazing," Yumi said defensively. "Fash-Forward just ranked in *Demur Magazine* as a Top 10 fashion company to watch. She's growing content and reach every day. The company is worth three million and counting."

"Whoa," Bear muttered, taking a sip of his beer. "Claire, that's amazing."

"It *is* amazing," she said with a flick of her long, curly ponytail. "I'm amazing. I'm an app-developing, fashion-loving, boss bitch alpha."

"A soon-to-be married boss bitch alpha," Yumi added with a wide smile.

Bear glanced between them and Yumi slowly lifted her hand, wiggling her fingers. In the firelight, a massive diamond twinkled on her ring finger. Bear felt a tightening in his chest, even as he smiled. "You finally caved, huh? You're really gonna be stuck with her now," he said at Yumi.

"The bite kind of took care of that," Yumi replied, her cheeks blooming pink. "But we just wanted to make it official in all ways."

"We're gonna belong to each other in every way that matters," Claire said to her beta, blowing her a kiss. She turned back to Bear. "So to answer your shitty, big brother question, no. My company hasn't folded, it's thriving. Yumi had some drama in her program, and we decided there's no point killing herself in a program she hates just 'cause she's too proud to quit."

Bear glanced over at Yumi. "Wait, so the doctoral program is..."

"So over," Yumi said with a smile. "And I've seriously never been happier. The day I left the program, Claire proposed, and we packed up all our stuff. We've been driving around for the last three weeks in a rented RV, just being free while we decided what we wanted to do next. Claire's been working where we can get wifi, and I've been doing a little bit of everything—hiking, yoga, swimming. I think I want to take up kite boarding."

"And you?" Bear said, glancing at his sister.

"Me?" She smiled again. She let out a long, exaggerated sigh. "Oh, Henry, I wanna come home. Yumi's been asking me every day where I see myself living, and in the back of my mind I just kept coming up with the same answer: Lake Beresford. I know it's a long way from any major fashion hubs," she added. "But my app is *online* for a reason. As long as I make some regular business trips to the city for fashion weeks and the big celebrity events, there's no reason we can't live here."

Bear raised a wary brow. "Here as in..."

"As in we bought a house!" Claire cried.

Bear glanced at Silas, who had sat quiet though the entire exchange. "Which house? Where?"

Yumi started giggling.

Claire shushed her. "Umm...remember the old Roberts place?"

Bear frowned. "You mean the cabin two down from mine? The one with the red dock you can practically see from here?"

Now both girls laughed. "That's the one," Claire replied with a megawatt smile. "We just closed on it two days ago! We've still got about a week before we can move in, but we have all these plans to fix it up. We'll practically be living with our contractors for the next few weeks because..." She paused, biting her lip as she glanced from Yumi back to Bear. "We're getting married in four weeks, and Henry I *really* need you to say you'll be there! Daddy's going to walk me down the aisle, obviously, but I need you there too. I know you have your scent thing and your pack avoidance thing but...I just...*please* say yes."

Bear sucked in a breath. This was a lot of information to absorb over one can of beer. "I—wow—of course, Claire." He blinked, swallowing down all the shit swirling in his head. "Of course, Yumi. I'll be there with bells on, you know that. Just tell me where to stand."

"And Dean is invited too, obviously," Yumi added.

"Yes, definitely. Dean, you can be Henry's plus one," said Claire.

Yumi cocked her head to the side, her eyes narrowed. "You know...you don't look like a Dean."

Silas blinked. "What?"

Yumi shrugged. "You just don't really wear the name Dean very well."

"What name do I wear better?" he muttered, giving the hood of his hoodie a little forward tug.

She pursed her pierced lips. "Hmm...something cooler than Dean. Shadow maybe?"

"Jasper?" Claire chimed in. "Or—*oooh*—I like Bastian."

Silas grimaced. "Bastian? You want Bear to walk around your wedding introducing me as his date Bastian?"

Both girls fell into fits of laughter.

Bear ignored them. He had eyes only for the omega who was casually referring to being his date. Bear had a sudden image of it—the two of them dancing under a canopy of twinkling patio lights, holding Silas's hand as he watched his little sister say her vows, catching his eye across a crowded room. He blinked the images away, shifting uncomfortably in his chair.

Silas looked just as miserable, but the girls didn't seem to notice. They were twittering to each other about something, using half sentences in that way bonded mates do, both of them absently checking their phones.

"And Henry," Claire murmured, glancing up from her phone.

Bear met her gaze again.

"I didn't want you to feel blindsided or anything...but I think Reed is coming to the wedding."

All the air left Bear's lungs. "Reed? You're in contact with him?"

Claire nodded.

Bear took a sip of the beer that now tasted like liquid trash in his mouth. "How long? Did you go looking for him or—"

"He contacted me," she replied, tears in her eyes. "About a year ago now—"

"A whole year?" Bear growled. That was a long fucking time for Claire to keep this a secret from him—from the pack. Or was it a secret? Did everyone know about Reed but Bear? Leaving the pack didn't mean Bear left the family... and Reed was...

Bear took another swig of his beer.

"We started slow with texts and the occasional call," Claire went on. "He came to see me in Wells. He wants a relationship with you too," she added. "But I think he doesn't know where to start. I think he's afraid you'll reject him. He wants to come to the wedding, but he understands if—"

"It's not my call," Bear muttered. "I'm not pack alpha anymore. And even if I was, it's still not my call. It's not Boyd's either. The only vote that should count is Liam's."

Claire nodded, dropping her gaze to her lap.

In the chair next to him, Silas was tense. Bear knew he wanted to know more, but he wasn't going to ask questions here. Bear got to his feet. "I'm tired. It's been a long day, and I've got work in the morning. Where are you two staying tonight?"

Yumi and Claire exchanged a look. Claire spoke for the both of them. "Well, our rental place changed the reservation on us last minute. We can check in there tomorrow at eleven..."

Bear sighed. "So, you need a place to crash."

"It's only one night," Yumi said quickly.

"But you need a place to crash," Bear repeated.

Claire gave him her best baby bunny eyes. "Would you mind terribly? We promise to make breakfast in the morning as a 'thank you.'"

Bear glanced at Silas. After everything they went through this afternoon with Ray, he couldn't just pull the rug out from under him again. He raised his brow in silent question.

Silas chewed his lip, clearly uncomfortable. But in the end he nodded. "Yeah, of course it's fine."

39

Silas

This was the opposite of fine. In the span of a few hours, Silas went from standing wet and naked in the living room having his scars gawked at, to standing alone in his room with the scent of a new alpha and a bonded beta clinging to his skin.

Bear had flat-out refused to allow Silas to give up his room. As soon as they were alone he called it omega rule number three. Claire and Yumi were cool about it. In the end, Bear helped them blow up a pair of air mattresses down in the TV room so they could have more privacy.

Silas stripped out of his hoodie and sweats, tossing them in the hamper. Even his t-shirt carried the faint scent of the girls. Claire's reminded him of a fruity drink. And Yumi's was softer with a little spice. But they still made his skin feel itchy.

He sat down on his bed and picked up his pillow, pressing it to his face and breathing deep. A groan tore from his throat. The rich notes of Bear were little more than a memory against the fabric. He wasn't going to be able to sleep like this. He wasn't going to be able to calm down.

Snatching up a clean t-shirt, he tugged it on and grabbed one of his crutches. He left his room, seeing Bear's door cracked open with a light glowing inside. He hobbled down the dark hall pausing in front of the door. Before he could even raise a fist to knock, he heard Bear call from within.

"Come in."

Pushing the door open, he found Bear sitting up shirtless in bed, his hair down around his shoulders, with his librarian glasses on his nose and an e-reader in his hand. The dog was curled up on a massive checkered pillow beside the bed.

Silas held Bear's gaze for a moment as he took a few deep breaths. "I can't sleep."

Bear glanced over his glasses. "Need to talk about it?"

Setting aside his pride, Silas opened the floodgates. "Okay, so...I feel unsettled and stressed...and I *hate* that they're here, but I couldn't let you turn them away, because they're family. But they asked me all these questions about my scars. And then they fed me so many goddamn s'mores that I feel sick, and I never wanna see a marshmallow again. And your sister smells like a daiquiri. And Yumi touched me like fifteen times. She didn't mean to," he added, watching the alpha's eyes narrow.

"I think she just couldn't help it," he went on. "And I used your shower without asking, and that's when I thought they broke in. And I almost attacked your sister with a bat, and then she saw me naked. And the pillow you gave me stopped smelling like you. And I just realized as I was saying all this that I forgot to feed the dog tonight and I'm sorry."

When the last words left his lips, he sucked in a desperate breath, shoulders sagging.

Bear just sat there, one leg propped up. Slowly, he reached over and flipped back the covers on the empty side of the big bed. It was a silent invitation. Silas had a choice to stay or go.

Stifling a whine, Silas shut the door and crossed the room over to the bed. He flopped down on it, letting his crutch clatter to the floor. Then he buried his face in Bear's pillow, lying on his stomach on the soft mattress. The bed smelled so strongly of his alpha—the sheets, the pillows, the blankets and throw. Best of all was the comforting smell of the alpha himself sitting inches away.

They were both quiet, Bear waiting as Silas tried to get his racing heart under control. He shifted on the mattress, still not quite comfortable.

"Silas...would you like for me to touch you?" Bear murmured, keeping his movements small as he set aside his e-reader and glasses.

"Please," Silas replied, his face still buried in the pillow.

Bear immediately reached over with his left hand, not closing the space with his body, and began stroking Silas's back over his t-shirt. Slow, gentle strokes that acted like an all-natural muscle relaxer.

With a deep sigh of relief, Silas turned his face to the side, glancing up at the alpha.

Bear was looking down at him. His posture was relaxed, but his facial features were tight. Those hazel eyes held him captive as he said, "Do you want more?"

"Please," he said again. "Bear—"

"Thank fuck," Bear muttered, dropping down to his side and pulling Silas into his arms. "Come here."

Silas went willingly, wrapping his arms around the alpha and pressing his face against his chest.

Bear tangled their legs together.

"I couldn't breathe," he whispered against the alpha's warm skin.

"I know," Bear soothed, his hands slipping under Silas's t-shirt to rub his back. It's like Bear was seeking out every inch of him that smelled like the intruding alpha and beta, determined to neutralize it, to reclaim Silas for his own.

Silas couldn't be more grateful. "I was standing in my room, and their scent was all over me, and I panicked."

"I'm glad you came. It was driving me crazy too," Bear replied. He dipped his head down, resting his face in the crook of Silas's neck. His beard bristled against Silas's scars. It should have had Silas launching away from him, and yet, his body was a live wire.

"They saw my scars," he said again. "Claire and Yumi. I wasn't wearing a shirt when they came in and...they had questions."

Bear's hand stilled for a second before he resumed stroking up and down Silas's spine. "What did you tell them?"

"Nothing. I distracted them with questions and let them talk about themselves. We didn't really get to me. But I know they're curious. People are always curious," he added bitterly. People needed to mind their own damn business.

"Do you want them to know the truth?"

Silas considered for a moment. "Do you trust them with it?"

"I do," Bear replied. "But it's not about what I think. It's your story, not mine."

"Why were you going crazy?" he asked, his lips all but touching the alpha's bare skin.

"Truth?" Bear murmured.

Silas stilled. "Always." Bear's calloused fingers stroked down his spine, making him swallow a moan.

"You looked so goddamn beautiful, I couldn't breathe," the alpha, admitted. "The fire made your skin glow and you were sitting so still, so quiet. It's like you were...untouchable," he said, trying to find the right word. "And I was... fuck, I wanted you," he whispered. "*Want* you."

Silas exhaled, his warm breath fanning over the alpha's skin.

"But then I could sense your unease, and I just wanted to climb over the fire, throw you over my shoulder, and bring you back inside. Make you safe. But you're strong," he added quickly. "You can take care of yourself—"

Oh god, Silas did it. He pressed his lips to the alpha's chest. It wasn't a kiss...but it definitely wasn't *not* a kiss. And if the way Bear went still was any indication, he was waiting to see what happened next too.

But this couldn't go any farther. There was a nosy alpha in the house. Bear's sister, no less. She and Yumi would definitely know if anything happened, and Silas didn't want to make Bear uncomfortable. He didn't want to lead the alpha on either. Because the awful truth was that Silas didn't know if he was ready for more...whatever that meant. Wanting it and being ready for it were two very different things. But he also didn't want Bear to read his inaction as indifference. His panic was mounting again.

"Bear, I—"

"It's okay," Bear soothed. "I'm just glad you're here. I was going mad trying to stop myself from going to you. I reread the same page of my book fifty times."

"When you got to the fire pit, I wanted to crawl in your lap," he admitted. "Bear, I want to live inside your scent."

Bear groaned. "God, I know. I've never felt anything like this. Never."

Silas stilled leaning back until he could rest his head on the pillow and look up at the alpha. "What did your sister mean...about your scent thing and your pack avoidance thing?"

Bear sighed. "I was always meant to lead Pack Beresford, but pack life just isn't for me. Almost from the moment I presented, I've struggled with scent signatures," he admitted. "I tried for about three years when I got back from the military. I lived the pack alpha life, but it was killing me. And when we started earnestly looking for an omega to replace my mom, I knew I needed out. The pack needed me out. I was no good for them. No good for anyone."

"You're good for me." The words were out before he could stop them. Once out, Silas leaned in to the sentiment. "You're good *to* me. Bear, you deserve more than me. Better—"

"Stop," Bear muttered with a deep frown.

"I'm broken—"

"You're not."

"The evidence is etched across my skin—"

"I don't care about the scars. And you are not a reflection of the shit that's been done to you. You don't have to carry it or live inside it anymore."

Silas scoffed. "You don't care that dozens of alphas before you have claimed me, and fucked me, tearing me with their teeth—"

"Stop," Bear growled, the hint of a bark in his tone. He gripped Silas tight under the chin and tipped his face up. "Nothing you can tell me about your past will make me stop wanting you. Stop trying to push me away. You get a choice in this, but so do I."

Silas sucked in a sharp breath. "I'm not going to let you throw away your life—"

Bear silenced him with a kiss, his lips firm yet inviting. Silas sank into it with a sigh of relief, opening his mouth to take in the alpha's seeking tongue. They played with each other, their lips moving in sync as their tongues explored. It wasn't rushed, but it also didn't last. Before Silas could really let himself get lost in the taste of the alpha, Bear was pulling away.

"You're not ready for more right now, and that's fine," Bear murmured, brushing his tattooed fingers over Silas's lips with a reverent stroke. "But I'm not going anywhere. I want to know you, Silas. And I want you to know me. Ask your questions."

Silas swallowed, still swimming from having the taste of the alpha on his tongue. "Umm...who is Reed?"

Bear stilled, his jaw clenching tight as all the romantic energy in him was leeched out like a popped balloon. "Reed was one of my mother's bonded pack mates."

"And...what happened to him?"

Bear leaned away, rolling on his back to look up at the lazily spinning ceiling fan. "When my mom died, it broke her alphas. My dad Henry took to the bottle and it killed him quick. Claire's dad Liam is still at the pack house."

"And Reed?" Silas murmured, readying for the worst.

Bear's frown deepened. "Mom's death broke him too. He walked away and left the pack as we were all grieving our omega. He left his kids," he spat with utter disdain. "He was my dad, same as Henry and Liam. And now apparently he's sucking up to Claire, playing her like the fiddle she is, while still hiding from me."

"I'm sorry," Silas replied, stroking the alpha's tattooed arm. "How long has it been?"

Bear gave a heavy sigh. "I had just turned eighteen when she died, so that was...god, like twelve years ago."

"And now he wants to come to Claire's wedding," Silas summarized.

"Apparently."

"And you...you'll see him? You'll still go?"

"Of course," Bear replied with the hint of a growl. "I'm not going to give him the satisfaction of thinking he broke me—broke any of us. I'm not gonna be run out of my baby sister's wedding because one sorry excuse for an alpha wants to show up and eat some bacon-wrapped shrimp."

Silas smirked. Bear was a force of nature, so strong and beautiful. Silas loved hearing the passion in his tone, the determination, even if the subject matter was heavy. Silas wanted to be there. He wanted to see Bear as a pack alpha, taking care of his family.

Okay, and he also secretly thrilled at the idea of having people see him as Bear's date at the wedding. "Can I really go with you?" he murmured. "Would that be weird or..."

Bear let out a ragged breath. "Si, we won't know if it's safe for you yet. Floyd could still be in town. We're lying low—"

"But the wedding is weeks away," Silas replied, his voice almost a whine.

"So we have a weeks to let the heat die down and keep checking for signs of Floyd or anyone from Pack Rainier," Bear reasoned. "We'll wait and make the decision then."

Silas nodded, trying to ignore how deeply crestfallen he felt.

Sensing his change in mood with the precision of a medical scanner, Bear rolled back over on his side and brushed a hand over Silas's cheek. "Hey...it's not a 'no,' okay?"

Silas nodded again.

"If it all works out, I'd love for you to be there, but your safety has to come first," he went on. "Speaking of which, I'll talk to them in the morning before they go. I'll say enough to make sure they know to keep their mouths shut about you being here."

Silas was still skeptical. "You really trust them to keep quiet?"

Bear snorted, his hand absently stroking Silas's arm, his chest. "Poor choice of words. They won't say anything about you," he clarified. "Otherwise they quite literally never shut up."

As if on cue, from beyond the closed door Silas heard the soft sounds of the girls' bubbling laughter.

Bear groaned, rolling onto his back again, covering his eyes with his tattooed hand.

A question sat on the tip of Silas's tongue. It was fighting to escape through his clenched teeth. Did he dare? Was this crossing a line?

He smirked. He was lying in bed with the shirtless alpha, burrowed under the covers, skin touching skin. Lines were already thoroughly crossed. "Can I stay in here tonight? Just—while they're here it's easier for me. I—just tonight," he added quickly, his eyes locked on the geometric pattern of lines and dots wrapping around Bear's elbow.

The alpha kept his hand over his eyes. "Is that what you want, Silas?" came his deep, honeyed voice. "Then say it."

Each time the alpha said his name, it felt like a gift. He nodded, reframing his question as a command. "I want to stay in here tonight."

Without another word, Bear rolled over and clicked off the lamp on his bedside. He plunged them into darkness lit only by the softest of white glows coming from the security panel on the wall.

Silas let out a breath, willing himself to give over to his fatigue. He rolled on his side facing away from the alpha, tucking his arm under the pillow as he closed his eyes, his body still humming. After a few minutes of nervous agitation, he felt the alpha shift behind him.

"Silas...do you want me to hold you?"

"*Yes*," he breathed, even before Bear had finished saying the words.

Bear rolled over, wrapping his body around him, nuzzling his bearded face at Silas's scarred neck. His arm came around Silas's middle. Silas sought him out, entwining their fingers together. The darkness helped, acting as a shield to embarrassment. He could take what his omega instincts needed without fear or judgement.

In moments they settled, both of them breathing easier. Bear brushed his lips over Silas's shoulder. It wasn't a kiss... but it wasn't *not* a kiss. "Goodnight, Silas."

Silas dared to let himself sink fully into this feeling of pure and utter contentment. "Goodnight."

40

Silas

S ilas woke in an empty bed. *Bear's* bed. He sat up, rubbing a heavy hand over his face. He slept like a rock. No dreams. No tossing and turning. It was amazing how restorative a good night of sleep could be.

The alpha's side of the bed had the blankets flipped back, sheets cold. The window shades automatically rose at sunrise, so the room was bathed in golden morning light. Silas looked around, feeling totally relaxed. He'd slept next to an alpha and nothing terrible happened. Bear held him, their bodies fitting together like a pair of puzzle pieces, and they slept. No pain, no tension, no awkwardness at all.

Just...*peace*.

A clang of pots and pans followed by a peal of feminine laughter had him rolling out of the alpha's bed. He rifled through Bear's closet until he found a cable knit sweater that would cover his neck scars. It was thick and warm and smelled like he was drowning in Bear.

He turned the corner from the bedroom to find Yumi sitting cross-legged on top of the kitchen island, phone in hand, calling out directions to Claire.

"Yeah, the big one," Yumi said, pointing at something Silas couldn't see.

Claire's arm shot up in the air behind the island, wielding a large skillet. "This one?"

"Yep, just put it there and—oh *no*—Silas, did we wake you?" Yumi cried.

It took a second for Silas to notice she'd used his real name. His breath caught and he shot his gaze over to her. She was smiling at him sweetly, no hint of revulsion. What had Bear told them exactly? He couldn't just leave this elephant in the room, could he? "Yeah...uhh, sorry about lying last night," he muttered.

"You don't owe us an apology," Claire said. She was back on her feet, rattling the skillet down on the stove top. Her hair was a massive bun of dark curls on top of her head. She turned, crossing her arms under her breasts, pressing them up in her tight sports bra top. "Henry told us why you did it. I mean, we weren't gossiping about you," she added quickly. "But he told us you're in a tight spot and sorta hiding out 'cause you're unbonded. Sorry I was a bitch about it last night. And your secret's safe with us."

"Totally safe," Yumi added with a nod. "And sorry if we woke you."

"No, I was already awake," he replied. "Where's Bear?"

"He had to run something into town, and we're making him grab some bacon on the way back," said Claire.

"And he gave us strict instructions not to wake you, but to give you a mug of the medium roast coffee with a dash of cream and two sugars when you woke up," Yumi added.

"You really have him whipped," Claire snorted. "I lived with him on and off for like fifteen years and he never once bothered to memorize *my* coffee order."

"It's the omega dazzle," Yumi replied, her attention back

on measuring out flour into a mixing bowl. "Plus your coffee order is ridiculous. Do you know how long it took me to memorize it?"

Claire looked affronted. "If you're about to call me high—"

"Maintenance!" Yumi shouted over her, dusting her with flour with a flick of her fingers.

Claire gasped, wiping at the flour on her nose with the dish towel. "Don't listen to her, Silas. I like what I like, and there's nothing wrong with that."

Yumi choked on a laugh. "What you *like* is a tall, no whip, decaf iced mocha, with two pumps of chocolate, extra almond milk, lite on the ice."

"Because I have taste," Claire replied.

"Because you're a monster. We call it the Gutless Wonder," she threw at Silas with a roll of her eyes.

Claire stepped forward, brushing her freckled nose against her beta's, a wide smile on her face. "But you love me anyway."

Yumi stifled a giggle, cupping the alpha's face with her flour-dusted fingers. "So freaking much—"

Claire silenced her with a kiss. In moments, the girls were moaning into each other's mouths, feminine sounds of delight that had Silas wishing he could sink through the floor. He glanced down to see the pair of dogs watching the alpha and beta going at it on the counter.

Swallowing his mounting anxiety, Silas loudly cleared his throat.

With a sound like a suction cup, the girls separated. Yumi went crimson as Claire brushed it off with a laugh. "Ooop, sorry, Silas. If you'd ever had a taste of my girl, you'd understand—but don't try it, 'cause I'll cut your lips off," she added with a little alpha snarl.

"Ohmigod, you are *so* embarrassing," Yumi laughed, giving her alpha a shove. "Start the bananas, or I'm not feeding you."

Their little scene of domestic bliss sank deep inside Silas. Like the roots of a climbing vine, it was working its way into the cracks of his walls, burrowing through the mortar. He wanted this too. Peace and security. Someone to want him and put him first. Someone to memorize his coffee order and boss him around. Someone to love. He wanted to believe he could have it. God, even admitting it inside his own head was fucking terrifying.

THIRTY MINUTES LATER, YUMI AND CLAIRE HAD MADE A disaster in the kitchen. Flour dusted the counter, and the dogs were still eating crushed pecans off the floor. But the cabin was bursting with the intoxicating smell of bananas foster pancakes.

Silas sat at the island with his mug of coffee in hand as Yumi slid a plate across towards him. The plate was heaped with a stack of three buttered pancakes smothered in bananas cooked in a gooey, delicious brown sugar glaze. The whole stack was dusted on top with the crushed pecans.

Yumi and Claire stood back, eyes wide, waiting for him to take a bite. He hated having an audience, but he picked up his fork and cut into the stack. He took a bite and his mouth exploded in a bouquet of flavors. Holy fuck, it was orgasmic. Without meaning to, he let out a sensual sounding groan.

Of course, that was the moment Bear stepped through the door.

"What the hell is going on?" Bear growled.

Silas was instantly on edge, the alpha's protective tone making him wary of danger. Both girls took two big steps away from him, practically compelled by the unstated warning in his voice. Silas glanced over at the alpha. Wait... was this mood about *him*? About them cooking for him?

No, idiot. It's about the orgasm sound you just made for someone other than him.

"Morning," Claire called in a sing-song voice.

"We're feeding your omega, like you asked," said Yumi. "Bananas foster pancakes."

"And I think he likes them," Claire added with a wink.

"Do you?" Yumi said, glancing back at him.

Silas nodded, already chewing on a second bite. "Yeah... this is amazing."

Yumi clapped while Claire took a dramatic bow with her spatula. "Pull up a stool, big bro, and you can have the next batch." She turned back to the mess on the stove, the heat from the skillet making the loose curls around her face spiral tighter.

In moments, Bear was right behind him, the alpha all but pressing against his back. Silas was surrounded by his scent. Damn, the combination of Bear and bananas foster pancakes was lethal. Silas stuffed another bite in his mouth, ignoring how his cock was suddenly twitching with interest.

Not the time, you needy omega bitch! Eat your damn pancakes.

But then the alpha dared to lean over him, setting a pair of grocery bags on the counter. His breath was on Silas's ear as he said, only loud enough for him to hear, "Are you gonna eat those, or have sex with 'em?"

Fire licked down Silas's spine as he went still as stone, his every nerve awakening to the proximity of the alpha.

Heart racing, he tried to keep control of his raging omega instincts. "Maybe a little of both," he whispered.

"I can tell," Bear replied.

Silas swallowed, mindlessly cutting into the pancakes. "Wanna try?"

"Yes." The double-meaning in that one-word response wasn't lost on either of them.

Holy fuck, he's flirting with me over pancakes. He's trying to make me hard.

Then Silas had to fight the urge to laugh. Was Bear...*competing* with the pancakes? Trying to see which turned Silas on more? Were his little alpha feelings hurt by Silas finding pleasure in a breakfast food? Because no offense to the pancakes, but Bear Beresford was the 6'3" bearded tree of a mountain man that Silas was quite literally desperate to fucking climb. If Bear slipped those fuck-hot librarian glasses on, Silas might just bend over and present right here at the bar.

Oh god, oh god, shut it down—

Holding his breath to stop any more of the alpha's scent from invading his senses, he slid the plate over a few inches in invitation. Goddamn it, but that just gave Bear a chance to get closer. His chest brushed against Silas's back as he wrapped an arm around him to reach for the fork. Cutting a triple layer of the pancake, Bear turned the fork and stabbed a banana. Then he lifted it over Silas's shoulder and put it in his mouth.

Bear groaned and Silas wanted to die. The sound exploded inside his chest, making him drop his hands to the cold granite of the counter, holding tight to it. "So fucking good," Bear hummed in his ear, reaching around him again to set the fork down.

It was all Silas could do not to turn around and bury his

tongue in the alpha's mouth. He wanted to taste Bear and the cinnamon sugar together. He stared down at his plate, unsure of what to do next. How did life keep moving forward?

Pick up fork. Cut food. Eat.

A feminine squeak had him lifting his eyes to gaze across the counter.

Oh shit...

"I umm...We should..." Yumi looked drugged, her eyes unfocused, her pierced nostrils flared.

"Goddamn it!" Claire slapped the spatula down. "I can*not* be turned on right now. I'm freaking the fuck out."

Yumi turned to her alpha. "Claire," she whined. "I need—"

"Come on." Claire snatched her beta by the hand, dragging her out of the kitchen.

"We can't," came Yumi's panicked voice. "It's too weird!"

"It's the omega dazzle," Claire snapped, leading the way down the stairs.

The girls disappeared and in moments the telltale sounds of lovemaking filtered up from the floor below.

Bear stepped around the island to turn off the stove, still wearing that satisfied smirk. "I guess I'm not getting any pancakes."

Silas was spinning. It was only then he noticed that a new scent had overtaken the kitchen. Layered on top of a beta, two alphas, and bananas foster pancakes, was the cloyingly thick perfume of an aroused omega. Of *him*.

His overwhelming scent told him two things. First, his attraction to Bear was undeniable and growing increasingly painful to ignore. Second, and more distressing...his scent blockers were most definitely *not* working.

41

Silas

Silas was sitting outside on the deck the following morning, wrapped up in his grey sweats, faded hoodie, and a knit blanket he snagged from the living room. He had a mug of coffee in one hand and his phone in the other, shooting off texts to Ollie.

They'd spent the past 24 hours trying to figure out what was wrong with his blockers. Ollie was sending him some new pills, and in the meantime Silas decided to add a third pill to each morning dose. He hated taking them. They twisted his stomach into knots, making it hard to eat. He spent an hour that morning hugging the toilet, losing his breakfast as his stomach cramped. He was worried he was losing weight again. It was a double bummer because Bear's cooking was amazing.

"Hey," the alpha called, stepping outside. He was also wearing sweats and a pair of thick wool socks. He was bare-chested under a half-zip fleece. His hair was up in a bun and he was wearing those damn glasses.

"Hey," he replied, slipping his phone in his pocket. If

Bear noticed how often he was texting Ollie, he said nothing.

"I wanted to show you something before I head over to the shop," he said, closing the distance between them. "Can I sit?"

"Yeah." Silas eagerly curled forward, trying to reach the outdoor coffee table to set his mug of coffee down. Bear trotted forward the last couple steps and took it from him, setting it down. Silas budged over, making enough space for Bear to sit.

They'd somehow wordlessly agreed to call a truce on raising the heat level on their simmering sexual tension. Yesterday had been a disaster, with the pair of them all but tumbling out of the cabin to avoid the pheromone storm created by Yumi and Claire fucking like rabbits.

At least someone got to enjoy the results of Bear's pancake tease show.

The girls cleared out around lunchtime, and Bear and Silas kept to themselves for the rest of the day. Silas was relieved to have the alpha close again. He'd been too chicken to ask Bear if he could sleep in his room for a second night, so he'd suffered alone, tossing and turning and whining into his sheets like a hot mess.

Bear brushed his arm against Silas's leg as he lifted up his tablet, setting it on Silas's lap. "I wanted to show you this."

Silas glanced down at the screen to see some kind of fashion website. *FashForward.* "Wait...is this—"

"Claire's website, yeah," Bear replied. "It's actually pretty inventive. You can make these mood boards. See, here?" He tapped on the top of the screen with his stylus, pulling up a new page. "And you can give them names and pull color palettes, seasons, styles. There's a planning side, where you can just get inspired," he added, tapping a side bar on the screen. "And then if you click here, you can shop the looks. So you can build a whole wardrobe based on pictures you like, and then the app helps you hunt down pieces from the pictures. That way, you can recreate the look."

Silas nodded, watching Bear click around. "That's pretty cool..." He glanced up at the alpha. "Why are you showing it to me?"

Bear was quiet for a minute, his eyes still on the screen. "It was something Yumi said at the fire pit. I can't get it outta my head."

Silas smirked. "She said like seventeen thousand things. You gotta be more specific."

"About how you don't look like a Dean," Bear replied.

"Well...I'm not a Dean, so that tracks," he said with a shrug. "I'm not a Shadow either. Or a Talon or Sebastian or whatever other stupid names they said."

Bear nodded slowly, lost in his thoughts. "Yeah...but are you a Silas?"

Silas glanced up at him again. "What do you mean?"

The alpha held his gaze, those devastating hazel eyes boring into him. "Who *is* Silas? I want you to feel and look like yourself, but I don't think you know who you are. Seven years is a long time to push down all the parts of you that make you Silas. I think you need to find him again...or find him for the first time. Fashion is a great way to do that," he finished with a shrug.

Silas felt suddenly deeply vulnerable. "How does fashion help me find myself?"

Bear's beard twitched as he smiled. "Fashion is self expression. It's a way to have your outsides match your insides. And this—" He gestured at Silas's ratty hoodie and thrifted sweat pants. "I don't think these clothes are a reflection of who you are. Silas deserves a chance to be seen for *all* that he is. You deserve to know yourself and express that self to the world."

Silas looked down at the tablet in his lap, fighting the surge of omega emotions threatening to drown him. "So... where does the website come in then?"

Bear cleared his throat. "Yeah...I uhh...I made you an account, and I'm assigning you some homework. I want you to rest this morning while I'm out at the shop. You've been pushing yourself too hard," he added, his voice stern as he shut down Silas's ready protest. "Play with the app for a bit. Explore. Get inspired. Save some stuff to the boards. You can show me at lunch."

"Let me get this straight," he said, sitting forward. "You want me to *not* work this morning. No chores, no sanding. You want me to sit here with my coffee and your dog and put together a dream closet?"

"Yes."

Silas crossed his arms over his chest. "These are working hours and I need the money. Are you gonna pay me to do this instead of chores?"

"Yes."

He groaned. This was ridiculous. "I just...*why*?"

Bear growled, that alpha sound making Silas sit up a little straighter. "I already told you my reasons. You want to make choices, so here you go. Choose what you want to wear. You're on the clock, and I'll expect a full report at lunch." He held out the stylus, his determination clear.

Silas narrowed his eyes on the stylus. "Wait...what happened to all your big alpha talk about all my choices being mine? This feels a lot like telling, not asking. What if I don't want to online shop today? Maybe I want to get paid to watch *The Secret Diaries of a Teenage Omega*."

Bear just smirked, poking him in the chest with the stylus. "Who says you can't do both?"

With an eye roll, Silas took the stylus. "I hope you don't expect me to dress like you. Flannel and work boots are so not my style."

Suddenly Bear leaned in, his alpha scent filling Silas's senses. "You know you like my style." The sound of his deep voice sent a zap of electricity through his entire body. The alpha dared to brush his fingers down Silas's arm. "And just maybe...there's a small part of me holding out hope that if I'm the one who puts you *in* a sexy new outfit...I get to take you out of it too."

Dead.

After tossing that sexual tension grenade, the alpha dared to wink and then walk the fuck away.

42

Bear walked back up to the cabin a little after noon to find Silas sitting at the kitchen island, still tapping away at the tablet. Damn, but he was gorgeous. Each day that passed, Bear saw the way the omega bloomed. His color was better, he was stronger. As he shed the layers of his past away, he was emerging as the confident, beautiful soul within. Pure Silas.

And Bear craved him. Longed for him. *All* of him. He'd been distracted all morning, worried that he might have taken things too far. It was hard to tell with Silas when he needed a push and when he needed a more gentle, guiding hand. Bear didn't want to make him do anything he didn't want to do, but he also didn't want the omega to be afraid to take risks or demand what he wanted—from himself, from others, from life.

"Hey," Silas called, his tone bright.

Not too upset then. *Good.*

"This website is really cool," Silas went on. "Your sister has a great thing going here."

"Tell her that, and you'll get showered with free stuff for

the rest of your life," Bear replied, filling a cup with water at the sink. "Gifts are her love language."

The omega's scent hit Bear's nose, and he let out a relieved exhale, taking a sip of his water. He refused to investigate what it might mean that he was quickly reaching a time limit for how long he could go without a fix.

"When is my report due?" Silas asked, still focused on the screen. "Before or after you make us something amazing for lunch?" He lifted his gaze, a smile in his eyes.

"How about we keep it simple for lunch, and I'll spoil you rotten for dinner instead?"

Silas raised a brow. "What's your idea of simple?"

"Uhh..." Bear moved over to the fridge and checked inside. "Ham and cheese sandwiches and chips? My sister left a pack of that shit water that's supposed to taste like fruit..."

"Way to sell it," Silas laughed. "Hey—what do you think of this?" He flipped the tablet around, showing Bear a photo of a guy in sharply creased caramel colored dress pants, a cream turtleneck, and a navy peacoat with the collar popped.

"It's...do you like it?"

"I'm asking what *you* think," Silas pushed. "I need a second opinion."

Bear's smile spread as he picked the tablet up off the counter and inspected the photo more closely. He let his eye flick from the photo to the omega and back. "I think it's cool."

Silas crossed his arms. "Cool? That's it? Why do I feel like you're trying to say you don't actually like it?"

Bear sighed. "My opinion on the clothes doesn't matter. What matters is that *you* would be wearing them. So the real question becomes would I like to see you in these clothes.

265

And the answer to that question is, of course. You'd look hot as hell in this. The cream would play well with the bronze in your skin. But you look great in sweats, so I can't be trusted to have an opinion."

Silas rolled his eyes. "So you're saying you're not gonna help me."

Bear came around the island, leaning his hip against it as he held the omega's gaze. "I'm saying the clothing you wear needs to reflect *your* self expression, not what you think *I* want you to wear—or anyone else for that matter." He reached across the island for the tablet and handed it back to Silas. "What do you like about it?"

Silas frowned, his dark brows pinched as he stared down at the photo. "I don't know. It's just...cool," he finished with a shrug.

Bear laughed. "Then add it to your board. Now, come help me make these sandwiches. I gotta get back out to the shop, and I'll need to make a delivery to town this afternoon."

TEN MINUTES LATER THEY WERE SITTING SIDE-BY-SIDE AT THE bar eating their ham and cheese sandwiches and dipping pretzels and veggies into a creamy dill dip. Bear had the tablet, flicking through Silas's mood boards. Next to him, the omega hummed with nervous energy, waiting for him to comment.

Bear was impressed. The omega clearly took the assignment seriously. It was an interesting look inside his brain. If Bear had to summarize the mood boards in three words he'd say: smart, stylish, and modest. Silas liked tailored looks—dress pants and layers, everything long-sleeved, and most looks paired a cool jacket.

It didn't escape Bear's notice that everything Silas starred as a favorite look would cover his scars. His style was almost...preppy? But in a way that felt modern and utilitarian. Pieces could be mixed and matched to make a cohesive, almost uniform look.

The exception was the shoes. Silas had saved pin after pin of modern and funky shoes—colorful high top sneakers, pointed-toe loafers, fashionable motorcycle boots. Bear had to stifle a smile. He wore exactly two pairs of shoes: his boots for work and his running shoes for exercise. If Silas had his way, he'd apparently like to have a wall of shoes. A pair for every mood.

"This is all really great," Bear said, taking a bite of his sandwich. "I can see you in this," he added, tapping his finger over a photo of a guy wearing tailored green khakis, black leather high tops, and an oversized white cowl neck sweater. It was accessorized with a baseball cap and a fancy watch.

"Listen...I've had an idea," Silas began, dipping a carrot stick into the dill dip. "But I want you to hear me out before you say no..."

Bear tensed. "Why do I already feel primed to say no?"

"I want to get a tattoo," Silas said in a rushed breath.

Bear set his sandwich down and glanced over at him. "Why would you think I'd say no to that? Have you seen me?" he added, gesturing with his gaze down at his exposed tattooed forearms.

Silas shrugged. "I don't know...alphas get weird about seeing their omegas in pain, right? I just assumed you'd get all noble and say no. Like a 'do as I say, not as I do' kinda thing..."

A tense moment stretched between them as Silas quickly realized what he'd said. Meanwhile, Bear inconveniently forgot how to breathe. Desperate to stop Silas from taking it back, Bear cleared his throat and snatched for his sandwich. "Tattoos can be painful, but it doesn't last," he reasoned. "And it's your body, Si. You want one, get one."

Silas let out a relieved breath. "Good. Tonight?"

Bear choked on his sip of soda. "What—*tonight*? Where the hell are you gonna get a tattoo tonight?"

"I figured if anyone would know where to go to get a tattoo it would be you."

Bear could tell this was important to the omega and he didn't want to stifle him, but... "Silas, we're trying to keep you hidden—"

"*You* could do it." Silas's dark eyes were wide with eagerness. "We could do it here or out in the shop."

Bear snorted. "Oh, now it's *me* giving you the tattoo? And you think my shop is a magical shop that has tools for all occasions? Furniture, check. Automotive, check. Tattoos—"

"Have you ever done a tattoo before?" Silas pressed, leaning his elbow on the bar.

Bear pursed his lips. How was he getting roped into this? "Yes," he said slowly, dragging out the 'e'. "But—"

"And do you know any tattoo shops in town that would let you borrow a gun?" Silas's eagerness was bubbling over now.

Goddamn it. Nate would give him a gun no questions asked. "Yes, but—"

"Cool, so get the stuff when you're in town, and we can do it when you get back," Silas said, his decision clearly made. He slid off the bar stool and did his stupid pogo stick jump around the island, dropping his plate and cup into the sink.

Bear crossed his arms over his chest, eyes narrowed at the omega. As Silas started to wash the dishes, Bear glanced around. Had the omega cleaned up in here even though Bear told him to rest? The counters were spotless, the mail was organized, their shoes were in a row by the door. Had he vacuumed the dog bed? It definitely looked less hairy...

He glanced over his shoulder at the living room. Subtle changes were everywhere. The backs of both couches and the chairs all sported a blanket or throw. Silas had even taken some of the pillows from downstairs and added them to the couches up here. A trio of electric candles were on in the middle of the coffee table, creating a soft glow.

The omega was nesting.

Silas was nesting.

That's when Bear really *looked* at him. He wasn't wearing the hoodies anymore. He wasn't hiding himself—not from Bear. Not here in this home where he felt safe. He stood calmly behind the sink in a t-shirt, his neck and wrist scars on full display.

Son of a— Bear fought a groan. *That's my fucking shirt.*

Silas was a little thief, pilfering all Bear's favorite clothes for himself. And fuck if Bear didn't want to go to his closet and give it all to the omega. Silas may not care for his fashion, but he cared for *him*. Silas craved his closeness, even if he couldn't admit it. It was enough to have Bear hard, fighting the urge to rip off that shirt and replace it with his own skin. Silas wanted to be wrapped in his scent? Bear was more than ready to oblige. All the omega had to do was ask.

Please, god. He sent the silent prayer to the heavens. *Please, let him ask.*

Anything. He would give this omega anything he wanted. Any part of him. He swallowed, breath tight in his throat as he said, "Well...what kind of tattoo would you want?"

43

Silas

Bear made good on his promise. When he returned from his furniture delivery in town, he made Silas an amazing dinner of pistachio-crusted halibut and roasted potatoes with a goat cheese and arugula salad. Silas had never tasted a halibut in his life, and he had no idea pistachios could be used to 'crust' things, but it was amazing.

Not bananas foster pancakes amazing...but Silas was a sucker for sweets.

They were sitting in the dining room for once, and Bear had music playing softly through a speaker on the kitchen island. Silas glanced down at the empty stretch of plates between them. "Where did you learn to cook so well?"

Bear shrugged, taking a sip of his beer. "Self taught, mostly."

"Your mom wasn't a gourmet cook?"

The alpha snorted. "Hell, no. Mom's idea of cooking was pouring the cheese packet over cooked macaroni and stirring. My dad was the chef. He liked to grill and bake. He made amazing sourdough and pizza crusts."

Silas pursed his lips. "You call him 'your' dad..."

"Yeah, just a habit. Mom wanted everything to feel equal with the pack mates, so she wanted a kid from each of them. I came out fine. Henry was my bio dad. But she really struggled to get pregnant with Reed. Had a couple miscarriages and some other health stuff. Claire is Liam's...but they were all my dads. It's not like I treated Henry any different," he finished with a shrug. "What about you?"

Silas stilled. "What about me?"

"Did you grow up in a pack?"

Silas sighed, reaching for his water. Apparently they were sharing now. His own fault for asking the question. "My dad is an omega," he replied. "Most omegas are women, but in our genes it runs strong in the men. I grew up in a pack, I guess, but it was...sterile."

"What do you mean?" Bear prodded gently.

Silas let himself think back to those early years. There were some happy memories, but mostly there was just... nothing. "They were all career types, you know? Dad worked long hours in a lab. I think he cared more about his work than his pack. He was an odd omega in that respect. But his pack mates were the same way. I mostly raised myself as they all pursued their careers. I never lacked for anything, I just...I can thank them for my independence," he said with a shrug. "They didn't really even notice when I took off around sixteen. Then I presented at seventeen and went to the Omega Center, and you know the rest."

"They never looked for you? Never questioned where you'd gone?"

Silas shook his head. "We were never close. It's not like I was calling once a week to check in before I left the Center. And to them, Centers are a safe place where omegas get supported and adored. They didn't know any better. Most people don't."

"Do you want to reconnect now?" Bear murmured.

Silas shook his head. "Nah, I'm good. They're living their lives, and I'm living mine. They don't need to take on any of my shit or blame themselves. I don't resent them," he added quickly. "I just...don't need them. Not all families are tight like yours. And I made my own family."

He paused, glancing up at the alpha. He suddenly felt the urge to tell him the truth. "I have a friend...an omega from the Center. We got back in contact when you gave me the phone. We talk every day—I've—we've been talking..."

Bear's gaze shot up, his face unreadable. "That's great," he said after a minute. "Have you told him where you are?"

Silas nodded. "I'm sorry I didn't tell you. I wasn't trying to hide it—well, I *was* but—but it's not like...bad." He was stumbling over his words now. "We talk about *The Secret Diaries of a Teenage Omega* mostly, and he complains about his alphas. He's bonded. He's got four alphas."

"What's his name?"

"Ollie."

Bear nodded. "I'm glad you have a friend, Silas. I'm glad you have another omega to talk to."

Silas let out a relieved breath. He didn't understand why it felt so strange, like he'd been carrying the weight of the secret on his chest. What did he think Bear was gonna do, take his phone away? Ban him from talking to anyone but him?

Yes. Both.

Silas sat in that realization for a moment, knowing it was true. He'd been afraid that Bear was going to treat him like other alphas had treated him. Control him. Cut him off from family and friends. But Bear would never do that. Silas had to *trust* that Bear wouldn't do that. Telling him about Ollie was an important first step in building that trust. He found himself leaning across the table, wrapping his hand around the alpha's larger hand and giving it a squeeze. "I know you would never hurt me."

Bear smirked, his lips twitching under his beard. "You say that as I was about to ask if you're ready for your tattoo."

Fifteen minutes later, the kitchen was clean, the dishes were done, and Silas was sitting on a folding chair in the middle of the garage watching Bear put together the pieces of a travel tattoo kit.

"If you're lookin' for anything more artistic than a stick figure, you're gonna be disappointed," the alpha said, unraveling an extension cord.

"Did you do any of your own tattoos?" Silas asked, eyeing the alpha's forearms.

"A couple," Bear replied.

Silas leaned forward, curious. "Which ones?"

"The shitty ones."

Silas rolled his eyes.

"So...what did you have in mind?" Bear said, taking the chair opposite him. "Where do you want it?"

Silas didn't know why he was suddenly nervous, but there was definitely a flutter in his chest. "I was thinking maybe on my hand. I like—" He swallowed his buzzing emotions. He could admit to this and not make it weird. "I like your finger tattoos. I was thinking maybe something there."

Bear smirked, still setting up the kit. They were using an old TV tray as his work station. "Finger tats hurt like a bitch. And this kit doesn't have a micro needle, so we can't do anything with fine lines or it'll look like shit."

"Okay, so...what do you recommend?"

Bear frowned, lifting his gaze to him. "This is your tattoo, not mine. You tell me what you want, and I'll tell you if I can do it."

Silas groaned, glancing wildly around the garage in search of inspiration. "I don't know. I just—you pick something."

"What?"

Silas leaned forward. "Yeah...you've got cool tats. You pick something and do it."

Bear's frown deepened. "Silas, *you* have to choose—"

"I *am* choosing," he replied. "And my choice is that I want *you* to pick. I can't decide. It's too huge! I'll pick the wrong thing. I'll pick something stupid like a pentagram because I think it looks cool, but I'm not even Wiccan. And then for the rest of my life I'll have to explain to every Wiccan I meet that I'm not *actually* a Wiccan and I can't come to their meeting and—what—don't you *dare* fucking laugh at me, Bear," he growled, crossing his arms tight over his chest.

The alpha's lips were curling up in a smirk. He quickly schooled his emotions. "Well...if you don't know what you want, then why are we doing this?" He was trying to be all calm and reasonable and it was setting Silas's teeth on edge. "We don't have to do this—"

"I *want* to do this," Silas snapped, his voice rising. "I want a tattoo!"

"Why?" the alpha growled, matching his tone. "Silas, tell me *why* you want a tattoo so badly that you don't even care what it is—"

"Because!" He was shouting now.

"Because *why*—"

"Because it's *my* fucking skin!" He bolted out of the chair, hobbling on his good foot. He hated this alpha for pushing him. Hated him for prying, for cracking him open. "Because this is *my* skin, and I want to know there is a mark *I* put on it. It's my choice, Bear, and this is what I want. Now, pick up that fucking gun and stab me in the hand with it!" He was panting, his whole body wracked with the movement.

Bear was sitting cross-armed in his chair, his expression veiled. Silas didn't miss the way his eyes dropped to his neck. All he wore was a t-shirt so his scars were on full display. He didn't back down, squaring his shoulders. He waited for the alpha to decide his fate.

After an excruciatingly long moment, Bear gestured at the chair. "Sit down."

With a sigh of relief, Silas sat.

"Left hand or right?" the alpha muttered, eyes on his work.

Silas held them both up. "Left," he decided, sticking it out.

Bear ripped open an alcohol wipe and cleaned the top of Silas hand, wiping over the knuckles of each finger. "You want one tattoo on one finger, or something across the fingers?" he murmured, still rubbing the wipe over his last knuckle.

"Umm...maybe across the knuckles? Do you have any ideas?"

Bear just hummed low in his throat and picked up a pen. "I'm gonna free hand it first and show it to you. If you like it, we'll do it. If you don't, we'll wipe it off and try something else."

Silas nodded, focusing all his attention on the fact that the alpha was holding his hand. Bear inched forward, bending his head over Silas's hand. Silas took in the sweep of his hair behind his ear as it tucked into that messy bun. A few tendrils framed his face. One brushed against Silas's arm in a featherlight touch as Bear shifted.

"What was your first tattoo?" he murmured, soothed by the feel of the pen tickling his knuckles.

Without looking up, Bear tilted his forearm, flashing the side of his wrist where the name 'Georgia' was scrawled in a feminine script.

Silas knew what it was, but he still asked. "Is that your mom's name?"

"Yeah," Bear replied. "I got it the night she died."

"How did she die?"

"Cancer."

He didn't push any harder. They sat in silence as Bear finished whatever he was sketching on Silas's pinkie knuckle. In moments, he was sitting back and capping the pen.

"Well?" he muttered, catching Silas's gaze.

Heart in his throat, Silas glanced down at his left hand. Bear had sketched a letter in purple ink on the top knuckle of each of his fingers in a bold, block script. Together the letters spelled out FREE.

"If you don't like it we can—"

He stretched his hand out towards the alpha, willing him to take it. "Do it," he whispered. "This is what I want."

"Right...set your hand down on the tray," Bear directed. "Tell me if you want me to stop, or if you need a break. We're not gonna use any numbing cream because it can affect the work."

Silas nodded, laying his hand flat.

Bear fished in his pocket for his phone, turning on some rock music at a soft volume, just enough to break the tension of their shared silence. Then he snapped on a pair of blue surgical gloves. He picked up the tattoo gun in his right hand and gave it a flick. Buzzing filled the air, echoing over the slowly pulsing rock music.

Clearing his throat, Bear picked up Silas's hand and held his gaze, those hazel eyes boring into him. "Speak now..."

Silas exhaled and nodded again. "Do it."

Ducking his head, Bear hovered the gun over Silas's hand. Silas fought the urge to close his eyes. He wanted to watch the moment the needle connected with his skin. He gasped, holding impossibly still, as the first prick of the tattoo gun zapped the top of his finger.

44

Silas

Bear was tattooing him. His alpha was marking him, and now Silas would carry these marks forever. He had to fight the urge to whimper. He'd always thought tattoos were sexy, but who knew that *getting* a tattoo could be such a turn-on? He had to look away. He needed a distraction.

"So...do all your tattoos have deep meaning?" he asked, trying to keep his hungry eyes off the alpha.

Bear snorted, not looking up. "Nope. Most of these are proof I had two hundred dollars to burn and nothing better to do," he replied. "A few were planned out, like the lion," he added, gesturing with a side nod to the large, expertly shaded lion head on his upper bicep. Half of it was concealed under the sleeve of his t-shirt.

"Can I?" Silas murmured. Bear nodded and Silas reached out with his right hand, tugging Bear's sleeve up enough to expose the whole of the lion's face. "The detail is amazing."

"I definitely can't do that level of work," Bear replied. "You'll need an actual tattoo artist for a piece like that."

"What about the sexy lady?" Silas had noticed her before, trailing down the inside of his forearm. It was done in a pin-up style—a curvy woman pressing her breasts together, flashing a wide smile.

Bear groaned. "I got that one on a drunken dare while I was in the military. Apparently we flipped for it. Heads was this, tails was a mermaid. My buddy got the mermaid but his artist was shit, so instead she looks like a scaly sharkmaid."

Silas grinned, imagining Bear waking up with a wicked hangover to find a naked woman tattooed on his arm. "Why go with the full sleeves?"

Bear shrugged, wiping at Silas's finger with a cloth to remove the excess ink. "The first one was for my mom. The day she died I was feeling all kinds of things I didn't wanna feel. The tattoo let me feel just one thing: Pain. All the rest faded away, and I could just be in pain for the hour it took my friend Nate to bury her name under my skin."

While Bear talked, he kept moving the tattoo gun. The sharp prickling sensation set Silas's teeth on edge, but he didn't move or complain. He wanted this ink in his skin. He wanted Bear to be the one to put it there.

"My dads hated my first couple tattoos, so then it was about rebellion," Bear went on. "As shit went to hell after mom's death—dad drinking, dad dying, pack breaking apart —I used it to escape. I guess it became like my own brand of therapy. Feel too much? Get in the chair. Not feeling anything? Get in the chair. Therapy probably would have been cheaper," he mused with a dry laugh.

They fell into silence as Silas watched Bear work, letting himself get lost to the pain. When Bear started on the third knuckle, Silas couldn't take the silence anymore. "Is this just biology?"

Bear's shoulders stilled, the tattoo gun hovering over Silas's ring finger. "What?"

Silas swallowed, his chest rising and falling as he held his left hand still. "Between us...it's just biology, right?"

Slowly, Bear looked up, those hazel eyes piercing through him. "Is this just biology for you? Does your interest in me begin and end with my designation?"

"No," Silas said quickly. "Of course not—but...I don't know—*fuck*," he groaned, sensing immediately that wasn't what the alpha wanted to hear. "You have no idea what it's been like to live for seven years as a corpse. I could barely scent an alpha before. Betas were nothing to me. I've been so numb."

He closed his eyes, taking a few deep breaths. "And now I'm feeling again, and it's like I have no memory from before to guide me, no way to know what this is or what I feel. And I'm freaking out, because I feel so much. *You* make me feel so much. I feel like I'm drowning in you. It doesn't feel real. It *can't* be real...can it?"

The alpha lowered his gaze, moving the tattoo gun over Silas's knuckle. "Why do you think it can't be real?"

Silas hissed, shutting his eyes again as he held still. This finger hurt worse than the first two. He had the feeling his pinkie would hurt worst of all. He grit his teeth as he growled out, "Stop answering all my questions with a question and *talk* to me. Tell me what you're thinking, Bear. *Please*."

"I'm thinking that I can't be your firefighter," the alpha murmured.

Silas blinked, staring down at the top of the alpha's head. "What the hell does that mean?"

"You know, your firefighter," he repeated. "Your life was a burning building, and I pulled you out—"

"Don't put that on me," Silas growled, his hand tensing. "I didn't ask for anything. I told you to keep driving—"

"I know," Bear replied. "You made your choices, and I made mine. I don't regret it, Silas. I helped you of my own free will, and now you're feeling things for me. Only you can't tell me if what you feel is more than biology. I'm the first alpha you ever scented that hasn't hurt you, so of course you think you feel something. Chances are it's nothing more than your omega senses coming back to life, right?"

Silas felt punched in the gut. He had to fight the urge to pull his hand away. "Got it...yeah. Chances are it's nothing. We're nothing." He felt dead inside. Empty. Hollowed out.

"That's not what I'm saying."

"You *just* said this isn't real. That it's probably just our biology—"

"No, you *asked* me if it was just our biology, as if you don't know. You're still so turned around, you don't know which end is up, and you don't trust yourself *or* your omega senses *or* me. I can only control what I feel, but what I feel doesn't matter because you don't know how *you* feel."

Silas sucked in a sharp breath, his eyes locked on the alpha. Bear was staring back at him, hope and confusion and hesitation dancing in his eyes. "Oh, Bear," he whispered, very aware of the way the alpha was still holding his hand. "You want it to be real...don't you?"

The alpha swallowed, the motion moving the pulse point in his tatted throat. He didn't speak, he just held Silas's gaze.

"What you feel for me is real," Silas went on, putting the pieces of Bear's argument together. "You don't doubt yourself, but you doubt me...don't you? I'm the mess. I'm the broken omega who can't let you in. Can't let myself in." He groaned, his emotions spinning like a top inside his chest.

"Bear, *help* me. Tell me what you feel. If I'm feeling any of what you're feeling then we'll know, right?"

Bear took a deep breath, his dark lashes fluttering closed. "It's your scent," he began. "I won't deny it drew me in. But it's so much more. Your taste. Your...everything." He raised his gaze, drinking Silas in. "You're so goddamn beautiful," he murmured. "So graceful—"

"Graceful?" Silas snorted, eyes going wide at the heated look Bear gave him.

"You *are*," the alpha pressed. "You don't see yourself the way I do. You don't give yourself an inch of space for love and acceptance. You're so handsome, it sets my heart racing. You enter a room, and it's like I've been hooked up to a pair of damn jumper cables. And you're graceful—the way your hands move, the way your expressions change. You're like... water," he said on a breath. "Smooth and deep, rapid and churning. Powerful. And you have no fucking idea, which makes me want you even more. I'm crawling out of my skin over here. Do you know how hard it is not to touch you? Hell, looking would be enough, but even that sets you on edge and I'm dyin'—"

"I'm on edge because I *feel* it," Silas countered, leaning forward in his chair. His heart was racing so fast. "Down to my bones, I ache with it, Bear. I can't breathe with your eyes on me...but I can't breathe when you look away either. And it's not fading, it's getting stronger. And I'm scared. You make me want things I've been afraid to want all my life. You make me think I could have things...that I *deserve* to have them—"

"And you think this is somehow easy for me?" the alpha growled. "Two weeks ago, I stood in that road, rain pounding down, and *everything* that was my life was unraveled and remade. The tapestry I'd woven over years of hard work and sacrifice became a rope and it ties me to *you*. I thought you were a beta, and I was ready to burn the world for you. Nothing has ever felt more real in my life. *Nothing.* Not my work, not my pack or my family, my life in the military. God, *I* don't even feel real anymore, Silas. You are my real."

Silas was flying and falling all at once. He was tumbling through the air, a skydiver without a parachute. He reached for the alpha with his free hand. "Bear—"

"*Don't*," the alpha growled, his body coiled tight. "Don't speak. Don't move." He was pleading. "I don't want to hear you speak. You need time. Don't say something now that you'll later regret. Don't make promises you can't keep. So, just don't speak."

Tears in his eyes, Silas kept his mouth shut. Bear didn't trust him not to break his heart. The alpha's heart was his to take, but he had to earn it first. Slowly, he nodded.

"I'm gonna finish this tattoo, and then you're gonna go upstairs and get some fresh air away from me where you can think, alright? I'm not mad at you," he added quickly. "I just...need you to take some time."

Silas nodded again and the alpha turned his attention back to the unfinished tattoo. The tension mounted between them as neither spoke.

Everything Bear said was true...painful, but true. Silas was a mess. He didn't trust himself. How could he trust others if he didn't trust his own instincts? He was terrified of being an omega. Terrified to want and be wanted. From the moment he started feeling again, he'd been doing everything in his power to revert to being numb. He was secretly taking blockers and hiding it from Bear. Blockers that were making him sick. Blockers that weren't even working. And the only reason he was taking them was so that, when he inevitably lost his place here, he wouldn't be as much of a moving target on his own. Because he didn't trust Bear to want him. He didn't trust the alpha to want him to stay.

This had all been too easy. Bear was the first alpha he met outside the life and he was supposed to gleefully become his bonded mate? Silas frowned, once again watching the top of the alpha's head. But scent-bonding was a real thing. Silas remembered that from his textbooks. Scent-bonding was as close to soulmates as alphas and omegas could get. It was a biology thing, nature pairing people by matching their pheromones. But it was also about personality matching. It was the rare unicorn in A/O bonds. Is that what this was? This undeniable urge to be near Bear, to drown in him?

Claire had been here, and he hadn't felt a thing except anxiety. Yumi and Ray, Jared—all betas with perfectly tolerable scent signatures. He felt nothing for them. Meanwhile, Bear only had to inhale and it's like Silas was fighting the urge to climb over the furniture and claim his every exhale for his own.

This was different. *Bear* was different. Silas wanted to be different too.

"I'm done," the alpha muttered, turning the gun off and giving Silas's fingers another wipe with the cloth. "We'll check it in a couple days and fill in where needed."

Silas glanced down to inspect the tattoo. The tops of his knuckles looked raised and irritated. The four newly inked letters were black and shiny. FREE.

Stripping off his blue gloves, Bear tossed them on the tray and took Silas's hand again, inspecting the work one last time. With his head leaned over, elbow on his knee, it almost looked like Bear was bowing over his hand.

Silas had a sudden urge to be bold...to be *free*. He lifted his hand while Bear held it, bringing it closer to the alpha's lips. Bear leaned back slightly, not intuiting Silas's want. Silas lifted the hand again, bringing it to the alpha's lips.

Bear went still. His only movement was his exhale onto Silas's skin. He flashed his eyes up. Holding Bear's gaze, Silas closed the space between them, pressing the back of his hand against the alpha's lips again.

Ever so slowly, Bear moved his lips, turning the awkward gesture into a kiss. Silas sucked in a needy breath, watching the alpha kiss his hand. One peck, and Bear was daring to lift his head away. Silas gave chase, bringing his hand back to Bear's soft lips.

The alpha groaned, taking Silas's newly tatted hand in both of his own. He kissed the top of his hand again, breathing out against his skin. Then he traced soft kisses over the tops of the new tattoos. Each kiss was featherlight, not giving Silas nearly the attention he craved. He wanted this alpha. Bear deserved to know how badly Silas wanted him.

"More," Silas whispered as Bear kissed his smallest knuckle.

With another groan, Bear was gripping his hand tighter, dragging his tongue over the top of the fresh tattoos. It stung, even as it sent an aching jolt of need straight to Silas's cock. He moaned as it hardened, pressing against his leg.

"Does it hurt?" the alpha murmured, his voice impossibly gentle.

"Yes," Silas said on a breath, that one word covering all manner of pains. It hurt to breathe in this alpha's presence. It hurt to stay away from him. His fingers hurt from the fresh tattoos. His cock hurt, alone and untouched. Aching. Needing.

The alpha kept caressing his hand with tongue and lips, flipping it to kiss his palm.

"More," Silas begged, leaning forward in his chair.

Bear lifted his gaze to him while turning his hand back over. With his eyes on Silas, Bear opened his lips and sank them around his finger, caressing it with his tongue as he pulled it fully inside the warm heat of his mouth, right to the edge of the new tattoo. Bear dragged his teeth lightly over Silas's skin as he sucked.

"Oh, fuck," Silas gasped, the tip of his hard shaft weeping with need.

Bear sucked on the length of Silas's finger, tracing his tongue over the sensitive pad as he let it pop out of his mouth. Then he took two at once, his saliva coating Silas's fingers, caressing them with that clever tongue.

Silas wanted to die. It wasn't enough. Not nearly enough. He tasted his own pheromones in the air, a needy omega desperate to be fucked. The words had him stilling as nerves took over. Is that what he wanted? Could he let this alpha fuck him?

No—too much. He wasn't ready. And Bear didn't trust him. But he needed something more. Anything. "Please," he whispered. "Bear, please—"

"What?" the alpha replied, returning to placing open mouthed kisses along his knuckles.

"I need—"

Bear lifted his gaze, his parted lips brushing over Silas's knuckles. "What? Tell me what you need."

"I need more," he admitted, dropping his right hand to cup his aching cock. Even just that bit of added pressure had him squirming on the metal folding chair.

The alpha growled, the sound shuddering through every atom in Silas's body. In moments, Bear was sliding off his chair to his knees, rattling the TV tray out of the way. He still held tight to Silas's hand, bringing it back to his lips. He murmured against Silas's skin, "Tell me what to do. Tell me what not to do—*fuck*—I'll do anything."

Silas knew what he wanted. He had to trust this alpha. Bear would let him have this. Silas licked his lips, heart pounding. "I...don't move," he whispered, taking his left hand out of the alpha's grip and dropping it to the top of his sweats. He slipped it under the elastic band, palming his hard shaft. "Oh—*god*—" He wrapped the fingers slicked with Bear's saliva around himself and stroked once.

Bear's eyes heated. The pools of amber green were swallowed by black as he leaned forward.

"I said don't move." Silas used his right hand to free his cock from the confines of his sweatpants.

The alpha's gaze flicked down, desperate for a glimpse of Silas touching himself.

"Don't look down," Silas panted, giving his shaft two sharp pumps. "Alpha, look at me."

Bear's eyes flashed to his face, a growl low in his throat. "Silas..."

"Look only at me." Silas already felt himself on the edge of release. "Don't touch. Don't move. Just let me—*ah*—" He squeezed himself tighter, twisting his fist a bit at the tip. He was leaking like a fountain, his cum slicking his hand.

Bear breathed heavily, his eyes locked on Silas as he drank in his every look and sound.

Silas squirmed in the chair widening the spread of his legs as he felt that tension build, a low burning in his gut. "I wanna come," he whimpered. "Alpha—I need—"

His words died as he buckled forward, his right hand clutching to the alpha's shoulder as he stroked himself with his newly tattooed left hand. The pain in his fingers mixed with the pleasure of chasing his orgasm.

"Do it," the alpha growled. "Look at me and fuck yourself. I want to watch you come."

Silas cried out. Lost to the euphoria of release, he watched as his hot cum spurted from his tip, hitting Bear's chest. His release soaked into the alpha's shirt as he pumped himself, moaning on the chair. More and more of his cum leaked from his tip until he was shaking.

"Oh *god*—I can't stop coming. Bear—"

"Don't stop," the alpha ordered. "Fuck that hand 'til you finish. Give me everything."

"*Ahh*—" Silas pumped his shaft a few more times until every ounce of his omega seed was spent. Bear's shirt was soaked with a giant wet spot right over his sternum. If Silas wasn't reeling in a state of bliss, he might feel embarrassed, but the pleased look on his alpha's face removed all doubt. Bear was happy. A rumble in his chest built, cascading out in a slow rhythm. He was purring for his omega.

Silas let his still-hard cock go, his hand slicked with his release. That's when he noticed the purring had stopped and Bear was looking at him, a pained expression on his face. His post-orgasm haze cleared a bit. "Bear?"

"Silas, please," the alpha groaned, shutting his eyes tight.

Silas noted how carefully Bear was trying not to move. He glanced down lower and saw the massive bulge in the front of Bear's jeans. The alpha was pleased to watch Silas come, but he needed release too. Silas slipped off his chair, dropping to his knees. "Are you aching, alpha?"

Bear shut his eyes again. "Please...don't tease me."

Silas leaned a little closer. "Are you desperate for my touch?"

Bear's eyes snapped open. "I said *don't*."

"It's not teasing if I mean to follow through," he replied, his voice coaxing. "Take your cock out for me, and I'll wrap my cum-soaked fingers around it. I'll fuck you with my hand until you blow on my chest."

"Fuckin' hell," Bear growled, his alpha scent spiking sharper.

In this moment, Silas felt all-powerful. He stripped out of his t-shirt, leaving him bare-chested on his knees before the alpha wearing his cum. "Take out your cock, Bear. Don't make me wait."

With a low groan, Bear dropped both hands to the front of his jeans. Silas kept his eyes locked on the alpha as Bear worked open his belt and unzipped his jeans. Then he reached inside his briefs with his tatted hand and dragged out his cock.

Silas glanced down. Sweet mercy, the alpha was big. Silas wanted to taste, to devour. He'd felt that cock pressed against his ass before, but that was always between layers of clothing. Now he was seeing it all on its own and his inner omega wanted to burst with happiness.

He reached out with his slick-covered hand, wrapping his fingers around Bear's shaft. At that first touch, a shudder wracked the alpha. "Eyes on me," Silas murmured. "Look only at me. Know who's making you come."

"Silas—"

"No speaking." He stroked the alpha tightly in his fist. The slide of his hand was so slick and smooth. "I don't want to hear you speak," he added, echoing the alpha's words back at him. "Spill your seed on this skin that aches only for you. Cover me in your scent. Claim me so no one doubts who calls you 'alpha'—"

"Silas, please—"

"Speak again and I'll stop," Silas crowed, slowing his hand to stillness as he smiled. Now it was the alpha whining, his cock pulsing in Silas's hand. Silas felt like a king, a conqueror. Bear was *his*. This alpha belonged to *him*.

Bear begged with his eyes, his teeth biting his lower lip to keep from asking for what he wanted. Silas rewarded the alpha for his silence, inching closer until they were all but brushing chests. He fisted the alpha's cock tighter, working him with both hands, stroking and twisting as they panted together. The alpha's thick knot grew, and Silas knew he was ready to release.

With a surge of adrenaline, he leaned forward and licked Bear's scent gland. At the same time, he squeezed the alpha's knot and rasped in his ear, "Come for me. *Now*."

With a guttural groan, Bear released, splattering his hot cum all over Silas's bare chest. Silas gasped with pleasure, pumping the alpha again and again, until the cum was dripping down his stomach. Silas sighed, his senses utterly filled with Bear's intoxicating scent.

At last, he dropped his hands away from the alpha. They sat there on their knees, staring into each other's eyes, wearing the other's release. Silas felt warm all over, like he'd been plunged in a hot bath. Bear looked dazed, his lips slightly parted, his gaze unfocused.

Slowly, Silas raised the hand slicked with both their releases. Eyes on the alpha, he sucked the tip of his wet finger into his mouth. The taste of them together was an explosion of riotous flavor on his tongue—sweet and salted, warm, and so goddamn smooth. He whimpered, closing his eyes as the taste wrapped itself around his soul, burying itself marrow-deep.

He opened his eyes to see the heat burning in Bear's gaze. The alpha was molten, and his cock was already hardening again. It was clearly all he could do to hold still.

Dropping his hand to his side, Silas let out a shaky

breath. "Thanks," he murmured. "For my tattoo...and the orgasm."

"Any time," the alpha replied, voice tight.

Anxiety was starting to creep in. Silas needed to take the alpha's advice and separate. He needed to breathe. Scrambling back up onto his chair, he snatched for the crutches leaning against the utility cabinet. Then he got to his feet, and headed for the door, leaving the alpha on his knees.

45

Bear

"So...what's this I hear about you harboring a fugitive?" Jared's voice crackled through the phone as Bear took a turn in the dipping valley between Spring Hill and the cabin.

He tensed, fisting the wheel tighter. "What?"

"Oh, you know, the *fugitive* you're hiding in your cabin?" Jared repeated. "Boyd told me all about it at the baseball game last night—and thanks for skipping out on us by the way. We had to put Jerry on short stop and he fuckin' sucks. What the hell, Bear?"

Goddamn it. Bear knew he shouldn't have picked up Jared's call. He was distracted when it rang and felt compelled to answer in case it was Silas. But the omega never called. Probably giving Bear the damn space he asked for. Huge fuckin' mistake.

It had been three days since their moment in the garage. Three days since his life flipped itself inside out for the second time in as many weeks. Three days since he had the best damn orgasm of his life. He watched the omega taste their joint release, and a feral need to claim had flooded him. He wanted Silas more than coffee, more than a lakeshore run on a crisp fall morning, more than fucking air.

But since then it had been radio silence. Silas was hiding out. He was like a ghost in the damn house, his omega scent haunting every room. Bear was at his wits-fucking-end.

He pressed the accelerator to climb the last hill before home. "What the hell are you talking about, J?"

"I'm talking about *you*, Bear! Did you or did you not buy that beta a bus ticket? Because I swear to fuck, I dropped him at the depot. Did your crazy ass go and pick him back up?"

Bear growled. "It's complicated."

Deafening silence greeted that admission.

Finally, Jared spoke again. "Bear, what the hell is happening? Why did you go get him? I thought he had a whole damn criminal alpha pack chasing his tail. He was supposed to be on a bus to Redrock—"

"Yeah, *you* know that, I know that, and the alpha hunting him knows that too," Bear barked into the phone. "We laid a trail with proof of a ticket and proof of life. Silas got on that bus. The cameras saw it. He got off the bus where the cameras weren't watching. So for all the alpha pack knows, he's somewhere between here and Redrock. He's laying low, J. The heat is dying down, and then he'll be free."

"Free to do what?"

Bear's breath caught in his throat. He knew what he wanted, but it wasn't up to him. He'd never felt so paralyzed by fear. "Whatever he wants."

"I just don't get it, man," Jared replied. Bear could almost see him shaking his head. "This isn't like you. What is it about this beta that has you so twisted up?"

Bear's eyes traced the serpentine of the double yellow

line down the middle of the road as he drove. All around, the beauty of the fall leaves created a canopy of red and orange. Shafts of bright sunlight filtered through the trees, shining down on the road in patches of glittering gold. There was a stillness. A quiet peace.

Bear held tighter to the phone. "Jared...Silas is an omega."

Silence.

"What the hell are you talking about?"

"It's a long story, but he's not a beta. He's an unbonded omega."

"You're crazy," Jared scoffed. "You need to get your senses checked—"

"He told me what happened, and I believe him. I did some digging. You ever heard of SunaCorps?"

"Yeah, they're a big pharmaceutical company."

Bear flicked his blinker on as he made the turn down his gravel drive. "Yeah, well a while back they had this drug they rushed to trials. It was supposed to be the best omega blocker on the market. It would let omegas practically mainstream, even unbonded omegas. They got funding because they were sellin' the idea that the government would save so much money when they closed all the Centers. Omegas wouldn't need Centers if they could safely mainstream, right?"

"Yeah...but those drugs always come and go. They're never as effective as they say," Jared replied.

"Well, this was a shot," Bear went on. "Sunapraxin or some shit like that. A bunch of omegas were put in the trials. But it didn't block their hormones, J. It turned them the fuck off. Numbed them completely. Silas said he wasn't even told what the shot was for when they gave it to him."

"Oh...shit. That's awful. Well, what happened?"

It was hard to keep his emotion from his voice as he said the words aloud. To know what this omega had suffered was a near-constant pain tearing at Bear's soul. "His Center fuckin' sold him, J. Dumped him like trash."

"Damn...did that happen to all the omegas in the trial, or was he like a freaky accident?"

Bear parked the truck in front of the garage, keeping it running as he stared down at the steering wheel. "I've been doing some research this week," he admitted. He hadn't even told Silas yet. He didn't want to get his hopes up for nothing. "It looks like there was a medical malpractice case filed about four years ago and they won. Some of the omegas in the trial that had the same thing happen sued. It was millions in settlement."

"Holy shit. Well...that's something, I guess. Silas should look into it. Hell, for his pain and suffering he deserves to get paid."

"I agree," Bear muttered darkly. "But it would mean coming forward, giving his name to lawyers and courts and shit. He doesn't need that heat right now. And I can't keep him safe with that kind of spotlight on him," he admitted.

"Yeah...I get it." Jared was quiet for a minute. "Bear... what are you doing? What's the endgame here? Are you falling for this omega? You thinking you want him to stay?"

Bear swallowed, raising his eyes to glance out the window at the serene vista of the lake. "I think we're scent-bonded."

"Oh...shit," Jared rasped. "Wait—well, does Silas agree? Does he know, or is he still numb?"

"I think he knows. But I think he's fighting it. He's fighting being an omega at all. He's scared, J. Seven years is a long time to live as less than a beta. And now all his omega senses are flooding in at once. And he was at the Center for less than a year before he was sold out," he added. "He might not really know what scent-bonding means...but I can't walk away. I can't—*fuck*—I feel crazy even saying it out loud but...I don't think I can live without him. I'm moored to him now. Whatever happens..."

"I get it," Jared said again. "Scent-bonding is super rare, but if any alpha would know when a scent is meant for him, it would be you, Bear. I believe you."

Bear let out a shaky breath. He needed someone to know, needed someone to understand. He'd been carrying the weight of this alone for over two weeks, afraid to talk about it to the one person he wanted to speak to the most. But Silas wasn't ready to admit to a scent bond. He wasn't even ready to admit to being an omega.

"I gotta go, J," he said, turning the truck off.

"Yeah...yeah, you go and...shit, I think you need to talk to Boyd though," he said on a sigh. "Cause he's still running his mouth, and the last thing you want is him getting Silas in trouble."

Bear's alpha urges flared, anger like white-hot fire blazing in his chest. "Don't worry about it," he growled into the phone. "I'll handle Boyd."

Phone call ended, Bear got out of the truck and went into the cabin, mind still reeling as he considered what to do about Boyd. His cousin had always suffered from big-mouth syndrome. He loved to talk. More accurately, he loved to brag. Boyd Beresford was the kind of guy that always caught the biggest fish, slept with the hottest betas, and knew all the best dirt on everyone.

That alpha needed a damn muzzle. Bear just had to decide how best to accomplish it. A permanent ball gag might work...but then punching his fucking face until his jaw shattered might make Bear feel better. You can't gossip or brag with your jaw wired shut.

He was pulled from his dark thoughts by an ominous feeling.

Where was the dog? That floppy-eared idiot always met him at the door.

"Zeus!" he barked.

The dog came trotting around the corner from Silas's side of the hallway, tongue lolling out of his mouth. That feeling of anxiety spread.

Something's wrong.

Before he could take a step, he heard it—a heaving, retching sound. He rushed across the living room and down the short hall. The smell of sick smacked him in the face as he turned the corner into the open hall bath. Silas was on his knees, head buried in the toilet, puking his guts out. Fear and panic blasted through Bear as he dropped to his knees beside him. "What's wrong?"

The omega jumped in fright and then groaned, turning his face on the toilet seat to glance over at him. His eyes were red and watery. "Just sick," he muttered.

Bear was already reaching for him, feeling for fevers. No heat, which was a relief, but Silas's skin was slicked with sweat and clammy. His color was off. "Is it something you ate?" Bear pressed. They had the same thing for breakfast hours ago—two eggs over medium and avocado toast. Bear felt fine all day. "What did you have for lunch?"

"Nothing," Silas groaned. "Couldn't eat—"

Bear leaned back as Silas dry heaved again. Nothing came out. Silas laid his head back on his arm on the toilet seat. "How long have you been like this?"

"Hour maybe."

Annoyance churned in Bear's gut. His omega had been sick like this for an hour and hadn't bothered to call or text? Bear would have come straight home. He would have helped. Why wouldn't this stubborn damn omega let him in? Taking a deep breath, he pushed down his own frustrations. Silas needed him. "Where does it hurt? When did it start?"

"Stomach," Silas panted. "Cramping—burns—" He heaved again. This time some mucus came up.

Bear leaned over and flushed the toilet, even with Silas's face perched over the bowl. The worst smell of the sick washed away, and he saw Silas take a little relieved breath. "Baby, talk to me," he pleaded. "I can't help you if I don't know what's going on. Do you need to go to the—"

"No hospital," Silas whined, pushing himself off the toilet with shaky arms. "Just wanna sleep. I'll be fine."

Something was wrong, Bear could feel it. Aside from the obvious illness, there was something else wrong with the omega. Silas was hiding something. It was all Bear could do to keep himself from barking at the omega, pulling forth his truths like a human lie detector. It might help him get to Silas's truth, but it would break his trust. Which mattered more?

Silas flopped over, waving his hand blindly for his crutches, as if he meant to try to get to his feet. Bear took charge, wrapping his arms around the shaky omega. "Arms around my neck," he murmured.

Silas flopped his weak arms around Bear's neck and Bear awkwardly shifted up on one knee, rising to his feet in the narrow space. He bridal-carried Silas down the hall to his room, laying him on the bed.

Silas rolled on his side, curling up in a ball. He pushed against his stomach with both hands, as if pressure was somehow easing his pain.

Bear felt totally helpless. "Silas, please. You're not telling me something. If you don't tell me, I'll have to take you to the hospital."

"I said no hospitals!"

"You're giving me no choice!"

"It's *my* choice," Silas whined. "You told me—you promised! Everything would be my choice—"

"Well, right now it looks like you're choosing to kill yourself, and I'm not okay with that!" Saying the words made a light click on in Bear's mind and he was suddenly sinking onto the edge of the bed, turning Silas at the shoulder. "Silas, look at me."

The omega groaned, eyes shut tight.

"Baby, look at me. Did you take something?"

Silas blinked his eyes open. He had to work on his poker face because Bear saw the truth shining there. Terror sank into the pit of his stomach.

"Oh...shit." He grabbed the omega by the shoulders, shaking him gently to keep him awake. "Silas, what did you take? Sleeping pills? Pain relievers?"

"No," Silas groaned, trying to turn away from him.

"Silas, for fuck's sake—"

A loud ding echoed on the bedside table and Bear glanced over to see Silas's phone screen light up. Silas could hate him for this invasion of privacy later. He snatched up the phone and read the new text message.

Ollie: Sorry, man. That sucks. I told you to stop taking them. You officially have me worried.

Dread filled Bear as he flicked his thumb against the screen, letting the flood of texts between Silas and this other omega fill in all the gaps of missing information.

Ollie: New pills working any better?

Silas: No. Still feel like *shit emoji*

He flicked higher up.

Ollie: New pills show delivered. These are 200mg. Take two in am. Lmk if they work better.

Was this omega a pharmacist? A drug dealer? Apparently Bear had another name to add to his ass-kicking list under Boyd.

Ollie: I just don't get why you wanna go back on blockers. Aren't you done with all that shit? I would be.

Silas: We've been over this, Ol. I've got three weeks before I'm out. I can't just wander the streets like this, asshole. You want me starting riots?

Bear's heart stopped. Silas was taking omega blockers again. Apparently, they were counterfeit, or whatever this other omega could scrounge together for him. Fuck, it all made so much sense, even just to explain the last three days —his weird moods, the stomach complaints, his obsession with checking the mail. The sneaky omega was getting drugs delivered to the house. Shit drugs that were making him sick.

Bear glanced down at the phone again.

Ollie: I keep saying it, man. I think you're allergic. I can't say for sure b/c I. AM. NOT. A. DOCTOR.

Silas: Yeah, but you're bonded to one. Ask Heath about Omestra

Ollie: No

Silas: I haven't tried that one yet

Ollie: *middle finger emoji*

Bear set the phone aside. He'd seen enough. He glanced down at the omega curled up on the bed. Silas was a runner. That's all he knew how to do. He'd spent the last seven years trapped—trapped in his own body, trapped by alpha packs. In a shining moment of strength and purpose, he'd escaped one trap. He was physically free.

But he was still running. This broken omega was terrified to feel, terrified to be himself, terrified to dare and step into the power of being an omega. Silas deserved to live free. If he wanted to live as an unbonded omega for the rest of his life, Bear would make it happen. He'd never question, never push. But Silas had to *live* first.

46

Silas

S ilas woke with a groan. His head was spinning. He sucked on his tongue, trying to moisten it. Rolling over, he opened his eyes. He was lying shirtless in Bear's dark bedroom. The smell of the alpha surrounded him, calming him. But the last thing he remembered was being on the floor of the bathroom, hugging the toilet.

Oh shit.

Did he black out? Did Bear find him passed out in his own vomit? Is that where his shirt went? Shame flooded him as he sat up, rubbing at his face with his tattooed hand. Outside, the sun had all but set on the far side of the lake, the far hills outlined in dusky pinks and purples.

He sucked on his tongue again, noticing the minty fresh taste in his mouth. So he'd at least managed to brush his teeth between vomiting and passing out. And he was clean, his skin not sticky with sweat. What the hell happened last night—

He gasped. Bear was sitting in the chair in the corner of the room by the window. The alpha sat still as a statue, his eyes on Silas. His mood was impossible to read—angry, sad, scared, frustrated. What happened? Was he really mad at Silas for getting sick? Silas couldn't help it...sort of.

"What happened?" he muttered.

A muscle twitched in the alpha's jaw. "You tell me."

Silas swallowed down the nerves fluttering in his chest. Why did he feel like he was entering a bull-fighting ring? "I was sick," he said with a shrug. "It happens sometimes."

Bear's scowl deepened. "Yeah...when you overdose on counterfeit scent blockers, shredding the lining of your stomach. That's when you get *sick*...right?"

Shit. Shit. Shit.

"Bear, I—"

"Is this all of them?" The alpha lifted a plastic bag off his lap full of various prescription bottles. Over the past few weeks, Silas had tried them all. They all made him sick. Something in his biology was rejecting them.

"Bear..."

The alpha turned one of the bottles through the plastic, reading the label. "Crapweasel, Reginald A." He wasn't smiling and Silas understood why. Nothing about this was funny. "Is that your real name?"

Silas shook his head.

"Then why do you have his prescriptions?" He gave the bag a violent shake, rattling all the bottles.

Silas pursed his lips, daring to be obtuse. "It's a free country—"

"You're poisoning yourself!" the alpha barked. "Fucking hell, Silas! You lived through seven years of this shit, and you wanna keep drowning your system in this toxic trash?"

"I don't know what else to do!"

"Stop taking the blockers would be a start," Bear snapped. "They're making you sick!"

"Some brands are, but I haven't tried them all—" He

quieted at the look of righteous fury on the alpha's face. "Bear, please..."

The alpha got to his feet. "This is finished." He shook the bag again. "I'm flushing 'em right now." He stormed off towards the bathroom.

Panic filled Silas. "No! Bear, don't you dare—" He scrambled off the bed, not caring that he didn't have his crutches. He hobbled on both feet after the alpha. "Bear, no!"

Bear was standing over the toilet, the bag tucked under his arm as he opened the first pill bottle, dumping all the pills into the bowl. He threw the empty bottle to the floor with a clatter.

"Bear, you can't do this! It's my choice—I *need* them!" He snatched at the alpha's arm.

Bear jerked away, popping the lid off the next bottle and making it rain tiny blue pills into the toilet.

"I hate you!" Silas cried.

Bear turned with a growl, dropping the bag to the tile floor as he snatched for Silas, gripping him tight by the jaw as he jerked him forward. "Well, I fucking *love* you, and I'm not gonna watch you hurt yourself out of fear of being who and what you are!"

Silas wrapped both hands around the wrist holding him captive. "Bear—"

"You're an omega, Silas!" Bear barked. "You're *my* omega, and I love you!" He lowered his face inches from Silas's lips. "Whatever else happens, we're starting there. You don't want a bond, fine. I'll never ask. You wanna live here, stay. You wanna move to the moon, I'll start building us a damn rocket. You can go anywhere and do anything, but *first* you have to be an omega. Stop fighting yourself!"

Silas was breathless, staring into the depthless hazel eyes of the angry alpha. "You love me?"

Bear growled again. "Of course, I love you. And it's not just our damn biology. I've been falling more in love with you every day. Silas, you are the strongest man I've ever met. You are a hurricane of passion and hope and strength. I wanna stand at your center and feel your chaos."

The alpha's every word filled Silas with such warmth, such sense of purpose. But the shame lingered. Silas had been such a fool, taking pills that made him sick, all because he was terrified to feel, terrified to live on his own terms. Terrified of the freedom that was now within his reach.

He looked around at the mess on the bathroom floor—pills strewn about, the bag of bottles. Realization sank deep into the pit of his stomach. He was letting his fear win... letting *them* win, the alphas who sought to control him, to scare him and make him smaller. They wanted Silas weak, afraid of his own shadow, dying to chase that numbness.

No more.

He leveled his gaze at the alpha who stood so calmly at the center of his storm. Bear wasn't looking for an exit, and he wasn't trying to control him. He was trying to help. He'd only ever tried to help Silas see what was so plain: Silas *deserved* to live.

"Bear," he said again, his voice softening.

Bear's grip softened too, his thumb brushing along Silas's stubbled jaw. "I was a ghost, Silas. I wandered these hills living half a life, resigned to being alone forever. No pack, no home. I couldn't bear it. Couldn't breathe. Not after mom's death and—" He caught himself on a groan, dragging a hand through his hair.

"I stumbled out of my truck, rain pounding down, and *you* were there," he went on. "You think I saved you, but Silas you saved *me*. I was nothing. I was...*god*, I was so alone," he whispered. "You saved me in that road, Silas. I'm yours. I will do anything, *be* anything—your friend, your lover, whatever you want." He dropped his face forward, resting his forehead against Silas's. "Only don't make me watch you hurt yourself anymore. Silas, please. I wanna be yours. Omega, *please*—"

His alpha was begging him. Silas saved him. Silas could still save him. It was his choice. Power flooded through him, coating his very bones in iron. He was strong. A hurricane, Bear called him. The chaos part was fitting too...but the strength is what Silas harnessed now. He held the alpha's gaze, raising his hands to place them on Bear's shoulders. "Kiss me," he demanded.

The alpha couldn't comply fast enough. Wrapping his free arm around Silas's waist, he pulled him forward and pressed their lips together. In moments they were both drowning in the flood of their shared pheromones as they kissed like two people who would die if they stopped.

Silas gripped tight to Bear's shoulders, pressing his whole body against the strong alpha. Bear dropped his hand from his jaw, wrapping it around his bare shoulders as he pulled him closer. His other hand trailed down Silas's lower back, sliding over his rounded ass until the alpha pressed into him, the hardness in his pants finding Silas's aching cock.

Both men groaned again, their hips moving as they sought desperately for more friction, more pressure, more everything. Silas tugged at the fabric keeping his alpha's skin covered. "Take it off," he ordered. "Off—"

The alpha loosened his hold on him, and he wanted to die, but then Bear was jerking his shirt off one-handed, dropping it to the floor. Silas smoothed his hands all over the firm planes of his alpha's chest and arms, biting his lip to contain his whimper. No person had ever been so beautiful.

Bear swallowed the sound, burying his tongue in Silas's mouth. Silas opened willingly, letting their tongues dance and their lips tease as he wrapped his arms around his alpha, dragging his hands over the taut muscles of his back.

With a possessive growl, Bear slid both his hands over Silas's ass. Gripping him tight by the thighs, he hauled him up against him. The pressure was exquisite as Silas wrapped his legs tightly around the alpha's waist. Bear carried him over to the vanity, setting him on the edge. He stepped between Silas's spread legs, pressing their cocks together.

Silas was flying. Everything was possible in Bear's arms. He felt invincible. His scent pheromones spiraled through the air, meeting Bear's in a symphony of unbridled passion. Their scents wove together like the strands of an unbreakable rope, surrounding them both as they drank of each other.

Bear broke their kiss with a gasping breath, his large hand cupping the back of Silas's neck. Silas stilled as he felt the alpha's thumb brush purposefully over the edges of his raised neck scars. Fear and doubt hammered at the doors of his mind, threatening to ruin this perfect moment.

"Do you trust me?" the alpha murmured.

Did Silas trust Bear?

Yes. Only Bear. Always Bear. My alpha. My mate—

Silas moaned, repeating the first word aloud. "Yes."

Bear dropped his face to the crook of Silas's neck. His nose brushed over Silas's scarred scent gland as he took a deep breath in. Silas moved his hips, pressing his hard cock against the alpha's. He dropped his hands to Bear's waist, sliding them inside the top of his jeans, grazing his fingers over the top of his sculpted ass.

Perfect. My perfect alpha. So beautiful. So strong. So—

"Ahh—" He cried out, his whole body feeling like he'd

just been zapped by an electric fence. Bear ran his tongue over the scars of his neck again and he wanted to burst out of his skin. Nothing had ever felt this good. *Nothing.* No alpha before or after would ever compare to this. There was only Bear and that teasing tongue, healing the most broken parts of him, covering him in his scent and his love.

"Fuck me," he panted, twisting his face until he could scrape his teeth over the alpha's scent gland in return. The movement had Bear bucking against him, cursing under his breath. Silas did it again, adding a flick of his tongue, and Bear all but fell against him, his arms gripping tight to him, desperate for more. "Fuck me, alpha," he said again. "Alpha, please. Take me. Own me. Make me yours."

Bear pulled back, his hands on Silas's shoulders. He looked dazed, his eyes blown black with hunger. His mouth was open, and he was panting. "Wait—*wait*—what is that?" He took a shaky breath, resisting as Silas whined and pulled him closer.

"Bear, *please.* I want you. I'm ready. Make love to me. I want your knot."

"Oh...shit," Bear groaned, still pulling away.

Something was wrong and Silas was suddenly fighting the urge to cry out. Why was his alpha pulling away? Didn't he want him? He did, Silas could taste it, feel it through every bone of his body. "Bear," he begged.

The alpha sucked in a sharp breath, as if keeping himself apart was a physical pain. "Silas," he growled, dragging a tattooed hand over his face. His other was on Silas's shoulder. Slowly, his elbow locked, keeping Silas at arm's length as he looked him in the eye. "Silas...baby, I think you're in heat."

47

Bear

Silas was panting on the edge of the vanity, eyes wide. It was all Bear could do to keep his elbow locked. It put some much-needed space between them. He took gulping breaths of air, trying to clear his swimming senses.

"What?" Silas repeated. "What do you—"

"I mean you've gone into heat."

Bear was sure of it. Never been so sure of anything in his life. In the last five minutes, Silas's scent had changed. Before, it filled his senses as something smooth, spiced, and oh so sweet, like a shot of whiskey and a scoop of vanilla bean ice cream. Now, the scent was heavier, darker. It pulled at Bear's every shred of self-control.

The omega's eyes went wide. In an instant his scent went from spiced and cloying to sharp and desperate. "Oh, shit... no. Bear, I'm scared!"

"It's okay." Bear stepped in, smoothing his hands over Silas's bare shoulders. "We've got time before it really kicks in, okay? Not a lot of time, but enough to get things in order."

The omega's panic was fighting with his desire, which

was still a blazing inferno. Bear was achingly hard, desperate to tend to him, but it had to wait. Their window of consent was closing fast. He'd seen an omega in the peak of heat before and they often didn't remember their own damn names.

He framed Silas's face with both hands, taking control. Silas needed him to be the alpha now. "Silas, look at me."

"I feel like I can't breathe. I'm so hot—"

"I know. You're gonna feel fevered for the first day or so. We'll put you in a cool bath and that will feel good, okay?" Anything to slow the heat down. Bear went to step towards the bathtub, but the omega cried out.

"No!" Silas wrapped his legs around him. "Don't leave me—"

Bear slid his hands from Silas's elbows up his forearms, linking their fingers to loosen the omega's hold on the back of his neck. "Baby, I'm not going anywhere." He brought Silas's hands around to the front, kissing the knuckles. "I'm right here."

"I feel like I'm crawling out of my skin," Silas panted. "Bear, I need you—" He leaned froward, seeking Bear's lips for a kiss.

Bear gave in, letting the omega taste him, even as he kept still. After a few moments, he broke the kiss. "Okay, that's enough—"

"No—"

"We need to *talk* first, Si," Bear pressed. "We weren't ready for this. We need to set your expectations—"

"I expect you to *fuck* me," the omega growled, jerking his left hand loose and cupping Bear's crotch, giving his stiff cock a squeeze.

"Fucking hell," Bear panted, trying and failing to keep his hips from moving against the pressure. Would it be so bad if he just gave in? The omega was clearly asking for it. Begging—

Your omega is vulnerable. Tend to him.

The voice of reason won out, and Bear pulled back. Silas whined, but Bear shut him out. "Okay, here's what we're gonna do. I'll let you come," he soothed, brushing his fingers along Silas's sternum.

Silas shifted forward on the vanity. "Yes—*please,* alpha—"

"Once," Bear growled, a limit for himself as much as for Silas. "That'll take the edge off. Then I'll get you in a cool bath. Hopefully the bath will slow things down, and we can have our conversation...okay?"

Silas ran his hands down Bear's arms. "You are so beautiful," he murmured, his gaze full of longing and adoration.

Bear couldn't help but smile. "Thanks. Now, look at me." He placed a hand under Silas's chin and tipped it up. "*Look at me,*" he said again, his tone laced with a bark.

Silas's eyes shot up, dark and inviting.

"Would you like to come now?"

Silas nodded. "Yes, alpha."

"Do you want to do it yourself...or do you want me to help you?"

"Please, touch me. Bear, I'm aching for you."

"I will. I promise," he soothed. "Do you want me to use my hand or my mouth?"

Silas's eyes went wide as his breathing stopped. His lips quivered as he dared to answer with the truth. "Both."

Bear smiled, stepping closer. *Thank god.* He brushed his fingers over Silas's chest, letting the calloused pads of his fingers graze over his nipples. Silas flinched, biting his lip to keep in his moan. Bear's smile widened. "A few weeks ago, you said if I tried to gag on your cock, you'd stick it in my smoothie blender. Are we over that now?"

Silas turned that heated gaze back on him. He cupped Bear's face and pulled him forward. "You are *mine*."

Groaning with relief, Bear let the omega kiss him again. They swam in each other's fevered touches—tongues dancing, teeth teasing. When Silas dropped his hands to the top of Bear's jeans, Bear pulled away. "Wrap yourself around me," he growled.

"What—why—"

"I'm taking you to the bed."

Silas eagerly wrapped his legs around Bear as he hoisted him up, moving quickly through the bathroom back into the bedroom. He sank to his knees and bent forward, dropping Silas onto the edge of the mattress. Silas caught himself in a half-curl, spreading his wrists out behind him, his hands pressing into the sheets.

He was gorgeous. Bear sat back on his heels for a moment to appreciate him. His skin once again had a healthy bronze glow, his body burning with his heat, warming him from the inside out. A fine dusting of black hair crossed his chest and trailed down his stomach in a thin line, disappearing into his pants. The muscles of his stomach and chest were taut. He was leaner than Bear, but strong. His dark nipples were peaked, aching for attention. Bear had always appreciated the sharp planes of a man's chest. He wanted to lick every inch of this omega until there was no knowing where his scent stopped, and Silas's began.

"I trust you," Silas panted.

That was all Bear needed to hear. He lunged forward, gripping the top of Silas's sweatpants with both hands. With a swift jerking motion, he tugged off the sweats and briefs at the same time, leaving the omega naked on his bed.

Silas sank back to his elbows, his chest heaving as he watched Bear take him in. Bear's eye went immediately to the omega's stiff cock, already wet and twitching with need. It was beautiful; long and proud. Bear's own cock throbbed with want. His brain felt like it was scattering and reforming as he imagined all the ways he could bring this omega pleasure.

Focus. This is a marathon not a sprint. One step at a time.

One step at a time...more like one orgasm at a time. He smirked, spreading the omega's knees so he could crawl up between them. That's when he stilled, his passion suddenly doused with cold water. He narrowed his eyes on the omega's thighs. On either side of his inner thigh, Silas's skin was ravaged with more raised bite marks, the scars faded darker than the surrounding skin. Alphas had torn at his femoral arteries, thinking his omeganess might be theirs for the claiming.

"Bear," the omega murmured. "Hey...alpha, *look* at me."

Bear dragged his eyes from the scars, looking instead at his omega.

"They don't matter," Silas whispered. "Please tell me you don't care. Alpha, *please*—"

Bear crawled up between Silas's legs, pressing his body against him as he claimed his mouth in a heady kiss. He poured all his love and reassurance into the kiss, only pulling back when he felt the omega relax. He held Silas's gaze. "I would kill them all," he growled. "I would hunt them down and take their heads. Sink their corpses to the bottom of the lake."

Silas nodded, his chest rising and falling with each breath. "I would watch you do it." He swallowed, his eyes clearing slightly from the haze of the heat. "Bear..."

Bear raised a brow, leaning closer. "What, baby?"

"Fuck me."

With a groan, Bear sank back off the bed to his knees. Not wasting another moment, he smoothed both hands up his omega's thighs and filled his mouth with Silas's hard cock. He swallowed to the hilt, sucking with his tongue. That first taste of Silas made Bear ready to forget his own name. It was better than anything he'd ever tasted—smooth as whiskey, sultry as sin. He wanted to rut, claim, bite. He would ruin this omega for all other alphas. He would—

Cherish. Adore. Worship. Love.

Silas arched up off the bed, pressing his hips forward. Bear moved with him, his hands gripping tight to the bones of Silas's hips. Bear loved a man's narrow hips. He loved that velvety smooth patch of skin just next to the hip bone. He grazed his thumb over the spot and his omega whimpered for him, cock twitching in his mouth. Smiling around his feast, he sucked harder, bobbing up and down as Silas moaned.

His own painfully hard cock sat alone and ignored. He had to pace himself. If he had any hope of crossing this finish line with Silas, he had to ration his own pleasure. His mother ruined her alphas every heat, and she had three to work with. Bear was all alone. Just the thought of someone joining them made him growl around his omega's cock. No one was touching Silas but him. Ever. *Never.* Silas was *his.* He was just going to have to get creative to survive his heats.

One orgasm at a time.

He redoubled his efforts, pouring all his attention on the omega, working him with hand and mouth, dropping his other hand to cup his sack. Silas moaned louder, saying incoherent words as Bear teased him.

They'd have time to test each other's limits later. Bear liked games. He liked delayed satisfaction, and he wasn't opposed to some bondage or impact play. Sex with the right partner could be daring and fun. But now wasn't the time to discuss kinks. And it definitely wasn't the time to edge his omega.

As if on cue, Silas arched up on the bed. "Please—right there—*god!*" He loosened his hold on the bed and curled forward to grip Bear's hair with both hands. Fingers digging in tight, he took charge, moving Bear how he wanted him.

Fucking finally.

Bear groaned with satisfaction, letting his omega use his mouth. He relished in the feel of Silas's tight grip tugging at his hair. Silas pressed up, making him gag, but Bear didn't stop.

"I'm right there," Silas cried. "Alpha, *please*—"

Bear popped off the omega's cock just long enough to growl, "Come down my throat, Silas. Make me drown." He barely had his tongue back on the omega's tip when his mouth filled with exquisite release. He squeezed Silas at the base, holding his cock still as he sank down with his mouth, swallowing everything.

No drop of this first release would be wasted. This was a sacred moment: An alpha and his omega sharing seed. Bear wanted this feeling, this taste, imprinted on his memory forever. He groaned with feral need as he drank his omega's essence. The bonds tying him to Silas glowed golden-white in his mind. One word echoed through the ecstasy: *Mine.*

With a final sigh, Bear popped off his omega's cock. Sinking down to his knees, he rested his face on Silas's thigh. Above him, Silas was panting, his body splayed across the edge of the bed like a sexy, sweaty starfish.

Taking a breath, he crawled up the bed, laying down next to the omega. An alpha purr rumbled in his chest. He reached out a hand, stroking his fingers from Silas's collarbone, across his sternum, down his stomach. "How was that?" he murmured.

Silas's mouth quirked in a smile while he kept his eyes closed. Bear could tell he was breathing easier now, which made him breathe easier too. "So fucking good."

He matched the omega's smile, feeling pride swell in his chest as he glanced down Silas's naked body. "You're beautiful too, you know."

Silas blinked his eyes open. "What?"

Bear chuckled. "Nothing." Silas didn't remember calling him beautiful. Too lost in that first wave of the heat.

Silas rolled onto his side, looking more alert. "I feel strange...like I've got a hive of bees in my chest...and like I've taken a double dose of dick-hardening meds." He glanced down and grimaced. "Fuck, see? I could go again right now. I *want* to go again. It's all I want. If I tell myself no, the bees start buzzing and I feel like I'm being torn apart inside." He rubbed absentmindedly at his chest, as if he was soothing the invisible stings.

Bear gave him a sympathetic smile. "Best not to fight it then. You're an omega, Silas. There is nothing more natural in the world than an omega in heat."

"I just...wasn't expecting it," he murmured. "Not like this. And I...I didn't want to force you this way."

"Hey—" Bear turned Silas's face towards him. "Don't do that. Don't get in your head. If you think for one second I don't want to be here, you're crazy. You're the one we need to protect. We need to talk about your limits before the heat sets in and you're no longer in a frame of mind to consent."

Silas stilled. "Limits?"

"Yeah. Like...do you even want me to help you through your heat?" He couldn't believe he was saying the words. The alpha club was officially going to revoke his membership, but Silas deserved to know all his options. "I don't have to do any more than what I've just done," he went on. "I've got some toys you could use...lube...and your hands both work."

Silas chewed his lip for a moment, lost in thought. "That's what they did to me for my first heat...the only heat I ever had before the suppressant shot. They put me in a locked room with a box of toys, a gallon of lube, and a stack of A/O porn. It was awful," he muttered, suppressing a shudder.

"I'm just trying to keep you safe," he soothed.

Silas glanced up. "Is that what you want?"

Bear closed his eyes and exhaled. "This isn't about what I want, Silas. You're the one in heat. *You* have to choose— and this is not gonna be like the tattoo," he added, silencing Silas's protest with a stern look. "We're not playing the 'I choose that you choose' game."

Silas frowned glancing away. After a moment he murmured, "And...if I said I want you with me?"

Bear breathed a sigh of relief. "Then I would ask in what capacity."

Silas faced him again, his gaze heating. "I want...everything. I want *you*. I'm ready. I wasn't ready before, but I am now. I trust you, and I want you with me."

Thank god.

Bear's gaze dropped to the omega's parted lips. "You want my hands on your cock again?"

Silas nodded.

"My mouth?"

"Yes," he whispered.

Bear held his gaze. "And...what about *my* cock, Silas?"

Silas's omega pheromones flared, spiking the air. Bear was instantly salivating, ready to devour him. They were playing a dangerous game. They needed to have this conversation before they both got lost to the heat, but talking about putting his cock in Silas's ass for the first time was having him all kinds of distracted too.

Bear inched closer, brushing his fingers along Silas's side. "You can say no. If that's not what you want—"

"It is," Silas said on a breath. "Bear, I want you to fuck me. I want to feel like...like I'm yours. I want you to come inside me and fill me. Knot me. Own me—"

Bear crashed his mouth against the omega's, swallowing his words with his tongue. Silas moaned, wrapping his free arm around Bear as he rolled closer. Immediately he dropped his hand between them, cupping Bear's hard cock over his jeans.

"I want this cock so deep inside me that I feel it for days," he whispered against Bear's lips, lighting up every nerve in Bear's body. "I want you to lose yourself in me, alpha. Claim me until no one can question who my alpha is again."

"Silas," Bear growled, forcibly pushing Silas away. If he didn't get space now he was going to lose control. He rolled off the end of the bed, getting to his feet.

Silas sat up, his hard cock already leaking at the tip, desperate for more. He held out his hand in invitation. "Alpha..."

Bear closed his eyes, shaking his head. "We gotta slow down. I'll put you in a cool bath and that'll buy us an hour or two. Okay?"

"And then?" Silas murmured, lowering his hand to his naked lap.

Bear turned back to him, letting him feel the full effect of his heated gaze. "And then you're all fuckin' mine."

48

Silas

Bear was right, a cold bath was a great idea. Silas sat neck-deep in the cool water with his casted leg slung over the edge of the deep soaking tub in Bear's bathroom. Bear tucked a rolled towel between his leg and the tub's lip for better comfort. Silas stretched out in the water, letting the coolness ease his fevered body.

He knew waking up from his seven-year feelings coma was going to be a serious mind fuck. But to go from zero libido to this was...what was worse than a mind fuck? A soul shredding? A mauling at the fabric of his existence?

He took a calming breath.

That's what Bear told him to do. Deep breaths. Yoga shit. Mind over matter. Bear even lit a candle and turned on some spa music.

And then he left. Silas had been alone in the cold bath for what felt like forever. He knew it was probably more like forty minutes, but it felt longer. Any moment not in Bear's arms stretched the length of a painful eternity.

Bear.

The alpha loved him. He'd said it. Multiple times. He

said they were scent bonded. He bared his soul. Twice. He'd begged.

And how did Silas reciprocate? He said, "Fuck me."

He groaned, covering his face with his hands. God, he was messing this up. His fucked-up-ness was going to infect Bear and ruin him too. The best thing that ever happened in his life was going to walk away because Silas was too much of a mess to say anything other than how much he wanted to get fucked.

No. Stop it. Breathe through it.

Bear's words, not his. Silas's words were all still themed around self-deprecation.

Screw up. Hot mess. Useless, broken omega worth nothing—

"How are you feeling?"

He spun around so fast, he sloshed water over the side of the tub. Bear was here. The alpha stood in the doorway of the bathroom wearing nothing but his workout shorts and those fuck-hot librarian glasses with his hair up in a man bun. He didn't even realize he was whining until Bear smirked.

"That good, huh? You wanna come out?"

"Am I allowed?"

"Of course," Bear replied. "I think I'm about as ready as we can get given the short notice. Good thing is we have phones. Claire and Yumi are on standby."

"You *told* them?" Silas groaned, embarrassment flooding him.

Bear crossed his arms, leaning against the doorway. "We'll need reinforcements, Si. They just left with the dog, and they're swinging by in the morning with groceries. They'll leave them on the deck," he added.

This alpha knew him too well. He didn't even give Silas the chance to be uncomfortable with the idea of them coming inside the cabin. If anyone came near Bear right now, Silas felt ready to go full praying mantis on them. Even thinking of Bear on the phone with his sister made Silas want to climb out of this bath and grab him by the cock.

Mine.

He groaned, glancing down. Apparently, this cold water was doing nothing to encourage shrinkage.

"Si...I can smell you," Bear muttered. "Tell me what you need."

Silas closed his eyes, feeling the way his body was heating the cold bath. "I need you." It was the simplest way to voice everything he was feeling.

Bear crossed the bathroom, dropping to one knee at the other end of the tub. "Last piece of heavy we gotta deal with..."

Silas sat forward in the cool water, awkward with one leg sticking up in the air. "What?"

Bear slipped a hand into the pocket of his shorts and pulled two things out. One was a file packet of what looked like pills. The other was a shot. "I had to threaten Jared for this favor. We officially owe him a trip around the world, baseball season tickets, and ten fruit baskets."

Silas eyed Bear's hand warily. Didn't he just get the third degree for non-prescription drug use? "What are they?"

"You can change your mind about how you want things to go forward, but if I'm gonna be involved, you gotta take birth control."

Door. Slam.

"What?" Silas rasped. "Why do I need birth control?"

Stupid question.

"Mpreg is real, Silas. You said your dad was an omega too, right? I assume he was your carrier?"

Silas nodded.

"Well...do you feel ready to be a father?"

"Fuck no," Silas cried, sloshing water as he leaned away.

"Okay, well, do you still want me to be present for your heat?" Bear pressed.

Silas swallowed, eyeing the goods in Bear's hand like they were a pair of venomous snakes. Then he looked back up at Bear. The alpha was waiting. *His* alpha. "I need you there," he murmured, knowing it was the truth.

"Okay...so do you want to take pills, which are a monthly thing...or the shot, which lasts a year?"

Silas groaned. "Give me another shot, I guess. What could possibly go wrong?"

"The pills are always an option. As is me only partici-pating in a limited way," Bear replied, a sympathetic look on his face. "I'm sorry I had to spring this on you like this, but we had no time to prepare or discuss and—"

"Just give me the damn shot," he growled. "Hell, give me three at once. I don't ever want to have kids."

Bear stilled from slipping the packet of pills back in his pocket. "Is that really how you feel?"

Silas snorted. "Of course. Can you see me with a kid? No way. I'd just fuck it up worse than I'm already fucked. Besides, I'm never running the risk of bringing another omega into this world."

Bear frowned, flicking the protective top off the needle. "Gimme your arm."

Silas lifted up, tilting his right shoulder out of the water.

"We'll revisit this conversation in a year," Bear said with a level look, stabbing Silas in the shoulder and pressing down on the applicator.

"Ouch," Silas whined, even though it didn't really hurt. This was not how he envisioned spending his heat.

Bear tossed the used shot in the trash. Reaching down,

he pulled the plug on the drain. The sound of the sucking water drowned out the shitty spa music. "Let's get you standing," he murmured.

He held Silas under the arms and braced as Silas got to his feet—one foot in the tub, his casted foot dangling out. Then Bear grabbed a bathrobe off the back hook of the door and helped Silas put it on. The terrycloth felt like sandpaper against his skin. There was only one thing that he wanted touching him and that was Bear.

Bear wrapped his arm around Silas's waist and helped him hop out of the room. "Reminds me of the night we met," he said with a grin.

Silas remembered. It felt like a lifetime ago that Bear helped him hobble up the steps of the vet clinic. They passed through into the bedroom and Silas gasped. "Whoa...what the hell happened?"

The bed was missing. Well, not the bed frame, but the mattress and blankets and all the pillows were gone.

"Yeah...so I didn't really have a great space for a nest," Bear explained. "Nothing like what my mom had. Your room was gonna make you stressed out because it's so sterile."

Silas couldn't agree more. Even just thinking of going in there was making his heart race. "Yeah, no. This would have been fine though."

"I know, but you seemed to like the living room," Bear hedged. "You were nesting out there already, and you like taking naps on the couch. So, I dragged some stuff out there. If you hate it, I'll drag it back in here," he said quickly.

Silas was smiling like a loon. "Show me."

Bear helped him through the bedroom and around the corner into the living room.

Silas's eyes went wide. All the overhead lights and lamps

were off. The only light came from the fireplace, which was packed with over a half dozen electric candles that created a soft glow. In the span of an hour, Bear had somehow managed to take three sheets and string them up between the exposed beams of the living room, creating a closed in space that felt safe and homey. His king-sized mattress was sitting in the middle of the floor in front of the stone fireplace, piled with all Silas's favorite blankets and pillows, including a few from the couches Silas thought were soft.

"It's...too much," Bear muttered, worry in his tone.

Silas turned to the alpha, his heart fit to bust with all he was feeling. But rather than say a single word (because he was a damn coward), he sank back into action. He kissed the alpha, pouring everything he was feeling into the act—gratitude, love, friendship, happiness.

Bear quickly melted. His alpha purr rumbled in his chest as he wrapped Silas in his arms and kissed him back. Silas felt his heat mounting. His body practically quivered with it. Breathing in Bear's alpha pheromones was better than any party substance he'd ever taken. Proximity to Bear gave him an all-natural high and he never wanted to come down. He broke their kiss, dropping his mouth to the alpha's neck. He sucked on Bear's scent gland, grazing it with his teeth.

"Silas—" The alpha dropped his hands to the belt of Silas's ridiculous robe, tugging it loose. He flipped the robe off Silas's shoulders, exposing more of his fevered skin.

"Kiss me," Silas panted. "Kiss me everywhere. Anywhere. *Please*—"

Bear dragged his tongue along Silas's collarbone, sending a shiver through his body. He did the same on the other side, making Silas gasp.

Silas shrugged the rest of the way out of his robe, letting

it drop to the floor. Then he reached for the top of Bear's athletic shorts. With a sharp tug, he let those drop too. The alpha groaned as Silas took a daring step in, rubbing his naked front against the alpha's. Bear was a few inches taller, but not so tall that their cocks weren't touching.

"Oh, fuck me," Bear groaned, immediately wrapping his hand around both their shafts.

Silas gasped, wrapping his hand around Bear's so they stroked each other together. "Is that an invitation?" he teased.

Bear took his free hand and tipped Silas's face up, still strangling their cocks in a tight fist. "You can do anything you want to me, Silas. Anything. No limits. No shame and no questions. Are you with me still?"

Silas nodded. "I'm here. The heat is building, but I'm still here."

"Good," Bear murmured, kissing him again as he twisted his fist around their cocks. They were both leaking enough pre-cum to make it slick. "Tell me what you want first, baby. You want me to suck this perfect cock again? Want me to worship you? I have some toys too...if you're into that," he added.

Silas blinked. "Toys?"

Bear nodded, kissing up Silas's jaw to his ear. "But maybe we should start small—"

"I want you to fuck me."

Bear stilled, dragging his teeth off Silas's ear lobe with a little nip. "Or...you know, we can go big."

Silas cupped his bearded face with both hands, loving the smooth feel of that ashy brown hair. He held the alpha's gaze. "No holding back on me because you're afraid I might break. I'm strong, Bear—"

"I know," he said, closing his hands around Silas's

ravaged wrists. "God, I know." He rested his forehead against Silas's as they breathed each other in.

"Good, because I just had to get another shot for this. I'm an omega in heat, and I wanna be fucked. If you're not the alpha for the job, point me in the direction of the rubber cocks."

Bear growled low in his throat, a primal sound that set Silas ablaze. "Get on your knees."

49

Silas

Biting back his whimper, Silas dropped to his knees at the edge of the mattress. He crawled forward until he was kneeling in the middle. It was only once he was inside the makeshift nest that he realized Bear had strung up a few strands of twinkle lights. The sofa tables were set up in the corner, stacked with bottles of water, juice, fruit, granola, and other snacks. Silas even saw the bluetooth speaker perched on the bottom next to a charging station for their phones.

Bear thought of everything.

Silas closed his eyes, trying to remember to breathe.

The alpha sank down behind him, his hand on his shoulder. "Hey...are you okay?"

Silas turned, wrapping his arms around him. "You're too good for me." He kissed him, pressing himself against him, wanting to climb inside Bear's skin. "Please, alpha. Don't make me wait." He kissed Bear's neck, his collarbone, dropping his hand to stroke the alpha's hard cock. "You're aching for it. I can taste it on your skin. You want me, Bear."

"So fucking much," Bear groaned.

Feeling daring, Silas turned around, pressing his back against the alpha's front. "So take me."

Bear wrapped his arms around him, kissing his shoulder. "Is this how you want it? Are you going to present for me, omega? You want me to take you from behind?"

Silas shivered, his body going still. "Is—do *you* want that?"

Bear stilled too, his breathing heavy. "Silas, look at me."

Silas swallowed down all the shit that had somehow simmered up to the surface. Bad fucking timing. He wanted all that to disappear. Fuck Pandora and her twisted box of shit. There was no place for it between him and Bear.

"Silas..."

He glanced over his shoulder, meeting the hazel comfort of his alpha's eyes. He was still wearing those sexy glasses. As if he was just realizing it too, he slipped them off, setting them on the table by the speaker.

"I want you to face me." Bear was gentle, turning Silas back around and following him as he sank down on his back onto the mattress. "Look in my eyes," he soothed, running his hands all up and down his body—his arms, his shoulders, his sides, his stomach. These were Bear's hands. Bear's beautiful eyes and his strong, tattooed hands.

There was only Bear. There was no before. It didn't exist. There would be Bear, and everything that came after.

"Alpha, please. I need you so badly—"

Bear silenced him with a kiss, shifting his hips until he was between Silas's spread legs. Their cocks pressed together as Bear lowered himself. Silas wrapped his legs around the alpha, moving his hips to get a perfect slide along that massive, slick cock.

"I'm gonna use my fingers to prep you," Bear warned. "Do you want that?"

Silas nodded, keeping his eyes open, his attention focused on his alpha. Bear was here. Bear was touching him, loving him, pleasing him how he should be pleased. Bear slid his fingers up and down their wet shafts, coating them in slick. Then he lifted up slightly to make more room for spreading Silas wider.

At the first press of Bear's finger at his asshole, Silas gasped, his whole body going still. Bear pressed in and Silas shuddered. "Oh, please," he breathed.

"You're so tight," Bear groaned, working him with one finger, then two. "You really think you can take my cock?"

Silas's heat went from a steady burn to a blaze. He flexed his hips and grabbed at his alpha's hair. "That cock is all fucking mine. Give it to me, Bear. *Now.*"

Bear pulled out his fingers and gripped Silas under both knees, holding him in place as he pressed forward with the tip of his cock. "Look at me, Silas," he directed. "Eyes stay on me as I take you."

Silas lost himself in the look of joy and lust on his alpha's face as Bear pressed in and in and in, working with his hips to ease the way. With every inch he pressed in, Silas felt more complete.

"Look how well you take me," Bear crooned, leaning back to watch his cock slide inside Silas's tight hole. "So fucking perfect. So slick and tight. You feel amazing, baby."

"Bear, move. *Please*—fuck me."

The alpha started slow, moving those strong hips, burying himself deep inside. Silas's cock pulsed with aching need as the alpha thrusted again and again. Each time spiraled Silas's need a little higher. The tension was exquisite; a perfect sense of fullness. When he felt the pressure of that knot at his entrance, he became a whimpering mess.

"Touch your cock for me," Bear panted, his own eyes lost to lust as he drove in, his balls slapping against Silas's ass. "Wanna watch my perfect omega touch himself. Let me see you shatter all over my chest again. Want my skin dripping with you. Nothing more beautiful."

Silas didn't hesitate to wrap his tatted left hand around his cock, matching the rhythm of his alpha's strokes. His cock trembled with want as he gave it a twist and flick with his wrist. "I'm so close," he gasped. "Alpha, don't stop."

"Don't look away. Look right at me."

Suddenly, Bear rocked back on his heels, changing his hold on Silas's legs as he lifted his hips. The change in angle had Silas seeing stars. His vision went splotchy as he cried out, his own hand stuttering on his cock. "Don't fucking stop —*don't*—"

With a growl, Bear curled forward between Silas's spread legs. "Come on my chest. Give me everything. *Now.*"

One more stroke and he was coming, spilling his seed onto his alpha's waiting chest. With a matching groan, Bear released inside him. Silas clenched around his alpha's cock, feeling that hot cum fill him. With Bear's last few strokes, some of the cum leaked down Silas's crack and dripped onto the bed.

He felt used and cherished and so very full. His body went lax like jelly as Bear folded himself over top of him, kissing him senseless. When Bear pulled out, Silas felt an inexplicable sense of loss. "You didn't knot me," he murmured, trying and failing to keep the hurt from his voice.

Bear was unfazed as he placed another line of kisses along his exposed collarbone. "Baby, that was only round one. If you think I don't intend to knot your sweet ass, you are sorely mistaken."

"I'd be more *sore* if I'd been knotted," he muttered under his breath.

Bear growled, falling forward on his elbows to nip at Silas's jaw. "Careful what you wish for, omega. By the time I'm done with you, you're gonna sleep for a week."

AFTER THE FIRST SESSION IN HIS PERFECT NEST, SILAS'S HEAT slammed into him in full. He lost all touch with reality as the minutes and hours became a haze of sleeping, drinking fluids, and begging to be fucked. There was no enough. Almost as soon as he came, he felt his body ramping up for the next wave of heat to hit.

It didn't escape his notice that Bear was being conservative with his own orgasms. No such rule applied for Silas. Bear used his hands and talented mouth to make Silas come on his knees, on his back, and twice in the shower as they rinsed off under the cool water. Bear even pulled out the toys, letting Silas come in his mouth while a butt plug vibrated in his ass.

It was fucking amazing. Bear was amazing. He was attentive and caring, gently cleaning them up after each round. He made sure Silas was fed and hydrated and rested. He slept when Silas slept, and each time Silas woke him for more sex, Bear was ready to tend to him.

Silas was feeling completely fulfilled...except he wasn't. As the hours wore on, he felt an odd disquiet settling in him. Why wouldn't his alpha knot him? He was perched on a pile of pillows and Bear was between his legs, devouring his cock again. Euphoria had him spiraling higher with each soft grunt and sucking noise. Bear was desperate for him. He was eagerly swallowing him whole, teasing him with one finger curling in his ass to stimulate his prostate.

So why did Silas feel close to tears?

"Alpha, please," he keened. "I need you. Bear, I can't. Please don't make me beg."

Bear's lips were pink and swollen, glistening with Silas's pre-cum. "What's wrong?"

Silas whined again, gripping the sheet tight with both hands as he fought the urge to cry. "I need you. I can't do this. I feel like I'm dying—"

Bear crawled up his body, wrapping him in his arms, soothing him. "*Shh*...I'm right here. Tell me what you need, Silas."

"I need *you!*"

"You have me. Anything you want. Name it, and it's yours."

Why couldn't Silas just speak? He squirmed in Bear's arms, desperation clawing at him. He dropped a hand to cup Bear's cock. "*Alpha*," he begged. That one word meant everything to him now.

Bear let out a slow exhale. "Ohhh...okay, baby. Si, look at me." He tipped his face up and Silas lost himself in those hazel eyes. "Silas, do you want my knot?"

"*Yes!*" he cried, clinging to his alpha. "Bear, *please*. I can't breathe without you. Need you to claim me. Make me yours. Make us whole."

"Okay," Bear soothed, peppering kisses down his shoulder as he shifted away. "Okay, here. I've got something for you. Wanna see it?"

Silas nodded.

Bear stretched out his long, muscular body, reaching for something in his bag of tricks. Silas let himself feast on the planes of his alpha's body. He wanted to lick his way from Bear's perfect ass to those tatted fingers. Before he could roll over and start, Bear was turning back to him with something in his hand.

"Know what this is?" he said with a naughty grin.

Silas looked down at the electric blue rubber ring Bear held in his palm. "A cock ring?"

"Not quite," Bear replied, slipping it over two of Silas's fingers. "Hold still."

Silas swallowed his nervous excitement as the alpha held up a little remote and pressed a button. Instantly the ring sprang to life, buzzing around Silas's fingers. He grinned. "It's a vibrating cock ring—oh fuck—" Bear had pressed another button and the cock ring was contracting.

"It's an alpha lock," Bear explained.

Silas's eyes went wide. In his time at the Hotel Royale, he'd serviced the occasional female alpha...not that he'd ever really enjoyed it. But female alpha anatomy differed from male. Bear had a knot that would feel amazing in Silas's ass...but females had a lock that was like an orgasm vice for his cock. Bear was offering Silas the best of both worlds. Omega heat heaven.

Bear turned off the ring, slipping it from Silas's fingers.

Silas lifted his gaze back to the alpha. "What are you gonna do with that?"

Bear smiled, a wicked glint in his eye. He rolled Silas on his stomach, running his hands up over the curves of his ass. Lowering himself, he licked Silas's ass cheek, making him shudder. He did it again and again, on both sides, until Silas was panting against the mattress.

"Bear—"

Bear crawled forward, his hard cock pressing between Silas's cheeks as he whispered in his ear, "I'm gonna knot this perfect ass while I lock your cock."

Boom went the bars around Silas's heart. All hesitation and reservation disappeared in a puff of omega heat smoke. In a feat of strength, Silas shoved up onto his hands and knees, carrying the alpha's weight with him. Bear scrambled backwards, gripping Silas by the hips. Silas presented himself to the alpha, lowering down to his elbows, ass in the air. "Alpha, please," he panted. "Fucking do it. Knot me. Make me yours."

Bear was a growling, feral beast as he wrapped an arm around Silas's hips, slipping the electric blue lock down the length of his shaft. It was a tight fit. The only thing that got it in place was Silas's slick.

He wasn't ready for the ecstasy of that first buzz. "Holy fucking god," he gasped, his whole body zapped by the feeling of his cock suddenly vibrating.

Behind him, Bear sank in with two fingers, easing him open. Silas's lips parted on a silent scream as Bear's thick fingers pressed down on his prostate. It was already stimulated by the lock, and now Silas felt ready to ascend to a higher plane of existence.

"Get inside me," he growled. "Don't you dare make me come without that knot!"

With a dark laugh, Bear leaned over him. "I want you saying my name the entire time I'm inside you. There will be no mistaking whose knot you wear."

Dead. Deceased. Ascended.

"Bear, *please*," Silas panted. "Need it. Need you. Oh —*fuck*—"

Bear was pressing his thick head at Silas's entrance, using his hands on his hips to hold him still. Inch by inch Bear worked in, saying naughty things in his ear while his cock buzzed, his tip already leaking with cum. "I'm gonna fill this ass so full," he warned. "Look at you, perfect sweet omega, taking your alpha's cock."

"Yes—Bear, please. *Alpha*—Bear...Bear..."

Bear was seated to the hilt, that thick knot pressing against Silas's entrance. Silas wiggled his hips, trying to force himself back onto the knot, but Bear growled, holding him still. "Not yet. First you're gonna take your lock. Beg me for it."

"Alpha, please," Silas said on a gasp. "Lock me. Bear, do it."

Silas let out a strangled cry as the vibrating intensified, joined by a pressure that had stars dancing in his eyes. The ring contracted around the base of his shaft, squeezing the orgasm out of him almost against his will. The euphoria was indescribable. Then Bear's hand was there, fisting his tip to provide additional stimulation.

Furious with himself, Silas couldn't hold the orgasm back. Cum soaked his alpha's hand as he writhed backwards on that big alpha cock. But he wanted Bear's knot too. He'd die without it. "No," he cried. "No—*ahh*—"

Bear slammed forward with his hips, burying his knot inside him. Wave after wave of ecstasy barreled through Silas, sending him twisting and spiraling through the tumult of a release that seemed never-ending. His alpha wrapped him in his arms, lifting him off the mattress until their bodies were pressed together. Bear fisted Silas around the lock, his hand slick with cum. His warm breath was at Silas's neck as he sucked on his scarred scent glands, not caring about the alphas that came before.

Need hammered through Silas. A need for more—more closeness, more release. He wanted to crawl inside this alpha and never leave. Safe forever. Home forever in his arms.

Alpha. My alpha.

"Bite me."

50

It was all Bear could do to hold back his rut. His knot was buried deep inside the omega. They were one, breathing in sync as they came together. Silas was so beautiful. So strong. So fucking perfect. How did Bear get so lucky? He wanted to stay in this moment forever. Their pheromones mixed in a perfect blend. A new scent—*their* scent. All Bear had to do was—

"Bite me."

He stilled, unsure if he'd heard the words. Panting for breath, still coming, he tried to clear his head. "What—"

"Bite me, alpha," Silas begged again, his voice almost a sob. "Bite me. Make me yours. Claim me. Yours forever."

"Silas," he breathed. That name was his new reason for being. He was knotted inside an omega who was begging him for a bond.

Yes, please god. Bite him now. Bite him everywhere. Mine forever. Seal the bond—

He lowered his mouth to his omega's neck, but then his gaze settled on the scars. Dark and raised, they were a tapestry of the omega's pain and survival. Silas had been torn apart by other alphas who thought this gift was theirs for the taking. A bond with an omega, freely given...but was it?

Bear's confidence stuttered as his body still rode the cresting wave of his orgasm. His perfect omega was seated on his knot, taking all his cum, begging for more. Silas wanted forever.

Bite him. Make him yours—

"No," he growled, his teeth clenched so tight he thought they might crack.

Silas moaned at the same time, not hearing Bear at war with himself.

Bear focused on the scars, letting them tether him to reality as the rut pressed in all around him. Silas hadn't consented to this. Saying it in the heat of orgasm was one thing, but would he still mean it in the harsh light of morning? Bear would rather die than cross that line. Silas was his to protect, to cherish—with or without a bond. He wasn't going to take advantage now.

Besides, a bond was forever. A bond was partnership and total trust. A bond was sharing your very life force with another person, binding yourself to them in the sacred act of taking blood. Bear wanted that with this omega, but he had to be sure Silas wanted it too.

"Bite me," the omega whined, sinking back down to the mattress.

Not like this. Please, let us wait, Bear wanted to say, but he didn't want to upset Silas or sow a single seed of doubt in his mind.

Instead, he fell with him, his knot still buried deep, and rolled them on their sides, caressing Silas and kissing his shoulders. They'd be trapped together until his knot went down. His lips hovered right over that pulsing scent gland. It would only take one bite.

Just one...

With a growl, he rolled back on top of Silas, pulling the omega up to his knees.

Silas was nearly delirious. "Bear, what—"

"I'm not done with you yet," he panted, lifting his upper body away from the omega. If his mouth stayed too close to that neck, he'd break. The urge to bite was too strong. Better to rut and keep his distance. "Come for me again, baby. Wanna feel you take this knot." Reaching for the remote, he pressed the top button, sending the cock ring buzzing again.

Silas howled, his tight hole clenching around Bear's knot. "Oh, fuck yes!"

Bear held tight to the omega's hips, grinding as he pulled Silas tight against him. His knot kept him locked in, buried deep. He canted his hips forward, changing his angle, and Silas cried out with pleasure.

"Don't stop! Bear—dontfuckingstop—"

"You feel so good, baby," Bear groaned over top of him, his heart fit to burst with longing and need. "So tight—so goddamn perfect—"

"Turn it up," Silas cried, clenching him tighter as he fisted his own cock.

Bear clicked the remote higher and Silas moaned, body shaking as he lost himself to another release. This, Bear could do. He could please his omega. He would do anything to keep Silas happy, to help him through this heat. Regardless of whether a bond was in their future, Bear had this moment. He would worship Silas and love him as he should have always been loved.

Gentling his strokes, he caressed the omega's hips and lower back as he gazed down at him in wonder. Silas's beautiful skin glowed in the candlelight, his muscles tense—so much strength and passion.

"Silas, you're a gift," he murmured, knowing he wouldn't be cogent enough to remember. But the words were in his heart and on his tongue and so they had to be said. "Precious...loved. Give me a chance, and I will never let you down. I will never stray. Silas, I'm yours."

51

Silas

The smell of sizzling bacon woke Silas from his deep, dreamless sleep. He blinked his eyes open, delirious for a moment as he took in his odd surroundings. Why was he staring up at the exposed beams of the living room ceiling? And...was he in a tent?

He glanced around as a flood of memories washed over him.

The heat.

Silas had been in heat, and this was the nest Bear built for him. It was so cozy, permeated with the paired scent of their ceaseless lovemaking. Silas never wanted to leave. Flashes of the last few days filled him. He was struggling to remember specifics, but he did remember feeling one sensation overriding all the sweat and writhing and endless orgasms: *Peace.* He was sure his serenity had something to do with the alpha who saw him through it. Bear had been there the whole time. The alpha took care of him—feeding and washing him, making him rest.

He quickly took inventory of his body. He was naked, but his skin felt fresh and clean. His heat fever must have finally broke. The sheets were clean too. He sat up with a soft groan. He was a little sore, yes, but he felt relaxed and rubbery, like his bones had become jelly and weren't quite finished being remade.

The bacon sizzled as a metal spatula scraped along the skillet. Silas smiled. He knew what he'd find when he emerged from the nest. Looking around, he snatched up his discarded bathrobe. He slipped it on over his shoulders, rolling to the edge of the mattress.

He found Bear standing at the stove cooking breakfast. The alpha was showered and wearing a grey long-sleeve t-shirt and a pair of black briefs that hugged his toned ass. His hair was down, curling at his shoulders.

Silas didn't see a crutch close by, so he just used the back of the couch as a support. "Hey," he called, inching towards the kitchen on one foot.

Bear stilled, glancing over his shoulder. "Hey." He turned back to his work.

"What time is it? How long was I out?"

"Almost noon. Your fever finally broke last night," Bear called over his shoulder, now busy whisking some eggs. "You've been asleep for the past fourteen hours."

"Well...shit," Silas said under his breath. He rarely slept through the night. The two times on record were now both with Bear—the night he slept in the alpha's bed, and last night. "How long were we...was I, you know..."

"A little over three days," Bear replied. "It's Monday morning."

It felt strange to have entire days of his life missing from his memory. Well, the memories were all there, but they felt almost unreal. Some of the sensations felt too good to be true—the euphoria, the unbridled passion. Silas had never been 'unbridled' in his life. He turned his attention to his alpha, taking in the firm set of his shoulders. "Have you slept? You must be exhausted."

"I'm fine," the alpha muttered. "I'll have this ready in a minute."

Silas hopped from the back of the couch over to the island. He couldn't wait to get this stupid cast off. Using the island as his support, he moved around it towards the fridge. While Bear cooked the eggs, he got out a carton of juice and some sliced strawberries.

"I can get all that," Bear said. "You just sit down."

"I can help." Silas shifted past him to open the cabinet and pull down some plates. He wobbled as he turned and the alpha's hand shot out, wrapping around his wrist.

"I said I'll get it." He grabbed the plates from Silas, placing them on the island by the strawberries.

"What's your problem?" The words were out of his mouth as soon as Silas thought them.

"Nothing."

No way. If Silas wasn't allowed to play the withholding game, neither was Bear. He reached for the alpha's arm. "Hey, talk to me—"

Bear hissed slightly, his forearm tensing as he slipped it from Silas's grasp.

Worry bloomed in Silas's chest. "Bear, what—"

"It's nothing." Bear clicked off the stove as he scraped the scrambled eggs onto the waiting plate of bacon and grilled tomatoes.

"It's not nothing, and you're gonna talk to me," Silas pressed. "Are you hurt?" He stepped into Bear's space, tugging on the sleeve of his shirt to expose the edge of a taped bandage. "Bear—"

"I'm fine," the alpha growled. "Let's just eat breakfast. You need to eat a square meal. No more grapes and granola.

You need protein and a proper serving of all the food groups."

Silas crossed his arms over his chest. "I'm not eating a damn bite until you tell me what the fuck is going on. I woke up five minutes ago feeling blissed out and ready to come kiss you and *thank* you. Now you have me panicking thinking I did something or said something...or more likely *didn't* do or say something I should have said or done. And what happened to your arm?"

Bear groaned, dragging a tatted hand over the back of his neck. "I don't want to frighten you."

"Mission failed."

Bear met his gaze. "I...seeing you through the heat was harder than I thought and...I almost did something reprehensible. To avoid doing that awful thing, I did something else and...Silas, I'm sorry. I thought I could be enough for you. I thought I was strong enough." He dropped his eyes away, busying his hands at the sink.

Silas stepped forward. "Bear, what are you talking about? You were amazing. You were perfect. You—"

"I almost bit you," Bear said on a breath, dropping the dishes into the sink with a loud clatter.

Silas stilled, his hand brushing over Bear's stiff bicep before falling back to his side. His memories were so fuzzy. "You...but *almost* means you didn't...did you?"

Bear groaned. "Believe me, you would know it if I'd forced a bond on you, Si."

Silas swallowed. Yeah, he'd been asking Ollie about the bonding process. All he knew about it he learned from force-bonded omegas and *The Secret Diaries of a Teenage Omega*. Neither source seemed like the best teacher.

A bond was a spiritual connection, like choosing someone to be your soul mate. And there was no revoking a bond once made. It's what Silas had been afraid of for seven long years: being forced to share an existence with alphas in his heart and in his mind that he didn't put there. "But you didn't bite me. So...we're all good, yeah?"

Bear leaned against the counter, facing away from him. "Do you remember begging me to bite you?"

"Um...everything is kind of hazy," he admitted. "You know, like a really good dream, the kind that feels so real when you first wake up...but then fades with every minute you're awake? If you say I did that I...yeah, maybe I did. I'm sorry, Bear. I'm sorry if that was hard for you."

"Hard for me?" His hazel eyes were unyielding in their intensity. "No, Silas. What was *hard* for me was juggling your constant need for orgasms, knowing I had to give you three for every one of my own. Otherwise, I would have been a useless, sex drunk corpse, leaving you in need by the end of the first day. *This* was impossible." He dragged a shaky hand over his face. "You kept begging me for it, Si. You don't even remember, but you did. Denying my omega again and again when I'm knot-deep and he's whining for my bite...it fucking tore me apart."

"Bear," Silas murmured. "I'm sorry—"

"Don't you fucking apologize," Bear growled, stepping forward to cup his face. "You did nothing wrong." He dropped his gaze to Silas's mouth rather than his eyes, unable to look at him.

Silas raised his hands, wrapping them around Bear's wrists. "Bear...what did you do?"

"I...had to bark to make you stop," he admitted, his self-loathing evident in his clipped tone. "Silas, I controlled you. I silenced you. I couldn't hear you beg me again," he murmured, brushing his thumb over Silas's lips. "But I also couldn't rip my own fucking heart out by saying 'no' to you again. So, I barked you into silence...then I rutted you into submission. I kept you on my knot for hours...kept you under me. Past passion. Past endurance. I used you, Silas. To keep myself from hurting you I...fuck, I still think I hurt you. Please, *god*, tell me I didn't." He dropped his forehead to Silas's, breathing him in.

Bear's version of events didn't align with Silas's at all. What was a beautiful, cathartic experience for Silas was apparently a horror show for the alpha. It broke Silas's heart. "Bear, look at me."

The alpha let out a heavy exhale and glanced up.

"Show me your arm," he whispered. It wasn't a request.

Bear tugged back the sleeves of his t-shirt. He had three square bandages taped on his arms—two on his left, one on his right.

Silas ghosted his fingers over the bandages. "What happened?"

"Deep in the rut I lost control and bit myself to keep from biting you," he admitted. "I broke skin, but they're not deep. Bruised more than anything." He tugged the sleeves back down, looking dejected and tired.

"I'm sorry I put you through that," he soothed, brushing a hand over Bear's furrowed brow.

Bear grimaced. "I said don't apologize."

He pulled away and Silas wanted to snarl. "I can apologize if I want to apologize," he replied sharply. "You were my partner in this, and you were hurt. That deserves an apology. Everything fell to you, and that's not fair."

Bear shook his head. "I should have asked you about bonding while you were still cogent enough, but I think part of me was afraid. Even then, I knew you didn't want it. I knew you would never consent to a bond. I...it was a close call...a few close calls, but I didn't break." He was quiet for a moment before adding, "But getting through your heat was the hardest thing I've ever done, and I honestly don't think I have the strength to do it again."

Silas stilled, his heart suddenly refusing to beat. "What are you saying?"

Bear faced him again. "I'm saying I refuse to hurt you or trap you in a bond you don't want. I'll protect you with my life, Silas...even if that means protecting you from myself. For your safety, I don't think I can be in your heat again."

A thousand pounds of bricks could come smashing through the ceiling for all Silas cared. His alpha was rejecting him. His alpha didn't want to help him through his heats anymore. Silas was too much work, too needy, too desperate.

"This isn't a punishment," Bear was quick to add. "I'm not upset with you, and I'm not saying I want anything to change between us. Silas, I *love* you," he declared, squeezing his hand. "That hasn't changed. And I'm not trying to force a bond—"

"But I'll give it to you," Silas cried, desperate to keep his alpha close. "Bear, I want it. I was asking for it, and I think maybe it's because some part of me really must want it. And I want *you*—"

The alpha shook his head, eyes closed. "No. Silas, *stop*." He opened his eyes, his gaze firm. "I'm not interested in you offering a bond to placate me. And I'm not interested in knowing that some small part of your omega subconscious *might* want my bond."

He reached out a hand, cupping Silas's cheek again. A tear slipped out as Silas leaned against it. Bear swallowed, tears in his eyes too. "I want *all* of you, baby. Every part. But I want you brimming with confidence, eyes wide open, sure as a fucking sunrise when you ask me again—*if* you ask me again. Until then, you need freedom. You *deserve* freedom. I don't own you, Silas. I would never try to own you. That's not what a bond is for me, but *you* need to know that too."

"I don't want to lose you," Silas whispered, speaking his new greatest fear aloud. "I don't want to mess this up because I can't give you what you want."

"You can't lose me," Bear replied, smoothing his hands over his shoulders and pulling him into an embrace. "I'm right here. I'm not going anywhere."

Silas cried, his face pressing against the alpha's chest, breathing him in. "All my life, this is the only thing that has ever felt real to me, Bear. *You* feel real. This. *Us.*"

"I know," Bear soothed, rubbing his hand along Silas's back.

Silas leaned back to gaze up at the alpha. "I think... maybe my head just needs a little more time to catch up with my heart."

Bear nodded. "I know. Take all the time you need."

52

Bear

Four days after the heat, Bear and Silas had reached a kind of equilibrium. Neither of them discussed what happened during the heat—the good or the bad. The only evidence that it happened was the presence of the nest still covering most of the living room. Bear hadn't felt ready to take it down. When Silas didn't push him to do it either, he kept it up. They'd slept in it each night.

And thank fuck they were beyond the awkwardness of even a week previous when Silas jerked off on him and then went radio silent. No, the omega was proving every hour of every day that he had no intention of running. He was present in the house—cleaning, working, nesting (that last only when he thought Bear wasn't looking). He was attentive to Bear's needs, striving to be an equal partner.

And at night, they found each other. When it was dark and the only world that existed was the two of them in the nest, Silas let his head take a rest and led with his heart. Outside of his heat, Silas was still passionate, a playful lover willing to take risks. Bear only had to ask or offer something new and Silas was eager to try it—new toys, new positions.

Knotting the omega again was a gift, precious and rare. Silas gave everything, letting Bear worship him. And fuck if Bear knew how he would ever get enough.

On Tuesday night they walked along the lakeshore over to Claire and Yumi's new place to pick up the dog. The kitchen was being demo'd, so the girls made wood-fired pizzas out on the sweeping back deck. They stayed late into the night, drinking and placating Yumi while she did tarot card pulls for everyone. Bear drew the line at palm reading. He wasn't about to sit there and watch the beta paw at Silas while she talked about love lines and mounds of Venus.

Bear was out most of the day on Friday. He somehow got roped into helping Ray with a big delivery over in Greenville. Two hours one-way in the truck got boring real quick. Curious to try something new, he reached for his phone and called Silas. The omega actually picked up. It felt strange to think this was their first time on a phone call. Their mutual awkwardness only lasted a minute or so before Silas started live-reacting to the episode of *The Secret Diaries of a Teenage Omega* he was watching. Bear sat with the phone on speaker, smiling like a lovestruck idiot as Silas ranted about Destiny's ruined prom night.

He stopped in Spring Hill on his way home to pick up some groceries. He was in the mood for something delicious and terrible. A heaping bowl of spaghetti with meatballs the size of his fist seemed appropriate. And he'd had this undeniable urge for vanilla bean ice cream. Just thinking about that taste on his tongue had him picturing Silas naked... which had his cock twitching...which absolutely no one shopping in the Spring Hill Food Mart needed to see.

He rounded the corner out of the spaghetti aisle, pushing his cart in front of him, and nearly ran right into Boyd. His cousin had a basket on his hip with some essentials—bananas, bread, eggs—and a case of beer under his arm.

"Hey Bear, how-ooooly shit," he said, his eyes going wide. He looked momentarily dazed and shook his head to clear it. "Cuz...you smell like a blackberry pie fucked a magical forest. Shit, I can't be gettin' hard over my damn cousin." He laughed, taking a dramatic step back as he adjusted the beer under his arm. "What's up? You missed Sunday dinner."

Bear sighed. Boyd was the last person he wanted to see right now, but this conversation had to happen. He'd delayed it enough already. "I was busy."

"Yeah, I won't ask what you were doing. Or...maybe I should," he added with a wink. "Shit, would that be weird? We've talked about hookups before. Should probably wait and crack one of these open first," he added, shifting the beer on his hip.

Bear's jaw clenched tight. Silas wasn't a random hookup, and hell was going to freeze over before he gave Boyd a single detail of their life together. His irritated body language clearly gave him away, because Boyd was smiling like an imp.

"So, it *is* true! That side piece you're hiding really is an omega?! Shit, cuz...I mean, why all the secrecy? Are you two bonded yet? When does he get to meet the rest of the fam?"

"It's not much of a secret since you've been blabbing your mouth all over town," Bear snapped, pushing his cart aside. Slowly, he crossed his arms over his chest, giving Boyd his best 'fuck around and find out' glare.

Eyes wide, Boyd dropped the case of beer at his feet, setting his basket on top. "I haven't been blabbing," he countered, daring to look offended. "Who have I gone and blabbed to?"

"Well, let's see...the pack for a start, the vet, the whole fuckin' baseball team," he said, counting them off on his fingers. "Hell, I wouldn't be surprised if the cashiers here know. You have no idea what you're walkin' into here, Boyd. You could do real damage—"

Boyd snorted. "If they know, it's 'cause they smell it on you. I mean, Jeeezus, B. It's coming outta your damn pores. That is totally not my fault—"

"But you admit you've told people about him," Bear pressed, taking a step closer. "You don't know what the fuck you're talking about—you overheard me with Terry, or you snooped in his office after I left—but you *think* you know something, and you're runnin' around town running that mouth, and it stops right the fuck now. You hear me, Boyd? You're gonna get someone hurt or worse."

Boyd's mouth opened in surprise. Glancing sharply around, he snapped it shut and glared at Bear, his dark brows narrowing. "Who do you think you're talking to right now? I'm not some bottom-feeding beta you can push around," he snapped. "I'm a fucking pack alpha. I'm *your* pack alpha."

"I'd have to be in your pack for you to be my alpha," Bear countered. "No fuckin' thanks."

"Your name's still Beresford, right?" Boyd growled. "That means you're *my* responsibility. Everyone in this town knows what the name Beresford means. You goin' rogue is making us all look bad, Bear. Me especially."

"You don't need any help from me there, Boyd," Bear muttered, done with this pointless conversation.

"The fuck you say?" Boyd snarled, his tanned cheeks flaming crimson.

Other shoppers around them had noticed their standoff. Those curious had paused to watch.

Bear tuned them out. This was between him and Boyd. He lowered his voice. "Are you gonna keep your mouth shut about Silas?"

Boyd flinched, his eyes heating. "Hmm...I'm thinkin' I wanna see you try and make me. I'm tired of you walkin' around here acting like your shit doesn't stink!"

Bear growled deep in his throat, raising a finger in the air. "That's one, Boyd. One chance to piss me off and walk away. One is all you get." He leveled the finger at his cousin. "You're gonna leave Silas's name out of your mouth before someone gets hurt. And in case you're missing any of my damn subtlety, that someone is gonna be *you*. Mouth shut, Boyd." He finished his speech with a bark lacing his words.

He knew what was coming before it happened. The moment the bark hit Boyd's psyche, the alpha reacted. He wasn't going to be told what to do. The only way to put Boyd in his place was going to be to physically put him there. *Boot, meet fucking face.*

Boyd lunged and Bear was ready, bracing with his back leg as his cousin barreled in with his shoulder, trying to knock Bear off his feet. Bear got his arms around Boyd and then it was on. The pair of alphas growled and grappled, smashing into the aisles and knocking over a big display of pumpkin pie fixings.

Glass shattered and the shopping cart went wheeling off as Bear threw Boyd into it. Boyd scrambled to his feet, lunging mid-crouch like an animal, slamming Bear right in the gut. Both alphas tumbled backwards, rolling in the mess of broken jam jars. Boyd clocked him in the jaw and he saw spots. The tang of iron hit his tongue and he knew he was bleeding.

In the chaos, someone screamed. Bear tuned it out. All he could hear was the pulse of his own blood pumping in his ears. He fought with Boyd, chest heaving, until he got the upper hand. Straddling Boyd, he pounded him in the face. His hair was in his eyes, jam sticky on his neck, his hands. He punched Boyd again, and blood smeared with the purple jam.

"Keep—" *Punch.* "Your fucking—" *Punch.* "Mouth—" *Punch.* "Shut!"

Under him, Boyd was groaning, his own hits not landing.

Then suddenly everything was in motion. Strong arms had ahold of Bear, dragging him backwards.

"Alright, that's enough! Break it the fuck up!" The voice was familiar.

"Bear, you gotta stop now," came a softer voice, lower in his ear. He shook his head, the red receding from his vision, as he realized he was wrapped tightly in the arms of a burly stock boy...and Jared.

The beta vet had an arm around his waist, his body pressed in close to trap Bear's arm. On his other side, the stock boy was doing the same.

"Just breathe, man," Jared said. "He's not worth it."

Across the aisle, another store employee held tight to a groaning, bloody Boyd. The other pair of arms on him was that first voice Bear heard. It was Val Tanner, a beta trooper in the sheriff's office. Bear and Boyd had known him all their lives and went to school with his kids.

"Break it up, before I write you up," Tanner shouted, still grappling with a cussing Boyd. "Look at this damn mess! You're like a pair of animals. Scarlett's gonna have kittens."

Bear groaned. Scarlett Owens was the seventy-something owner of the Food Mart. Like the Beresford's, the Owen's had lived in Beresford County for ages. Scarlett knew them both in diapers.

Boyd struggled against Tanner and nearly got a fist raised. Tanner smacked it down. "Swing at me again, Boyd, and I'll drag your ass to the station—don't think I won't! I bet Terry'd *love* to watch you stew overnight in the tank."

But Boyd wasn't listening. Blood was streaming from his nose and he had eyes only for Bear. "What the hell happened to you?" he barked. "You leave us 'cause you can't stand to be in a pack. You break the whole family's fuckin' hearts, hidin' out like some miserable hermit in the woods. Now we find you're shackin' up with an unbonded omega, keepin' him all to yourself? You're selfish, Bear!" He spat blood on the mess at Bear's feet.

"Shut up, Boyd," Jared growled, dragging Bear back another step.

"Yeah, man. That's enough," said the big stock guy holding Boyd's left arm.

"He's a fuckin' traitor," Boyd bellowed. "Selfish alpha-hole! Our pack is in pieces 'cause of you, and you don't give a fuck! Go home to your omega, you piece of shit. I'm done with you!" He turned away, chest heaving.

The air left Bear's lungs as the fight ended. Boyd argued a few muttered curses at Tanner with his back turned before they let him go. Jared and the kid loosened their holds on Bear too.

"You good, man?" Jared asked, knowing full well he wasn't.

"Fine," Bear muttered, dabbing at his cut lip with the back of his blood and jam-smeared hand. "Tell Scarlett to send the bill to me. I'll pay for every inch of damage." Glancing around at the chaos he'd created, he turned on his heel and left, stomping over a sea of broken glass down the aisle and out the door.

53

Silas

D *ing dong.*
Zeus went off barking as Silas stilled, holding a pair of Bear's dryer fresh jeans in his hands. He stood in the laundry room, heart suddenly racing.

Someone was here.

Bear would never ring his own bell, and Claire and Yumi had a key. They'd already let themselves in once this week, surprising Silas while he was in the bathtub with bags of sandwiches and chips. They said their contractor kicked them out because they were being too vocal with their opinions about his tile-laying technique.

It's them, a dark thought hissed. *They found you at last. You thought you were clever, but you'll never escape.*

He'd been having dreams about Dallas again, hanging dead in the SUV. He dreamed of Floyd too, raising a gun to his chest and saying, "Sorry, Si. Ava's orders." No matter how long he stayed out, the thoughts remained, threatening to pull him right back in. His dreams weren't safe, even sleeping in Bear's arms. Would he really be free from the shadows that haunted him?

He flinched and closed his eyes as the doorbell rang again. Zeus was going wild. Someone was definitely out there.

Snatching up his crutches, he worked his way up the stairs, pausing at the top until he could peek around the corner. The wall of lake-front windows glowed bright and cheery with late afternoon sunshine. There, in front of the door, sat a pile of boxes.

Silas watched as a man in a lime green polo shirt and khaki shorts came trotting up the steps with another box in his hands. He tugged a scanner out of his cargo pocket and scanned the barcode on the box. Then he rang the doorbell again.

Zeus trotted over towards Silas, eyes bright, body relaxed. His demeanor helped Silas relax too. Silas came out from around the corner and hurried over to the door, tugging it open just as the guy looked ready to leave.

"Afternoon," the guy called. "You Silas Beresford?"

Silas's heart did a little flip as he nodded. "Yeah…"

"Great, sign here," the guy said, handing over his scanner to show a signature pad with a bright screen. "Need help getting them inside?"

"No," he replied quickly. "I got it."

"Well, cool. Have a good one," the guy called, trotting away down the stairs.

Silas dragged all the boxes inside. With the nest still set up, the couch had been pushed back almost to the kitchen island. Silas sat down, Zeus hopping up next to him, as he reached for the box marked "1 of 6." He ripped the tape off the seams and peeled back the flaps to find a sparkly envelope sitting on top with *FashForward* emblazoned on the front. He tugged out the note and read:

Dear Silas,
Just a little gift from your friends at FashForward. Omega slay
all day!!
kiss emoji

Inside the first box were two pairs of jeans and a hunter green sweater. He glanced from the clothes to the dog. What was this foreign feeling...joy? Contentment? Was he getting spoiled like a proper omega?

"Did he do this?" he asked the dog. "Was this all Claire?"

The dog just blinked, stretching out.

Feeling like a kid on Christmas, Silas tore into all the boxes. They were packed full of stuff he'd saved on the app —shoes, belts, sweaters, an awesome double-breasted peacoat in navy blue. The last box had a pair of combat boots with red laces and silver studs on the heel and toe. They were punk and cool and Bear was gonna hate them. Silas smiled.

He was sitting in the mess, inspecting the boots on his lap, when Zeus leapt from the couch with a bark. Silas knew that bark. He glanced up, eager to accost Bear about the boxes. The front door lock beeped and Bear stepped in.

"Hey, did you—what the *fuck*?" His panic shot through the roof as he scrambled to his feet. "What happened?"

Bear was a mess. He was covered in something purple. And red...and sticky? Was that...food? It was slicked in his hair and stained down his shirt, which he was already tugging off as he stomped past. That's when Silas smelled the blood.

"Bear—"

"Don't ask," the alpha muttered, heading towards his room.

Silas was completely taken aback, blinking after the

357

retreating form of the alpha. Recovering his wits, he narrowed his eyes. "You think that's how this is gonna work?" he called, chasing after him.

Bear was already in the bathroom, stripping out of his boots and jeans, leaving them in a gross mess on the floor with his shirt. He flicked the shower on. Zeus sniffed at the pile of soiled clothes.

"Tell me what happened before I freak the fuck out," Silas ordered.

"Ran into Boyd in town," Bear muttered, stepping naked into the steaming shower.

"Literally from the looks of it," Silas replied. He scrunched up his nose as the dog licked Bear's jeans. "Is that...jelly?" He glanced up to see Bear standing naked under the shower's spray. He was turned away from him, one hand bracing against the dark tiled wall, as he used his other hand to drag shampoo through his hair and beard, washing the food mess away.

With a sigh, Silas stripped his shirt off. Then he stepped right into the shower, moving in behind Bear.

Bear stiffened, glancing over his shoulder. "What are you doing?"

Silas dropped his shorts and briefs, leaving them on the floor of the shower. "Tending to my alpha."

Bear gave him a stern look. "Si, your cast."

"I don't care," he replied, stepping under the spray. The leg didn't hurt to walk on. Once he was standing, he just kept his weight off it. "I did some research and I think I can get this off, trade it for a brace. I used the card you left on the counter and ordered one. It'll be here in the morning. Now, turn around."

The alpha raised a brow at him.

"Relax," Silas teased, wrapping his arms around him. "I just want to hold you."

They stood under the spray, their bodies pressed skin-to-skin. Slowly, Silas leaned back, opening space between them as he smoothed his hands down Bear's ribs and over his hips, cupping his firm ass. "You've got such a great ass," he murmured, kneading the muscles with his fingers.

The alpha growled, dropping his forehead to his arm as he leaned against the tiled wall. His growl turned into a soothing purr as Silas massaged him. He worked the muscles, sliding his hands up to Bear's lower back, kneading with his knuckles.

Silas's cock was so hard. He would never get enough of this alpha. His beauty, his strength and kindness. Silas stepped in, wanting the alpha to know how he affected him. He nestled his cock right between those perfect cheeks.

"Silas," Bear growled, need thick in his voice.

Silas slid his hands around, smoothing them over Bear's hip bones, grazing them along the sharp "V" of his muscles to grip his rock-hard cock. He held the alpha with both hands, working him with slow, loving strokes. Then he rested his forehead on the back of Bear's neck. "Tell me why you're upset. Trust me to carry it with you."

Bear's shoulders stiffened slightly. "Am I selfish?"

Silas stilled his hands, lifting his head. "What?"

"Is keeping you to myself selfish?"

"Are...do you *want* to share me with other alphas?"

Bear made a possessive sound low in his throat, his hand wrapping around Silas's on his cock. "*Never.*"

Silas sighed with relief, inching closer as he moved his hands again. "Then why is this bothering you?"

Bear was quiet for a minute, his cock twitching in Silas's

grasp. "Omegas need more. They need a pack. What if..." He sank into silence and Silas stilled his hands.

"Say it," he murmured.

Bear tensed, letting out a heavy breath. "What if I'm not enough for you? I'm just one alpha."

Silas pressed wet kisses over the alpha's back and shoulders. "I don't want anyone else."

Bear groaned, pulling himself away until he could turn in Silas's arms. He faced him, his hands rising to rest on his shoulders. "But you don't know that. You don't even know if you want me—not the way alphas and omegas are meant to be together."

"Omegas don't have to bond all their alphas to be a pack," Silas reasoned. "I've been talking to Ollie about it. I just...wanted to understand it better," he admitted.

"That's good," Bear encouraged, stroking Silas's collarbones with his thumbs.

The motion had Silas ready to forget how to speak, but this was important. He pressed on. "He has four alphas, but he's only bonded to two. The others are still his pack. Total ride or die."

"Is that what you want for us?" Bear murmured, unable to keep the pain from his voice. "You wanna be pack mates? Platonic life partners?"

"No," Silas said quickly, holding his gaze. "I want us to be...*us*. I wanna be yours. Does it have to have labels?"

Bear sighed, sliding his hands over Silas's shoulders and down his arms. "But what if you want more, and you just don't *know* that's what you want? I can't stand to think you're settling for me because you've never let yourself explore anything else."

Silas snorted. "You think I'm settling for you? Have you *seen* you?"

Bear was clearly in no mood for jokes. He closed his eyes and shook his head. "You could have a real pack...a family."

Silas frowned. "Is this about kids again?"

"No, it's about living a full life," Bear pressed, those hazel eyes piercing in their intensity. "I want your life to be so full, Silas. I want you to get everything you want. I want you to be so deliriously fucking happy that everything that happened before you met me just fades away. Don't think I haven't noticed your nightmares getting worse," he added. His tone was full of pain, as if it was *his* failing that Silas couldn't keep the monsters out of his dreams.

"Bear, my shit is not yours to carry," Silas soothed.

Bear dropped his forehead to his, wrapping him in his arms. "I want to be everything you need. I just wanna be sure. I don't ever want to hold you back."

Silas smiled, placing his hands flat on the alpha's chest. The water pounded down, running over the tattoo on his left hand. *FREE*. "I'm alive because of you, Bear. I'm safe and happy. I've got friends...Claire and Yumi, even Jared. And I've got *you*. I don't need anything else. I don't want anything else. I don't have to meet every alpha in existence to know I don't want them in my life or in my bed." He placed a hand under the alpha's bearded chin, drawing his gaze. "You have to trust that I know my own mind."

Bear sighed, nodding his head under the spray. They were quiet for a minute before he glanced up again. "So... you gonna tell me what the hell happened in the living room?"

Silas shook his head. "Nah-uh. No way. Your story seems way more interesting. Tell me what happened with Boyd."

Bear growled, his left hand lowering to grasp Silas's ass, as he pulled him closer. He brushed the fingers of his right hand over Silas's mouth, pausing to apply just enough pressure to pull his bottom lip down, letting the tip of his finger graze inside.

Heat flooded Silas from head to toe and his cock twitched, desperate for more. He leaned in, sucking on the tip of the alpha's finger. Then he shifted his hips, grinding against Bear's hard cock.

The alpha let out a low groan. "New house rule. I don't want another alpha's name on these lips," he warned. "Not when you're naked in my arms, in *my* fucking shower."

Silas smiled, feeling oddly comforted by the alpha's territoriality. No mentioning other alphas while naked in Bear's arms. *Duly noted.* Power coursed through him as he glanced up. "Bear?"

"Hmm?" the alpha replied, his gaze now trailing down Silas's chest as his hands explored his hips. Open desire glowed in his eyes.

Silas took a deep breath, letting the steam of the shower fill his lungs. The warmth matched the fire burning inside him. He cupped the alpha's face, holding his gaze. "I don't know what happened today. You're gonna tell me later," he added, his voice firm. "But now...in this moment..." He trailed a hand down Bear's front, wrapping his fingers around the alpha's cock again.

Bear groaned, a look of such fierce longing on his face. Silas leaned in, licking the alpha's mouth, tugging on his bottom lip with his teeth. Bear's hands dropped to grip Silas's hips as he chased his kiss. But Silas shoved him backwards, pressing the alpha against the tiled wall.

Bear's brows raised in slight surprise, but it morphed seamlessly into eagerness as he gripped tighter to Silas's hips. Strength flowed through Silas as he stroked his alpha, loving the feel of his twitching cock in his hand. It was power. Control. Trust.

"Silas, please—" Bear panted.

"I know what I want, Bear," he growled. "I want you. You're *mine*." He kissed him again, losing himself in the alpha's taste.

Bear met him with equal passion, his own hand finding Silas's cock and giving it a tight squeeze. Bear dropped his mouth to Silas's neck, sucking on his scars and dragging his tongue over them until Silas's cock was aching with need. His whole body quivered.

"Bear, I want you," he said in a breath. "I want to have you."

"I'm yours," Bear replied. "Baby, I'm yours. Take anything."

"Want to please you," Silas said, dropping to his knees. He pressed the alpha to the wall with both hands, holding his hips still, as he sank his mouth around him, sucking the alpha's cock down his throat. He took him so deep, his lips brushed the alpha's growing knot. Bear's precum soaked his tongue, and he was flying.

Bear cursed, dropping his hands to Silas's shoulders as if he meant to pull him back up. "You don't need—wanna make you feel good," he said on a groan.

Silas let him go with a soft sucking sound, holding his gaze. "This *does* feel good. Bear, *you* make me feel good. Let me have this," he murmured, placing a few soft kisses to the tip of the alpha's cock. "Let me make you feel so fucking good."

Bear's gaze softened as he nodded.

Joy flooded Silas's chest and he sank back down on his alpha with his mouth, sucking him deep. He played with him a little, bringing Bear right to the edge, before dropping his mouth down to suck on his balls.

"Holy—*fuck*—Silas—" Bear panted, his grip tightening on his shoulders.

Feeling bold, Silas snaked a hand between the alpha's legs. "Spread," he growled, wrapping his eager mouth back around Bear's shaft.

Bear shifted his stance, letting Silas trace his fingers up the crack of his ass. With his mouth swallowing the alpha's delicious, salty precum, Silas played with his asshole, rimming him with one finger before pressing in.

Bear growled. "God—*fuck*—"

Silas pressed in deep, curling his finger to put pressure on Bear's prostate. The alpha twitched in his mouth, knees jerking. Then Silas started to move, mirroring the glide of his finger with the pulsing of his hot tongue on the alpha's shaft.

In and out. Deeper. Hold him there. Right fucking there.

"Baby, I'm gonna come—"

Silas moaned louder, already tasting Bear on his tongue. Tipping up his face, he gazed at his alpha through the shower spray, desperate to watch the moment he shattered. With a smile on his lips, he worked a second finger in the alpha's ass and sucked hard enough to hollow his cheeks.

"Silas—*ahh*—"

Bear released, shooting hot cum down Silas's throat. It was a flood of desire. With a greedy sound, Silas swallowed every drop. Never before had sucking a dick felt so good. This was primal, sensual. Taking in this alpha's essence felt like a sacred act. He never wanted to stop.

Because he's all fucking mine, came the possessive voice inside. *And I want to be his.*

The truth of those words anchored him. His own cock wept with need, but this wasn't about him. Not this time. His alpha deserved to feel cherished and wanted too. Beloved.

No other alpha would ever turn his head. No alpha could ever compare. There was only Bear.

The alpha sagged against the shower wall, chest rising and falling with each breath. He lovingly stroked Silas's face, gazing down at him as Silas stayed on his knees. Silas gazed back up at him, utterly at peace.

With a grin, Bear dragged a hand through his hair and pulled Silas to his feet. "Right. Your turn."

Silas's heart flipped, even as he said, "You don't need—"

Bear silenced him with a kiss, deep and seeking, his tongue claiming his mouth, tracing his teeth. Tasting himself on Silas's tongue, the alpha groaned, pressing his hips against him, pinning him to the wall. They sucked and teased, groaning out their desire for each other. When the kiss broke, Bear cupped Silas's face, eyes blazing. "I *want*."

Those two words alone had Silas ready to come. Licking his lips, he nodded, already gasping with pleasure as the alpha sank to his knees.

54

Bear

The following night, Bear and Silas made the walk down the lake to Claire and Yumi's. Their kitchen renovation was finished in record time, and they'd texted repeatedly for the pair of them to come over and 'break in the new floors with dancing and daiquiris.' Silas was eager to thank Claire for all the new clothes, so they went.

He looked like a new man, hobbling on one crutch in his designer jeans and boxy, cowl-neck sweater. Under the jeans, he wore the new brace, which was still too clunky for a shoe, but he could at least take the brace off to shower and relax. On his right foot he wore a military-style boot with bright laces and studs on the toe. It wasn't Bear's style, but Silas pulled it off with ease.

Jared was furious about the soaking wet cast. He was even more annoyed when Bear dragged him out on his Saturday morning to take it off. He warned Silas over and over that a cast was more secure than a brace, but Silas wanted it off. And apparently Bear had become the biggest pushover in the world, because Silas was going to get whatever he wanted.

Silas placated Jared with an invitation to Claire's for the dinner and daiquiri party. Bear rolled his eyes but said nothing. He knew exactly how long Jared had nursed a bleeding heart for his baby sister. Jared always stayed quiet about it for his own good. If Yumi caught wind of it, she was likely to go full velociraptor on his ass, which would at least make for an interesting night.

In the end, Jared got pulled into an emergency house call for a horse with a broken leg, so Bear suffered three rounds of daiquiris without him there as a buffer...or entertainment. It turned out 'dancing' referred strictly to wedding dances. The girls made Bear and Silas listen to a dozen different songs, trying to narrow it down to one for their wedding reception.

After three long hours of rapid fire conversation, Bear gave Silas 'the look' and they made their way for the door. As soon as they stepped into the shadows at the edge of the girls' lawn, Bear could feel Silas smiling. "What?" he muttered.

Silas's grin spread. "Admit it...you like it."

He raised a brow. "Like what?"

"You like spending time with them," Silas teased, wrapping his free arm around Bear's. "You pretend like you don't. I think part of you even *thinks* that you don't...but you like your sister and Yumi. They're loud and have absolutely no boundaries, but you're glad they're here."

Bear smirked. "I like seeing her happy," he replied. "Things were really tough when mom died. The pack unraveled. Henry drank himself to death, Liam went into ghost mode, and Reed literally ghosted. I'd already signed up for the military, and that's not a contract you can just get out of. She didn't have anyone left. She went from a full pack to...nothing."

"So did you," Silas murmured. He was quiet for a minute. Thoughtful.

"What is it?"

Silas opened his mouth and closed it. "I just...do you ever think maybe some of your reservations about me are actually meant for you?"

Bear stilled, glancing over at the omega in the dark. "What do you mean?"

"I mean that you had a pack once, and you were happy and loved and supported and...maybe you'd like that again. Maybe you're the one who needs more, not me," he finished with a shrug. "Alphas need a pack just as much as omegas."

Bear was quiet for a moment as they walked along the wet grass, going slow to account for Silas and his crutch that sank into the soft ground. The only light came from the soft glow of the nearest dock light. It was a beautiful night—crisp and cool, with the crickets chirping and the frogs humming in the mud. The clouds covered the stars, and the lake sat still like a sheet of black glass.

Bear turned back to the omega. "You're right. I miss pack life. But pack isn't a number...it's a feeling. It's peace and center and home. It's that feeling I've missed so goddamn much that sometimes I can't breathe." He smiled, cupping Silas's cheek, loving the warmth of his skin. "I get that feeling with you, Si. You're all the pack I need."

Silas's dark eyes went wide, his full lips parting in surprise. "I...the only packs I've ever know have been awful. I see Claire and Yumi together and I feel what they have... what *we* have. I want it too, Bear...but I don't know how to trust myself. I don't know how to let myself feel worthy of having it." He covered Bear's hand on his cheek. "But I want this to be real too...I want to trust it."

Bear smiled in understanding. "Trust has to be earned.

I'll keep trying to prove myself worthy on my end. But you have to let yourself in too. Trust yourself. Trust that you know what you want. It's not easy for an alpha to sit back. I wanna fix everything. I want to protect you from the thoughts that tell you you're not worthy. But that's not my place. I know that...it just doesn't make it any easier for me."

"Yeah...I'm sorry I'm such a pain in the ass," Silas said with a wry grin.

Bear smirked as he shrugged. "Well, at least it's a nice ass."

Rolling his eyes, Silas dropped his hand and looped it around Bear's arm again. "Come on, mountain man. Take me home so this ass can get in bed."

They walked back to the cabin in companionable silence. As they reached the top of the deck stairs, Bear's phone buzzed in his pocket. He tugged it out, checking the name that lit up the screen: UNKNOWN.

A feeling of foreboding sank into his gut. He flashed Silas a weak smile. "Go on in, I'm gonna take this," he said, holding up the phone.

Silas nodded and kept moving. "I'm making some hot cider. You want some?"

Bear nodded as he pressed the call button and raised the phone to his ear, waiting for Silas to close the door. "Who is this?" he growled, voice deep.

"Watch the tone, son," Terry growled back.

Bear groaned. He'd been waiting for this call. Terry was sure to chew him out and say he'd been too hard on Boyd. "You interested in hearing my side at all, or you just wanna lay right in?"

The other end of the phone was quiet for a few seconds. Then Terry sighed. "I'm not calling about you and Boyd, Bear. Well...I am and I'm not. Scarlett isn't pressing any charges. She told me you want the bill sent to you, but I convinced her to split it and send half to me. You boys never tussled by halves, that's for damn sure."

"I'm willing to admit I pushed Boyd into it. I was pissed. Still am," Bear replied.

"Yeah, well, you got bigger fish in your frying pan right now. We gotta talk about...goddamn it, I think Boyd might have gone and done something really stupid this time."

Bear was instantly on edge, peering through the glass wall of the cabin to watch Silas move around the kitchen, talking to the dog with a smile on his face as he prepped their cider. "What did he do?"

"It's about your omega."

Bear's breathing stopped. An ominous feeling crept up his spine as he turned his gaze away from Silas, staring out at the dark lake. "What happened? What's wrong?"

Terry sighed. "I think...I guess I'm saying I *know* that Boyd found out his identity."

"How?"

"He went through my files in my office. The little shit took them," Terry admitted.

Bear was going to kill him. He hadn't even heard the worst, and Bear knew that was the only acceptable course of action. "Just tell me, Ter."

"I hadn't gotten around to talking to you because it all just came across my desk," Terry hedged. "We've been looking out for the Rainier pack, like you asked, and well...a new BOLO came through about two days ago for a Silas Wright, an unbonded omega that may be posing as a beta, known member of Pack Rainier." He was clearly reading from the paper as he spoke. "It's got his picture and everything, Bear. Young guy, medium build, handsome. Says he's got scars marking up his neck and wrists. Sound like your Silas?"

"What's the BOLO for?" Bear replied, ignoring the question. Of course, it was his Silas.

My Silas. The words echoed in his mind. *Mine.*

"That's the thing...it's bad, son. Says here he's wanted for murdering a congressman. Remember the Dwight Patterson case?"

Bear's mind flashed with images from the news from half a year back. Gnarly crime scene photos from a hotel room showing the dead congressman—blood on the walls, his body spread-eagle on the sheets. Then there was a flood of gossip about his gambling and whoring and hidden debts that took down his whole family. It was a huge story in the press for weeks.

Just thinking of the photos, Bear knew the truth with absolute certainty. "Silas didn't kill him, Terry. He wouldn't. Not like that."

"You sure?" Terry pressed.

"I can ask him, but I know," Bear replied. "I think this is a set-up. The pack wants to flush him out of hiding. They're hoping the BOLO will give them an alert in the system so they can come pick him up—" Bear stopped talking, his mind catching up with his words. "Oh god...oh fucking hell..."

"Yeah...got there, have you?" Terry muttered, his tone almost apologetic.

Bear stumbled forward, clutching to the railing of the deck. "Terry, what did Boyd do?" He already knew, but he needed to hear it.

Terry sighed. "Apparently, he told a few guys here at the station that he knew where to find the omega fugitive wanted in the Patterson case. Told 'em he's been hidin' out with you."

Bear closed his eyes, hand gripped tight around the phone. "And they sent it in?"

"This morning. I went out to lunch with Janine and came back to find the report on my desk and Cindy asking me to sign it."

Bear turned back around, peering through the glass. *This morning.* That was hours ago. Their window of opportunity was closing fast. His mind spun out all the possibilities. "So, what happens now, Terry? This isn't just a courtesy call."

Terry groaned. "Bear..."

"You gotta say it, Ter."

"You're in the system now too. Aiding and abetting."

Bear nodded. Did he expect any less? Guilty until proven innocent, right? Especially where a congressman's death was involved.

"They wanna bring down the hammer," Terry went on. "We're expected to pull the trigger early in the morning. They're bringing in a team from Greenville to lead since you and I are family—"

"But that won't matter, because all of this was orchestrated by Pack Rainier to get to Silas first," Bear replied, weaving all the threads of this shitty web of lies together. "If the calvary's coming in the morning, we can bet the pack knows and is coming tonight."

"That's my thought too. So, what are you gonna do?"

Bear held his gaze on his omega. "You believe me that we're innocent?"

"I do," he replied without hesitation. "I believe you, and you believe the omega. But the BOLO is out, and the cops runnin' the Patterson case are chomping at the bit. I can try and tell them it's all an elaborate set-up, but I don't have much of a leg here seeing as I have no evidence except the word of the wanted omega fugitive. Not to mention we're family, and by all rights you're supposed to be my pack alpha…"

Bear let out a slow exhale, his mind made up. "We gotta run." That was their only option. They had to get space from this. Stay alive and fight to clear their names. At least they had Terry on the inside.

"Right…well, I'm not hearing this, agreed? This is a burner phone. I never called, and this conversation never happened. And I have no fuckin' idea where you went or why, and *don't* say anything more about it," he barked, the sound almost a beg.

"Terry," Bear pressed, already moving towards the door. "I—thank you for this. You just saved our lives."

"Yeah, well…what are families for, huh? Stay safe, kid." With that, he hung up.

Bear shoved the phone in his pocket and rushed inside. "Silas, we need to go. *Now.*"

55

Silas

Silas's gaze shot up to Bear as he came storming inside. He looked like he'd just seen a ghost. Silas was immediately on edge. "What happened?"

"Let's go," Bear said again. "We gotta go. Now. Tonight. We're gonna pack our shit and leave. Come on." He rushed past Silas, running towards his room.

His panic on peak performance mode, Silas hurried after the alpha. "Bear, what the hell are you talking about?"

"That was Terry on the phone," Bear called. "He gave me a tip on a bollo!"

Where was he going? And what the hell was a bollo? Silas moved through the bathroom into the closet to find Bear in front of the massive gun safe with the door flung wide open. He was on his knees, dragging out the metal bottom drawer. He flicked back the lid to expose stacks of cash. The rest of the inside of the safe was a solid row of guns.

"Hand me that duffle," he said, pointing to a bag sitting on the middle shelf of the closet organizer.

Silas's hand moved automatically, offering the bag out to

the alpha. Bear took it and started dumping the stacks of cash in by the handful. It looked like several thousand dollars. Ten. Twenty? More.

"Where did you get all that?" he said, voice shaking.

"When my dad died, I sold both his trucks. Kept this as a rainy day fund," Bear replied, shoving the cash into the bag. "And it's not raining now so much as pouring."

"Bear, you're scaring me. Please just tell me what's going on. I'll help you pack, just tell me *why*."

Bear stilled. "Pack Rainier is coming for you. Tonight."

Silas's heart stopped. "What?"

"They put out a BOLO on you to help flush you out of hiding, and apparently my idiot cousin called it in."

Silas sank back against the door frame. "What's a bollo?"

"A BOLO. It means Be On the Look Out," Bear muttered, stuffing the last of the cash into the bag. "It's a cop memo they send system wide. Lets other departments know about wanted individuals."

"Wait—I'm wanted? Why...cause I'm unbonded?"

Bear huffed, zipping the duffle shut and getting to his feet. "No, because they're saying you killed a congressman." He stepped forward, placing his hands on Silas's shoulders. "Si, did you have anything to do with the death of Dwight Patterson?"

The buzzing in Silas's head grew instantly louder. It was a storm of sound, a great thundering. The lid on his dark box of memories blew back in the maelstrom, and all the secrets and shit he buried deep blew out.

That name.

That fucking awful night.

He closed his eyes and he was right there again, face pressed against a hotel bedspread that smelled faintly of lavender detergent. Music played through a bluetooth speaker, something slow and sultry. The congressman was a regular at Hotel Royale. Many of Pack Rainier's top clients came through the hotel to party. Everyone wants to set the rules, but no one wants to play by them.

Dwight Patterson liked to do lines before he partied with any of Ava's pack. And the alpha congressman liked the omega experience...liked to dominate. Silas shuddered, his neck tingling with the memory of the alpha's teeth buried deep, his hot breath on Silas's skin...

"Silas..." Bear's touch pulled him from his deep well of memories. "Silas, look at me," Bear soothed. "*Look* at me. Stay with me, baby."

Silas took a gasping breath, his tattooed hand pressed flat over his heart. What a fucking joke. He was never free. And he was going to drag this beautiful, perfect alpha down with him. "I can't—"

"Look at me and tell me what happened. You know the name Dwight Patterson?" Bear pressed, his hazel eyes right in his face, luring him in.

Silas nodded.

"How do you know that name?"

Silas swallowed the bile in his throat. "I um...he was a client. They made me...I was with him when they...when they came in." He closed his eyes, feeling the weight of the man pressing on top of him like it was happening all over. The door banged open and Floyd was there, gun in hand, Dallas standing just behind. Silas opened his eyes, focusing on his alpha. "They shot him," he murmured. He could still hear it...still feel the spray. "They shot him right in front of me...on top of me. His blood got all over me, and Dallas laughed and threatened to leave me under him."

"Oh, Silas," Bear whispered, tears in his eyes. "Why did they kill him?"

Silas looked down at his feet. "Ava wanted him to squash a piece of legislation...something about gun reforms, I think. He refused, said if she tried to control him, he'd end her, end the pack. Told her to stick to selling dick. He always came to the hotel armed. They used me to get him in the room, get his gun off his hip." He looked up. "I didn't want to. Bear, *please*—I didn't—I never wanted any of it—"

Bear stepped forward, wrapping a rough hand around his neck as he gave him a quick kiss on the forehead. "You did nothing wrong, and we're gonna take every last one of those fuckers down. We're not living on the run forever. We're taking them down, Silas."

Silas blinked, his mind still reeling from the flashback that flicked in his mind like someone was clicking through the channels with a remote. "I—what are you talking about?"

"The pack is pinning his murder on you to draw you out. The BOLO went system-wide, and my fuck-stain of a cousin told them you've been hiding out with me. So that was Terry on the phone saying the Greenville police are planning a raid for the morning to take us both in. You for the murder of Dwight Patterson; me for aiding and abetting."

Silas's heart sank through his chest, through the floor, and burned up in the core of the earth. *He* did this to them. He brought down this heat on Bear. He ruined his life. "Bear, I'm so sorry—"

"We don't have time for sorry. We have to go. *Now*. The police will be here in the morning, but Pack Rainier is coming tonight. We can't be here when they get here."

"I'll go," Silas said on a breath. "Give me your keys. I'll drive the truck. You can say I hit you and stole it. You can say you didn't know—"

"Absolutely not."

"*Please*, Bear." He stepped forward, grabbing the alpha's shoulders. "You've done enough to protect me. Let me protect you now. Let me run—"

"*No!*"

"I won't let you become a fugitive for my sake!"

"You think I care about that?" Bear growled. "I don't care about the BOLOs or the fake charges or any of it. I only care about *you*." He wrapped his hands around Silas's wrists and squeezed. "We have to leave now. *Together*. There's no running separate. Terry is gonna help us unravel this fuckin' mess, but we have to be alive to do that."

Silas was buzzing. He stepped back, dropping his hands to his sides. "I—you would really run with me?"

Bear's gaze softened. "Of course, I'll run with you. I'd do anything for you, Si. *Trust* me," he pleaded. "You're it for me, baby. You're my whole world now. That's what love is. That's what *pack* is."

Silas sucked in a breath, eyes glistening with tears.

Slowly, Bear extended out his hand. "The choice is yours. Ride or die, Silas?"

The workings of the universe slowed to this single moment as Silas gazed into the eyes of his past, present, and future. This alpha was his reason. This alpha was his *everything*. One circle without end. Love. Pack. Trust. Feeling a wave of peace settle in his chest, he reached out and took the alpha's hand. He'd never felt so sure of anything in his life. "Ride."

Bear squeezed. "Then let's ride. Get your shit packed as fast as you can. We're leaving in five minutes."

56

Silas rushed to his room and dug his small duffle out of the closet. He didn't even slow down to turn the lights on. He could see well enough with the hall light and he knew where everything was. He'd had to leave most of his new stuff, which broke his heart, but stuff could always be replaced. He ripped open his drawers, filling the bag with as much as it could carry.

"Two minutes!" Bear barked from somewhere in the cabin.

Silas rushed over to the bureau, sweeping all the toiletries off the top into a plastic bag. He stilled, fear pricking down his spine as lights flashed in the windows. He all but stumbled up against the wall, peering out through the curtain. Headlights.

Fuck.

"Bear! Someone's pulling up!"

Silas heard the telltale crunch of tires on gravel. The sound reverberated through his chest until he felt like *he* was the stones under the wheels.

The alpha barreled down the hall into his room. He peered out the window. "Make and model?"

Silas caught a better glimpse as the car cleared the trees. Wait...two cars.

Double fuck.

"They're dark SUVs." He didn't need to say more. Bear already knew the truth. They both did. He sensed the spiked change in Bear's scent.

"Well...it looks like our window to ride just slammed shut," Bear muttered.

Silas sank against the wall, heart breaking. "So...it's die then."

Bear growled low in his chest. "Not a fucking chance. I'm not dying here, and neither are you. Come on—" He snatched Silas's hand, dragging him from his room and down the dark hallway back to his bedroom.

Silas limped on his braced foot, feeling a slight twinge of pain shoot up his leg. His ankle didn't like being so constricted. "Bear, what—"

"I didn't find you after all this bullshit just to lose you. We're riding, Silas. I'm getting you out of this." Bear pulled out his phone and dialed, dragging Silas back into his walk-in closet. The gun safe was still open, the duffle of cash sitting zipped beside it.

The phone connected and Silas heard a deep male voice. "Bear, what—"

"They're here," Bear barked into the phone. "Two SUVs. Get the fuck over here and arrest us if you have to. I'm calling us in. 9-1-1. Full cavalry." Without waiting, he hung up the phone and shoved it back in his pocket. "Fuck, I should've taught you how to shoot. When we survive, that goes on the top of the fucking list," he growled, digging in the gun safe.

"Bear, what are you doing?" he cried, his panic spiking higher. "You're really gonna try and shoot your way out of this?"

Bear spun around, gun and magazine in hand. "Listen closely, and don't interrupt. The pack knows you're in here. They know what you're capable of, but they don't know what *I'm* capable of, which means we have an advantage. They don't know this house, or these woods. *We* do. That's an advantage too. I know this is scary, but we have an edge, and we need to use it."

Chest rising with each anxious breath, Silas nodded. Bear's strength gave him strength. His focus was calming Silas, centering him in the moment. "Tell me what to do."

"I'm giving you your gun back," he replied, clicking the magazine into place. "Once we give them proof of life, you're gonna get out of the cabin, and you're gonna run to Claire's as quickly and quietly as you can. Terry is on the way with the police. They'll take over. I only have to hold the pack off until then."

Silas couldn't be hearing him right. He shook his head, heart racing. "What—*no*. We run together. You said we run. If we can both get out, we both run—"

Bear shook his head too. "I need to lure them in here, Si. I'll keep their attention on me, so you can make a clean break. You'll be going at half speed. You need the distraction—"

"*No*—"

Bear grabbed him by the shoulder, his strong fingers digging in. "They think they can take you, Si. They mean to come in here and take you away from me. I'll make them rue the fucking day."

"They'll kill you," Silas whispered, his worst fears already playing out in his mind. Dallas's face in the car was replaced with Bear's, blood dripping down his forehead, and Silas wanted to scream.

"They can try," Bear said with an alpha growl. "Now listen, we only have moments. Here's your gun. Safety is off." He racked the gun back and Silas heard a bullet lock into place. "This is chambered now. You've got eleven shots with the round in the chamber making twelve. You got that? Twelve shots only." He shoved the gun at him.

Silas took it with shaking hands. "Bear—"

"You use two hands on it," Bear directed. "The gun has a kickback, so you aim low to hit high. Otherwise you'll aim high and hit trees. No head shots. Chest only. Got it?"

"Oh god," he whispered, his hands closing around the cold metal.

Bear stepped forward, both hands on his shoulders now. "You do *not* fire unless absolutely necessary. Firing will draw attention. Firing will get you killed. You will hide, and you will run, and you will stick to the shadows. Get to Claire's. Do *not* come back for me, no matter what you hear or see. Do you understand me?"

"Please don't make me do this," Silas whispered. "I wanna stay with *you*—"

"This is our only chance, Si. This is *my* fucking house. My woods. My lake. And you are *my* omega. I will burn these alphas to the ground. But I can't think if you're still in here." He raised a hand to his cheek, brushing his thumb over Silas's parted lips.

The doorbell rang, making them both jump. From somewhere in the house, the dog started barking.

"Zeus—" Silas turned for the door.

"Leave him," Bear growled, snatching for his arm. "They're not here for a dog. They're here for *you*. Now, listen to me. There's crawlspace access in this closet, takes you down under the cabin." He dropped to his knees and reached for a section of the floor that Silas had never noticed was cut squarely into the carpet. Bear gave a sharp tug and the floor opened up to reveal a short drop down to the packed earth below. He sat up on his knees. "You'll need to crawl in the dark, but not ten feet that way is a grate. You kick it out, and you run for the trees. Do you hear me?"

Silas's eyes followed where Bear was pointing.

The doorbell rang again, followed by a heavy fist pounding on the door.

"Silas, what are you gonna do?" Bear barked, getting back to his feet. He reached into the gun safe, checking a gun magazine. Then he pulled out a black pistol and clicked the magazine in, racking it. He tucked it in the back of his pants. "Silas," he barked.

"Down the crawlspace, ten feet, kick out the grate, and run," Silas repeated in a rush.

Bear leaned in to suck in a lungful of his scent and kiss his temple. "Good. Breathe. Deep breaths for me. You good?"

Silas nodded, wrapping his hand around the alpha's wrist. "I'm good."

"Okay, we only have seconds. Come with me." He held out his hand and Silas took it. Bear snatched up a shotgun with his free hand and led him through his dark room into the hallway.

The pounding on the door stopped, but Zeus was still barking like mad.

"Come on out, Silas! We know you're in there!"

Silas froze. He'd know that deep voice anywhere.

Bear glanced over his shoulder. "Is that Floyd?"

Silas nodded.

"He a good shot?"

Silas shrugged, his eyes on the shotgun his alpha now carried. Bear needed this information. It might keep him alive. "Decent, I guess. I only ever saw him shoot unarmed people at close range. Hard to miss, hard to fight back."

Bang. Bang. Bang.

"You knew I'd find you, little omega!" Floyd called again. "They sold you out! We know you're in there!"

"Oh, fuck," Silas whined, his panic spiraling higher. This couldn't be happening. This was a nightmare and he wanted to wake.

"Okay, this is it," Bear breathed, wrapping his hand around his arm. "When they speak again, I want you to answer. Nice and loud, okay? Really shout it out so they know it's you."

"Why?" he rasped.

"Because Floyd needs to hear you *in* the cabin. But the second you respond, you go straight for the crawlspace. Understood?"

Silas nodded.

Floyd's voice rang out again. "Silas, come on! Make this easier on yourself and come out now! Enough playing hide and seek! The house is surrounded!"

Bear glanced at Silas and nodded.

Centering himself in seven years of pain and suffering, Silas took a deep breath and shouted back with his whole chest, "Get fucked, Floyd! Stupid fuckin' alphahole, burn in hell!"

He heard voices murmuring. More than two for sure. Oh god, would Bear really fight them all alone?

Bear was leaning in, his hand wrapped around his shotgun. He reached out with his free hand and pulled Silas forward. "Kiss me, baby. One kiss."

Silas eagerly met his lips, pulling a taste of the alpha onto his tongue—spiced and woodsy and heaven sent.

Bear broke the kiss too quickly, pushing him back. "I love you, Silas. Now *go*." He didn't even wait for Silas to respond before he darted down the hall, ducking into the hall bathroom.

Silas wanted to stay. He wanted to follow his alpha unto the breach. He loved Bear, and he didn't even get the chance to say it. Not once. First he was too confused, then too chicken, and now he was too fucking late.

"Time's up, little omega!" Floyd called. "Dead or alive will be your choice, but we're coming in!"

"You better live, Bear Beresford," Silas hissed down the hallway. With that, he turned on his heel and darted back into the bedroom, headed for the crawlspace.

57

Bear

Divide and conquer. Distract and disarm. Separate and escalate. Bear ticked through his list of tactics in his head. He had to lure them into the cabin. Send them looking in different directions. That was key. Divide them up. Then he needed ways to distract them. Once they were separated, he could escalate one-on-one.

Silas needed him to focus. He needed him to survive. But there was no surviving without Silas, so Bear had to keep the fight on him. His omega needed time to run.

He pulled out the fire extinguisher from under the sink in the hall bath, taking it with him down the hallway. There was another one in his bathroom and another in the kitchen. He had to time this right, lure them in and—

Like clockwork, the lights all went out. The hum of electronics and ceilings fans all went dead at once. They'd cut the power. Joke was on them, because Bear didn't have a landline and the police were already on their way. He timed it at thirty minutes before Terry would arrive, lights and sirens blaring.

But a lot could happen in thirty minutes.

He took a deep breath, taking the fire extinguisher and the shotgun with him as he moved from the hallway into the dark living room. The nest was still up, the hanging sheets providing paper-thin cover, enough for him to move through into the study unseen.

CRASH.

Something was being used to break the glass at the front door. Zeus was beside himself, racing away towards the basement stairs. Bear couldn't think about the dog now. He had much bigger problems. Slinking through the study, he heard the crash and crunch of breaking glass as they expanded their point of entry.

"Don't make us hurt you, Silas," a female voice called. "You know Ava wants you in one piece. The Bridgeport pack needs to get what they paid for!"

"Yeah, and you're outnumbered too," called a new male voice. "We got the pack swarming outside. Just try to run, ya little shit."

Bear moved through the study into the dining room. He checked the windows as he moved, inching up to the front of the room by the kitchen. Leaving the fire extinguisher perched on the edge of the table, he folded himself into the shadows near the doorway.

"Whooooa, get a whiff of that," said the guy. "Our little beta is definitely an omega now."

"Goddamn it," Floyd growled. "Aw, fuck. Ava's gonna be pissed. That little omega shit went into heat."

"You think he's already bonded?" came the woman's voice.

"Fuck, man, I'm getting hard just standin' here," the third voice groaned. "That alpha smells amazing too."

"Focus, Nick," the woman hissed.

"Boss, want us to do a sweep?"

Fuck, that's a fourth voice. How many? Silas said two cars—three people in each? Four? More?

"He's a runner. Been running for weeks. He's gonna try and get out," Floyd replied, voice low. "You three take to the woods around the cabin. Spread out and watch the windows and doors. *Hurry*," he barked.

Bear heard heavy feet move off across his deck and down the stairs.

Please, let Silas be out already. Please—

He needed to get this party started, draw the focus inward. Taking a deep breath, he reached in his pocket for his phone. With the brightness setting on low, he held it against his chest and turned on the bluetooth speaker. Using the app, he turned the volume all the way up. Then he flicked through to his favorite heavy metal playlist. Sending a prayer up to the heavens, he pressed play.

Scream metal blasted from the speaker on the counter. As one, the trio standing in his kitchen spun on their heels and started taking wild shots at the cabinets.

"Wait—stop—*STOP!*" Floyd barked over the music.

The shooting stopped, but the heavy metal played on.

"Turn that damn speaker off," he growled. "Silas, I'm in no mood for your goddamn games! Ava's already gonna tear me a new one over all this bullshit. Now you come on out! No more Mr. Nice Guy!"

Bear raised his shotgun and cocked it, the *clack-clack* of the buckshot round hitting the chamber. He let out a slow exhale as he folded himself around the doorway to the kitchen. Taking in the scene in seconds, he pointed the shotgun at the man closest to the counter who was fiddling with the speaker. He fired.

BOOM.

The man screamed as he was blasted back, the sound

not quite covered by the screech and wail of the heavy metal. Bear didn't wait to take a second shot. He military-stepped backwards, rushing down the length of the dining room as the other two opened fire on his pantry.

Bam, Bam, Bam went their bullets, as wood splintered, and cabinets cracked.

"He's got a damn shotgun," Floyd barked. "Turn off that music—"

"I think Nick's dead!" the woman shrieked.

Rest in pieces, alpha trash.

Bear side-stepped around the end of the table, moving past the window to angle himself in the corner opposite the kitchen doorway. He dropped to his knees. Resting the shotgun against the chair, he pulled the pistol from the back of his pants and set up his next shot, bracing his elbows on the corner of the table.

"You just killed Nick!" Floyd bellowed over the music. "Silas, what the fuck!"

Bear took a steadying breath and waited.

The music cut off and the silence was almost deafening. It left Bear's ear's ringing. He pushed down his discomfort, eyes narrowed on the doorway to the kitchen.

"You're breakin' my heart, little O," Floyd called. "Get out here, or when I find you, I am gonna take that shotgun, bury it in your ass, and pull the fucking trigger!"

"First Dallas, now Nick," the girl snarled. "He's not worth all this trouble. I say we blow the house with him inside. Burn him the fuck up. Ava can just deal."

"Quiet," Floyd rasped.

Bear waited, trying to control his breathing.

Whispers. Hushed orders. They were splitting up. Floyd and his female crony. Bear could only imagine their 'you go this way, I'll go this way' bullshit conversation. Maybe they even had hand signals. He didn't give a fuck. Whoever came through that doorway was dying.

Suddenly, Bear heard the distinctive *pop pop pop* of gunshots. His heart sank through his chest. They were coming from outside. But there were no flashing lights. No sirens.

Oh, fuck. No!

Silas was outside.

Then Floyd was calling out in a hoarse whisper, "*No*, it came from outside. He's outside! *Go!* Don't let him get away!"

Fuck it. Bear had to act, had to draw them back to him. He squeezed the trigger of his pistol, firing two shots through the open doorway that hit the window of the far wall, shattering the whole pane and sending down a rain of glass.

"Whoa, backup. Take cover—"

"That came from inside!" the woman shrieked.

"He's still in here!"

"His alpha fuck buddy must be in the woods—"

"Or he's in here—"

"Quiet—"

Hushed whispers had the hair on Bear's neck standing on end. They were going to trap him in like this and he needed to get out to help Silas. He had to go on the offensive. Another *pop pop* of shots fired outside had him on the move. In a burst of speed, he ran the length of the dining room and darted around the end of the table, snatching up the fire extinguisher as he went.

This was madness. He just had to pray his aim held true. Dropping to his knees, he slid along the hardwood through the kitchen doorway. As he did, he tossed the fire extinguisher. It skidded across the floor, hitting the edge of the couch and spinning off.

"What the—" came Floyd's low growl.

Bear raised his pistol and fired once, twice.

The fire extinguisher exploded on the second shot, sending a huge plume of white smoke billowing through the air, straight up to the ceiling.

The woman screamed and Floyd bellowed again. Taking his chance, Bear popped up from behind the counter, aiming the pistol at the first moving target. He fired off two more shots straight at the tall woman's chest.

She dropped, her gun clattering to the floor. From across the room, Floyd returned fire in a wide arc that forced Bear to duck behind the island.

"You dead?" Floyd barked. It sounded like he was near the hallway to the bedrooms, maybe using the stone chimney as cover. Clever. Bear would do the same. "Jayla! *Jayla!*"

The woman groaned. Still alive, but she wasn't getting up any time soon.

Bear was already on the move again, ducking back into the dining room. He pulled his phone out as he ran, tapping the screen to connect to the battery-operated speaker in his bedroom. As soon as the blue light blinked, Bear pressed play and rock music came pounding out of the speaker.

That earned him another roar of rage and shots fired from the furious alpha.

He smirked, snatching up his shotgun and ducking into the study. He tucked the pistol back in the back of his pants, raising the shotgun so it was fire ready.

"You think this is *funny*?" Floyd shouted over the music. His voice had changed positions. He was moving back across the living room towards the kitchen, towards his fallen pack mates. "I am going to *bury* you, Silas," Floyd shouted. "No more fuckin' games! You're *dead*. You hear me?

Ava's wanted you dead for years, you broken piece of shit omega! You know too fucking much!"

The woman was still moaning, bleeding out on Bear's floor. "Boss...help me."

"I can't do anything for you, Jay. I'm not a medic. What the hell am I gonna do?"

The woman whimpered in pain.

The alpha cried out in a rage, furious at not getting what he wanted, forced to watch another one of his pack mates bleeding out.

Bear let his fury calm him. *Two down, one to go.* Then he needed to get outside to help his omega. He was going to enjoy this next part immensely. Floyd Rainier would never hurt Silas again.

58

Silas

S ilas crawled on his elbows through the dark, the smell of earth thick in his nose. He could barely see his hand in front of his face, but a faint grayish light guided his way. He reached the thin metal grate and smelled the fresh evening air beyond.

Bear told him to wait until the coast was clear, but how the heck was he supposed to know that? He couldn't see a damn thing! There was no hope for it, he'd just have to do it. Bracing his hands on either side, he gave it a hard shove. The grate didn't move. He tried again twice more to no effect.

Rolling awkwardly in the cramped space, he got his good foot pressed against the grate. He gave it a sharp kick. The sound of clanging metal reverberated far too loudly, but the left side had given out. Taking in a few puffs of air, he moved his good foot over to the right side and gave it a swift kick. The grate clanged loose, flopping into the dark grass.

Silas peeked his head out, noting the partial coverage of the shrubs. On the other side of the shrub, the HVAC unit let off a gentle, whirring hum. The flood light on the back corner of the cabin was shining down on the grass, creating a halo of soft white light. He could make it to the trees if he skirted right away from it.

But Claire's house was on the opposite side of the cabin. Silas would have to work his way around. There was no cover on the lake side. He'd have to move through the trees near the driveway.

He crawled out through the grate opening, keeping the gun clutched awkwardly in his hand. Then he curled up on his hands and knees in the shadows of the shrub, feeling the sharpness of the mulch under his palms. His vision was clearer out in the open. There was no way to move from this hiding spot without at least stepping on the edge of the circle of light.

Do it. Run. Your alpha told you to run.

He took two deep breaths, raising up slightly on his good knee and readying for pain. Running on his broken leg was gonna suck. Just as he was about to move, the floodlight clicked off. The HVAC made a whining sound like a powering-down robot and then went still.

Oh shit, this was it. Someone cut the power. He had darkness, and he needed to use it. Not waiting another second, he launched to his feet, and ran across the dewy grass, feeling the icy wetness on his exposed toes. It wasn't as painful as he thought, his left leg only twinging and his ankle fighting the constricting motion of the brace.

He panted through his mouth, sprinting his way into the cover of the trees. He darted around a wide trunk, pressing his back against it.

You're out. Step one done. Now, get to Claire's.

It was Bear's voice in his head. His alpha was guiding him, protecting him. He could do this. Bear needed him to do this. Bear would meet him at Claire's.

He held tighter to the gun with his right hand as his eyes adjusted fully to the darkness. Each second was precious. He needed to be at full capacity. All around the cabin, crickets chipped. An owl hooted, as if it didn't care that Silas's life was crashing down.

SMASH.

Silas swallowed his gasp of panic, curling around the trunk of the tree to look for the source of the sound. It came from the cabin, a huge breaking of glass. Fury burned in his gut alongside his fear. That was *his* window. His perfect, picturesque, lake-view window. They were breaking into *his* fucking house, daring to go after his alpha. He would kill them all. Rip off their fucking heads and—

Run. Hide. Get to Claire's.

With a soft growl, he pushed off the trunk, moving in the opposite direction of the crashing sound. Bear wasn't even here, and Silas felt him breathing down his neck, guiding his steps towards safety.

It was impossible to move quietly with the crunch of the fall leaves under foot, but he worked his way along the trees around the back of the house, pausing in view of his bedroom window. Not his room anymore. It was the guest room, and Silas was no guest. When they survived this, Silas was moving all his shit out of there. Bear loved him. Bear was *his*. His mate, his alpha. Silas was never sleeping apart from him again.

He took a step and nearly cried out when heavy metal music shattered the nighttime quiet.

Bam. Bam. Ba-bam. Bam.

Silas raised his own gun at nothing. Shots fired in his house. "Bear," he whimpered, unable to stay silent.

The shots quieted, but Bear's workout music continued to blare. Silas moved forward a few more feet, inching around the cabin until he was in view of the SUVs parked in the driveway, boxing the truck in.

The blast of another gun came from inside the house, this one like a cannon.

The shotgun. Silas knew that had to be Bear.

More shots. Rapid fire.

"No, no, no," he panted, his heart feeling like it was being ripped in two. God *damn* it! If he had a bond with Bear, he would know what was going on right now. He would feel Bear. He'd be able to soothe him and connect. Ollie said it was like sharing a consciousness; best feeling in the world.

And Silas had been a scared idiot. Scared of what? Letting Bear fully into his consciousness so he could see all the messed up shit in his head? Scared Bear might know all his deep dark truths and turn tail and run? Not likely. The alpha had a chance to split tonight, and he'd stood tall and proud, holding out his hand.

Ride or die, Silas?

Now his Bear was alone inside the house, drawing all the heat onto himself so Silas could escape. No, Bear wasn't going anywhere. If he could be so sure of Silas, then Silas could be sure of Bear. Silas was riding. Silas was living, and his alpha was going to live too. He rushed forward but quickly slid to a halt, left leg throbbing, as he heard voices.

"Circle the house," a man barked. "No one gets out. If it moves, you shoot it!"

"Garrett, take the back! Erica, get to the other side!"

Silas panted, ducking behind a tree. He knew the name Garrett. Big guy. Redhead. Tattooed all over, even on his face. And Erica was a pixie of an alpha who was always in close with Ava. She had crazy, long black hair that she dyed electric pink at the tips. It was strange for an alpha to be so petite, but she was by no means weak. She was mean and quick, and she didn't have a broken leg holding her back. Silas didn't want to race her in these woods.

He rolled against the tree trunk, peeking out the other side, as the bulky frame of Garrett came stomping through the grass not eight feet from where he was standing. He wasn't looking towards the trees. He has his eyes on the cabin, gun raised with both hands, as he scanned like a robot.

The music in the house cut, leaving the clearing ringing with an echoing silence.

"Wait—I think I see him," Garrett growled, his body going tense as he pointed his gun at the dining room window.

No fucking way.

Silas wasn't going to stand here in the shadows and watch this guy hurt his alpha. Raising his own gun with both hands, he came out from behind the tree, and took two big steps forward. Six feet of grass separated him from Garrett's broad back. Oh god, at this range he could smell the alpha—orange zest and coffee grounds. It flooded Silas's head with memories and fear. He blinked to clear his mind.

Aim low to hit high.

Not waiting for his fear to overpower him, Silas aimed for the small of Garrett's back and fired two shots. Garrett fired on reflex, the shots hitting the side of the cabin and the air as he fell forward with a cry, crumpling in the wet grass.

Silas panted, gun shaking in his hands. The recoil reverberated down his arms and he smelled the acrid smoke of the powder with his sensitive nose. Garrett groaned, his arms twitching as if he was going to try to push up off the grass. Not giving him the chance to regain his feet and keep fighting, Silas stomped forward. He leveled the gun at the back of the alpha's head and shot again.

The alpha went still.

"Garrett!" the other man barked.

"What happened?" Erica shouted.

With a gasp, Silas tore his eyes away from the alpha and all but stumbled back into the trees.

"Garrett's down! Oh, shit—"

"I saw him! There's someone in the woods! He got out!"

Silas ducked behind a tree, panting for breath, when more shots rang out from the house, followed by a shattering rain of more broken glass. He clenched his teeth, panting through the pain in his leg. His perfect home was being violated. His alpha's life was at risk. Every single one of these fucking alphas was going to die.

Someone moved through the shadows to his right.

"I see him!" Erica cried from the left.

Gunshots split the silence, with one cracking into the bark six inches from Silas's head. He swallowed his cry as he took off, scrambling over roots and crunching on leaves. The good thing was Erica wasn't being any quieter. He heard her stomping through the dry leaves. He turned and shot wildly in the air one-handed, feeling the recoil rattle his forearm. Then he darted quickly to the side, stumbling in a half arc as shots rang out.

From the house came a sound like an explosion and everyone stopped.

Silas was screaming inside. His inner omega was clawing at his chest, ripping open his very lungs, desperate to know if their alpha was alright.

"What the hell is happening?" the man bellowed.

"Looks like little Silas has some help," Erica jeered. "Silas, is that you out here? Come on, beta boy. Not so beta anymore, right? You got someone helping you in there? Still making others fight your battles?"

"Ava's gonna kill us if we let him get away," the man growled.

Erica huffed a laugh. "Nah, Silas isn't going anywhere. Not while his alpha is at risk. I bet our little omega friend would do *anything* to keep his new alpha safe. Right, Si?"

Silas knew Erica was goading him, trying to get under his skin and make him do something reckless. He took deep breaths, breathing out his fear and anxiety.

"Come on, Todd. Let's go back and help Floyd smoke out that alpha. If we can't get Silas, we can at least get him. Burn him the fuck up!"

They turned, the sound of the feet crunching on the leaves towards the cabin.

"No," Silas rasped, his words little more than a puff of breath. They wanted to hurt his alpha. With a growl, Silas darted out from behind his tree, gun raised, and started firing.

59

Bear

Bear ducked his head around the doorway from the study to the living room to see the woman named Jayla bleeding out on his floor. She was still groaning, still alive. Behind her, the body of the other alpha laid crumpled at the feet of the bar stools.

Floyd Rainier stood at the stove, burner on high. His massive body was silhouetted by the bright orange flame. *Oh shit...*Bear knew what Floyd was planning to do. It was the same thing Bear planned to do. Floyd was just beating him to it. Like hell he was going to let himself get trapped in his own damn house while Floyd fucking Rainier sent it up in flames.

Bear raised his shotgun, ready to blow off the back of his fucking head. Just as he pulled the trigger, Floyd ducked down. The buckshot shattered the tile behind the stove and the alpha bellowed.

"I'm gonna make you eat that shotgun," he barked from his hiding place behind the thick kitchen island. "Who the hell are you? Silas can't shoot like that!"

"You messed with the wrong fucking omega," Bear

barked. "Silas is *mine* now, and you're trespassing. In this house, we shoot first and ask questions later."

"I have the same rule," he called back. "Pity Silas doesn't. He could have saved himself all this trouble."

"Yeah, what the fuck, man! He told me he spared your worthless fuckin' life in that car crash. All you had to do was let him walk away! You owe him this!"

"You think it's so easy for me? I got people who depend on me too. Ava says jump, we all say 'how high.' What am I supposed to do? Can't just return empty-handed."

Bear wanted this alpha dead more than he wanted air. Floyd Rainier wasn't haunting Silas for one more sleepless night. "You overplayed your hand, Floyd," he called. "You came in here all cocksure, thinking you'd have things your way. But the police were called before you even finished pulling down the drive. I'd say you've got about five minutes tops to make your final play. And Silas isn't even here. You will *never* see him again!"

"Who the fuck are you?" Floyd barked.

He smirked, holding tighter to his shotgun. "I'm Henry fucking Beresford. And you're trespassing on Lake Beresford! You're in *my* territory! You wanna talk about packs? My pack owns this county. Even if you crawl outta here, I'll have Pack Beresford hunting your scent, hounding you into the fuckin' ground."

Floyd huffed. "You don't know me—"

"Floyd Oren Rainier. 280 pounds. ID number 775-217-340!" Bear barked. "We've been watching you for weeks, Floyd. My uncle's the sheriff of this county. He's been following you. I've had my eye on you since you first stepped foot in Spring Hill."

"Oh, yeah? Well how come I got the drop on you? How come I'm here in your house?"

Bear gripped tighter to the shotgun. *Because Boyd Beresford is a stupid, selfish fucking alphahole dead man.* "You think you got a drop here?" he said with a laugh. "I knew you were comin' asshole. My uncle called me. Silas and I set this up to lure you in. This is a fuckin' trap, and you walked right into it! You're done, Floyd! We'll bury you where you fall. And your shit pack is finished too!"

Silence followed his speech. Then the alpha called, "What do you want?"

Bear rolled his eyes. "What makes you think I want fuck-all from you?"

"Every man has a price! We got money. Some of it could be yours in a matter of minutes...I just gotta call Ava. She'll make it happen."

"Keep your blood money," he called back.

"You want me to leave here without Silas? Fine. You promise me that you'll keep him quiet, keep him away from the cops, and I'll never come after him again! I'll tell Ava he's dead for good this time!"

Lying alphahole. "Not interested! The only thing I want is you dead and in a shallow grave!"

"Fuck you, you piece of shit mountain man!" Floyd roared, his fury and panic boiling over. "I'm not dying in here!"

Oh, yes you are.

Bear swung around the corner of the doorway. Racking his shotgun, he aimed right for the flaming stove and fired.

60

Silas

Silas fired his gun at the moving shadow until he heard a yelp of pain.

"Fucking hell, he got me!" Todd yelled.

Before Silas could take cover behind a tree, another shot zinged past him, clipping his arm. He stifled his cry, dropping one hand from his gun to slap it over the intense burning in his left forearm. He dragged his hand away from the sleeve of his sweater, seeing red blood coating his fingers.

Pain in his arm. Pain in his leg. Silas was reeling. His vision was getting spotty. The human body could only take so much. His adrenaline pumped in overdrive. He had to get away from these alphas, get back to Bear.

"Where are you hit?" Erica hissed from somewhere to his right.

Todd wheezed, his voice sounding garbled. "My side—think he broke a rib—breathing hurts—"

"Oh shit, *shit*," Erica cried. "Silas, get out here and fight us like a man!"

Silas needed to finish Todd. He was already hurt. He was the weaker target.

Aim low to hit high.

He rolled off the tree, darting left. He didn't make it five steps before two shotgun blasts echoed out from the house. Then a massive explosion rocked the cabin. It was so big, it shook the ground. Red-orange flames burst from the walls and windows as the kitchen was engulfed in fire. Acrid black smoke billowed into the night sky.

Rather than scream or cry or do any of the thousand things tearing through his body, Silas used the moment to step forward, raise his gun, and fire two shots into Todd's back.

The alpha fell. Dead? God, Silas hoped so.

But Silas was too slow to duck away from the return shots fired off by Erica. Another bullet lanced his right arm high at the shoulder. This one went deeper, he could feel it. The pain had him choking on air as he spun and dropped to his knees, his own gun falling to the grass. In a blur of tears and pain, he tried to find the gun again. The bright light from the house fire was messing with his vision. And how could a hit to the shoulder also feel like a punch to the gut? His insides twisted, making him want to throw up.

Focus. Find the gun. Find it now—

Behind him, the tiny alpha charged forward, gun brandished in front of her. Silas stumbled to his feet, hands empty. Two feet separated them. He was done. He closed his eyes and spread his hands wide. "Bear, I love you," he whispered.

The last thing he saw was the sneer on the alpha's face as she raised her gun and pulled the trigger.

61

Silas

lick. Click.
The gun didn't fire.

Silas flicked his eyes open, injured arms dropping to his sides, as he watched the alpha wrestle with her gun. It was empty.

Erica screamed in her fury, lobbing it at Silas's head. The heavy weapon cracked him in the forehead, making him moan in pain. Then she was slamming against him, dragging him to the ground.

They wrestled, Erica wrapping her legs around his waist and pummeling him with her sharp fists. His soiled cream-colored sweater made it clear exactly where he was shot. The alpha aimed her fists there, pounding against his wounds until he wanted to die. His arms went limp as pain became the only emotion he could identify.

"I'm gonna *kill* you!" Erica screamed in his face. "Worthless! Omega! Trash!" Each curse came with a punch. She exhausted herself, dropping forward to wrap her clawed hands around his neck.

He gasped, feeling her fingers constrict. Now was the time to fight back. Now.

Get up, Silas, and fight! came Bear's voice in his mind.

Another explosion rocked the cabin, sending a sea of shattered glass falling from the busted-out windows. Erica looked wild in the firelight, her lilac eyes glinting as her curtain of inky black hair with hot pink tips dusted his cheeks.

He raised his arms, flailing them at her. He didn't want to die like this. He wanted to fight. He was strong enough. One last fight. For Bear.

An ominous growl tore through the darkness. Was that him?

Silas stared up into the face of the vicious alpha stealing his air, watching as her expression turned from triumph to panic. Her eyes went wide as a feral bark echoed loudly in their ears. Out of the dark, Zeus launched himself on her, his teeth tearing into her forearm with a fury. The dog was feral, biting and snapping, forcing her off Silas. She stumbled to her feet, clutching her shredded forearm, rushing back towards Todd's fallen body.

The gun. She's getting his gun.

"No," Silas groaned, rolling on his side and up on his knees. His throat felt crushed. He could barely suck in air, but he managed to crawl towards the spot where his gun fell. Meanwhile, brave Zeus chased after Erica.

"Get away," she cried. "Call him off!"

Silas panted, vision spinning, as his eyes darted around the dark grass, looking for his fallen gun. She screamed again, the dog in her face as she tried to bend down to get the gun from Todd's limp hand.

There.

Silas breathed a sigh of relief. Ten inches from his

splayed fingers, his gun was lying in the grass. He crawled forward, picking it up with his left hand. His right arm felt too weak from the shot to his shoulder. He didn't even have the strength to stand. He just pushed off the ground onto his knees and raised the weapon.

That's when he saw him.

Striding across the dark grass, his hair blowing in the fiery smoke, was Bear. He marched right up to Erica, shotgun pointed at her head, and blasted her the fuck away before she even had a chance to raise Todd's gun. Zeus growled low as her body fell back on top of the other alpha.

Bear's fury tuned itself on Silas. "Are they all dead?" he barked.

Silas could only nod, chest heaving as he took grateful breaths of air. His alpha was alive. Bear was alive. "Bear," he cried, dropping his gun and leaving his fingers splayed open.

The alpha was already on the move, crossing the grass in a few strides as he dropped to his knees before Silas, wrapping him in his arms. "Oh, thank god," the alpha groaned against his neck, breathing him in with deep, gulping breaths.

"Floyd? The others?"

"All dead. I shot two. I took Floyd down by blowing the stove. Had to get out through your bedroom window."

"Good." Silas sighed with relief. Was it really over? Had they survived?

Bear's scent filled Silas's senses. It was all wrong now, tinged with the stink of gun powder and burning wood. Sharper too, made more potent by his adrenaline. Bear pulled back from him and Silas let out a whimper. "*No—*"

"Where are you hurt?" Bear's eyes and hands traced over Silas. "You got shot? Where?"

Silas didn't care about his pain right now. He only cared about this. He raised his left hand, cupping the alpha's bearded cheek. "Bear, I love you. I love you so goddamn much. I've loved you for days. Weeks. I should have said it before. I was afraid, but I'm not anymore. I love you—"

Bear silenced him with a kiss, a bruising press of lips that tasted like sweat and smoke and alpha. They moaned into each other, letting loose their fear and anxiety. Bear broke the kiss. "I love you, Silas," he breathed, lips still touching.

Knowing with total clarity what he needed, Silas held his alpha's gaze. "I want your bond," he declared. "Bond me, alpha. Never let me go."

Bear let out a sharp exhale, pulling back slightly. "Silas, you're—we can take a minute to breathe, okay? We're both alive. It's gonna be fine—"

"It won't," Silas cried, digging his fingers into Bear's shirt. "I just spent the worst night of my existence not knowing if you were dead or alive. Never again, Bear. *Never*. Bond me. Become part of me."

"Silas—"

"*No*," he barked, watching the alpha's eyes go wide in surprise. "This isn't the fear talking or my adrenaline or my biology or fucking *any* of it," he said with a slash of his shaking hand. "You said we ride or die. Did you mean it?"

Bear's gaze softened. "Of course, I did."

"Well, I'm riding," Silas pressed. "Bear, I'm riding with you. I want forever, and I'm not wasting one more fucking minute not being yours. Take me in your arms and do it. Bite me, alpha."

Bear's pheromones were spiking, his hunger overpowering the acrid smell of the gun powder and smoke. A low growl was building in his throat. "You want me to bite you right here? Right now?"

Silas met his gaze with determination. "If I was the alpha, it'd be done already."

Bear's growl turned feral as he lunged. He flipped Silas down on the grass, rolling him onto his stomach. Silas's arms screamed out in pain, but he didn't care. Nothing was stopping him from getting what he wanted. This alpha was *his*. He was going to wear this bond with pride.

In his heightened reactionary state, Bear was more alpha than man as he ripped at Silas's jeans, dragging them down over his ass. "I'm gonna fill you, omega. Knot and bond you. Mine forever."

"Yes," Silas panted, dropping himself down to his elbows to present for his alpha. His sweater slid down, exposing his lower back to the cool night air. Bear was right behind him, the fingers of his left hand digging into his flesh hard enough to bruise as he worked two fingers of his right hand inside Silas's ass.

That first breach had Silas crying out, moaning his alpha's name. "More," he demanded. "Take me, alpha. Fill me. Rut me senseless. Yours. Only yours."

"You are so goddamn perfect," Bear growled above him, removing his fingers to replace them with the tip of his hard cock. He pressed in with a groan, working himself inside Silas's tight hole. "So fucking slick. You're made for me, baby. *Mine*. Say it."

"Yessss." Silas moaned with pleasure, pressing eagerly back with his hips to bury the alpha further. His own cock was painfully hard, weeping with need. "I'm yours. Only yours."

"I love you, Silas," Bear breathed, burying himself deeper with each thrust. "Love your heart; your strong heart.

Love your body. Your resilience—*god*—" He was seated to the hilt, Silas clenching him tight.

"Bear, *please*. Need your knot and your bond."

"I know, baby. I know—"

"Don't make me wait, alpha. I'm dying for you. Been dying all my life. Wanna live for you—" He was incoherent with need, waiting for that moment of connection that had once scared him half to death. But there was nothing scary about this. Bear was his everything. His lover, his friend, his home. Being bonded to Bear would be easier than breathing.

And then the beautiful truth hit him: Being bonded to Bear would make it easier to *breathe*. He sighed in his relief, utterly at peace, even knowing there was carnage all around them. It didn't matter. There was only this. Silas glanced over his shoulder, meeting his alpha's depthless hazel eyes that glowed from the light of their burning house. "Bear...now."

The rut cleared in Bear's eyes as he held Silas's gaze and nodded. He folded himself over Silas, reaching with one hand to turn his head. "Give me your mouth," he panted. "Kiss me. *Silas*—"

Silas eagerly complied, lifting up on his left arm and arching his neck over his shoulder to kiss his alpha. Their mouths moved furiously, a clashing of angry teeth and tongues. Silas couldn't wait another second for the bond. He was about to scream out his desperate need when a sharp pain suddenly broke through his haze of lust.

Oh god...

Bear bit him. The alpha had his teeth locked on his bottom lip, sinking down until the coppery taste of Silas's blood coated both their tongues. The taste in his mouth quickly changed from salty iron to...*euphoria*. Everything that was Bear's essence and everything that was Silas's wove together into a complex layering of scent and sensation, wrapping itself around them both.

Silas opened his eyes wide, staring into the eyes of his alpha, as the bond burrowed itself under his skin, sinking deep, all the way to the marrow of him. That pairing of their essences became like a new life's blood, working itself through his bones and spreading outward. He was warm, he was cold. He was made new.

They both sensed the moment the bond flared to life. Suddenly, it's as if everything Silas was before became strengthened, even as it diminished. He felt full up of himself and his own essence, but there was a new presence too. It bloomed inside his chest, his mind, his very being. That scent that he loved so well was no longer something he experienced outside his body. It was in him. It *was* him. Bear's scent, Bear's essence, it was part of him now.

Bear's teeth released Silas's lip and the alpha licked the blood away, panting as he looked down at him. It was almost like Silas could feel and see Bear looking down at him, even as he looked up.

Opening the doors of his heart, he let the alpha fully inside. He was awash with new sensation and emotion— love, adoration, worship, protection. They weren't Silas's feelings, they were Bear's. Bear loved him. He was proud of him. He'd protect him with his life. Only wanted his happiness—

Silas had to close his eyes, reeling from the sensation of such perfect trust and love. He panted, licking his bitten lip. "I feel you," he whispered. "Alpha..."

Bear smiled, his expression one of bliss. "And I feel you, baby. I feel your love for me. There's no hesitation in it," he said with a sigh of relief. "God, you really love me."

Silas felt that smile like it was pressed against his skin. He knew all that he was feeling, glad for Bear to share in it. Hope and salvation. Trust. Longing. So much longing on both sides. "I love you so much, Bear. You're mine now. Mine to love forever."

Warmth and contentment washed over him from Bear's side of the bond, but there was also a primal need to rut, to claim and own. The bond wanted completion, and Silas was desperate for the same. "Knot me, Bear. Alpha, I'm yours."

He repeated the words in his mind, feeling the gentle caress of Bear's love like a stroke down his back. That stroke ended with a pair of firm hands on his hips as his alpha pressed forward, sinking his knot inside him. Silas moaned with relief, bracing against the wet grass as his alpha rutted into him with wild abandon.

Bear folded over him, one of his hands wrapping around him to grip his aching cock. "We come together, Silas. Ride or die. Forever."

"Ride or die," Silas repeated, his face pressed against his arm as his alpha stroked him so well. "Together."

They chased their release, their bodies coming together as one. The bond hummed between them, perfect and pure and shimmering with the promise of this new forever.

Just as they came down off their high, the forest behind them lit up with a fury of red and blue blinking lights. Sirens blared and tires crunched on the gravel. The cavalry was here.

Bear and Silas stilled, the alpha knot-deep inside him. All around them was utter, devastating carnage. The cabin was fully aflame now; there'd be no saving it. Smoke from the fire billowed a mile high. Bodies lay scattered in the grass mere feet away. Guns littered the ground around them. And Silas was doubly shot and still bleeding.

Closer than the sounds of the sirens came a pair of panicked voices, followed by dogs barking.

"*Henry!*" Claire screamed. "Silas!"

"Ohmigod, Henry!" Yumi echoed. The girls were running up the lakeshore, the dogs barking at their heels. Their attention was all for the burning house. They hadn't spotted them yet in the dark of the grass.

Embarrassment flooded Silas as he realized their awkward predicament. "Uhh...Bear?"

"Shit," Bear panted, giving Silas's ass a soft smack. He was still knotted and hard as stone. "Well...this is gonna be fun to explain."

62

Silas

Bear and Silas spent eight days in the hospital under 24-hour police custody. Their "arrest" was madness. Cops from three cities swooped in on the cabin in full tactical gear to find them in the yard, Bear knot-deep, with bodies strewn around them on the grass. Not their finest moment, but it was hard to care while riding the high of a new bond mark.

The awkwardness didn't end there. The police dragged Silas and Bear to Greenville Hospital in cuffs and then promptly split them apart, intent on interrogating them separately while the doctor's treated Silas's gunshot wounds. But separating a wounded omega from his alpha? Yeah, bad idea. The bonding acted like a mini heat trigger and Silas was crawling the walls within the hour, incoherent with need for his alpha. He sent chaotic messages down the bond that made Bear frantic. Bear nearly strangled a cop who tried to keep him from getting to the door.

In the end, the police threw up their hands and put them back together. For half a morning, they fucked like rabbits on every surface of Silas's tiny hospital room.

Working around the IVs and monitors was a feat, but they managed. Eventually, a blushing nurse came in while Bear was knot-deep and just unplugged the machines. Silas wasn't going to die from too much sex; Bear would gladly make sure of it.

Once the intensity of the bond heat wore off, the police resumed questioning Silas. He gave over thirteen hours of testimony. It was brutal and breaking and so very difficult, but each story he told, each piece of evidence he provided, became one more reason to dismiss all the charges against them.

Within 32 hours, the charges against Bear were dropped. By the fourth day, Silas was told the charges against him for the congressman's murder were also being dropped. It was Terry who let it slip that they weren't going to be charged for anything that happened at the cabin. Their testimonies, coupled with evidence collected from the SUVs, made it clear that Pack Rainier never had any intention of letting Silas live.

Luckily, Floyd's big play didn't work. He and five pack members were dead. The rest were being brought up on a shopping list of charges. On the sixth day, the police conducted a raid at the Hotel Royale. Seventeen trafficked betas were rescued, and Ava Rainier made her last stand on the third floor, dying in a haze of bullets. The media went into a frenzy, with TV crews pressing in at the hospital doors trying to get the 'unidentified source' to make an official statement.

Hell would freeze over before Silas got in front of a camera.

In between all the police interrogations, Silas had the enjoyable little chore of getting stitches in his left arm and surgery on his right. They had to put a pin in his shoulder to fix a chip in the bone from his gunshot wound. They wanted him in a sling for a few weeks, and he hated it. At least the running hadn't made his leg fracture any worse. In fact, the doctors cleared him to start reapplying weight.

On the day Silas was finally discharged, he found the whole of Pack Beresford waiting in the lobby—Terry and his mate, Claire and Yumi, even Boyd. Bear was pushing Silas in his wheelchair down the wide, pea-green hallway when he caught sight of his cousin. Silas felt Bear's rage and resentment flare in the bond.

Silas had never met Boyd before, but he knew him instantly from that guilty fucking look on his face. He was handsome, broad-shouldered and tall like Bear, but his features were dark—black curly hair, olive-toned skin. A tiny strawberry blonde stood next to him holding a squirming baby.

Bear halted the wheelchair, eyes only for Boyd. Silas well understood his simmering rage. This alphahole nearly got them both killed. The other alphas framed themselves around Boyd, placing him in the center of the waiting room. It was time for him to atone.

Silas didn't even realize he'd reached up to place his hand over Bear's on his uninjured shoulder. He gave Bear's hand a squeeze of consent. This had to happen.

Not waiting another second, Bear stomped around Silas. The other alphas took a collective step back and Boyd raised his hands. "You know I'm sorry—*wait*—"

Bear wound up, slamming Boyd hard in the jaw with a firm fist. Boyd reeled, spinning around and dropping to one knee. Next to him, the strawberry blonde gasped and sobbed, clutching her crying baby. One of the other women put a firm hand on her shoulder, pulling her back.

Panting slightly, Boyd spit blood onto the floor and stood. He faced Bear and nodded. "Again."

Bear unleashed his fury, pounding Boyd down to the floor, raining down his fists as Boyd groaned. The pack watched on. No one lifted a finger to pull Bear off. Silas sat in his wheelchair watching too, feeling out the edges of Bear's control through the bond, making sure his mate wasn't falling in too deep to his alpha rage.

After less than a minute, Boyd rolled to his side, raising his arms to cover his face. "Alright, enough," he growled. "Fuck—Bear—*enough!*"

Bear paused, now straddling his cousin on the hospital floor. His exertions had loosened his hair around his shoulders. It hung in an ashy, tangled mess. He panted, chest heaving, knuckles bloody. "Oh, you think it's enough? You sold out my mate to the cops, Boyd. You broke pack rules, and almost got me fuckin' killed in the process! And for what? Tell me why!"

"Jeez," Boyd groaned, dabbing at his bloody mouth. "I think you broke my fuckin' tooth—"

"You tell me *why!*" Bear barked.

Even Silas felt it. The order had him curling his toes. Boyd tried to fight it, clenching his teeth, but he was no match for Bear. Silas's mate was so beautiful, so strong. He couldn't help but flood their bond with pride.

"Fine," Boyd panted. "I was jealous, alright? I was jealous of you, and I was worried you were angling to come back and take over the pack. But you had your chance, and you fuckin' left. I stayed, Bear. *Me.*" He jabbed his thumb at his chest. "I know I'm not smart like you, or as good a leader, but I fuckin' stayed when it all fell to shit. But no one was ever gonna pick me over you, not with a shiny new omega in tow."

"So you tried to get me *killed*?" Bear bellowed.

Boyd shook his head. "No—I didn't—I had no idea that would happen—"

"Then you *are* a fuckin' idiot, Boyd! You don't *think*!"

"I'm sorry," Boyd said with a sigh, his body relaxing on the floor. "Shit, you know I am. You know I'm a fuckin' screw up. Just...don't exile me, Bear. Please...I got kids."

Silas felt the jolt of surprise rock through Bear as he rolled back on his heels and got to his feet, staring down at his cousin. Boyd sat up with a groan, still dabbing at his busted lip.

"I'm not pack alpha," Bear muttered. "It's not my call what happens next."

Boyd huffed. "Yeah, right. So you're just gonna waltz off into the sunset with your omega? You're really such a selfish alphahole? Nah...I know you better than that, Bear." He glanced over his shoulder, eyes narrowed at his father in his police uniform. "Admit it, Pops. You think it should be Bear too. It was always supposed to be Bear."

Oh god...Bear as pack alpha? What would that mean for Silas? For their life together? Silas was suddenly filled with dread. Bear felt it all through the bond and groaned.

Terry frowned, glancing from his son to Bear. "I think Bear has to make the right choice for him and his mate. I don't want any alpha in my pack who doesn't want to be here."

"Agreed," chimed a pretty blonde alpha girl with bright blue eyes.

"He doesn't have to decide now," said a tall, dark skinned man with a thin mustache. Silas sensed a warm feeling from Bear followed by a word: *father*. This had to be Liam. Claire's father. "You can come home and see what feels right."

Bear glanced sharply over his shoulder at Silas. "I can't

just...I have to think of Silas first. Alphas are a problem for him. I can't shove him into a pack against his will. Omegas have to choose their pack—"

"Bear," Silas called softly.

Bear glanced over his shoulder.

"Let me make my own choices, okay?"

Bear crossed over to him and took his hand, giving it a gentle squeeze.

Silas glanced over the group of assembled alphas and betas, watching as the strawberry blonde helped a shaky, bleeding Boyd to a chair. His eye settled on Boyd. "Are you sorry for what you did?"

Boyd swallowed, his tangy alpha scent sharpening at being addressed directly by an omega. He licked his busted lip, almost afraid to even look at Silas. "I...yeah, of course I am."

Silas narrowed his eyes at him, searching for any word of a lie. Then he glanced to Bear. "I want him spared. Penance is owed to us and the pack," he added. "But I don't want any more blood shed for me." He glanced back at Boyd. "The next time you think to do something so reckless and cruel, remember that I'm a person first, Boyd. You nearly took my life. You nearly cost me my mate. I will forgive, but I cannot forget." He gestured to his injured shoulder. "Your betrayal is a scar that will linger on me as lasting as the other scars inflicted by cruel, selfish alphas. When you look at me, I want you to think of that. Know I will carry your betrayal on my skin forever."

Boyd's bottom lip quivered as he held back his tears. "I'm sorry," he muttered again.

"Don't say you're sorry," Silas replied softly. "*Be* sorry. Show us you're sorry."

A pregnant pause filled the air.

A tall man with ebony skin and dark eyes standing by the vending machine cleared his throat. "The omega has spoken. Boyd is abjured as alpha, but he will be given clemency. He stays pack."

Slowly, Terry nodded. "I second Leo. I'm sorry, Boyd, but you're abjured. I can't follow an alpha who'd knowingly risk the life and safety of an omega."

Around the waiting room, the pack muttered and nodded their agreement as Boyd hung his head.

Silas glanced around at the assembled group, a nervous fluttering in his chest. "I just need you all to know that... well, you might have already heard some stuff about me. Bad stuff. There's been some shit floating around in the media...but I *never* meant to hurt anyone in this pack or upset the balance. I'm sorry for any pain I've caused—"

"You've done nothing wrong," Liam soothed.

Next to him, Claire nodded feverishly. Standing together like that, Silas could see the resemblance of father to daughter.

"Since the moment you entered my brother's life, you've been bringing him back to us," said Claire. "You brought him back to himself. You saved him, Si." She flashed her brother a smile. "You're clearly good for him...and just maybe we could be good for you too...if you let us."

"I..." He glanced back at Bear. "Would we have to move into the pack house?"

Bear shook his head. Stepping forward, he addressed the pack, his hand once again finding Silas's shoulder. "Silas and I mean to rebuild on the lake. I want a life of solitude with my mate...but I *do* miss the pack. And I'm sorry for the way shit went down," he added, glancing from Liam to Terry. "I left in body and then...well, I left in spirit too. I checked out. At the time, that felt easier than trying, easier than making pack life fit me when it didn't. I was a terrible pack alpha—"

"But you weren't," said Terry, his gaze soft on his nephew. "You didn't even give yourself a chance to try before you folded."

"And you didn't give yourself a chance to *heal*," Liam added. "You weren't the only one who lost Georgia, but you carried the weight of it like it was only yours to feel. Then you added Henry on top...and Reed...and me. In our own misery, we broke the pack...and we broke you. We didn't make a home for you. We didn't try. You're not to blame for walking away, Bear."

"Dad..." Bear murmured, wiping at his eyes with his tattooed hands. Claire was crying too.

"Come home," Liam repeated, his own voice thick with tears. "In whatever capacity that looks like for you and your mate. Please...think about it?"

Bear glanced down at Silas, a question in his eyes. Was Silas willing to consider pack life? Would he ever let himself get close to these alphas and their beta mates? No...not alphas and betas. *Family.* Bear's family.

Swallowing his nerves, Silas cleared his throat and addressed the group. "Look, I don't know the first thing about being in a pack. Not one like this. Not one that's a real family. I don't...I can't guarantee I'll be any good at it," he admitted. "And I definitely don't know *anything* about being an omega. Bear's been having to teach me shit for weeks. I think he might make a better omega than me." Several of the alphas chuckled as Bear flashed him a warning look. He smiled and turned away. "So uhh...yeah...maybe we could go slow? Figure it out together?"

"Sounds good," Terry replied.

"Why don't you start with telling them all your name...*Dean*," Claire teased, flashing him a wide smile.

Silas returned her smile. His name was as good a place as any to start. "Yeah, I'm Silas...Silas Beresford."

Liam beamed. "Another Beresford, eh? Well, it sounds like you're exactly where you're supposed to be. Welcome to the family, son."

63

Bear

Two weeks later

"Dance with me."

Bear groaned, letting Claire pull him up out of his chair and onto the dance floor. He couldn't deny her anything. It was her wedding day, after all.

She was all smiles, a stunning bride. Her dark curls flowed like water down her back, while her ivory dress cinched in at all the right places, showing off her full, hourglass figure. It trailed to the ground in silk folds, fluttering around her feet as she pulled him forward.

On the other side of the dance floor, Yumi was wrapped in the arms of her father. She looked gorgeous too in an edgy, all-white pantsuit with a sequined top. Her ebony bob was slicked back with a cool pomade, making a stylized wave pattern.

All around them, couples danced and swayed to the music.

"Thank you for coming," Claire murmured, taking his left hand as her other hand slid around his waist.

"I wouldn't have missed it, Clairey. You're both beautiful. The ceremony was great."

Almost overnight, the girls' backyard had been transformed into a haven. Twinkle lights lit the place from the trees, the deck, the dock. A large white tent was set up with a dining area at one end and the dance floor at the other. Up the sweeping expanse of grass to the deck, people mingled, drinking and laughing. It was the largest crowd Bear had dealt with in...hell, years.

"How bad do you wanna slink away and hide out in the woods til it's all over?" She teased, reading him like a book with a squeeze of his hand.

He groaned. "Just keep dancing."

She giggled, stepping closer to him, as if she was afraid he really might dart off into the dark like an overgrown bat. He was wearing the right suit to complete the look. His black tux was a bit too small. It was a rental. All his own suits burned up in the fire. He'd quickly ditched his bowtie, stuffing it in his pocket.

It had been an exhausting two weeks since Silas was discharged from the hospital. They'd been staying here with Claire and Yumi, which was a blessing and a curse. The blessing was knowing Silas was safe. Until all the drama with the raids on Pack Rainier died down, they were all at risk. And Bear figured it was only a matter of time before someone doxed Silas to the press. They had to be ready.

Terry kept round-the-clock eyes on Claire's house and the pack had their own system. The house was never without at least two additional alphas. No one complained. In fact, they seemed eager, curious to meet Silas and experience what Claire and Yumi insisted on calling his 'omega dazzle.' Silas hated the term. Bear planned to get t-shirts made.

The curse was that...well, they were staying with Claire and Yumi. Two alphas, a beta, an omega, two dogs, and whatever members of the pack and police were also camped out made for a full house very quickly. Bear struggled to get a moment alone with his mate that wasn't found in the dark of night.

But at least they were together. They survived. Pack Rainier was finished, and Silas was well and truly free. They'd rebuild the cabin and live such a full life together. Bear would accept nothing less for his mate.

Speaking of...where the hell was Silas? Probably hiding out. Even being bonded, he was still an omega. Crowds like this were difficult for him too. He drew attention just by breathing, luring people to him like moths to a devilishly handsome flame.

Bear craned his neck, waiting for his bond sense to guide him towards Silas's hiding place. He stilled as his gaze fell on a familiar, yet wholly unexpected face. "Oh shit..." he muttered. "He's here."

Claire gasped, spinning in Bear's arms. When her gaze landed on Reed standing at the edge of the tent, she let out a sob, covering her mouth with her hand. She left Bear's side immediately, crossing the stretch of the dance floor until she was wrapping herself in the alpha's arms. "You came!" Bear heard her cry. "Ohmigod."

Bear stood still, emotion flaring in his chest. He thought, seeing Reed again, he'd feel nothing but hate and rage. He'd storm over to the coward and clock him out cold. Reed checked out. He left when his pack needed him most.

So did you, came a quiet voice.

The realization settled in his chest. The twinge was so painful he actually lifted his hand, rubbing the spot over his ribs with a wince. In the bond, he felt a fluttering of concern and confusion. Wherever Silas was hiding out, he knew something was wrong. Bear sent a calming thought down the bond.

Reed had changed quite a bit in twelve years. More lines crissed and crossed the tawny skin of his face, more grey at his temples. Like Bear, he wore his long black hair in a high bun. His dark eyes peered over Claire's shoulder, locking on Bear's face.

Claire turned, following his gaze, and waved her hand, beckoning him over. Her makeup was smudged, and she was using the handkerchief Reed offered to dab under her eyes.

Bear didn't even realize that his feet were moving until he was halting behind her shoulder, his gaze still locked on the older alpha.

"Hey, Little B," Reed said in that deep voice.

"You're late," Bear muttered, ignoring the feeling of eyes on them. They were drawing attention. Most of the people here knew Reed...knew he left. Busy bodies and lurkers—were they expecting a damn show?

Reed gave Claire another apologetic grimace. "Yeah, I got a flat tire out on Route 8. Then my e-jack crapped out and I had to call for roadside. I meant to get here on time—"

"It's okay," Claire soothed. "You're here now. Have you seen Daddy yet?" She glanced around, looking for Liam.

"Claire," Bear murmured, his hand on the small of her back as he lowered his face to her ear. "Maybe we should take this somewhere private."

She stilled, her teary eyes darting from Bear back to Reed. "You're not—are you gonna make him leave? Henry, I *need* him here. He's my dad—"

"Whether he stays or goes isn't my call," Bear replied. "I'm not the pack alpha."

Reed's eyes went wide with surprise.

"But...we don't have one right now," Claire whined.

"Liam is the ranking Beresford, and he's Reed's pack mate. It's his call," Bear replied.

"No, it's not," came a soft voice behind them.

Shit.

Bear turned to see Liam standing there, a glass of whiskey in hand. It was strange to see him in his tuxedo. He looked great, but he didn't quite fill the jacket out anymore in the chest and shoulders. Bear blamed his damn wasting sickness. Wasting away without the love and light of his pack. Without Reed.

Without you, came that voice again. *You left him too.*

"Hey, Li," Reed said on a breath, tears in his dark eyes.

"It means a lot to Clairey that you came," Liam murmured.

Reed nodded. "I..." Words failed him as he glanced from Liam to Bear, back to Claire. A tear slipped down his tawny cheek.

With a sob, Claire wrapped her arms around him, giving him another hug. He held to her like she was his life raft and he was being tossed in a storm at sea. Liam stepped in behind Bear, his gentle hand on his shoulder, and gave it a squeeze.

Claire pulled away from him, craning her neck to look over her shoulder at her father and brother. "I want him to stay," she declared, her amber eyes fierce with determination. "I've come home, Henry's come home. Reed gets the same chance."

Slowly, a smile pulled at Bear's lips as an idea settled in his mind. He knew it was right the moment it sparked to life. "It's your call...alpha."

"Henry, *please*—" Claire cried, not hearing him at first. Then she sucked in a breath, eyes wide. "Wait...what?"

Bear glanced from Reed's surprised face back to Claire. "Pack Beresford needs an alpha to guide us. Liam would be great, but he's never wanted the job. Reed's too flaky. Terry's too busy. And I'm a fucking mess. I'm barely holding the pieces of my life together. And my priority will always be Silas," he added. "You should be the alpha, Claire—"

"Agreed," said Liam, before Bear had even finished the sentence.

Claire's red-painted mouth puckered like a fish out of water. "But...I'm not...I'm...*me!*"

"Yes, you're you," Bear replied with a smile. "You're caring and clever. Loyal. Forward-thinking. Sensitive to the needs of others. You'd make a great alpha, and you have my vote."

She just blinked again. "Vote?"

"You have my vote too," Liam said with a gentle smile.

"And mine," Reed murmured, tears still in his eyes. "I don't know if I deserve a vote...but you're the only reason I'm still alive, Clairey. You brought me back to myself. You brought me back here...brought me home."

Her tears were falling again. "This is crazy!"

"We'll have a proper vote on it later," Bear soothed, giving her shoulder a pat. "For now, go enjoy your wedding night."

"Reed missed the father-daughter dance," said Liam. "Maybe he'd like to take you for a spin."

Claire was a blubbering mess as she pulled Reed away, dragging him wide-eyed onto the dance floor. The crowd oooh'ed and sighed, as he took her in his arms.

Liam stood still at Bear's shoulder. "That was kind of you," he murmured.

Bear shrugged, watching his sister's face crack into a wide smile, Reed whispering something in her ear that made her laugh. "I just...wanna see her happy," he replied. "I want to make up for what we did after mom died. I want to pick up the pieces and start new."

Liam nodded, handing him his glass of whiskey. "Will you hold this? I want to dance with my baby girl again."

Bear took the glass with a smile, as Liam walked onto the floor. Rather than cut in, he joined them, one hand around Claire's waist and one around Reed. The two older alphas breathed each other in, a lifetime of memories flashing in their eyes. Together, they danced.

64

Silas

It was official, Silas hated weddings.

Okay...so maybe he didn't *hate* weddings, but he definitely hated crowds.

And loud music.

And people making the *clink clink clink* noises with forks on the sides of glasses.

He peered into the flute of bubbling champagne he'd been carrying around all night. He wasn't actually drinking it, he just held it so people would stop asking him if he needed a drink.

No, he was stone cold sober...and he hated weddings.

Okay, that wasn't fair. Claire and Yumi made for two beautiful brides, and their backyard had been transformed into a fairy land. Later tonight they would stretch out blankets on the lawn and shoot off fireworks. It was a lovely party, and everyone seemed to be having an amazing time.

Silas was just feeling...unsettled.

It had only been two weeks since the events at the cabin. Two weeks since he found himself shot and bonded and homeless all in one night. Claire and Yumi had been great, taking them in without question. Silas hated to put them out, but they wouldn't hear a word about it. They practically force-fed him baked goods every day, which was getting old. But they loved *The Secret Diaries of a Teenage Omega,* and gleefully watched reruns with him.

Living in a house that had a constant rotation of new people cycling through was stressful for him to say the least. And now he was at a wedding packed full of people he didn't know...but who all seemed to know him. Or as least they knew *of* him. And the more the people at this party drank, the easier it became for them to ask him intrusive questions like, "What did you feel when you pulled the trigger?" and "You must be *so* glad to be out of there, right?"

So now Silas was hiding out in the corner of the top deck, looking down at the sea of party goers. He set his flute of champagne down on the edge of the rail, his eyes scanning the crowd. He felt him before he saw him. *Bear.* He could always feel him. His alpha was standing down on the dock, which was lit from end to end with strings of twinkling lights.

He said his name like a caress down the bond, so the alpha's head turned, looking for him in the crowd. Smiling, Silas stepped back from the railing, pulling his face into shadow. He loved the idea of gazing down on his alpha. It felt like a stolen moment. After hours and days of shared intimacy with others, this moment was just for him—and for Bear through the bond.

Fuck, but he looked good. Bear stood in his perfectly tailored black suit, tieless, with his top button undone. He had a glass of whiskey in his hand. He swirled it once as he laughed at something Liam said. Silas could almost hear the clinking of the ice in that glass. He suddenly pictured getting Bear alone. He wanted to lick the condensation off his lover's tattooed fingers...dragging them into his mouth... sucking on the tips—

He gasped, rocked by the flood of lust that hit him through the bond. Bear approved of this plan. Could they? Was that allowed? Would anyone notice if he sort of... dragged the bride's brother away and fucked his brains out?

Easy, tiger. This is not your night. You should be mixing and mingling and...doing whatever it is that normal people do at parties.

Silas groaned. He didn't want to do normal people shit. He wanted to stare at his alpha, worship him with his eyes. Bear's hair was pulled back, and a curl of his new neck ink was just visible over the collar of his shirt. Silas was there when he got it. Just last night, he'd traced his tongue over it. It was inked in the same style as his first tattoo on his wrist. One word. *Silas.*

Picturing his name on his alpha's skin had him getting harder. In a daring move, he traced his tongue over his bottom lip, setting off fireworks in his chest. The bond mark was still so sensitive. Down the bond, he could practically feel Bear growling with need. He smiled, loving the feel of Bear wanting him, wanting to *find* him.

He peered down, gasping with nervous excitement to find Bear was on the move, striding purposefully off the dock and up the dark grass. Silas was in so much trouble. He licked his lip again, biting down on it until he made his cock twitch. Down on the edge of the dance floor, Bear went still, his eyes darting around, still looking for him. Silas knew that face. Bear was hard...and hungry.

Silas closed his eyes, holding onto the deck rail with both hands as he tried to quiet the riot of emotions inside him. If he didn't pump the breaks on this game...

He opened his eyes and gasped again. Bear was looking right at him, a smile curling his lips. Bodies moved all around him, swaying to the pulsing music, but Bear stood impossibly still. It was one of the most sensual moments of Silas's life, keeping his eyes locked on his alpha as Bear prowled forward, coming to him. They kept their eyes on each other, the swirl of partygoers fading into nothing around them.

He lost sight of his alpha at the stairs. Heart pounding, he considered his options. Did he really want to let Bear find him here? With the way he was feeling, he was afraid he was going to do something truly memorable like present right here at the railing. He could go inside and lure Bear to their room. Or he could—

Too late.

Bear was up the stairs and walking right towards him. Silas stood still, his heart beating wildly as his alpha approached, that damn glass of whiskey still in his hand. His senses filled with Bear's intoxicating winter morning scent, layered now with a sweetness, a smooth spiciness. It was Silas. Bear smelled like himself, but he smelled like Silas too. It made Silas want to crow with happiness. This alpha was *his*. Owned, claimed, cherished.

The alpha stepped right into his space, lowering his face to breathe Silas in. Silas felt his neck going limp as he tipped his head to the side, offering himself to his alpha. This is what Bear liked best, right over the scent gland. He took a deep breath, rumbling his approval in Silas's ear.

"Baby, do you have any idea what you do to me?"

God, Silas was so hard. "Alpha..."

Bear's growl intensified, his nose brushing gently along Silas's jaw. "Say it again."

Silas was panting, his chest rising and falling under the

silk of his dress shirt. "Alpha," he whispered. "Alpha, please..."

"Please what? What do you need? Tell me."

Not breaking eye contact with his alpha, Silas took the glass of whiskey from his hand and set it on the railing next to his champagne flute. Slowly, he raised Bear's hand to his mouth. His fingers were wet from the glass, just like he imagined. Without saying a word, he licked down the length of Bear's first two fingers, dragging them into his mouth and sucking the tips.

"Fuck," the alpha growled, pressing forward until Silas was pinned against the railing. Bear's rock hard cock pressed against his own. The alpha shifted his hips to give them both friction. "I swear to god, if I'm not knotting you in the next two minutes..."

Silas smiled around the fingers in his mouth, letting them go with a tease of his tongue. "Eager?"

"Always."

Silas held on to Bear's hand as he leaned forward and claimed his lips. The alpha groaned, his free hand wrapping around Silas's neck as he opened himself deeper, giving and taking in perfect rhythm. To have Bear kissing his bond mark lit Silas up like a firecracker. He felt drunk and dizzy and damn near desperate to come.

"I need you," Bear panted against his lips. "I need —*Silas*," he begged.

"I know," Silas soothed, breaking their kiss.

"I've needed you so goddamn much," Bear whispered, momentarily flooding the bond with his doubt and worry and frustration. "I've been trying to keep it all together—"

"I know," Silas said again, taking it all, every worry. He was strong enough. They were strong enough together.

"My dad is here," Bear muttered, brushing his fingers over Silas's lips.

"Liam?"

"Reed," he corrected. "He came. He's here. And I think I just made my sister the pack alpha."

Whoa. That was a lot to digest. "Are you okay? The bond felt a little messy, but I just thought—"

Bear pressed in, kissing him again. Silas lost himself to the feel of his alpha. Bear broke the kiss. "I'm amazing," he said on a breath, his mouth curling into a smile against Silas's lips. "I feel...*free*, Si. I feel whole. With you in my arms, Reed here, Claire as alpha. I—*god*—you're my whole fucking world, baby. You and me. We'll have the pack, but *this* is what I need," he said, taking Silas's hands, and kissing his knuckles. "I just don't want to mess up again. I don't want to hurt you like I hurt the pack. I don't ever wanna lose you—"

Silas took Bear's hand in both of his. He slid it under his jacket, pressing Bear's palm flat against his heart. "Look at me. *Feel* me. Feel my heart beating?"

Bear nodded, his worries fading as he splayed his hand over Silas's chest. "I always feel you."

"This is the only thing that matters now," he whispered, brushing the loose tendrils of Bear's hair behind his ear with his free hand. "Whatever else comes our way, we can face it. Strongest together."

"Ride or fucking die," Bear said with a loving smile.

Silas's lips quirked into a smile too, a sly glint in his eye.

Bear felt it all through the bond. "What? What is that face?"

Silas's smile widened as he leaned forward and nipped at his alpha's bottom lip. "I was just thinking about other ways we can put 'ride or die' to the test."

Bear purred, low in his chest. "Baby, if you're asking me to ride you until you die of pleasure, the answer will always be yes."

"Come on then, *baby*," Silas teased, leading his alpha by the hand towards the house. As they reached the door, he leaned in to Bear's ear and whispered, "But tonight, I'll be the one doing the riding."

Bear groaned with aching need, stumbling after his omega into the house.

EPILOGUE

Silas

One Year Later

"No matter what happens in there today, you'll be fine. *We'll* be fine," Bear assured him, kissing his tattooed knuckles.

Silas nodded, taking comfort as always in his alpha's calming presence. Bear shored him up, filling in the cracks.

"Are you ready, Mr. Wright?" the court bailiff asked. She was a cheery, grey-haired beta with black-framed glasses.

Silas nodded again. No point in delaying. He'd come this far. "Yeah, I'm good."

"Great. There's gonna be some press inside today, but I think your counsel warned you about that right? High profile cases always attract a bit of media attention. And we have a spot reserved in the front row for your bond-mate," she added at Bear. "You can follow us in, Mr. Beresford."

Silas gave his tie a nervous tug. His navy-blue suit was a birthday gift from Yumi and Claire. Bear looked confident in a charcoal grey suit. As always, he skipped a tie, seeming to prefer using his ink as his neck statement.

For the last year, Silas's life had been a near-constant parade of legal affairs—interrogations, depositions, hearings. If he never saw the inside of a courtroom again, it would be too soon.

This case in particular was one he was eager to put behind him, because a case like this carried with it labels like 'high profile' and 'media magnet.' It had been Bear's idea originally, but it was actually the soft-spoken words of Liam that brought Silas to the courtroom today. He was suing the Suna Corporation and the Omega Center in St. Albans for medical malpractice. He was only the fifth omega to come forward and demand restitution. Silas knew for a fact that at least eight other omegas from his Center got the shot with him.

He never wanted to do this, and he'd been determined to tell Bear no. Bear's approach had been to stomp and rage about the injustices of Silas's life and argue how he deserved restitution.

But then Silas talked to Liam, and the older alpha took a different approach. He was thoughtful, and after a moment of reflection said, "I think it's important that you do this, son." When Silas asked why, Liam replied, "Because I'd like to think we live in a world where actions have consequences. SunaCorps and that OC took actions. Can they now live with them?"

It was as if, by taking Silas out of the equation, it somehow made the whole process seem less daunting. This wasn't about Silas earning a payout or getting rich off his own suffering. He didn't give a damn about the money. He'd happily tip the whole lot into the lake if he won. Bear made more than enough money to support them in a comfortable life.

No, this was about making it clear to the world that even

major multinational corporations can be held accountable for their actions. Silas agreed to come forward and press his case, and now ten long months later it was verdict day.

He followed the court bailiff into Courtroom C of the St. Alban's City Courthouse. As expected, there was a stretch of seats off to the left reserved for press. Cameras clicked and flashed as Silas walked up the narrow aisle between the chairs. The bailiff lifted the little wooden barrier blocking off the gallery from the front. Silas passed through, glancing over his shoulder at Bear. His alpha nodded, taking a seat in the row right behind him.

Behind Bear, the next three rows were already filled by a collection of their nearest and dearest. Claire and Yumi were holding hands right behind Bear, nervous expressions on their faces. They shared a row with Ollie and his four alphas. Ollie gave him a half-smile and a shrug, his round glasses crooked on his olive-skinned face. Behind them sat members of the pack—Liam and Reed together, Terry and his beta mate Janine. Solemn Leo gave him a nod of quiet support. Even Jared was there, wedged next to Leo.

"Good morning, Mr. Wright," Holly murmured, pulling Silas's attention back to the front. She was the ace young member of his legal team that led closing arguments. He'd have to thank Claire and Yumi again for his counsel. Claire used her wealthy connections in the fashion world to get a team willing to work pro bono. Like Silas, they were committed to upholding the truth that actions had consequences.

He sat nervously in his seat for a few minutes, trying to ignore the open stares of the fancy suits sitting at the table across from him. SunaCorps had a team of intimidating alpha lawyers that always made Bear so upset he took a double shower after each session of court.

Finally, the judge came in and took her seat. After a debrief with both legal teams, she called in the jury. Bear sent supportive thoughts down the bond as they waited for all thirteen jurors to file in.

"Right, I understand the jury has reached a verdict?" the judge called.

"We have, Your Honor," replied the foreman.

"Okay, you may read it out."

The foreman, a tall man with frizzy white hair and bright red glasses picked up a piece of paper and read aloud, "In the matter of Mr. Silas Wright versus the Suna Corporation, we the jury find the defendant guilty of the charge of medical malpractice. In this instance, they did knowingly and with malice administer the drug Sunapraxin, a drug that had not gone through the proper trials. Furthermore, we find that they acted in bad faith, not informing their patients properly as to what medical practice or intervention they were receiving. It is here proven that Mr. Wright was one such patient, and he is eligible to pursue a punitive settlement."

Silas let out a shaky breath, feeling Bear's relief and joy flood through the bond.

"Very well, and did you reach a damages settlement?" called the judge.

"We did, Your Honor. We the jury unanimously award Mr. Wright a settlement of five million dollars, to be paid by the Suna Corporation immediately."

A cheer went up from the collection of supporters behind him, followed by the flash and click of the cameras. Joyous vindication flooded Silas through his bond as Bear breathed a deep sigh of relief for them both. The judge had to bang her gavel to calm down the gallery.

Silas tuned out the rest of the exchange between the

judge and the foreman, faintly aware that his counsel was still patting him on the back and whispering words of congratulations in his ear.

How was this his life? One year ago, he was alone in the world, a broken omega on the run with nothing and no one. Now he was sitting in a court room, his bonded alpha by his side, listening to a jury award him a medical malpractice settlement of five million dollars?

He had a new cabin, built largely by the hands of his bond-mate. They made a few modifications to the old design, including adding a third bedroom for a nest and extending out their bathroom (Silas wanted a two-person jacuzzi soaking tub). They'd been in it for half a year already.

His sister-in-law and her beta mate lived two houses down, and they were the reason Silas was now employed. He was a content creator at FashForward, helping to put together looks and style guides, focusing on menswear.

Oh, and he had a pack. And not in the sense that the pack had him and there was no escape. No, he had a big, loud, beautiful family of a pack that accepted and loved him and called him things like 'swell' and 'treasured.' He refused to even entertain bonding any of them, but no one seemed to mind. They just...*liked* him.

And he liked them. Terry was his knight in black polyester, working round the clock in those early days to make sure he was safe, and all their loved ones were safe too. Liz and her twin brother Jake were hilarious. They were teaching him to fish, which mainly involved telling jokes at his expense. Quiet Leo went on morning walks with him around the lake. And Liam was quickly becoming the father he never had.

And then there was Bear. Silas couldn't help it. He

glanced over his shoulder, making eye contact with his alpha. As their gaze's met, Bear sent such a feeling of love and pride down the bond that it nearly took Silas's breath away. This quiet, proud alpha was his everything. It felt like another life that they met in the dark of the night on that winding mountain road. Was there really a time when he didn't trust this man? When he'd considered leaving him behind?

The pounding of the gavel brought him to his senses. Was it over? He stood because everyone around him was standing. From the far wall, flashes and clicks went off like crazy. He tuned that all out. He only wanted one thing. One person. He pushed back his chair and moved over to the rail.

Bear leaned across it, wrapping him in a tight embrace. "I'm so proud of you, Si," he murmured in his ear.

With his arms wrapped around Bear and his chin on his shoulder, he could see the sea of smiling, supportive faces looking back at him. Claire and Yumi were both sobbing. Ollie had his eyes on his phone, thumbs flying across the screen. He was probably feverishly texting the omega group chats that had been following the case. The row of pack mates behind were all whispering excitedly and flashing him wide grins.

Bear pulled back and cupped his cheek. "Well, how does it feel to come out on top?"

Tears stinging his eyes, Silas took a breath. Slowly, he smiled too. "Good," he murmured, feeling a lightness in his chest he hadn't felt in years. His smile grew. "Really fucking good."

. . .

A FEW HOURS LATER, SILAS AND BEAR WERE BACK IN THE truck on their way home to Lake Beresford. The rest of the Beresford crew caravanned behind them. Bear cranked one of his old cassette tapes on the radio, humming along to the scratchy country music.

If there was one thing Silas would change about Bear, it would be his taste in music...but even that found ways to be endearing. Goddamn it, the man had to have a flaw. Something Silas could hold on to and remind himself that Bear was only human too. Old Silas would have said his green smoothies, but damn it they didn't taste good...and they were healthy.

"What are you thinking about so hard over there?" Bear said, his eyes still on the road.

"You," he replied honestly.

"Oh, yeah?"

"Yeah...just trying to come up with a list of all your flaws."

Bear frowned. "Shit...well...can I see it when you're done? I'm curious."

Silas shrugged, pulling out his phone to check his messages. There were dozens, with more pinging almost every minute. Reporters, well-wishers, random strangers. It had been a total shit show for weeks leading up to this verdict. Silas didn't want to do media appearances. He just wanted to move on. In the morning he'd give his phone to Yumi and make her be his P.A. again. She didn't mind telling people 'no' for him. It'd be a huge relief when it all died down.

"So...five million dollars, huh?" said Bear, still drumming with his thumbs. "Plus, an additional million from the Omega Center. What are you gonna do with all the cold hard cash, Mr. Wright?"

Silas looked up from his phone. "I have some ideas."

Bear glanced over at him with a smile. "Oh, yeah? Like what?"

"There are some sales coming up on Fash. I've got my eye on a few pairs of shoes, and I swear to fuck if Jameson outbids me for them again, I'm gonna pull the 'your boss is my sister card' and...well, I can't get him fired, but I'll do...something."

Bear snorted. "Mail him a box of bees."

Silas blinked. "What?"

"It's a prank I did once in my misspent youth. I think tequila had been involved beforehand. I mailed my high school baseball coach a box of bees when he wouldn't start me."

Silas was speechless. "Where—"

"I read about it in a book once," Bear replied. "Turns out my coach was allergic though, so it wasn't very funny...so yeah, maybe let's scrap that idea..."

Silas narrowed his eyes at his mate. "Yeah, probably for the best."

"Well, what else? You've got six million dollars and all you want is to outbid some guy named Jameson on some shoes?"

Silas smiled. "Actually, there is something I'd like to do."

"Name it, baby. The world is your oyster now."

"I think I'd like to take a trip."

Bear glanced over at him. "A trip? Where to?"

"Anywhere," he replied with a shrug. "Shit...everywhere. I've never really traveled. I want to see everything...or at least some cool stuff. I'll make a list of like my top 10 sights and hit them all."

"And...am I invited on this trip?" Bear said with a smile.

"Of course. I was uhh..." Why was he suddenly so

nervous? He kept his eyes on his phone. "Actually, I was thinking it could be kind of like a honeymoon sort of thing...or whatever."

Zing went Bear's heart through the bond. "A honeymoon as in..."

Silas sighed, slipping his phone back in his pocket. "As in I just spent the last year of my life going through endless legal dramas, signing my name to shit, and getting summoned to appear in court. And today I heard a judgment for a man named Silas Wright and I was sitting there the whole time thinking, 'But...he doesn't exist anymore.' You know? Silas Wright is dead. He died on that road the night we met. I'm Silas Beresford now. I'll always be Silas Beresford. And I think we need to make it official. I can just change my name if that's easier," he added quickly. "But we could also...you know..."

Bear was positively floating in the bond, his happiness riotous. "No, I don't think I do know, Mr. Wright. I think I need you to tell me. Maybe I need you to *ask* me."

Silas rolled his eyes, his own happiness echoing with Bear's. "Henry Calhoun Beresford III, I want you to make me the happiest omega on this earth, and I want you to marry me. I'm Silas Beresford in my heart. I want to be him in all ways. I want to be yours. Forever. Be my mate, my husband and my love. Just...be mine."

Bear was vibrating with emotion, but he kept both hands on the wheel. "You know...nowhere in that declaration was I asked a question—"

"*God*, the—" Silas groaned, pressing the palm of his hand against his forehead. "The question was clearly implied. And maybe I don't want it to be a question," he added, glaring down the bench seat at his mate. "Maybe I'm not asking. Maybe I'm telling. My choice, remember?"

"Yeeeah...I'm still gonna need you to ask me," Bear teased. "If I'm gonna have a husband who is infinitely more attractive than me, and now wealthier than me, I have to cling to something. If you don't ask, I'll start to doubt myself." He gave a heavy, dramatic sigh. "My confidence will shatter...it may break us apart in the end..."

"I am going to take you so hard when we get home," Silas growled.

"Sounds great. Still gotta ask me."

"Bear, will you marry me?"

Bear smiled, his lips twitching at the corner of his mouth. Inside the bond, his answer was already bright and true and forever. "Yes."

BONUS EPILOGUE

Would you like more of Bear & Silas's story? There is now a bonus epilogue, available exclusively to my newsletter subscribers. Sign up now, and you can read the all new epilogue!

Sign up HERE

ACKNOWLEDGEMENTS

In July, I took a five-hour drive through Georgia into South Carolina. Between the long drive, the scenery, and the music, I think I entered another plane of consciousness. By the end of the drive, I had a full novel in my head. In ten days, I had over 40k words on the page.

In a way, this story feels like it wrote itself. Silas and Bear *needed* to meet. They needed to share their sad boy fall moment. They swept into my life and stole my heart. I hope they steal a tiny piece of yours too. So here you go, a fever dream of a novel. Read it, love it, review it.

Let's thank a few people. Firstly, to Ashely, my intrepid alpha reader, who read the worst and best possible versions of this story. To my dear friends at the JAX-SFF writer's group, who challenged me to dig deeper, thank you.

Thanks to my beta reader team: Katie, Nikki, Amanda, Alex, Lauren, and Michelle. Each project is a little different, and I thank you all from the bottom of my heart for just rolling with it. You know my chaos brain will always lead us down a fun path with lots of kissing.

Acknowledgements

To my ARC team: I can't say enough great things! Thank you SO MUCH for helping me launch Silas & Bear into the world.

In addition to my beta and ARC teams, this book benefited from the careful attention of several paid sensitivity readers. The team all identified as BIPOC, with a range of sensitivity specializations: LGBTQIA+ identity, sexual assault survival, and living with anxiety/depression. It was essential to me that Silas's story be one of strength, resilience, and joyful recovery. I so appreciate the insights and feedback from these readers.

Lastly, to my husband, my Bear. The world is less lonely with you by my side. Thank you for your patience and your love.

HELP IS A PHONE CALL AWAY

Call Now

If you or someone you know is a victim of human trafficking, there are resources that can help.

U.S.

National Human Trafficking Hotline
Call: 1-888-373-7888

U.K.

Modern Slavery Helpline
Call: 08000 121 700 (in an emergency call 999)

Australia

Australia Federal Police
Call: 131AFP (131237) or use the online form

Canada

Canadian Human Trafficking Hotline
Call: 1-833-900-1010

BANANAS FOSTER PANCAKES

Want to recreate the infamous bananas foster pancake scene?? Use this recipe and just add pancakes (or vanilla ice cream). Below, I walk you through the bananas foster part:

STEPS:
1. Prep the bananas foster ingredients and set aside
2. Make pancakes and set aside
3. Make bananas foster and top the pancakes

INGREDIENTS:
1/4 cup butter
2/3 cup dark brown sugar
3.5 tablespoons rum
1.5 teaspoons vanilla extract
1/2 teaspoon ground cinnamon
1/2 teaspoon nutmeg (optional)
3 bananas, peeled and sliced lengthwise and crosswise
1/4 cup coarsely chopped nuts

DIRECTIONS:

Step 1: melt butter in a large, deep skillet over medium heat. Stir in brow sugar, rum, vanilla, cinnamon, and nutmeg and bring to a low boil.

Step 2: Place bananas and walnuts in the pan. Cook until bananas have softened, ~3 minutes. Serve at once over pancakes (or ice cream).

LEAVE A REVIEW

If you enjoyed this story, please consider leaving a review! All the usual places like Amazon and Goodreads are amazing and so greatly appreciated. Please also consider leaving a review on your favorite social media site.

Early reviews are the key to indie author success! The new frontier is social media reviews. No matter where you feel most comfortable (TikTok, Instagram, Facebook, Twitter) your honest review means everything to me. You can find me at @emilyrathbooks

ALSO BY EMILY RATH

SECOND SONS SERIES

Spicy 'why choose' Regency Romance

#1 BEAUTIFUL THINGS

#2 HIS GRACE, THE DUKE

#3 ALCOTT HALL

STANDALONES

Contemporary MM Omegaverse

WHISKEY & SIN

JACKSONVILLE RAYS SERIES

Spicy hockey romance

#0.5 THAT ONE NIGHT

#1 PUCKING AROUND

#2 PUCKING WILD (Summer 2023)

ABOUT THE AUTHOR

Emily Rath is a romance and fantasy author. A university professor by day, she lives in Florida with her husband, son, and cat. They regularly comb the local beaches looking for shark teeth.

- Join my FB Group for monthly live sessions, exclusive first looks at art, and chats about ongoing and new projects
- Join my Newsletter to get all major publishing news

Printed in Great Britain
by Amazon